I
WILL
SURVIVE

A Divorcee

I WILL SURVIVE

iUniverse books may be ordered through booksellers or by contacting:

iUniverse
1663 Liberty Drive
Bloomington, IN 47403
www.iuniverse.com
1-800-Authors (1-800-288-4677)

ISBN: 978-1-5320-8506-2 (sc)
ISBN: 978-1-5320-8505-5 (e)

Library of Congress Control Number: 2019917186

Print information available on the last page.

iUniverse rev. date: 01/03/2020

This book is dedicated to my father whom I loved dearly and who was a very avid and passionate reader. He predicted, among many other things that in the year 2000's, many would write their own book. I wish he was here to share mine with him.

Contents

CHAPTER 1

INTRO

The Beginning Of The Book

One night my youngest daughter, Lisa asked me if I was going to write a book. She must have caught sight of me jotting down notes that I have been amassing for some time now on My Life and Other Lives. She probably observed me writing bits and reminders on scraps of papers, pamphlets or bills in the car or in my notebooks to elaborate on later. So, I answered "yes", because I felt it was the least, I could do to live up to some expectations. I thought it was my way of making up for not being a "perfect" mother like the other mothers, like "all the mothers?". But is any mother really like "all the mothers?". Probably not, but divorced mothers are even less so. Later, after I was halfway through the book, I realized that she had asked me that question because she did NOT want me writing a book.

Children sense that only the tip of the iceberg is showing where their parents are concerned (perhaps even more so where divorced mothers are concerned). There were things she probably sensed about her mother, with a child's intuition, that she did not want to know, or even less have the world know. But by then, it was too late; the book was a torrent I could no longer stop, but anonymity seemed like a welcome solution. It appeared to prevail like a peaceful island that my personal waves could wash up on and occasionally slam against. I also reasoned that the new generation does not like to read and for once this observation was one that had a silver lining.

"Bonnie and Clyde", sung by Serge Gainsbourg and Brigitte Bardot, seems to be the right song to listen to while starting to write this book. The song feels like what Life has felt like so far; an ongoing, steady and constant drumbeat in the background representing the irrevocable advancement of time. It is jazzed up in the forefront with a rhythmic but much less regular rhythm of hurdles to be jumped. The tempo can be likened to the escape of a gangster who is running for survival. Survival is the theme of this song and of Life itself. Running, jumping a hurdle, running, out of breath, turning a corner, surprise another hurdle, obstacles that come up unexpected, hurdles you see from far and anticipate, more running...running to something and away from other things but always running. That is the general feeling of this song and of life so far.

Bonnie and Clyde
By Brigitte Bardot, Serge Gainsbourg
Vous avez lu l'histoire
De Jesse James
Comment il vécu
Comment il est mort
Ça vous a plus hein
Vous en demandez encore
Et bien,
écoutez l'histoire

Bonnie and Clyde
by Brigitte Bardot, Serge Gainsbourg
(You read the story
Of Jesse James
How he lived
How he died
You like it, huh?
You still ask for more
Well,
listen up good to the story)

The Secondary Title: The F*cking Fifties

At one point, the title of this book was supposed to be the F*cking Fifties but somehow, I still must be old school and did not want such a violent word. The reason for such a title though, was evident. By the time you get to 50, you have survived at least one of three d's…Divorce, Death or Depression.

The son of France's most famous actor, Alain Delon, recently opened a leather jacket store in Paris. He said he named it after a Japanese term that means falling down seven times and lifting yourself up again. It is his way of expressing that what counts is rising up again and again. Being the son of France's most adored actor must have been tough. I used to see him as a spoiled daddy's boy, but he has aged as well, and I found his vulnerability rather endearing.

Indeed, with all the past events and struggles I have lived through myself or witnessed through the lives of women (and men) around me, the title just appeared as evident as it was perfect.

The alliteration did give the deserved full force to the theme. And then the word F.ck was the one word I truly missed when living in France. Because yes, I grant you the French language is perhaps more complex, nuanced and richer than the English language as a whole, but I defy you to find in the French language ONE word that is more powerful than the word F.ck. When the French are mad, their "putain" or "merde" are very lame. This single word is what makes for a tie between both languages in terms of expression.

By the time you are fifty, you usually have not pranced through life unscathed. This is what builds your soul. I am told. Having lived a soulful life gives you a real soul if nothing else.

A friend recently faced the sudden death of her soulmate. She had only spent three years with him. But had spent 30 years in a very lonely marriage, with a husband she had absolutely nothing in common with. I came up with a lame, "what can I tell you, it's the fucking fifties." She nodded in agreement. Somehow it seemed to pacify her and explain it all away. It stuck.

The Real Beginning: Divorce

To really start in life and really KNOW oneself, one must divorce. That is the real beginning.

Divorce is real self-discovery. If life were logical (lol), we should start life with a divorce. That way, we would grow progressively from the start. The only problem is we would have to start a marriage really early and who wants that? Funny that all the letters of the word divorce are in the word discovery....

Divorce is underrated. Some things in life are overrated. Like drinking champagne or riding in a limo or first-time sex. Did you ever notice how disappointingly dusty glasses are in a limo? Champagne is too sweet. As for first-time sex, I need not elaborate.

But divorce is definitely underrated. It is so talked about you would think it is an everyday occurrence, but it is about as normal as a tsunami. In a tv series like "Desperate Housewives", if a heroine were to get divorced, she would have a good scotch, explain it away in a luncheon (not lunch but luncheon) with her 4 perfectly blow-dried friends all wearing complementary colors, lose another effortless 3 pounds (lucky her) and continue hopscotching through life on heels. Of course, you cannot portray on TV the lump in her throat, the newfound friend cigarettes can become and the horrid emptiness of weekends. Divorce wipes out all the regular routines of your life exactly like a tsunami wipes out a bustling hotel that was on the edge of the beach.

I read in a French article in Paris that in a woman's life, the most traumatic experiences were death, divorce and moving. I lived through all three at the exact same time. Divorce was perhaps not the most painful in the long run, but at the moment it hit, it wiped out everything else and relegated the other two to second place.

The Move

There was no reason for me to stay in France when my ex-husband decided to quit our family. Montreal, my hometown offered the best option for my four daughters and myself. I had very little family in France. The friends you really want to keep when you divorce are only the ones who refuse to see your ex-husband for their entire life. The other ones can no longer be considered friends; don't kid yourself. You want to save yourself from silly, gauche or unknowingly at best, hurtful remarks.

When you divorce, you more than ever need a real family environment if you can get one. So, I brought my kids home to their grandmother, aunts, uncles, cousins of all ages; a big extended family and a close-knit community.

Like Marshall McLuhan, our great father of communications said (I got that out of my Master's in Communications!) it takes a village to raise a child. Not a big city like Paris that feels like a very beautiful, but coldly elegant and slightly depressed woman continually reflecting and philosophizing while smoking cigarettes under the rain. Not a city where on a Sunday afternoon you are alone in the sandpit of the beautifully manicured lawns of Park Monceau, with your five-year-old, trying to contain your tears and fears and breathe regularly while painstakingly counting the minutes before you can decently say, "let's go home and have a goûter now". Just so you can find a corner to cry for a few minutes.

It had been negotiated that my ex-husband would pay for the move, and I had hired a moving service that came to pack every single thing we owned. Yes, I indeed got to keep all the furniture. But like I told my neighbours Anatole and Dan, a charming couple that owned the most beautiful circus in France, what would a single man do with a very ornate Gustavienne dining room? I tried to make people laugh even when I was crying inside.

I was so dazed and confused by the divorce that I had lost track of the weekdays. When the movers arrived one morning at our apartment, all I could do was throw on my bathrobe and push my sleeping mask on top of my head. I was a sorry and slightly funny sight with my pink fluorescent sleep mask with glitzy lashes embroidered on. I answered the door to eight movers who marched into my house, their footsteps resounding on the old Parisian wooden floors and pounding reality again deep inside my head.

I braced myself for yet another painful episode in the Boxing Ring of Divorce. Because that is the type of rude awakening divorce gives you. Constant punches. Right Hook, the first lawyer letter you receive where your ex-husband summons you to get rid of you. It feels like a left hook the first time you have to take out your Livret de Famille, to be filled with the dirty word Divorced. Until now you took it out only on beautiful occasions to be filled in with the names of your newborns. Punch in the stomach, you are not going as a couple to your best friend's son's bar mitzvah; it's you and your girls. Low Blow, it's Saturday night, two of your girls need to be driven, and he is free for neither one. Yeah, he must have a date. Then one day, you get a low blow, right in the stomach. You bump into one of your best friend's sister, the one with the big mouth that always put her foot in her mouth. She lets slip that your husband has been seeing this really horrible woman for a while now, didn't you know? Oh sorry…

This move represented another punch that I had been bracing for since the date had been set. I was reeling with its force to the other side of the boxing ring. And to the other side of the world. We were moving back to Montreal. I kept bouncing off the boxing ring ropes. Boing! Boing! I was amazed that I could still feel anything after all the punches I was the recipient of. I wished I were numb, but I wasn't. You feel each blow, and that is what divorce is. Blow after blow and you being bounced off the sides of the ring in the craziest scheme of things. Total loss of control as your body is seemingly flung to all sides like a rag doll.

The movers entered, took possession and proceeded to pack every article of clothing, furniture and dish we owned to ship out to Canada while my children and I looked on. Important belongings we would need until the container arrived in Canada, two months later, were packed in a few suitcases. The suitcases stared at us, forlornly from a corner of the apartment. All the rest was packed and put on a boat towards our new land.

They packed. I cried.

My help cried too. "Madame, must you leave?". Gladys, the nounou as they say in France had given me for my birthday that year a hardcover copy of "The Devil wears Prada".

"Because Madame, I know you like Prada", she had proudly commented when she presented me with the book.

"Not because I am the devil, then right?" I chided her.

She had already more than once complained to my children in her lackadaisical way "Ah, la vie serait plus facile si votre mère était moins maniaque". (Life would be so much easier if your mother were not such a clean freak). But when my ex-husband asked her to work for him after I left, she nobly refused. She considered this a betrayal.

I cried again while tears streamed down her round face. I had found out that when I had hired her seven years earlier, the ID she had presented me with were "faux papiers" (fake papers). Her real name was Bernadette.

I looked back and remembered that I had remarked during the interview, "Wow, you look so mature for your age. Are you really 20? It must be all those responsibilities you had at home as the eldest child". She nodded and smiled, no doubt, laughing inwardly at how I had rambled on and provided her with the answer to my question. I had never doubted a minute that she was telling the truth. Many years later, she confided her true identity to my children, who laughingly reported it to me. By then, I was very attached to her and cared very little about the scam. I simply told her not to expect me to call her Bernadette after nearly eight years. She shrugged her shoulders. She came from Cameroun where she had practically single-handedly raised 8 younger brothers and sisters. What did she care if I called her Gladys or Bernadette, she seemed to say.

Very shortly after her firstborn, she had a second child. She confided to me, "it's less complicated to have two kids with the same father. Once I have my kids if he wants, he can leave, but at least my daughters will be real sisters". I was impressed by her practical evaluation of the marital situation. She was not surprised by her boss's departure. She took it all in stride like old souls do.

The week of the move, Bianca, one of my very best friends, came to the rescue, as usual, to support us through this difficult time. As soon as she entered the apartment, she quickly retrieved, from a thankfully still open cardboard box, the kettle for coffee and an ashtray. She then proceeded to give the movers clear instructions that these would be the last to go.

"These," she gesticulated to the French and English-speaking movers "are the last -'dernier'- in the box, only when you finished all the rest". They were so happy to accommodate finally a sane woman in this household who was somewhat giving instructions.

They packed. We smoked. I cried.

On the last day of the packing, my ex-husband came to check the last item being placed into the container that would cross the ocean. With his usual practical sense, he pointed out that he hoped the movers hadn't taken advantage of my tear-filled blurry vision to steal any furniture. Needless to say, I hadn't kept an eagle's eyes on them.

This heartless stranger, inspecting the apartment with a matter of fact efficiency, was not what I was mourning. It is not what divorcees lament, I am sure, 9 times out of 10. Why would anyone cry over a man that wants to leave us and therefore does not love us? It is the end of life, as we know it that we lament. It is the fear of the unknown that looms before us. The ruins of a life that must be picked up all alone. Who has the energy after a tsunami to rebuild? Compared to most women who must stay in a city or even in lodgings where they were happily (or not) married, I got off easy assured me, my therapist. My new surroundings would spare me nostalgic links to the past. I was going for a clean slate. After 23 years.

I was moving back to Montreal, to home, to my family, hoping they would help fill in the void and help rebuild a new life for my daughters and myself.

Like Eliette Abecassis says in the book "Une Affaire Conjugale":

"To do things well, in a marriage, you would have to start with a divorce. And then get married. You don't know a man in marriage. You don't know your spouse when you make love to them. (...) No, the only way to really know your spouse is through a divorce. There, one takes the full measure of his human, moral and psychological quality."

Death

In the middle of this horrible divorce, in the middle of the most horrible winter, the person that I was closest to on earth, my father, passed away. Did G.d want to spare him the pain of seeing his eldest daughter and adored grandchildren abandoned and suffering cruelly?

My husband and I had found an eye of calm in the tornado of divorce. And that is when I was urgently called to Montreal. My uncle called me with a tremor in his voice that I can still hear today telling me to come. I kept repeating that I could not come, I had work etc., as if I was trying to avoid the truth of how bad the situation was. I was just trying to make this horrible phone call go away. He told me my father was still alive, but not doing well. He didn't dare to tell me the truth, and I know it was his compassion for me that robbed him of this courage. My husband was devoid of any compassion; he had been told the horrible truth, but he was too "busy "to accompany me. During the whole plane trip there, I rocked back and forth praying, but it was too late. I lived for the next ten days the nightmare that all my life I feared of.

The day my father had turned 60, I had been struck with the

realization that he would not be around forever. It was about at that time that I started bothering my parents with neurotic phone calls just to check up on them. Sometimes I would stay up late because of our time difference between Montreal and Paris, incessantly calling until they finally picked up. This was before cell phones, but as soon as they came out on the market, I insisted they get one. The day I had dreaded for so long had come. Immense sadness and emptiness put my marital problems in the background, but not for long.

I landed back in Paris after the Shiva (mourning period). Soon after, my ex-husband greeted me with the cruellest blow, right in the head this time, making my ears pound and pain resonate in my whole being. He refused that I sleep in our bed because I was in mourning. All I longed for was to find refuge in my bed after the flight, to hide under my duvet. I felt that his hatred was becoming too destructive and not to spare me in this cruel moment was more than I could accept.

I asked him to take his belongings and leave. A few days later, he did. He had acted this cruelly, perhaps unconsciously, because he knew that is what it would take to make me abandon the marriage and finally ask him to leave.

I thought I would be able to mourn my father and that divorce would be relegated to the second level of importance. But a divorce equals everyday life that is torn to shreds and filled with sorrow, emptiness and disorientation. The sudden absence of my husband and the father of my children was unbelievably cruel, and to my stunned surprise, it took center stage in my sorrows.

The loss of my father was not given the place of honor it deserved because my life was overcome by divorce. Many years later I have survived and (mostly) gotten over my divorce. I once heard that to calculate how long it typically takes to get over a divorce, you should count a ratio of one year for every five years of marriage. My marriage lasted twenty odd years, so it should take me roughly 5 years to get over it. Normally. I still mourn my father, and this pain will last forever. The pain of divorce cannot and should not last forever. One cannot and should not mourn a person that has chosen to no longer be with us. Seeing pictures of my ex-husband now leave me cold, even if on the spur of the moment, the pain was intense. Seeing pictures of my father still makes me very sad, and I often miss him even many, many years later.

Nevertheless, the destruction of divorce was overruling my whole life, even the pain caused by the death of my father. A man I owed everything to. Perhaps my father's death had made me even weaker, and I wished not to cope with divorce. Maybe divorce is so destructive it always takes center stage.

Survival

That was my divorce. But in my divorce was my survival.

Because no matter how shocked and terrified I felt, I never missed once a day of work or any of my usual habits and obligations. I ran through them all, going through the motions with the constant lump in my throat and loud heart thuds filling my entire body. Even the ritual chore of going to the dry cleaners on Saturday mornings was religiously executed. Once we were all finally ready to get out of the house, my children, feeling relieved that I had plans for us, would pile into the Citroën and we would start out. By first going to the dry cleaners no matter what our plans were.

"Mom, do we have to go? Can't we go straight to Bon Marché to meet Bianca and Pascale? I am so hungry for lunch".

"This will take two minutes. Why didn't you eat a little

something at home? You know it's our family tradition to go to the dry cleaners." In the grimmest moments, I cling on to my sense of humor, thinking these are the memories and strengths I will leave to my children. Some mothers may leave as memories the smell of home-baked cookies or "choucroute" or "dafina" or itchy knitted sweaters or whatever their signature trademark for motherhood is. Humor and grosgrain bows adorning everything are the heritage I hope to leave.

We could have done without this family tradition. It was my way of clutching on to sanity. I needed to maintain a semblance of control over my life by staying on top of things. I needed to keep to our everyday schedule and NOT let things PILEUP and spin totally overwhelmingly and irrevocably out of control.

My life was a mayhem of sadness and tears, and I was petrified that only ugly emptiness lay ahead. I clutched onto my routines and errands helplessly. As if I could not afford to also lose control of these unimportant errands that were the ONLY thing, I had control over. At least I would be up to date on my dry cleaners. Not to skip a beat in the usual rhythm of my life. And all the other tiny niggling errands that kept me going. I focused on crossing off missions and chores from my blackberry to get a sense of achievement. I needed to stop feeling, at least for the time of a task, that my life was not being totally overrun by folly.

Every time I waited my turn at the dry cleaners, I observed the other customers with envy and fascination. These people were probably lucky to be living their ordinary everyday lives and not one like mine, where major catastrophe had hit. How I longed to be one of them; how I wanted for my old life with only minor qualms. Where was MY ordinary, everyday life where ALL was routine? When I could go to the dry cleaners without the non-stop thumping in my throat.

I did not miss a single day of work either. Not because I loved my job, which I did, but because I could not afford to lose control of this too. I chose my clothes as usual with care and tried to maintain my typical face painted with bright lipstick and adopt my habitual cheerful, efficient and controlled manner with everyone. The constant thumping in my throat forced me to periodically go to the bathroom, lock the stall and cry silently.

I had close work friends in whom I confided and will forever be grateful for. Some spoke from experience, having themselves gone through a divorce and offered successful examples that gave me a tiny hope.

Unlike the paramedic who came to collect me one particularly depressing Sunday when I was so anguished that I had a hard time breathing. He did not help any by telling me in the depressing ambulance on the way to the depressing Parisian hospital that his own mother had NEVER gotten over her divorce. Typical scene of french realism.

This book is not about Love and Divorce or Children and Divorce or Adultery and Divorce. It is about Survival and Divorce and Women. Because when you divorce, whether or not you love your spouse, (how could I love this man who didn't mind hurting me), whether or not there are children (I thank G. for my four wonderful daughters), whether or not there is adultery, (obviously there was) the toughest thing about divorce is surviving it.

For every divorcee out there, there exists a real Survivor story. This is the story of my fight for survival. And in my battle for survival are woven in my children, my work, men and most especially, women. That is what makes the fabric of this story.

Movement, Momentum

Before I start jabbering about all the silly anecdotes that surrounded my life of a divorcee, I should explain WHY, in my humble opinion, there are so many silly anecdotes. Divorce is also about becoming a teenager all over again. In my case, this was at the generous age of 46. That is what the newfound single status does to you. Especially if you were married to an overly macho, to say the least, Israeli/Moroccan/Jewish man for twenty-three years. And a change of life always comes with the good, the bad, ….

Divorce is surrounded by a lot of movement. It is preceded by a sudden movement that can be very subtle, and then there is a big bang, and it all gathers momentum. It disrupts life precisely like a stone thrown into the water. You do not expect the stone to be thrown, so that sudden plop surprises you. Then all of a sudden, there are ripples all around. And when the movements start, it takes a lot of time for everything to calm down again in your life (or the lake). That is why it is a crazy time in your life. Like my friend and neighbor's daughter remarked to me one day, "There is more happening here than at the Kardashian's." As lives are reorganized, physical and emotional whirlwinds occur. Vacations are organized with ex-partner, budgets and schedules discussed. Add to that some inevitable divorce drama…

That is in big part what this book is about and what every divorce does. My divorce was also about moving from one country to the next and all of a sudden discovering and rediscovering a new environment, cultural differences, the web, creativity and independence. And myself. Because like I said, divorce equals discovery.

A divorce releases you in many ways. Since high school and Mr Faigen's class in Mass Media, I had wanted to become a Creative. One of those professionals he talked about that sat in offices and dreamt up logos and stories and images. And throughout my marriage, I had struggled to find creative opportunities, but was always held back. When finally, my "dream job" opportunity came, after many years of working docilely for my husband, I had to seize it. He felt frustrated by my decision, and it was the first crack in our porcelain marriage. I was like a tiger holding the prey between his teeth and not willing to let it go even if it meant sacrificing my marriage. This, of course, I realized afterwards. Like most of the essential things we do, it was probably done knowingly, to get out of a marriage that would have made me lose myself.

I smile when thinking of one creative project I had worked on in Paris and how I had tried to hide it from my husband. I avoided telling my husband about this project because to him a plan with no real profit involved was devoid of interest and he would just scoff at it.

I had hooked up with a photographer, a make-up artist and hairdresser. We would get together once a month and shoot carefully composed images just for the pleasure. Like musicians getting together for a jam session. Beforehand we would choose the theme. As the Creative Director of the project, I had to get together all the elements for the day of the shoot (clothes, decors, etc.).

One day after a particularly intense shoot day, I was racing home because it was Shabbat. The table had to be ready with 14 different salads, or my husband would not be happy. I rushed. At a red light, I turned around and looked at the back of my car. We had just done a shoot full of vegetation sponsored by florists. My car looked like an Amazonian jungle. I prayed he would not approach my vehicle. That day it struck me. If you are with a man that you must hide a jungle from something is wrong. But I was not ready and thus continued to hide in my jungle.

Ready or not, the divorce came. And it released me. In a way, divorce is like those creams and treatments that promise to release the production of collagen. During and after divorce, your mind and body must react to adapt to a new life. Thus, you are in a regenerative state, and you are producing new vibes. Things happen. Especially right after. It is the law of momentum. And being with a heightened sense of awareness, everything that happens hits you with intensity.

I was free, and my creativity was released. Just like collagen.

Active ingredients were running amok.

But you realize afterwards that active ingredients had started peaking before visible results came. Because divorce does not happen overnight. To understand a divorce, one must analyze every life and all of life's many divorces that lead up to it. So, let's start at the beginning.

CHAPTER 2

IT ALL STARTED IN CASABLANCA

Casablanca

I was born in Casablanca. Like many Jews, for some weird reason, we felt safe under the French protectorate. Since 1906, the Algeciras Conference had formalized France's "special position" and entrusted policing of Morocco jointly to France and Spain.

The sultan Mohammed V remained the country's leader, but only in theory. In practice, the sultan had no real power and the country was ruled by a colonial administration.

French civil servants allied themselves with the tens of thousands of French settlers or colons who entered the country and backed by their supporters in France, they controlled Morocco. They all benefited together from the best the country had to offer, such as generous tracts of the fertile agricultural land. The French government focused on the exploitation of Morocco's mineral wealth, the creation of a modern transportation system and the development of a modern agricultural sector geared to the French market.

French protectorate brought a European way of life with stores like Galeries Lafayette where all the children of modern "enlightened" Jews would have a picture taken in a shiny red car next to a Muslim paid to be dressed as Santa Claus. Little girls would wear dresses that replicated the Parisian style for children and have professional pictures taken from the in-vogue French photographers. Like all the French, they had come to reap all the pleasant benefits of living in a sunny city offering a more laid back rhythm of life than France. Plus plenty of very inexpensive help and employees to make life "douce". The photographers would add hand-drawn eyelashes on portraits of us taken in their fancy studios with French furniture. We admired everything that was French, and in Casablanca, we studied only the history of the French and had books depicting blond children. The history books we read started with "Nous les Gaullois", Us the people of Gaulle...

My parents were a beautiful and glamorous couple living in Casablanca and enjoying all the capital had to offer. For this generation, the ideals were French. The chic and enlightened way of life was to send the children to the nun's nursery school (yes, even if you were Jewish) and to have them checked by French pediatricians. I was a frail child, and when the French paediatrician highly recommended that I eat ham, although it was formally forbidden by our Jewish religion, there was no way my loving parents would deprive me of it. It would be backwards to do so by the following of religion over science! When I had lunch at my grandmother's house, although she kept a strictly kosher home, she asked my mother's younger sisters to run down and buy ham from the grocery store and to serve it to me on a bench in the building's hallways. I was her first grandchild, and if that ham was good for me because all the children in France had it for lunch, then it would be served to me.

My mother came from a family of 11 children. My grandmother was a loving, extremely responsible and discrete woman. She had lived through the scandal of having a very eccentric mother who had fallen in love and taken off with a younger man.

This younger man was a musician who loved to play the oud, a five stringed guitar used in music throughout the Middle East and smoke hashish. Hashish in Morocco was called kif which now means "pleasure" in French slang. My grandmother fell head over heels in love with this man. No doubt she had married too early and yearned for freedom and romance. She left her protected family life for the unknown and worked as a seamstress to support her independent lifestyle. The artsy hashish smoking musician could not support her. This was a huge deal in the '50s and in Morocco and in the Jewish community. I found this out at a very late stage in my life and wish I had met the romance-seeking, gutsy woman.

My grandmother and her daughters were all very conservative-way-of-life-abiders. As if trying to always make up for that bout of passion and eccentricity that had appeared in our family by means of their scandalous grandmother.

They all simply aspired to bring up their children with rules, discipline, order, propriety and a lot of home-cooked meals. Food was very important in our family. In fact, many years later, when my husband left me, the general feeling in the family was that he would not have left me if had I cooked more. Right before my second marriage, one of my aunts suggested that this time round I cook the entire Friday night Shabbat meal rather than resort to store-bought appetizers. This would give this marriage all the advantages and efforts it took for it to succeed.

In a family of 9 girls and two boys, seriousness and reputation were of the utmost importance. My grandparents were blessed with 8 daughters before (finally) having twins: a boy and a girl. The joke in Safi, the little fisherman's town where my grandparents raised their children was, "Jacob finally had a boy, but he came accompanied by yet another girl!". Finally, they topped off the family with one more boy. Thank G.d for my uncle Adam as this procured him the company of the youngest brother Marc in this family predominantly of women.

My mother and her siblings had been raised in the cramped quarters that could be afforded by my grandfather, an earnest and respectable bank employee.

In spite of a tight budget, when Passover came, my grandmother would buy rolls of fabric and sow new dresses, tablecloths and napkins. My grandfather was pleased that his daughters were elegantly attired. Reputation was important. The family moved to Casablanca because one of my grandmother's sisters insisted it was the thing to do for her nieces to find eligible Jewish bachelors and be married. My mother and her sisters appreciated the big city of Casablanca and its sophisticated European flavor.

Even in Casablanca, my grandfather kept a close watch on them. My mother or one of her equally beautiful sisters won prizes each year for the Miss Miami Beach beauty contest. This was the chic private beach, they would go to on Saturday afternoons. Afterwards, they were always faced with the dilemma of how to get rid of the first prize they could not bring home without an explanation. This was usually an oversized lamp. My grandfather would not have wanted his daughters to enrol in these contests.

My mother and her sisters all lived the same life but, what was interesting was how they all perceived or experienced it so differently.

The oldest of my aunts always felt the crushing responsibility of a new baby arriving home. The youngest ones never gave a second thought to living in a big family. They coped with it and simply tried to borrow clothes from their older sisters as much as they could. One of the middle sisters confided that when they would all go to the beach, for a family outing, she would look wistfully at the perfect European families. They were often very neat and controlled families with only two children that were given perfectly wrapped party sandwiches. She would dream that a family exactly like that one was her real family and was waiting for her somewhere in another country. Later that was precisely the family that she reproduced with her husband. One boy, one girl. European education in France and carefully prepared party sandwiches. Another one of my aunts, a middle child, said that often she would hide in the closet for hours to see if she would be missed. She remembered that no one ever looked for her. "Who had time!" the older sisters scoffed at these self-centered memories.

My father came from a smaller family and was quite spoiled for that era as the eldest son. He was an intellectual, one of the rare Jews to have gone to France to study and obtain the baccalaureate in those days. His friends would tell me with pride many years after the fact: "You know your father has the Baccalaureat, "as if he had obtained it for the whole community. Years later, even the rough diamond, self made millionaires were impressed by my father's diploma.

My father came from a family that did well; they owned a big hardware store in Casablanca, and my father was given favored treatment by his parents. His lifestyle was the same as that of the golden youth of Casablanca. Being sent to Paris for the baccalaureate was a rare luxury at the time. Add to that the fact that in Morocco when you were born and raised in the capital of Casablanca, you were as close to nobility as you could possibly get. In my early twenties, I briefly dated a young man in Paris. He introduced me to his mother, who was known for being extremely snobbish. Upon hearing my family name, she gave her seal of approval by informing her son that my father was "un vrai Casablancais", like herself. She now lived in Monaco, a city that had attributed to her the most prestigious of nationalities. But as she smiled at me from behind her armor of diamonds and minks, she was still sensitive to the pride of pointing out that her family also came from our capital. As if this were indeed a sign of great lineage.

I had such great love and admiration for my father that no matter the reason, I was always happy when someone said my father was extraordinary. Indeed, he was. This handsome young man was referred to as "the playboy of Casablanca". But he was more than that. He was principled but tolerant, ethical but not judgemental and very well-read: his great passion was philosophy although he could be found reading books on subjects as diverse as math, algebra, history or world politics. Later, when he would come visit me in Paris, we would go to the FNAC and he would stock up on the latest books on philosophy. We would leave the store, these dense and heavy books in bags and my father was as jubilant as a young boy leaving a candy store. My down to earth mother was always a little upset at the huge expense, but no doubt impressed by her husband's erudite passion.

My father was not perfect. That is probably what made him so special. He loved his books and philosophizing, but he also loved nightclubs, travel, friends and had so many different interests. He had favorite pastimes such as collecting prints of ships, hot air balloons and maps. He followed the political situation of every country of the planet, not limiting his curiosity to big headliners.

He was as impulsive as he was thoughtful. Sometimes it was a bit much for my cautious, sensible mother. But she always had great admiration for this extraordinary man she had fallen head over heels in love with.

He was a thinker and a dreamer, but would willingly engage in a fistfight for the cause of any underdog or to defend a friend. Friends were real allies. My father told me that they never had any financial debts towards each other. Whoever had money paid drinks, dinner, hotels for those who didn't have any, without ever keeping track. That was just the way it was done. When sojourning in Paris or elsewhere with his friends, as soon as any of them received money wired from their parents in Casablanca, they would all immediately fiesta together. Courtesy of the freshly arrived sum, they would land at Regine's nightclub and order a bottle of whisky to get VIP treatment and a table. This was at a time when the celebrated French actor Alain Delon was just another young, good-looking man hanging around the clubs.

Once when my father shared an apartment with his friends in Paris, it became very quickly crowded with friends of friends from Morocco looking for a place to stay during the summer vacation. A few too many arrived, after a late-night of doing the round of nightclubs, and they had run out of all feasible sleeping spots. My father's friend took off his tie, laid it out in an elegant gesture on the carpet, and told the newest arrival, "Here is your bed". The tie was probably a Francesco Smalto, one of our dandy king's favorite brands that all the young men of Casablanca also favored. I think it was their way of respecting and recognizing our ruler's excellent taste for European finery but also his occidental values in an Arab country and his kindness towards the Jews.

My father had a great variety of friends: the intellectuals that studied voraciously, the golden boys that partied, the strong men that would fight for a cause, the poker players that would lose their shirt. Years later, when he would come to visit me in Paris, he would do all the rounds going from the chic Polo club to the seedy bars that hosted poker games. Many of his friends had moved to Paris.

"Bon, maintenant je vais voir la racaille," (now I will visit my sleazy friends), he would say laughingly but also affectionately before going to check up on them in their dubious quarters in dilapitaded bars of small Parisian side streets.

As I grew older, I recognized in myself, my beloved father's quirkiness. He would suddenly leave a dinner party, we were hosting to look up something in a book or read just a few stolen lines on philosophy or history or even in an algebra book. He loved these dinner parties and was always there to distribute advice or encouragement to young and old alike. But all of a sudden, he would surreptitiously vanish, and we knew he had been pulled away from us, by his books. Then I would enter the room where he was reading, and he would guiltily look up at me and say "J'arrive Cherie". He would quickly get up and come back with us and be the charming and cultivated host he was.

Books were very important to him. A short time before he passed away, from the prostate cancer and the treatment that was wearing him down, one of the last questions he asked me was to count how many books were in his library. How many English and how many French. When I gave him the numbers that were very close, as both languages were equally represented, he was pleased.

My father was a businessman, but he did not have the thirst to make a lot of money like many of his friends. Often I noticed the same pattern among his friends. The more modest the circumstances they had lived in growing up, the greatest was their hunger for the (North) American dream. He was an educated man, so he was often the advisor or consultant of these men. But he did not understand their drive to buy bigger and bigger homes or more and more expensive cars. He was too taken up by the world and its problems to center on his life.

What do we need a house with x number of bathrooms and bedrooms he would say.

He was not inhabited by the American dream of success in terms of money. Yet he had been the first to interact with the "Americans" in Casablanca.

In the Moroccan community of Montreal, he was often seen as an advisor because of his excellent mastery of the English language, thanks to his years working at the American airbase of Casablanca. American soldiers based at the USAF airbase had developed out of the Allied presence there at the close of World War II. In Casablanca, he had been impressed as a young man with them. He was not only in admiration of their cool aviator jackets, ray ban glasses, but also of their friendly, unaffected manners and good ethics. This era marked the start of his love for America and what it stood for.

He applied at the American base in Casablanca for a job, and before the interview, he asked for a quick vocabulary lesson from an American he had met on the circuit of the Casablanca nightlife.

"When they ask me if I speak English, I want a better word than just "yes", what can I answer ?" he queried.

"Fluently." the young military offered.

And that is how my father impressed them, landed the job and eventually became a fluent speaker. On the strength of the well-chosen word.

Life in Casablanca was kind to us. My parents met and were married in Casablanca. My mother was the first of her sisters to be married. She always felt guilty about disrupting the family order and marrying before her older sister, who ended up marrying a year later. I was born soon after and in the fashion of the era, I was named after a French actress or singer. In Morocco, all of our names were influenced by French colonialism. Our generation was either called Sylvie, like Sylvie Vartan or Catherine (Deneuve) or Michèle (Morgan). Later in France, I was to discover that many parents had the same source of inspiration for naming their children. When I joined the BGBC team's European headquarters, I found 23 Sylvie's, 20 Catherine's and 24 Michèle's listed there. My father's friends would always hum songs of girl's with names from France.

Aline
By Christophe
Sur cette plage
Dans cet orage
Elle a disparu
Et j'ai crié, crié
Aline
Pour qu'elle revienne
Et j'ai pleuré, pleuré
Oh! J'avais trop de peine

Aline
By Christophe
(On this beach
In this storm
She disappeared
And I cried and cried
Aline
For her to come back
And I cried and cried
Oh! I was too sad)

My loving parents were the most attentive parents a girl could ask for. Besides my adoring grandparents, I had 8 aunts and two uncles who doted on me, the first grandchild in the family. To complete this protective circle, my parent's closest friends were ever-present in our lives.

It was an era that was economically thriving and made it a wonderful place to live in, among many other things; Casablanca under the European influence had much to offer.

In Casablanca's best streets, many stores were filled with clothes and delicacies imported from Europe. Saturdays were spent at the private beaches named after faraway places like Tahiti and Miami, where Jews rented "bungalows" or small cabanas overlooking the pools and restaurants. In the morning, chauffeurs and help would lug elaborate lunches, or if it was Saturday, the traditional dafina to be shared with friends. Men played cards which led to many heated conversations. The women picked with great care the bathing suits, but also dresses and hats they would wear to go sit at the elegant restaurants overlooking the beaches with their families. After a day of swimming, there was always a group ready to go eat a French crepe at the latest Creperie or play a game of tennis at the Soc. The Soc tennis club was mostly filled with Jewish members. There were also the snobbier and very vied in vogue clubs where the French went as well as Jews who enjoyed basking in their ways.

Parties, bar mitzvahs, weddings, and all special occasions were celebrated with great energy, enthusiasm and no efforts were too demanding. French seamstresses brought the latest fabrics and trends from Paris and outfits were plotted and planned weeks before. The style of actresses like Sylvie Vartan and Catherine Deneuve was emulated right down to their perfect blond bobs or "chignons". Cooks were hired for wedding preparations. Delicacies were prepared for days beforehand, and usually, the festivities lasted at least a week. One of my aunts once rented an apartment for three weeks, solely to cook food for her daughter's wedding. She installed ovens and freezers and hired 12 cooks, she supervised relentlessly to prepare every dish, dessert, chocolate, pastry or bread roll that was made from scratch. Even the chickens had to be plucked.

There were the nightclubs where one could have dinner while listening to music. After dinner, we strolled to the "glaciers ", along "La côte", (the coast), where ice cream sundaes were served by Muslim waiters dressed up in white coat tails imitating the French garçons de cafes. And the cafés overlooking the sea where each café served as a pretext for the longest of conversations. With a cigarette, of course.

King Mohammed V was proud of the Jewish presence in Morocco. It meant that we were a country where all religions were respected. He also enjoyed the company of Jewish men in his entourage of advisors and felt that they were trustworthy and had a different way of thinking that he could benefit from. After all, a Jewish advisor would never dare compete with him and try to overthrow him like his friend General Oufkir had tried in vain. (The man and his family were to pay for that crime: Oufkir was killed and the family imprisoned in a gated home for nearly twenty years).

The Jews lived in a comfort zone between the French protectorate and the kindness of our King, who had protected us from being deported by the laws of the Vichy government.

We emulated and admired the French, and they seemed sophisticated, "enlightened" and worldly to us, but our soul was closer to that of the Muslims. It was the Jews and the Muslims that went to the same communal ovens. Even when we had ovens at home, only those special clay ovens afforded the very particular earthy taste to our traditional Saturday lunch dish, "the dafina". Muslim women were hired as help and raised us as their children, often living with us. Muslim men worked in our businesses or were partners with us. Our communities also overlapped for a game of soccer, our country's favourite sport, played with the same passion by all. The French preferred the more "chic" sports like tennis and golf.

Of course, certain borders were not to be overstepped.

F. Amor the creator and fashion designer of the much celebrated, by the French press, "Plein South" would lament about these borders many years later. After too many drinks in the bar of the Ritz or any other super trendy restaurant he brought his entourage or staff to, he would reminisce.

Farid was born of a German mother and a Muslim father. He was handsome, tall with blue eyes and long blond hair. His German angular side was softened by the traits of his Muslim father. He was part of the golden Casablanca youth where Muslims, Jews and sometimes, but to a lesser extent the French frayed together. Among his closest friends was a young Jewish man whose sister inevitably fell in love with Farid. He returned the sentiment. He never understood the panic of the family at the thought of their daughter falling in love with a Muslim. This was more than highly disregarded and would hail the end of her eligibility among young Jewish men of the community. The girl was quickly and surreptisiously sent to Paris by her family.

This was because her family was wealthy and could afford to do so. If not, she would have been sent to Israel by an impromptu Jewish organization in Casablanca. My paternal grandfather had been part of that organization. The families would call on him and his group of volunteers. They would buy the young girl pretty dresses, distract her with attentions and have her shipped off to Israel.

But in this particular case, the family had an apartment in Paris. Farid found out and immediately flew there and stalked the apartment. The girl was shipped to Israel. Finally, she married a Jewish young man, the taboo of being in love with a Muslim, too difficult to affront. Later she divorced. Much later they were to bump into each other on rainy afternoons avenue Montaigne or in trendy Parisian restaurants. And reminisce. Their culture, country and upbringing could have made them one. But religion had its voice and had divided in the end their oneness.

And then he would find himself in those same places, with his staff who was the closest he ever had to a family during his adult life. And party and drink and reminisce. Probably not just about his love for a Jewish girl, but also about the loss of his brothers whose limit he had seen in spite of their closeness. And also, about those golden days of youth.

So, if we kept to our borders all was good for all sides.

But in spite of this our lives were precarious.

France's exile of Sultan Mohammed V to Madagascar in 1953 and his replacement by the unpopular Mohammed Ben Aarafa, had sparked the first opposition to the French protectorate by the nationalists and those who respected the sultan as their religious leader.

Two years later, faced with a united Morocco demanding for the sultan's return and rising violence in Morocco, the French government brought Mohammed V back to Morocco. The following year negotiations began that led to Moroccan independence. In late 1955, in what was known as The Revolution of the King and his People, the Sultan Mohammed

V successfully negotiated the restoration of Morocco's independence and this finally culminated in the independence of Morocco being declared on March 2nd, 1956.

Mohammed V's son "Hassan II of Morocco" Hassan II, became King of Morocco on March 3, 1961. His rule witnessed significant political unrest and dissent. This insecurity culminated in 1971 and 1972 when the regime was challenged by military coups. The King was most certainly desired by their G.d the Muslims claimed. After all, he had survived at least ten attempts on his life. In 1971, army rebels invaded the king's birthday party with gunfire, killing 98 guests, including the Belgian ambassador. His British counterpart survived by jumping over the palace walls, while the king saved his life by locking himself in a lavatory. Only a year later, his faithful minister, General Mohammed Oufkir turned renegade and sent up fighter aircraft to shoot down the royal jet flying home from France. The king is said to have grabbed the controls and radioed "The tyrant is dead", fooling his would-be assassins into letting him land. Once safely on the ground, he sent the rebels, like so many of their countrymen, to the torture chambers and dungeons of his desert forts. That is how Moroccans came to believe that Hassan must be a godly ruler as he had so much baraka, a God-given mixture of luck and grace that defied death and demise.

Jews felt insecure in this atmosphere. The King Hassan always had a particular fondness for the Jews of his country, but the question that preoccupied the community was what would become of them if he was overthrown. He was more lenient with the Jews that opposed him than the Muslims. When one of ours declared himself a communist, King Hassan never was able to take him seriously or really get angry with him. He treated him like the unruliest of his children for whom he had a particular fondness.

We always trusted the King Hassan and even when we emigrated to Montreal a picture of him was always hanging somewhere in our home. But we felt the insecurity that the end of the French protectorate had come to symbolize, and my family and community broke apart. Jews left in all directions: Spain, Belgium, France, United States, England or even South America. We were to go to Canada and my loving grandparents, aunts and uncles would all go to Israel. That was perhaps the first abandonment I felt in my life.

My parents sold all their beautiful French furniture to a Muslim businessman. Years later, my father loved to recount how the Muslim businessman after exchanging ideas with my father on the situation in Morocco became a friend and told my father, "please keep this furniture, stay here and I will give you a great position in my company. This is your country too. We need men like you". This goodbye was of a great comfort to us as it confirmed to my father that Morocco had not sent us away. We were wanted there till the end.

The Empress Of England

We were to take a cruise ship. The cruise ship was a lot more expensive and would make for a longer trip, but my father had a fear of flying. On that ship while my parents fought sea sickness, I learned my first words of English. I was made to repeat "Please, thank you, how do you do", by the captain and waiters who doted on me while we crossed the Atlantic Ocean. I loved, welcomed and savoured every word I learned.

CHAPTER 3

IT CONTINUED IN MONTREAL

The Other Side Of The Bridge

Their names were Susan and Sally. The boys were named Mike and Jeff. Is that partly why I am now in love with Jeff.

The girls had thin golden hair. My hair was so different : it was thick and curly. I asked my hairdresser aunt if she could cut layers underneath in order to make it look thinner like the girls I admired. She refused of course, saying one day I would appreciate my hair's thickness.

Their mothers served them the same meals as the children in the books we read about: meat, potatoes and gravy. In Morocco we were not like the children in the books, and once again, I felt no resemblance to the children in the storybooks. These Anglo-Saxon meals were unseen in our home. My mother cooked either Moroccan or French. Nothing similar to what was eaten in our newly adopted country. They had library books on Eskimo art and the fathers would build treehouses in the summer and watch hockey in the winter. Everyone loved hockey. The day the Canadians won the Stanley Cup even the meanest boy in school gave me a big smile.

My sister was born in Montreal. She was the "real Canadian". I remember the day my mother brought her home from the hospital. There was a snowstorm outside and my mother was worried about the cold. If my mother had brought her home in Casablanca, we would have been surrounded by family and overwhelmed with help. Here, we were alone, in a snow-covered city. When my mother resumed her job as a coordinator at the University of Montreal, she picked up my sister from the nursery after work and came home by bus, often in snowstorms. My father came home from work later.

I realize now how different this life must have been for both of them.

When it was minus 20 the boys could be seen running around with open jackets and the girls went ice skating. My mother made us wear so many layers, that once I caught the teacher and another parent commenting in an exasperated tone on the overabundance of complicated layering my mother imposed on me and my sister. We were marked or even stamped, I felt, with the immigrant's fear of the cold. They all had matching jackets and ski pants. Once my mother bought one of those outfits for my sister and I was proud to parade her when we walked to school together. As if we belonged. Like all children of immigrants, we were marked with our differences that ran through us and permeated all aspects of our lives : food, clothing, leisure and maternal tongue. Even our French maternal tongue separated us with its accent and vocabulary from the French the Canadians spoke.

We had arrived in Montreal and for the first 6 months we lived in the Cote des Neiges area that has greeted all immigrant groups successively.

Then we moved to Town of Mount Royal. We lived in an apartment building on the outskirts of this wealthy suburban town. We had chosen it because two couples, friends of my parents had also recently emigrated from Casablanca and lived in that building. Birds of a feather…

I went from being doted on by 8 aunts, two uncles and grandparents to having a French-Canadian babysitter and then becoming a "key child". My father became an advisor for a businessman and my mother found a job at the University of Montreal. She called, went for an interview and started that same day. Those were the days when jobs were around and if you did not have one it was because you did not wish to work. We had the responsibility to rush home after school and call our mother to say we had safely arrived. My sister still remembers that first phone number she had to learn by heart. Far off where the days where my grandmother and all her sisters helped her take care of me, leaving her to a still carefree life.

Later one of my aunts, her husband and children arrived in Montreal and also came to live in our building. Birds of a feather flock together. I would accompany my cousins, who were in the same grade school, for lunch at their house and was mildly envious that their mother didn't work. I had started out crossing the bridge over the train tracks that led to our grade school alone, then later with my cousins and later still with my little sister. There was something romantic about crossing a bridge every day and we pretended there was a little stream running underneath. Those were the days when we could spend hours playing in a park nearby or at the entrance to our building. Stones represented kingdoms and bits of sticks made huts or magic wands.

I loved having my cousins around and walking home with them. It gave me a sense of security and belonging to know that we had the same grandparents somewhere in Israel. Sometimes we would not play with the other children in the neighborhood, and just sit on the steps and enumerate all of our aunts and uncles in Israel, strengthening our bond with each name. It was also so reassuring to go with them for lunch, especially when my dear and sweet cousin Sophie and I did not squabble. I feel that was always my fault, she has always been obstinate but truly good. My cousin's presence in our building was very welcome after having been a key child for two years. During those two years I was instructed to call my mother at the office as soon as I entered the apartment and before I left. Lunch waited for me in the fridge and I ate it while watching the Flintstone's for company. I was eight. We were many with our keys hidden under our school uniform, but I always felt as if I was the only one.

I felt so different, and thus, was born my need to excel in school. I realized instinctively that as an immigrant I needed to work twice as hard to succeed.

I worked diligently and sat in the first row and was basically a teacher pleaser.

My competitive streak was born in grade 1 because of a Bristol board choo choo train.

It ran across the wall of the classroom, assembled by our teacher from multicolored cut out Bristol boards representing different compartments in a train. Cue cards with each pupil's name fit neatly into each compartment. Underneath our name was listed the titles of all the books we had read and shared a short report of with the class.

I was an avid reader, bringing a book with me wherever I went, even when I accompanied my parents and their friends anywhere from the hairdressers to restaurants or jaunts in the country. I assumed I would always hold the first place and see my card throne in the compartment at the front. It was the case until a new pupil arrived shortly after school had begun.

Her name was Peggy and her father had been hired to be the janitor of our school. She smiled good naturedly all the time and we soon became friends. One day, to my amazement after our book reports, I observed the teacher advance Peggy's card to the front of the train and put mine right behind.

Peggy continued to smile good-naturedly in the playground, oblivious to the emotions arising in me.

But all of a sudden, her smile seemed eerily smug. I was very unsettled by my new unfavorable position in the second compartment of the train. I vowed to no longer read just for pleasure, but also with the pressure of speed to regain my position. During weekends, I imagined that Peggy rarely put her book down because her parents were probably anchored to the school, fulfilling many responsibilities. Meanwhile I accompanied my parents on a whirlwind of activities, distracting me from reading and thus relegating me to number two.

Revigorated with purpose, born from my newly discovered competitive streak, I doubled my quota of library books and read, certainly still with pleasure but also with purpose. My goal now constantly present in the back of my mind.

When I finally retrieved my first position, with great satisfaction and pride, I realized that Peggy did not even flinch. She really had been reading and smiling good-naturedly totally oblivious to my designs of out reading her.

I felt a little guilty at my carefully executed plan of action to surpass her on the reading train. Still, it was nice to be back in first class.

That was how I discovered my competitive streak; on a choo choo train. I was to use it later in the corporate fashion world.

There were many other immigrant groups, but we were each closed off in our circle, probably because we were each different, differently. Town of Mount Royal was mostly inhabited by the wealthy Anglo-Saxons, but it was bordered by the Lacadie neighborhood where other immigrant groups settled. There were primarly Greek immigrants at the time. One of these families moved to the wealthier TMR and tried to anglicize their children. Vasoula became Betty and we were soon best friends. Scattered all over their coffee tables, you could find books on Eskimos from the library. No Greek food was found in that house, but meat, potatoes and gravy. I wonder if Betty is still Betty or became Vasoula today.

Things seem so simple for everyone else, but appearances are always deceiving. One of my friends seemed to have a white picket fence life, but time told us otherwise. Randy lived in a spacious rambling house with older brothers who seemed to always be washing the family Volkswagen with a dog at their heels. To complete the picture, her mother always seemed to be baking cookies and wiping her hands on a flowered apron like in story books. Her father was a math professor at the university where my mother worked. I admired and aspired to be as "white bread" as they seemed. But years later her father wrote a letter to the Math department to announce that he had waited for his youngest to be in university to get a sex change operation. When we get older, we see things are not so simple but, at that age, their family seemed the ideal I wished for.

Most of the other children lived in big homes and I had noticed that their parents did everything very differently. Our different cultures dictated that we did not spend money in the same way. One of my friends, who lived in a considerably sized house complained to her mother, "Valerie always has steak dinner at her house, why can't we ever have steak?". The mother replied, "Valerie's mother works so they can afford those extras". Somehow it did not add up to me. They could not afford steak, yet lived in this beautiful, huge house that I would have gladly sacrificed steak dinners for. One day at a birthday party in a huge TMR home, the older sisters of the birthday girl drove me back. I was indicating the route. At the end of a street I prompted them, "Turn right in". They misunderstood and turned into one of the biggest homes in my neighborhood. The sisters looked at me admiringly. I pointed to the apartment building, further down. "No, that is where I was telling you to turn in".

They drove me over in uncomfortable silence. Maybe I wouldn't have minded so much if I wasn't always feeling different.

So we ate steak dinners and I had the most awaited for birthday parties. This was because my parents, like many Sephardics, spent lavishly on little comforts. They would order from the expensive convenience store that delivered nearly every night. When you come from Morocco, of course, it does not seem like such a luxury to avoid facing a snowstorm to buy milk. To make the delivery fee worth their while, the habitual phone call would be preceded with "I am ordering cigarettes from 'la voleuse" (the highway robber), do we need anything else?".

After school, I watched the "Brady Bunch" but knew that my mother would arrive from work in the middle of "The Price is Right". On a few occasions, my mother was held up by snowstorms or a delayed bus schedule and the "Price is Right" was over and she had still not arrived. I could not breathe, my anguish was so immense until she came. I would look out the window at the streetlights, imagine the worst and pray silently till I heard the key in the lock. Then the door would fly open and my mother would exclaim terms of endearment, often in Arabic, and would shower my sister and me with attention to make up for the lost time.

My parents often resorted to the language from back home, that they missed, and was solely reserved for extreme feelings (great love or great contempt).

Each night my mother would make us take vitamins. When I would ask why, she answered that we needed these to get used to the cold of our country of adoption. As if with a simple prescription we could be programmed to adapt to this country.

As if we were a light switch to be turned "on" to this country. I have waited all my life to hear the click.

Even when my mother signed me up for ballet like all the other girls, I did not fit. The teacher looked at my knees and said they didn't bend properly. Years later, I looked at pictures of the show we had put on for the parents (where I was actually playing the role of a marshmallow with a huge white foam on my head) and noticed that there was not one single picture where I was in the same position as the others. By then I had decided to become a Creative, so it didn't bother me as much. Creatives are supposed to be different.

In those days, especially when you came from Casablanca, where you lived in a community, you did not worry unduly about children's security. Just look at the series "Mad Men", a true rendition of our lives back then. Parents smoked in closed cars with children or even around newborn babies. Children were just not the main preoccupation.

On two occasions, when I walked home alone men pulled their cars over and asked me to accompany them to the candy store. Both times as they talked to me, I could see their hands vigorously rubbing flesh under their steering wheel. I had never seen a man's private parts. With my child's wild imagination, I thought it was the small arm of a child. Some invisible hand protected me by bringing that thought to my mind and made me run away. And dream of a machine that all men would have to walk through and that would beep if their soul was bad, so they could be sent to another planet. So that we could all feel secure again. Later when I had my own children, still traumatized by the incident, I would occasionally spy on my help to make sure they were the first ones at school pick up and never missed a school outing as an accompanying parent.

Thankfully, the end of the school year came each year and with it our ritual trip to Israel. The last day of school I would run out, knowing that soon my haven of security would be within reach. I would be in a cocoon of warmth and safety. There was a long plane ride and once again I would be smothered by love and attention. My grandfather awaited us at the airport and my grandmother cried with joy upon our arrival.

My aunts worked at the Tel Aviv Club Med and they would take me with them to the private pool and spoil me with gifts and attention. In Morocco, when my mother made them babysit me, they often brought me to parties, without her knowing, and here they continued to take me along with them. Sundays we would lazily read magazines and comic strips or novellas with black and white pictures of heroines, their words in speech bubbles. Extended family life would once again comfort, soothe and envelope me like a generous, loving blanket.

Then we would go back to Montreal and being different. Slowly, other friends and family came from Morocco and with each arrival a bit of back home came to us and reinforced us. I still remember the night we went to pick up my family at the airport. My grandmother had passed away after fighting liver disease. My grandfather and all the youngest aunts and uncles left Israel on my mother's urging to come establish themselves in Montreal. One balmy summer evening we all went to the airport to welcome them to Canada. Our hugs mixed with tears of joy. They took an apartment in our building and we were reunited again. We were all greatly saddened by the loss of my grandmother, but the arrival of my extended family felt like my safety blanket had finally arrived and enveloped me that night.

I was happy my extended family had arrived but of course losing my grandmother had caused us all great sadness. My grandparents had a great love for each other. My grandmother was the pillar of the family and everything had always revolved around her. At exactly the same moment she passed away, I became obsessively clean and neat, to the great exasperation of my family. Looking back, I realize that I wanted to exert some control over life, after this great loss in our lives, by creating order. It annoyed my parents and sister when I would clean up a stray glass of milk they had not finished or even brush the fringes neatly in place on each side of the carpet. We had a navy carpet and I was always vacuuming it. Years later, unthinkingly, I had a navy wall to wall carpet installed in my basement and my uncle Adam remarked, "I hope it won't make you vacuum incessantly like when we all lived in TMR". Everyone remembered my obsessive neatness from one day to the next.

My parents were different from most of the other parents at school, but they were decidedly the most glamorous couple. They were so young and good looking, and sometimes when they came to parent's meetings at school, I was worried that they would stand out too much and then to my surprise a teacher or classmate would comment on how good looking or stylish they were next to most of the dowdy but so reassuringly normal Canadian parents.

On weekends we would go with all their friends from Casablanca to Schwartz's to have brunch or smoked meat sandwiches. My greatest memory is of my father bringing me for lunch at Casa Pedro's on Saturday while my mother was busy. We would enter the restaurant on Crescent Street, and I would feel important and grownup as we followed the hostess to a table with a starched tablecloth overlooking the busy de Maisonneuve street. The waiter would bring my favorite: seafood soup. So different from the Dafina we used to eat in Morocco on Saturday lunch; after all our religion prohibits seafood and spending money on Saturdays. Yet my father and I would revel at this moment. We would talk and invariably he would take out his newspaper and I would daydream and just feel happy and safe in his presence.

Later we rented country homes and the whole crew of my parent's friends would go first to the French pastry, The Duc de Lorraine and indulge in European epicurean pleasures such as (forbidden) smoked ham and camembert (it is doubly forbidden to mix ham and cheese), that would have truly shocked their parents. Their parents would have perhaps been shocked but would never have reprimanded them. That generation lived their religion with only tolerance for others and most especially for their children. They would have said "Bsartek" (eat in good health in Arabic) and imposed kosher eating only on themselves like my loving grandmother had.

The women still wore European fashions and the men who had made a lot of money wore raccoon coats. We would pile into cars and ride to the country houses and devour the fine French foods we had brought with us, incapable of eating the poutines and hotdogs available up north. Skiing was something that was encouraged for our generation, but the thought of actually going on skis was not for most Moroccans. They had after, all left behind an average temperature of 29 degrees C to land in an average temperature of -15 degrees Celsius. Those who skied were very proud and boasted they loved the sport as if it was the hilt of integration and solid proof of their adaptability. We belong here, they seemed to say when they skidded on their Solomon skis and confidently manipulated their poles. That is no doubt why as a teenager, I would always secretly fall in love with teenage ski instructors. My father was content to watch these adventurous types and puff on his cigarettes or pipe and read his newspaper.

Always his newspaper. One of my aunts said that one day, during a Cape Cod vacation, they were all having fun and being rowdy and my father was a few feet away reading a paper till a gust of wind carried it away. Ten minutes later it seemed the gust of wind brought it back and he matter of factly picked it up and resumed his reading as if it were the most natural occurrence. This is one of my favorite images ingrained in my mind as if I had witnessed it.

Slowly but surely arrivals from Casablanca increased. Men who had arrived with nothing quickly became wealthy and it was a beautiful thing to see, this American Dream unfolding before my eyes. Many of this happy crowd was befriended by a Montreal radio personality of the time, Douglas Leopold, otherwise known as "Coco". They gaily followed him to the nightclub "Regine's" and other jet set events of Montreal's glorious '80s. The chicest stores on Crescent Street boasted locations in Montreal-Paris-New York. The names of the stores were inspired by chic international stores: Rive Gauche, Carnaby Street, Les Createurs or Grège proning the new chic minimalist and neutral toned wave in fashion. One of my mother's friends, Teresa, hosted a fashion show in her beautiful Crescent store.

Barefoot on the plush carpets, the models pranced around us while we reclined on poufs and oversized orange, gold and spiced colored pillows. This Marrakech style contrasted and enhanced beautifully the Victorian windows overlooking the snowy streets of Montreal illuminated by glass lamps. We admired models that had been flown in from New York to parade the new collections imported from Europe. One tall and extremely elegant thin black woman made a sensation and particularly impressed me with her audacity and style. With her head daringly shaved, she graced every exquisite dress imported from Paris. It was an era of pure, undiluted luxury edged with so much distinction and style.

The elegance of this crowd newly arrived from Morocco, influenced by French colonialism and enhanced by American success stories attests to the unique glamour of the 80's and the particular flavor these immigrants of Casablanca gave it. This crowd could be found crossing route 66 in a convertible, exploring an impressive America, but complaining about how awful the food was, or sporting the latest trends in the elegant clothing fairs of Paris where men whore ties and women harbored gold-hued fashions and jewelry enhanced by Cartier tigers.

All this was topped off with flights taken on the Concorde, extremely tantalizing and self-indulgent cakes from Lenôtre reminiscent of the decadent Tropezian, the epitome of dreamy desserts best savored with champagne bubbles during gold-tinged days of St. Tropez…. another favorite spot of this happy crowd.

They had the good fortune and great fun to use their elegance in as highly diverse fields as record-making, (here I imagine lives like in the "Vinyl" series by Mick Jagger), fashion, hair salons (see "Shampoo") and restaurants. Pleasure and more pleasure.

Luxury had a particular flavor back then. It was not beautiful in the cold and metallic, "apple computer way" it is today. It had more soul; it was artsy and still searching for itself and most importantly it had a lot of individuality. Now luxury is a well thought out goal that is professionally made and marketed; it is created through a tunnel of well-oiled branding machinery. In those days, luxury came out of passion, love and searching for personal ideals that were reflected in the diversity of goods and styles. Today if one wishes to create luxury, the path is well established: make black your color, slap on a minimalist logo and Helvetica font and don't forget to tell "your story". Before when you entered the world of luxury either by picking out a Kenzo dress, a Courrèges jacket, Chanel ballet slippers or even a mille-feuilles in a highly discerning pastry shop on avenue Victor Hugo, you had a diversity of legends, ideals and personalities to choose from. When you made the purchase and left the store with the bag or carefully wrapped pastry, you took with you a small part of a world of pleasure and refinement that was tinged with the warmth of golden sunlight. Today luxury is illuminated by LED.

The French protectorate was behind us, but it was still present in our ideals. We ate French food, imported French clothes, wore French clothes (even French jeans, branded Lothar's), read French novels and followed the lives of French actors and actresses in Paris Match and listened to French music. When we spoke of America, the country we were in, it was through the eyes of a French man. Indian summer by Joe Dassin. It was fall, Indian summer, a season that only exists in North America....

L'été Indien
By Joe Dassin
Tu sais
Je n'ai jamais été aussi heureux que ce matin-là
Nous marchions sur une plage un peu comme celle-ci
C'était l'automne
Un automne où il faisait beau
Une saison qui n'existe que dans le Nord de l'Amérique
Là-bas on l'appelle l'été indien
Mais c'était tout simplement le nôtre

Indian summer
By Joe Dassin
(You know
I've never been happier than that morning
We were walking on a beach a lot like this
It was autumn
A beautiful autumn day
A season that exists only in North America
There it is called Indian summer
But it was simply ours)

And when someone asked us where we were born if we said the truth it would lead to unnecessary complications. Morocco? Where is that? Africa? But you're not black?

So often I noticed some children or even adults of my community replied "France". Like the jeans our parents imported. And that very few Canadians bought or understood but that we kept importing.

(Flashback To The Glamorous Women Of My Childhood In Casablanca)

Women in Europe…woman in America now…and way before that, women from back home.

Jacqueline was my mother's best friend and one of the examples I grew up with. She was a product of the Casablanca of the 60's living under the French protectorate and the French ideals of elegance and sophistication in easy, sunny, laid back Morocco. She was the symbol of glamour. With her graceful neck atop a long slender body, held perfectly erect and made sublime with her aloof attitude, she would grace you with a discrete smile and an occasional, not a care in the world, and head-thrown-back-laughter. Her gestures were all slow and relaxed as she expertly held her hair tightly back in a ballerina bun at the nape of her neck or skillfully wrapped a pareo around her slender hips, so that it became infused with an haute couture elegance. As she walked towards you it seemed that she was walking down a Parisian Haute Couture fashion runway.

Her first love, Michel was also a man of that special era. Michel was a handsome, charismatic, articulate and charming man. Michel was intense and demanding and a little crazy which is what made his charm. Many years later he was to become the owner of the famed French restaurant of San Francisco "Chez Michel", where all the hip San Fransisco crowd gathered. My friend Jean Jacques worked there for a summer in the '80s like many young French boys attracted by the American Dream. (Once again, note that we are all separated by six pixels). He related to me, many years later that Michel once pinned him down to the wall for not following the exact protocol when serving a drink to a client. He told the story with no resentment; for him, it was just an example of the high standards and flamboyant temperament of a great man who was an example of the successful American dream.

Michel was a perfectionist and it showed in how he lived his life. He lived it with all the demands and elegance of the '80s that required it to be lived to the hilt. He was what we call in French "a seigneur" literally meaning a lord. One night we were at the casino and he came to pluck me from a 20$ a hand blackjack table insisting that my father's daughter could not be playing at less than a 100$ a hand table and generously financed my evening. This just made me even more nervous about the outcome of each hand I played. I was touched by the attention and will never forget how nice it felt to be taken care of just because I was the daughter of his great friend.

Jacqueline and Michel lived golden years as part of the youth of that era cavorting in the best places Casablanca had to offer. In their early twenties, still single but considered an item, they were one of the most glamorous couples of Casablanca's '60's. The end of the French protectorate separated them. The departure from Morocco of many Jews sent Jacqueline and Michel in different directions with their respective families.

How fitting that now the song playing is l'Été Indien de Joe Dassin. It could be their story just before they separated, one towards Montreal and the other towards San Fransisco after the carefree era of Casablanca was over…

Tu sais
Je n'ai jamais été aussi heureux que ce matin-là
Nous marchions sur une plage un peu comme celle-ci
C'était l'automne
Un automne où il faisait beau
Une saison qui n'existe que dans le Nord de l'Amérique
Là-bas on l'appelle l'été indien
Mais c'était tout simplement le nôtre

(You know
I've never been happier than that morning
We were walking on a beach a lot like this
It was autumn
A beautiful autumn day
A season that exists only in North America
There it is called Indian summer
But it was simply ours)

Like my parents, Jacqueline moved to Montreal in the early '60s where she eventually had 5 husbands - all very different and 5 homes – all consistently impeccably elegant and reflecting the glamour of the '80s. I can still smell the polished wood and hear the creaking floors of the elegant Westmount homes. The houses were sombre and elegant, but the décor was invariably white with touches of brass and elegant chandeliers, candelabra, cigarette boxes and heavy desktop lighters and crystal vases filled with white or red roses. All this was atop shaggy white carpets where gold pillows were piled high. She shopped in the beautiful stores of Crescent Street filled with the latest fashions from France and every time my mother told me we were spending Saturday afternoon with her I would complain, "Oh no, we are going to try hats on again all day". But I loved it and loved all the glamour and excitement she exuded.

Jacqueline once brought me to a Chanel fashion show at the Hotel Parc Monceau when I was living in Paris. This was after she had been hired by Holt Renfrew as a fashion buyer and she was sent on a buying trip. She picked only the most glamorous dresses with her very elegant, subdued, relaxed way of ordering. She pointed out all the dresses she loved with her perfectly manicured long slender fingers and smiled pleasantly to the person in charge of her account. She picked dresses that would be "outstanding" on her or her beautiful sister Gigi, forgetting the dowdier woman that often made up the core customers of Holt Renfrew. It was all a question of cultural differences in retrospect. Jacqueline was the product of the carefree exuberance of Casablanca in the 60's juxtaposed with the values of a French protectorate that admired the elegant style of Anouk Aimée, Sylvie Vartan, Catherine Deneuve and Coco Chanel. She was ill equipped to buy for the practical north American women of

Montreal's '80s vaguely unsettled by separation anxiety brought on by Quebec's premier René Lévesque.

Jacqueline loved luxury but never counted money. Later I reminded her of the beautiful home she had lived in with her first husband George.

"I could have kept that house if I wanted to" she told me. "Il me manquait juste les sous" ("I was just lacking the money"). With easy elegance of that era she sent the money issue flying to where it should belong...a very secondary issue. It was given the importance of an afterthought. "Real chic." I thought. Too chic to center on vulgar money.

Perhaps that is why her buying responsibilities were soon over. In retrospect the cost seems little, even to her, as we have spent many years looking back with delight at that beautiful afternoon. While eating French pastries in the ornate, delicate and refined setting of the Hotel Monceau of the '80s, we imagined ourselves wearing dresses fit for a fairy tale,.

Many years later with 2 or 3 marriages each behind them, Jacqueline and Michel revived their past love. He was now the owner of the famed "Chez Michel" and with his high-pressure responsibilities had become even more ADD, intense, demanding and capricious. In his favor he was a perfect gentleman in spite of his difficult temperament. He wooed Jacqueline with his charisma and old-world charm and plied her with gifts and compliments. But he was a constant whirlwind of desires and was too unsettling for Jacqueline who was as lackadaisical as she was glamorous, even after 3 tumultuous marriages.

Crossing The Bridge (The Teenage Years)

And while these people painted the background of my life, after grade school I joined High School. With my navy pea coat, braces and blow-dried hair I felt like I belonged. A bit.

With my new friends, we would walk to the pastry shop for sandwiches during our lunch break and sing noisily the hits of the season.

You Light up my Life
By Debby Boone

So many nights
I'd sit by my window
Waiting for someone
To sing me his song
So many dreams
I've kept deep inside me
Alone in the dark
But now you've come along

My father bought me my own record player. I felt so spoiled and privileged. He would buy Frank Sinatra and Dean Martin records and I would buy the Top 20 records with all the greatest hits.

I seemed to finally fit in the first year of high school. I was even invited to dance my first real slow dance at my first party by the cutest boy in class. The longest slow that meant something….the reputable" Stairway to Heaven". After the dance we each ran back to our side of the basement, girls on one side and boys goofing around on the other side.

I would study hard in school and dream of the American dream. My window overlooked the warm yellow light of the

National Film board. I dreamed of attaining the American dream and becoming a film maker…winning an Oscar.

For now, though when my mother came to pick me up with her rusty car I made her pick me up at the back door of the school. I only allowed my father to drop me off at the front door with his gleaming pale blue metallic Monte Carlo.

Immigrants always have something to hide. Years later, I found out that my mother was not dupe to my shame. She did not mind though. The down to earth woman knew that her car was not her.

Then we were to move from our apartment, to bigger and better. My parents had bought our first home, a town house. Our little piece of the American dream.

We've Only Just Begun
The Carpenters
We've only just begun to live
White lace and promises
A kiss for luck and we're on our way
We've only begun
And when the evening comes we smile
So much of life ahead
We'll find a place where there's room to grow
And yes, we've just begun

Burning The Bridges

But nothing had prepared me (or my parents) for a boyfriend like Conrad.

He was the boy next door. He was also your typical "bad boy". Blond curls, blue eyes, an angel's face. He looked like Peter Frampton on the cover of the album "Frampton comes alive", which made it very easy to fall in love with him during that era. He was my first encounter with sex, drugs and rock and roll.

The first time I went to his house, I heard his mother speaking to him in the other room.

"I do not want you influencing that nice new girl next door." It was the first time I realized that somewhere I enjoyed tempting the devil or playing with fire. Was it a reaction to my very cautious upbringing? There is no rule for this. And so I fell desperately in love with him as only a teenager could. Eternal teenager that I am.

He also went to the high school of my new neighborhood but rarely showed up. I smoked my first joint with him and fell in love with Pink Floyd, Supertramp, Led Zeppelin, Eddy Money, Peter Frampton and him of course. While our parents were at work, we would just hang around and listen to music or go to the swimming pool that benefitted our townhouses. He would climb on our living room table and mimic the gestures of a guitar playing rock musician. He loved all music and would go from hard rock to traditional Israeli folk music which I found so sweet. I was in love for the first time.

My parents soon found out how bad he was when one night we had a drinking contest. That was when I found out that my constitution does not abide well with alcohol. I came home very sick and had to be rushed to the hospital. To this day if I have two vodkas, I have to throw up. Our house was now off-limits to Conrad.

Summer nights he would throw pebbles at my window or I would hear a low whistle and run to my bedroom window. He would look up, hands in his jean pockets and we would chat. I was at my happiest.

Occasionally I would skip school with him, but always picked carefully the courses I skipped. Yes, I could skip home economics or typewriting but never math or English. I maintained my grade A average and my American dream.

The kids in my new high school knew I was dating the bad boy and that I smoked so they were always surprised to see my name on the honor roll. "Hey, they made a mistake, what is your name doing there", they would chide me.

It was of course not easy to have changed high schools and make new friends. Conrad was never in school and he was as unpredictable in our relationship as he was in general.

The first day of school to my surprise, I discovered a group of Jewish Moroccan girls talking together near me in the hallway. I could not go up to them and say, "Hey, I am one of you" but longed to. Because my hair and eyes were light, I felt I would never be recognized. Indeed, I went through high school hearing repeatedly "You are not like the other Moroccans".

It was the phrase that represented my high school years.

There was a clichéd image and apparently, I did not fit in. My personality, my looks, my demeanor and so once again I had no anchor point.

The first year during lunch I would avoid cafeteria and just hang out at the library not to be seen alone.

As a kid in high school, you could take one of three directions. These were represented by the three doors that kids hung out at during breaks. The main door was inhabited by the Japs (Jewish American Princesses), who were very well dressed, popular, wealthy or wealthy looking and smoked cigarettes and drove around in Volkswagens. The second door was destined to the nerds who all wore bad jeans, running shoes and had the best grades. Finally, the back door was the privilege of the stoners who wore lumberjack jackets (much later reinvented by Dsquared the high-end fashion brand), construction boots and smoked joints.

I dressed like a jap, smoked like a stoner and had the grades of a nerd. Once again, I did not fit in. I somehow got through high school.

There I took Mr Faigen's Mass Media class and discovered my future. Communications. Creating brands, logos and small universes. Since I seemed to have a blurred identity myself, I would create extremely legible brand identities. I would create coherent brands like the very coherent groups represented in my school. As a brand you could clearly define if a product was a jap, nerd, stoner or granola. You could even mix two brand types I would later discover with the advent of the Hippy Chic trends in brands (my favorite). But for the most part, brands could be made to be reassuringly one thing to get a coherent, constant and consistent (the three c's) brand message across. I am red or black or white if I wish to be seen, heard and understood.

High school was in a Jewish neighborhood and we were nearly all Jewish; Sephardic or Ashkenazi. There was one black boy and a only a few non-Jews. Dating them was highly prohibited. The only girl who dared to was to become much later on, quite ironically, I thought, the principal of a Jewish high school.

In Montreal, the neighborhoods were very segregated. It was and still is a mosaic of cultures. French Canadians lived in the East, Italians in little Italy, Greeks in Park Extension and Jews in the West. The only French Canadian we crossed was an occasional teacher and the 161-bus driver who invariably would treat the rowdy teenagers we were of "maudits anglais". When we had moved to Montreal, my parents had decided they did not want us to adopt a French-Canadian accent that was so different from the French of Morocco, fashioned on the French from France. That is why we lived in an English-speaking neighborhood and they had enrolled us in an English school.

We were the "maudits Anglais" because all of a sudden, a line had been drawn around Quebec. You were either a federalist like our elegant Prime Minister Trudeau with his so glamorous and beautiful albeit neurotic wife Margaret or a rebel like the burgeoning René Lévesque demanding independence for Quebec from the rest of Canada.

René Lévesque championed the rights and identities of the French speaking Canadians and their language. For the first time, they now stood up and expressed how they had felt repressed by the English language and an Anglo-Saxon culture so far from theirs. The French had called the English "têtes carrées" behind their backs. Up till now, this had been muttered under their breath. With the rise of René Lévesque, their feelings were expressed. This expression, meaning square heads, belied how they felt that they were intrinsically and psychologically different from what they considered to be a people reigned by reason and logic. The Quebecers identified with a romantic view of an exploited and melancholic people. Their literature such as the "Tin Flute" by Gabriel Roi, the equivalent of Victor Hugo's "Les Misérables" reflected the general sentiment that they were getting the sore end of the deal. Quebec had been "discovered" by France and England and now the two languages and mentalities of these descendants were at war. The French perceived that all of the establishment and their employers were English speaking.

The sovereignty movement had started in 1968 but peaked in 1976 when Lévesque and his party won a landslide victory in the 1976 election. The night of Lévesque's acceptance speech included one of his most famous quotations: "I never thought that I could be so proud to be Québécois."

His government's signature achievement was the Quebec Charter of the French Language (known as "Bill 101"), whose goal was to make French "the normal and everyday language of work, instruction, communication, commerce and business."

René Lévesque and his politics gave great insecurity to the English speaking and I saw many of my friends leave Montreal with their parents. The October crisis in 1970 saw members of the Front de Libération du Québec kidnap Pierre Laporte, the provincial Deputy premier and James Cross, the British Diplomat. The kidnappers murdered Laporte, released Cross and escaped to exile in Cuba, following negotiations. Huge businesses such as CP, Sunlight, BMO, Dupont and IBM were on the verge of starting the construction of new headquarters on Dorchester Boulevard in Montreal. This incident made them all cancel this project and head towards setting up main headquarters in Toronto. Ironically, many years later, Dorchester boulevard changed its name to René Lévesque Boulevard. I saw Montreal diminish as an international city because many businesses and employers favored Toronto. The balance of power between the two cities toppled in Toronto's favor very quickly. Many of us resented this separatist dream as we saw Montreal diminish in power and affluence.

Many years later, one night while vacationing in Marrakech with my estranged husband, I lit the tv and saw a documentary on René Lévesque. I had felt particularly far from home and lonely that evening and all of a sudden Rene Levesque and his familiar face and name seemed like home. I watched this film with rapture and saw a side to this champion of the French that I had not seen while living in Canada. Distance had given me perspective. He was a true idealist and cared about nothing but politics. His coffee table was a cardboard box for years; he cared so little about anything other than Quebec and its people. I watched with fascination images of my country of adoption in the '70s; the speeches, the manifestations, the desires and demands. As I watched in my hotel room in Marrakech, I felt for the first time a connection to the champion of the French Quebecers. Even if I was forced to admit that his dream had not benefited the city of Montreal, I admired the man who had a dream for the benefit of others.

We are not one culture; we are like onions with many layers of cultures absorbed and accumulated throughout our lives. That night, in Marrakech, I felt Quebecois for the first time.

After high school, I went on to two years of a Cegep specialized in Communications. In Cegep, we found ourselves with kids our age that were Greek or Italian. Still, no French Canadians were in sight as they went on to French Cegeps. We were not many of my high school to find ourselves there, so the popular girls from high school, inadvertently became my friends and finally, I seemed to fit in somehow.

The Popular Girls

Joelle looked like Mariel Hemingway. Everyone wanted to be friends with her. She was Jewish Moroccan like me and the best-dressed girl in school. She would amble into high school at around 11 am every day, rarely before, wearing the perfect casual chic outfit and smelling of French perfume. She never had a pimple.

The song **"I am a creep"** was not around yet, but was created for her kind.

Creep
By Radiohead
Couldn't look you in the eye
You're just like an angel
Your skin makes me cry
You float like a feather
In a beautiful world
And I wish I was special
You're so fuckin' special
But I'm a creep.

And of course, there was **Tia** with her perfect porcelain face, chiseled cheekbones, blue-green eyes and very delicate manners. She was the girl everyone wanted to be friends with. Already in high school, she exuded a classiness and intelligent restrain but could also wildly giggle at gross or silly high school jokes we indulge in at that age. That was, and still is, part of her charm.

Tia was as delicate, restrained and refined as Joelle was bold, outspoken and brazen. To add to their differences Tia is Ashkenazi and Joelle Sephardic.

Joelle would make jokes, often very dirty and Tia would shriek with laughter but even so Joelle would tease her:"oh, even the ashke got it", highlighting the quick streets smart humour that was a trademark of the hustling Sephardic she made herself to be reveling in stereotypes. Joelle loved to pretend that she had just left the mellah (Jewish neighborhood in Casablanca) and thus accentuated her earthy, direct and jolting sense of humour.

She would make jokes about how carefree the Sephardics were next to the Ashkenase. "While our parents are buying Chinese furniture, the Ashkenase are buying Rsps".

The most special friendships come from contrasts

Twenty years later we still have three-way calls that leave me in tears.

"Those Sephardics are always running after their dicks on fire". Tia scoffs. "Ashkenazi men have more morals."

"I can't get into those boring, bland Ashkenazi men", Joelle wails. "They are not sexy. I need Sephardic dick."

As usual, Tia and I shriek with laughter and shock at the daring comment; Joelle is once again heady with the power of shocking us. We perhaps shriek even louder than when we were teenagers, it feels so good. These were the vile jokes that only 50 plus women make, I thought. After 50 you become less picky, discerning and delicate: you boldly seize opportunities to laugh. Time is running out. And perhaps you also need to laugh more than ever.

And then there were the most popular girls in schools Cindy and Bonnie. The highlight of that era was going with them to the Cars concert and being handpicked by bouncers as we were running in to go backstage and meet the musicians afterwards. Bonnie actually ended up dating Ric Ocasek for the whole of two weeks, which brought her to the heights of stardom in our high school.

Years later I bumped into Cindy and Bonnie when we were in our fucking fifties and I could not have made Bonnie more pleased by reminding her of that day. I had gone halfway around the world and found myself back in my hometown at a restaurant that was popular with my generation. I was sitting at the bar with friends and, just as if I had never left high school, one of the girls from the Cindy/Bonnie crowd came to see me at the bar. "Hey, are you Valerie from high school? I am sitting with Cindy and Bonnie, they want you to come say hi." I did. I had gone halfway around the world and come back home and was being summoned by the most popular girls in school who had sent over one of their court jesters. I heard a few women whispering "Is that Cindy over there? I remember her; she was not nice to me in High school ". Some habits are hard to break, I thought, as I walked over. And at our age I realized they can be so reassuring. Even if Cindy and Bonnie were no longer what they had been…they were also in their fucking fifties.

The Disco Years

And when I wanted to be a good girl, I got over Conrad and Rock and Roll and went discoing with the girls, notably with Bianca. The best part of the evening was usually the very beginning as we entered the nightclubs in downtown Montreal. The energy and promise of the evening were palpable just like the promise of life to come.

I Love the Nightlife
By Alicia Bridges

Please don't talk about sweet love
Please don't talk about being true
And all the trouble we've been through
Ah, please don't talk about all of the plans we had
For fixin' this broken romance
I want to go where the people dance
I want some action, I want to live!
Oh I, I love the nightlife

Going Back To The Roots

Between disco and rock, and a short new wave period that kept me busy with safety pins assembling folds and rips in t shirts, there was never a dull moment. Then I met a new "movement". Through my parents I met new friends whose parents were still living in Morocco and who had come to study in our Montreal Universities.

These were girls that had not been "Americanized". They lived sheltered, protected lives growing up in Morocco. For Jewish people to still be living in Morocco their parents had to be making a lot of money. So, they were surrounded by personnel, chauffeurs and guards. They never lifted a finger. I saw girls my age calls out "Fatima" to come shut the lights in their rooms because they were too lazy to do it or even just to bring them a glass of water. Later when they all moved to Montreal or Paris where the cost of full-time help was prohibitory, they would complain that the cleaning lady had forgotten to take out a roll of paper towel from underneath the sink and that they had to bend to get it. That is how pampered they were.

And so spoiled. Like in ancient times the women were obsessed with amassing gold and jewels and their way to longtime security. Girls my age pranced proudly around with Levi's and gold Rolexes adorned with diamonds given by their parents. Women coyly asked their husbands to buy them the latest designs in jewelry. The middle class went to the souk and bought from weathered-looking stores hidden under crumbling passages and the moneyed classes went to the shops that claimed to be the King's jewelers like Azuelos. Many of course claimed to be our King Hassan's jeweler. Years later I met in Montreal a young woman who was a descendant of Azeroual and like her ascendants, she toiled to bend metals to her will. Her inspiration was First Nations culture and she abandoned gold for more down to earth silver. She had inherited her creativity and inspiration but had adapted it to this new land so far away in countless ways and yet maintained the legacy.

I now had a new crowd and was quite fascinated by their values and by rediscovering my roots. Something all immigrants are one day confronted by. These Moroccans still living in Casablanca were so different from the ones who had immigrated like me. This can be said of all immigrant groups. I remember talking one day to a hairdresser of Italian descent who also found that back home in Italy her community was so different.

They were proud of their traditions and lived them fully and in a non-diluted manner. They seemed more at ease, as if the fact that they were not trying to be something else had made them stronger. They were untainted by their countries of adoption and not embarrassed by their original culture.

All the money that was there also helped. I traveled with my new friends to Casablanca every summer and on our way there and back we stopped in Paris or Marbella where we met friends also originally from Morocco who took us out. They had old fashioned, elegant manners. Women never opened their purses. Men never tried to kiss you on the first date. They came in to fetch you for a date. They sent flowers. They were very polite and respectful to your parents. Wedding invitations were hand-delivered. When you were invited to a wedding all of your house guests accompanied you even to the most lavish occasions. They never ever rolled a joint. I was miles away from my Canadian high school in many ways.

Two of my aunts still lived in Morocco, so we often went to spend summers there and I alternated my time between family and my new friends.

My aunt Rita and her best friend Isabelle lived in the same

building, so mornings were spent running from one apartment to the next to organize at what time we would go to Tahiti, the private beach. We were focused on deciding what we would wear and that in itself was a memorable event. Isabelle, my aunt's best friend tried on numerous outfits and admired herself in the mirror, patting her flat stomach lovingly and ignoring her generous behind. All of a sudden, she would make us all laugh with a witty observation delivered tongue-in-cheek style on the latest love scandal happening in Casablanca.

At noon we were all ready to depart and once again, like in my early childhood, women and children were surrounded by "les bonnes" or the help and "les guardiens" or the guards holding numerous baskets of food, towels and other necessities. We would gaily pile into cars and head towards the private beach where we would make an entrance with our carefully planned summery outfits. The family that lived all year round in Casablanca always had summer passes to the private beach and would usher in those of us on vacation, so we wouldn't have to pay extra. "She is with me", they would tell the guards and slip them a small bill, a fraction of the official price displayed. All these privileged people had bungalows overlooking the pools and behind the pools was the ocean. The bungalows were not bigger than 15 square feet with a very small table, chairs and a single couch for babies and small children to find shelter from the sun. The real action was in front of the bungalow. The most vied for position was to lay on a mattress on the wall along the main walk of the beach because every arrival or passerby would stop and chat while you laid back languorously in a queen-like position. You could easily identify the most spoiled member in a family by whom held this place. One family nearby had a very beautiful daughter who was overly adulated by her family. Every single day of the season this daughter lay on her throne and was thus exhibited by her parents. The son was never allowed to occupy the choice seat. The "strategy" worked to its end as she ended up marrying one of the wealthiest families. She divorced years later, but that is another story.

Every day we would find our positions around the bungalow and the day would officially begin.

Newcomers would amble across the main "beach corridor" and stop to chat. Men came from Paris, Montreal and London with hopes of finding a nice Moroccan Jewish girl to marry and bring back home with them. Preference was given to girls who had never slept with a man. Nice Jewish girls were happy to be married and leave Casablanca for new frontiers. Only once they were established in Paris or Montreal would they long for Casablanca. "I even miss the grocer ", they would wail. " I used to holler down from my window and his son would run up and deliver even a pack of gum. Now I have to go to this cold 'depanneur' in minus 30 degrees".

But everyone that had stayed back knew they could not live in Casablanca forever. One day things might get nasty and they would have to leave. Meanwhile they watched the country simmer and as long as things didn't come to a boil, they amassed money and invested it outside of Morocco.

As for myself I enjoyed the summers of my early childhood all over again and renewed with the traditions of before.

Our routine was just like before we had left Morocco: Tahiti beach, then the "Creperie", then the tennis club, then tea, shower, dinner and nightclubs along the beaches. And all this heightened by big weddings, house parties and elegant Shabbat dinners. Heightened of course by a summer romance. It did lend a particular glow to your summer when a young gentleman got through the challenging and outdated phone system of Morocco to ask you for a date. The gentlemen had pleasantly old-world manners, such as sending you a rose every day and chatting with your parents and family every time they picked you up. Later, when you were in a formal relationship, you could run down and out of the dark building at the sound of the long-awaited horn in a car that had made its way through the bustling streets of Casablanca to pick you up. Dates generally consisted of either being brought to tame and elegant house parties or the retro-chic nightclubs lining the coast. The most special evenings though, were when you were brought to "Le Petit Cabestan". This restaurant was poised on the edge of a cliff complete with bay windows overlooking the ocean. With the discrete white-gloved waiters dressed like in Paris and its elaborate French cuisine menu, it still had the pride and standards of French culture that colonialism had left behind like a forgotten but very lovely silk scarf.

Reality
By Richard Sanderson for movie La Boum
Met you by surprise
I didn't realize
That my life would change forever
Saw you standing there
I didn't know I cared
There was something special in the air
Dreams are my reality
The only kind of real fantasy

I nearly married a young man from there and that would have been my pampered life forever. It was not in the cards. It was for the better even if it would have been easier. Like Isabelle said, when she left Morocco many years later, living in

Casablanca is like eating candy all day. After a while no matter how good it is, you can get sick of it.

At the time of my life when I spent most of my vacations in Casablanca, I was in my early twenties and studying Communications at Concordia University. I had been overjoyed, even relieved, to get in because I knew this was the only thing I wanted to do. We studied cinema, television and graphic arts as well as the theory of Communications. We also studied old films like "Casablanca" with Ingrid Bergman and Humphrey Bogart. I had mentioned to one of the other students that I would be going to Morocco to visit my boyfriend over the Christmas holidays. As I left a class a few days later, I overheard whispered comments: "She is going to Casablanca for Christmas", and in their voices I saw Humphrey smoke, the café, Ingrid's soft eyes brimming with tears, the music and the sound of the airplane taking off. I could even hear, "Here's looking at you kid". I smiled at how different Casablanca was from the general perception as is the case with everything that is viewed by a different culture. Especially since "Casablanca" was shot at Warner Bros. Studios in Burbank, California except for one sequence... at Van Nuys Airport in Van Nuys, Los Angeles.

Flashback To Glamorous Men Of Casablanca

Men also lived the pleasures of Casablanca to the hilt. They enjoyed the sun, the sea and the pleasure that is afforded when one exercises his charms in such an environment and lavishes them on cared for and highly pampered women.

Every detail of parties thrown were attended to with great care. The women prepared for these occasions with cloths, gold and beauty artifice. The men as well looked forward to these evenings. I remember during one henna party, one of

Casablanca's most renowned dandy and woman-charmer made his entrance.

Dressed in a white suit, simple foulard around his neck, hair brushed back and with a gleam in his eyes that reflected the promise of the evening, he entered the hall.

I noticed him catching a satisfied glimpse of himself in one of the hall's mirrors.

It was a glimpse I caught of man's unequalled vanity. A woman's vanity always seems to have a crack of vulnerability unlike the perfect armour that coats the male kind. Does it have something to do with the vulnerability of aging that is so much more pronounced for a woman than a man? He seemed to emit a contented purr as he glanced at himself in the mirror.

You're so vain
By Carly Simon
You walked into the party
Like you were walking onto a yacht
You had one eye in the mirror
And all the girls dreamed that they'd be your partner
They'd be your partner,
You're so vain
You probably think this song is about you
Don't you?

My First Boss

Bob was part of my parent's merry crowd in Montreal. Our families had been friends since Casablanca and Bobs' mother told me once that she had been at my father's bar mitzvahand it had lasted a week.

Bob had lost his father who had a bookbinding business at

the age of 14. His mother had single-handedly raised her family of 5 boys and one girl and managed the business. At the ripe age of 15, Bob, a very bright young man who felt he was already a man, set off to find fortune in Paris. He spent many years there but soon succumbed to the call of America through the voice of an uncle who met up with him in Paris and told him Montreal was a grand place to live in.

He requested immigration papers from the Canadian embassy in Paris and to his surprise, received them in 15 days. The Ajaias was a Jewish organization helping new immigrants flee Arab countries and settle in Canada. They financed his trip, giving him the option of travelling by plane or train. He decided to take his time, not having really gotten used to the idea that he was moving to Canada and so a long boat ride seemed like a good idea. He took the boat from Le Havre and landed in Halifax. From Halifax, he crossed a vast and barren snow-covered landscape by train till Montreal. He had worked as a salesman in a high-end clothing store in Paris and had the wardrobe to prove it. Dressed in his ultra-chic albeit extremely thin Cardin suit and leather moccasins that were the "dernier cri" in Paris, he must have contrasted starkly with the other passengers. Nevertheless, he hugged closely his jacket cut from the finest fabrics the continent had to offer and skipped on the snow with the lightness that is procured only by youth, supple Italian moccasins and a sense of adventure. He concludes his story with, "J'avais vingt ans et tous mes reves." (I was 20 and possessed all my dreams).

He was first greeted by his uncle, but this free spirit soon became independent.

He had a knack for business, but his real calling was to be a writer/poet/artist. After work he would go to the Café Prag he had discovered on one of his rambles, through his newly adopted town and recite his poems.

In spite of his taste for the arts, he concentrated on starting and growing a business and was soon able to send for his family in Casablanca.

His mother landed in Montreal, where many of her sisters, brothers, nieces and nephews already lived. During Montreal's glorious eighties, this family became very well-known pillars of our community, especially since each branch had more than their fair share of success stories either through making jeans, investing in movies, real estates or even being dentists. The uncle who had originally encouraged Bob to come was himself a Canadian success story entrenched in his Moroccan culture. He was a shrewd businessman and amassed real estate. In the penthouse office of his headquarters, he had a big part of his generous office decorated in the style of Morocco, complete with traditional tea glasses, pottery and moucharabia carved couches. That along with a cigar and whisky made for a perfect welcome when the ambassador from Morocco dropped by. The kindly man would even take 10 years of your Moroccan passport if you were good friends. Some things back home were easier, although one welcomed the security of this cold but safe country where the sky was the limit. When the man married off his beloved daughter she made her entrance atop a white horse, like those of the Fantasia or Moroccan horse shows back home.

During my summers in Marbella I often bumped into many representatives of this illustrious family. One evening, as I was having dinner with them at Bob's table in a restaurant overlooking Porto Banus, I was seated next to his mother who was wearing a leopard print blouse. She always had extravagant taste, as was practically the norm in that period and anything leopard was her signature style. She pointed with a heavily ringed finger to a Rolls Royce that crawled by, proudly commenting, "We have 7 like that in our family in Montreal". She was not boasting. She said it with the childlike charm of an ingénue simply pointing out a pretty hat.

Bob was the chief of his mother's branch. He took care of her, installed her in a beautiful home and doted on all his brothers and sister, involving them in his businesses.

He soon acquired a whole floor in one of the better buildings on St. Laurent boulevard across the street from the famed Schwartz's smoked meat joint. He had as much taste and style as he had charisma and energy. The office walls were all painted a very chic and avant-garde shade of grey, glass walls overlooked airy showrooms, offices and conference rooms. The glamorous office style was picture perfect thanks to the art that was exhibited on the walls as well as images of the brands his business represented. He imported many fashion brands from all over Europe.

During my summer vacations, I would work there as a receptionist. His mother would breeze in and kindly say, "My darling son Bob is so smart to have you at the reception, you are as pretty as a bouquet here. To your Mazal and wedding my dear girl, but before yours to mine!". Bob had undoubtedly inherited his mother's charisma, charm and joie de vivre.

Although his organization was very successful, soon after I started, I discovered his real calling. He asked me if I enjoyed reading and when I responded that it was one of my favorite occupations, he showed me a closet in his vast, luxurious office. "Just come in here and pick any manuscript. When you are finished reading it, no need to knock, just come in and replace it with the next one."

Between reading his novels based on growing up in Casablanca, his adventures in Paris and his first years in

Montreal and simply observing this spectacular man who commanded such energy, wit and personality, I never had a dull moment. And there was the great non-negligible benefit: the clothes. The most beautiful, luxurious clothes that I spent most of my salary on.

It was also here that I created my first advertisements and communication tools. Bob was eager to share the fun of creating with everyone and he soon paired me off with the youngest of his brothers, so we could collaborate on projects. We produced images, brochures, packaging and even videos by rolling a camera on a shopping cart borrowed from Steinberg's grocery stores.

He hired two directors, an English man and a French Canadian at precisely the moment when the Quebec Sovereignty movement was getting under everyone's skin. I always wondered if he did this purposefully because 'il vaut mieux diviser pour regner". (In order to reign, it is best to divide). These two men competed and vied for his favors endlessly. One day I found them in front of his office door, both hesitating to push the door open.

"You tell him."

"No! You tell him."

News of a huge outstanding payment had arrived and neither of them wanted to be the messenger that would get "shot". Bob's temper was as intense and as flamboyant as his character.

I pushed my way past them and entered his office to replace my manuscript. I was relieved and grateful I only had to contend with the "artsy" side of Bob.

Bob was reclining in his plush, leather seat, glass wall behind him overlooking Montreal's Parc Avenue, bubble gum machine nearby, feet on the desk speaking to his best friend in Paris as he did nearly every day. He had to have his international round of jokes.

"I just hung up with Lilo (in Los Angeles), did you hear the latest one yet? There is a Jew, a Muslim and a catholic and they walk into a café...".

In spite of his haphazard management, probably because he was so charismatic, generous and energetic his business thrived many years. He ended up marrying the heiress of a famous soft drink company, (that shall remain unnamed but yes one of the brown drinks with bubbles) and moved with her to her hometown in Mexico. He lived there a few years until his incorrigible, free spirit got the better of him and he went to Los Angeles to dedicate himself to writing, books, art galleries, public relations and event planning.

I saw him a short time ago in Los Angeles where he invited me out for dinner with a friend of mine. As we walked to our table, he said to me with his usual mischievousness but more than half serious,

"Listen, dear, I would sleep with any of your girlfriends but tell them not to ask me for commitment. I cannot be tied down. Unless I decide. And then I must be left the liberty to decide every day all over again. But it can last a long time in those conditions on my terms. Look at Marisa it lasted 14 years, but every day I did not commit till the next day ....hmmm waiter! Who are those two pretty women at that table over there? Bring me their bill! (nodding to them), Mesdames, mes compliments!"

Sacré Bob. That was my first boss.

Le blues du businessman
by Claude Dubois

J'ai du succès dans mes affaires
J'ai du succès dans mes amours
Je change souvent de secrétaire
J'ai mon bureau en haut d'une tour
D'où je vois la ville à l'envers
J'passe la moitié de ma vie en l'air
J'aurais voulu être un artiste
Pour pouvoir dire pourquoi j'existe

The businessman's blues
by Michel Berger

(I'm successful in business
I am successful in love
I often change secretary
My office is at the very top of a tower
From where I see the city upside down
I spend half of my life in the air
I would have liked to be an artist
To be able to say why I exist)

(Flashback To The Glamorous Women Of My Childhood In Montreal)

Gigi was Jacqueline's sister and extremely glamorous in her own right.

She always had a new scheme and would disclose it to you with eyes sparkling. You got the feeling that when she talked excitedly about upcoming events or ideas that she was biting into life as if she were crunching with great appetite into a delicious, gleaming red apple.

She had impeccable taste and was Montreal's star hairstylist. Think of the movie "Shampoo"; she was the female equivalent of Warren Beatty and worked in all-white glamorous salons with assistants flocking around her. The wealthy and hip crowd of Montreal's glamorous eighties vied for long-awaited appointments with her. They needed that glamour imbued moment when they would be sitting on her chair and she would look at their reflection in the mirror, tilt her head to the side and suggest a life-changing hair moment. Cause that is what hair could do to you in the eighties of Farrah Fawcett: bring an abundance of excitement and thrill into your life.

Hair had been part of her life changing moment. When she was eight, she started to coldly analyze herself in the mirror and came to an unsatisfying conclusion. She approved of all her traits and indeed they were not reproachable. Yet her general appearance did not come up to par with the high standards and expectations she had set for herself, already at the age of eight. She decided with great determination that something would be done because it was simply unacceptable to lead a life without being beautiful. She gave the matter thought and decided she must get a haircut like Jean Seberg in the "Les 5 femmes marquées" and new clothes. For a girl of 8 to go to the hairdressers at that period and in that country was extremely uncommon and in the realm of the unthinkable.

But Gigi and her aspirations were strong. In fact, my mother, who would go to their house to visit her best friend Jacqueline, still remembers Gigi always walking around with her head held high, seemingly in her own world. This was not the era of "l'enfant roi". Parents and elders were not at children's beck and call, questioning them on their dreams, aspirations and feelings.

Nevertheless her distinctive character was already defined. She managed a visit to the hairdressers to get the very short bob, bought red checkered pants at the thrift store and took from her elder sister a black top that she altered herself to her liking. To this, she added a belly piercing and her life changed. She had willed herself to become beautiful, crafted her way into becoming beautiful and now heads turned.

Years later she was the best at giving this life changing moment to others because she understood that a woman on a hairdresser's chair wants to feel, like commercials always imply, that the possibilities are endless. This was the era when women with thin stringy hair would walk in with pictures of Farah Fawcett's luxuriant flips and demand, "I want that". Yet Gigi somehow made them confident and happy, perhaps simply because she exuded this.

I loved walking into the hair salons where she worked: it felt simply exhilarating and my heart would start racing with the promise of her transformation and what it could bring. I also felt so privileged in the luxurious atmospheres she worked in.

Receptionists would welcome you in spite of being extremely busy, with phones ringing and interphones beckoning employees. Then would come the robe moment, shampoo, all leading up to the key moment when you were the subject of Gigi's attention.

Some people have such charisma that just being in their presence and basking in their atmosphere makes you feel like you are tinged with golden sunlight and the promise of events as exciting as spring are bound to happen. Gigi did that to you; looked at you with head tilted, analyzed the situation, touched your hair and whispered words with such enthusiasm you could absorb her aura. Then the scissors were poised dramatically in the air for a suspense-filled moment before she began. Instants later she was done and had managed, during the haircut, to pass on to you an exhilarating feeling of life. Finally, she showed you the result with her hand-held mirror and you both admired it from all facets. You rose from her chair still glowing with the aura of that moment.

Exciting things were always happening to her. Like the time a suitor brought her to Monaco for a horse race and she found herself double dating with Caroline de Monaco and Philip Junot. It was a cold wintry day and she had forgotten her gloves. Caroline, in a very elegant gesture offered Gigi a glove. I can imagine them chit-chatting and laughing and pointing at the horses, one with a left gloved hand and the other with a right gloved hand.

Life gave her exciting moments not only because she was beautiful, but because she was more than just beautiful.

My mother and Gigi bought Teresa's wholesale fashion business and very brazen faced they named it Chan'elle. When you called, they simply answered "Chan'elle, Good Morning". Simple and to the point. We are in fashion. We will be like the best.

Gigi was invited to a conference and because it was held at the Ritz, her favorite place, she went.

Gigi loved luxury and luxury loved her back because it suited her very well. The speaker was a very good looking and successful corporate head from Cartier jewelers of Paris and the theme was "Forgery and the offence it is to the market." Gigi walked into the hall a few minutes late, looking striking as usual in her sexy but classy businesswomen attire complete with heels and elegant briefcase, and stood at the back of the hall with a friend. As usual, heads turned but one particular gaze was riveted on her during the whole conference: the speaker himself.

Her friend, slightly envious whispered "Gigi, he is looking at you!".

"I thought so", Gigi laughed, as she coyly held back his stare.

"I don't understand! Ok, you are very good looking, but not soooo exceptionally good looking", the friend blurted out, mystified and slightly aggravated by the indubitable successes her friend accumulated with men.

Gigi nodded modestly, "I know what you mean".

That was Gigi, taking what life had to offer, never letting it go to her head with the secret and wise philosophy that G.d's gifts must simply be accepted and enjoyed.

The minute the conference was finished, the speaker pushed aside all the people scurrying towards him and made a beeline straight to Gigi with the stride of the successful man who knows what he wants. He held out his hand and introduced himself as if the whole hall didn't already know his name. Gigi simply answered her name and, on his request, handed over her business card. He briefly glanced at it.

"Chan'elle? Vous êtes pas gonflé vous. Bon vous m'attendez? 5 minutes, il faut qu'on se parle". (Chan'elle? Well, you have some nerve, don't you? Can you wait for me 5 minutes? I must talk to you). His issues with forgery had been handled with the first three words of his sentence and he had relegated them in favor of more pressing matters: a tête à tête with Gigi. That is how irresistible she was.

In the same way she savored life, she savored luxury. With panache and style. On a shopping trip to Holt Renfrew, she succumbed to the temptation of a long, voluminous, Yves Saint Laurent black taffeta skirt, edged with ruffles. It had the hefty price tag of 2500$ which was an outrageous sum in the '80s but Gigi always managed to "swing it". When she entered a wedding or party with this skirt offset by a fitted chiffon blouse the effect was regal. She was so generous that rich or poor, many of the Jewish Moroccan women of the community were to borrow it for their important events. You would hear, "and I wore this with Gigi's-black-Saint-Laurent-skirt". Even for my wedding in Paris, years later, my mother called to inform me, "I found the perfect top to wear with Gigi's-black-Yves-Saint-Laurent-skirt". It was a given nothing could equal this.

In the glorious eighties, Gigi made a lot of money and rented or bought homes in beautiful Westmount and Outremont. Disregarding if the home was a rental or purchase, all financial considerations were put aside. She would strip everything in sight and start a gleaming clean slate with her iconic all-white style. Everything was in the finest fabrics and of the best taste. The desired result was to offer up to the senses the very best the world had come up with. Her environments are till today pleasing to the eye with immaculate and tasteful environments, to the touch with only the crispest cotton, the softest velvets and the most natural linens and to the scents emanating from the freshest essential oils or better yet from the cooking that only a woman who enjoys eating can offer.

No expenses were spared to achieve this. One day as she left her beautiful Port Royal apartment on Montreal's elegant Sherbrooke street, she stopped in her tracks at the sight of the new Pratesi luxurious bed linen store that had just opened. A bed throned in the window that represented Gigi's style to the hilt: it was luxurious, white, refined and spelt out her signature clean team style.

The fit for royalty bed was complete with the finest embroidered sheets, a crisp white duvet cover, bed skirt and an overabundance of diverse shapes of pillows perfect for a queen to frolic in. It was up to par with the highest standards of Gigi's lifestyle. You could imagine her, after a busy "Shampoo" day, sweeping into her building with her elegant allure, saluting the doorman, entering her apartment laden with orchids and the finest produce, calling out,"Fatima, please put these away for me". Then, indulging in a luxuriating bath and finally slipping into those bed sheets and relaxing with a queen like posture. Or being served breakfast in bed with a Pinterest worthy tray.

She entered the store mesmerized and without taking her eyes off the set, whispered to the saleswoman to please wrap absolutely everything on that bed for her, yes, everything ; she was taking it all. Thirty minutes later she left the store with 10 bags of diverse shapes and sizes labeled Pratesi and adorned with ribbons and bows. She excitedly walked towards her apartment from where she called her friends.

"Hi guys, finally I can't make it to Marbella this year. I just spent all the vacation money on something else but well worth it".

Instant pleasure with the instant gratification of biting into that apple right now is what Gigi is all about to this day. Women with style just must live stylishly no expenses spared. Till today there is nothing as enjoyable as going to the Ritz with her and eating madeleines.

The Lady in Red
by Chris de Burgh
I've never seen you looking so lovely as you did tonight
I've never seen you shine so bright
I've never seen so many men ask you if you wanted to dance
They're looking for a little romance,
Given half a chance
And I have never seen that dress you're wearing
Or the highlights in your hair that catch your eyes,
The lady in red is dancing with me

(Flashback To The Glamorous Women Of My Teenage Years In Montreal)

In spite of myself, I have always been impressed by ruthless, cool, calculating, strong women who will stop at nothing to get what they want. I always hoped I would myself be like that in my life and career, although my "hot" temperament is the furthest as can be from this type of persona.

The salesmen at Prada were fascinated by Joan Collins of Dallas. In the back office, they loved to pretend to be her answering an important call. They would pick up the phone, flip their (imaginary) long hair impatiently to the back, pull off their (imaginary) bulky clip earring like Joan Collins did and very coolly whisper into the phone:"sell the pipeline".

They were fascinated by Joan Collins and many an ambitious woman must have tried to emulate her.

Our community had a Joan Collins. Teresa was the Jewish Moroccan version of Joan Collins and quite as fascinating.

Rumour had it that she had been poor, but very respectable back in Casablanca. That usually implied that even if you had only one dress, it was always washed and pressed. It also meant that you had the thirst, brains and instinct to go far.

She had emigrated to Canada with her husband who became very wealthy soon after. By a stroke of good fortune, he became partners with an uncle, and they became the kings of the shoe business.

He was the one who went to work every day, but nevertheless one always had the feeling that his success was in large part due to his strong-willed, calm, cool collected wife. She was the epitome of the woman behind the man. No doubt her modest background had given her strength of character and focus.

She was the type of woman who knew of her husband's

affairs but relegated them to the realm of issues of secondary importance that had to be swiftly dealt with. Rumour had it that she had even taken one of her husband's mistresses for an abortion, all the while sympathizing with her and probably just sighing and rolling her eyes disdainfully in the direction of her embarrassed husband.

Once she was present when her son and nephews discussed their shared "bachelor" apartment where they could bring their girlfriends, uhuhm "when needed" since they were still living with their parents. She cynically remarked, (no doubt over her scotch on the rocks, in a long and elegant housedress with a stiff blow-dry and immaculate red nails), "Armand, you should ask the boys if you could have a share in that apartment".

No wonder her husband respected and loved her till the end. Yes, such a woman can make a man feel emasculated, but such a strong presence would leave an impossible void to fill.

Her children were at the age of marriage by then and she adroitly chose a spouse for each of them with her indomitable will.

For her son, she decided that the Canadian girls were too easy and silly. She found him a Made in Morocco wife complete with old fashioned values and a good head on her shoulders. Of course, a made in Morroco bride would have been shocked to know that her "Canadian/Moroccan" husband smoked a joint every night, so he had to get a dog to be able to walk it every night and find a pretense to discretely have his smoke. This lasted quite a while, but he was eventually found out. By then this was one of the so many irreconcilable differences between their differing cultures. I pondered how much happier he would have been with my chill and cool girlfriend he had been in love with but whom his mother had not approved of.

Her eldest girl she encouraged to marry her high school sweetheart as he was to become a doctor.

The prize, her youngest was not to be pawned off so easily. She had many suitors because she was pretty and had all the wonderful trimmings of a future heiress that traveled all over Europe, including knowing how to tie a Hermès scarf with a perfectly perky but not overdone knot.

But Teresa found none good enough for her princess; not even a good-looking young man from a well to do family from France.

One day a friend landed in Montreal with the King of a Jeans brand that shall remain unnamed. He was indeed twenty years older. But there is a three-way chart to calculate matches: the ratio involves money, beauty and age. The bigger the age difference, the more money must come into play. And it did.

The nineties had arrived and brought with them an economic tide she felt withdrawing from Montreal. With her survival instinct, she decided it was time for the American dream. And this jean brand was part of the American dream. Her daughter would be happily married to this man and they would open a new division for this brand… shoes.

Her daughter was not thrilled at the prospect, but no one had a chance against Teresa. She once remarked in front of her daughter, taking me as an example, that I had also married an older man. I did not dare point out that my husband was barely eight years older. You did not oppose Teresa just like you would have a hard time opposing Joan Collins. She willed you into her direction with her smile and chanting yet throaty voice. She cloaked the throatiness of her voice by speaking with exaggerated softness, but you could hear the strength in the deep undertones of her voice.

The King of Jeans was no match for her either. She plied him with shabbat dinners and offered up to him a picture of a family life, a young girl with ideals that she made shine next to the "flashy" models he was dating. She simply branded her daughter. He gulped it all down.

Cinderella would thus find her shoe.

Teresa arrived at her fairy tale. Years later I went to visit them in their home. It was as huge and spectacular as any American dream I had ever seen.

Her daughter had ended up divorcing the king of the jeans brand but had gotten a nice hefty sum. One wonders if she ever did love him. But then they were all secondary characters. It was the Joan Collins, doting over and still directing her now elderly husband that fascinated me the most.

In the end, we come to the realisation that there is so little we can control in life. That is why when we are faced with someone so relentless, it is impossible to be devoid of admiration. Even if the goals were not altruistic, they were met and that in itself is not negligeable.

Elsewhere

Every summer and winter I traveled extensively. I worked on the weekends and my parents gave me pocket money and I followed my intuition mostly to Europe and its special flavor. The idolized and idealized Europe of my colonized upbringing understandably held unrivaled allure for me. I dragged along with me any of my different groups of friends that were available and not in a serious relationship with a boyfriend.

In Paris, thankfully the Canadian dollar was at its best and when luxury items were on sale, we gleefully indulged in Chanel earrings or Chacok dresses and Cacharel bathing suits that became the highlights of our wardrobes for the remainder of our vacation.

In Marbella, we had dinner late in the evening and then

strolled around Porto Banus and followed this with clubbing at Olivia Valere's or Regine's and then the "after" nightclub Pepe Moreno and on really special nights we ended up having a last drink watching the flamenco dancers and eating churros till 6 in the morning. The next day we slept in, arrived at the beach for a late lunch and to make new friends, then went home to nap, shower and start all over again. When my parents picked us up at the end of the vacation my mother always marveled that I had not gotten a tan after such a long time away.

In Cannes, St. Tropez and Monaco we went to the restaurants, nightclubs and beaches of the golden youth and tried to do as the Romans do by trying the topless thing but were soon very uncomfortable. We were still prudish Americans on some days...

Then for what was left of our vacation, once we had used up most of our financial resources we ended up in Casablanca where there was always an aunt to welcome us and we could be a rich American tourist with just a few Dirhams.

After summer was over, I would find myself in Montreal each fall where I continued my path in Communications. I loved every minute of my classes. But even though Montreal was home, I felt I needed to live in another city and not limit discovery to mere vacation spots.

I knew from all my travels that Europe had a strong pull and that my life would not be fulfilled if I did not set off for these new horizons.

Paris, with its "Haussmannien" architecture, wrought iron lace-like balconies, old fashioned bakeries devoid of franchise concepts and non-capitalist habits that permitted all shops to be closed Monday mornings so that the city would arouse quietly from a festive weekend was calling out to me.

Once my bachelor's in communications was obtained, my parents responded to my plea for an overseas experience and sent me off to Paris to work on a master's from the Nouvelle Sorbonne.

CHAPTER 4

RE IMMIGRATION
IN PARIS

Paris

I had arrived in Paris and was set on living my Parisian dream. I was 23. I wanted a career, but I equally felt the obligation to have a personal life complete with husband, children and a station wagon. Or Citroën.

It was simply the age-old mating season, and everyone was going off in twos and I felt the pressure to do likewise.

He was of Jewish Sephardic ascent like me. He was good looking, successful, rich. All of the criteria that since time memorial, when women were dragged into caves, made that he had, in theory at least, the makings of the ideal catch. The trophy husband dare I say. I recently read a book about it. It is called evolutionary psychology.

Wikipedia says: Evolutionary psychology is a theoretical approach in the social and natural sciences that examines the psychological structure from a modern evolutionary perspective. It seeks to identify which human psychological traits are evolved adaptations – that is, the functional products of natural selection or sexual selection in human evolution.

In other words, men aim to marry pretty for a pleasant life and with the aim of reproducing, women aim to marry rich for a pleasant (and safe) life and with the aim of reproducing. Evolutionary psychology and thus society dictate this. And somehow, I guess I did not feel strong or confident enough to make it on my own. In all the examples around me, the woman was the secondary breadwinner.

It took my reading about evolutionary psychology to understand why I was attracted to and married this man that I did not have much in common with.

Of course, I thought that our common Jewish Sephardic background would suffice to make us a real couple. I thought we would reproduce my parent's schema which my upbringing dictated. But we were a very ill-assorted couple. We were like birds who mated only because we felt the need to build a nest at the same time.

The problem was that my need to be protected and cared for had attracted me the biggest macho possible. Which was in total conflict with my Canadian upbringing. I sometimes feel guilty because it was not his fault that so many contradictions dwelled inside of me. He banked for a nice Moroccan Jewish girl that would raise his children, cook endless Shabbat dinners, fuss over him to wear a scarf. Instead he got a self-involved, to an extent jap or Jewish American Princess that worried about her career advancement. (Well, he probably got what he deserved for having such a macho outlook of how a woman should be!)

How can a woman who was raised in a Northern American culture where she is taught the ideals of independence and self-fulfillment get along with a man who was raised in Israel, a country that is focused on survival?

In the end problems are always cultural. My desires were seen as frivolous. His needs were seen as dictatorial.

Our first argument was about 30 seconds after the rabbi pronounced us man and wife as we were exiting the houppa and walking down the steps in the middle of the synagogue.

"We must stay here and accept congratulations," he said.

"No, let's just drive off" (I had images of American movies where the bride and groom run off under a torrent of rice).

This was not a good sign.

But we were married and tried to lose our differences in early married life. We worked and traveled and had dinner with many other often equally ill-assorted couples and soon we were blessed with children. Which does make it all worthwhile.

Devil Wears Prada

After my masters from the Nouvelle Sorbonne in Communications was obtained, I was fortunate to do an internship in a real fashion magazine. My parents were friends with one of the main brands, advertising in the magazine, "Infinitif" and this helped me get this extremely vied for - by all the privileged fashionistas of the world - internship.

I became the assistant of Anne Marie Paris (yes, she had a perfect name) and worked in a "Devil wears Prada atmosphere". Anne Marie had nothing to do with Meryl Streep. She loved my taste and sent me to Chanel, Yves Saint Laurent, Thierry Mugler and even the jewelers of Place Vendome in search of selections or "shopping's" to be photographed. She introduced me to her colleagues as Mlle De something thus making me a full-fledged member of the French aristocracy. She adroitly added the prefix to my name, and I pretended not to hear it to comply with her wishes.

She directed her cattiness towards the other fashion editors.

"Did you see that editorial Marion just did? She shot a scene in a Rolls Royce! How nouveau riche, how vulgar!"

When faced with each other the competing fashion editors would swat each other with pernicious, snide remarks but never overt hostility. They would be witty, condescending and bright with intellectual references peppered into their remarks. You could only admire their way of dealing with confrontation. That is the way of French women in corporate life and I have had many examples to prove it.

During lunch, I once accompanied Anne Marie further down on the Champs Elysées to see her twin at Radio France. Her identical twin had also come from Provence and was battling with her own corporate life in the Parisian media world. Mirrors of each other whispered, face to face, their latest reports of corporate schemes and intrigues, thus giving each other strength, while I the assistant waited patiently to the side.

Once their energy was renewed, they saw each other off with, "Ok allez a toute!" and we were off.

Off to fashion shows at the Louvre, presentations in the most beautiful halls of Hotel Concorde or the Ritz, product launches at the PR offices. We left after dousing the new products at launches with generous oohs and aahs while nibbling on macaroons accompanied by champagne. We were usually given by the PR firms a little bag of gifts, to encourage us to expose the new products in our magazine.

I loved every minute of my (unpaid but oh so glamorous job).

But when on a Friday night Anne Marie asked me to work late, I sadly had to quit my dream job. My husband could not serve himself the eighteen requisite salads as well as the fish and meat that were obligatory every Friday night.

The Sentier Or Fashion District

I took the easy way out. I did not have to face alone what I could be worth on the job market. I started working with my husband in the Parisian fashion district, nicknamed The Sentier after one of its metro stations, and put my career on the back burner.

I helped him with his company. Of course, it always irritated him that while working in his company I continued to strive for self-fulfilment and did not solely focus my efforts and energy on the important priority of helping him earn a living. Nevertheless, my efficiency and hard work made up for this weakness.

The fashion district was a very colorful, animated neighborhood to say the least.

My husband's company was on the renowned side street of la Rue Blondel. In front of our doors, prostitutes started their shift as early as 8 am. They had an easy relationship with the owners and salesgirls of the clothing companies. They would occasionally come up and ask to buy clothes at wholesale prices.

My husband would very simply and unflinchingly say, as he passed by, when he saw them purchasing clothes,

"You know the rule, please don't wear them on duty".

"Of course, not Alex! We would never do that!". This preposterous suggestion was out of the boundaries of the unspoken rules established by the fashion district insiders.

It was not the best building to walk out of. One day I left the office to walk over to the pharmacy and buy a chocolate Ovomaltine. I tucked a few francs into the pocket of my form hugging Azzedine Alaïa black jean skirt and sheltered myself from the rain under a black umbrella, quite unthinkingly. A young man walked up to me and stammered a few words. Due to the deafening environing traffic, I could not hear what he was saying. I made him repeat it three times. His forehead seemed to glisten with sweat. Finally, horrified, I understood. He was saying, "How much?"

It was an honest question on that street, especially since prostitutes never wear a purse. Poor man. I screeched that if he did not leave my sight, I would hit him with my umbrella and call the police. Cultural misunderstandings are quite unfortunate. A poor French man, no doubt an "habitué" of the illustrious rue Blondel faced with a Jewish Canadian sheltered young woman holding an umbrella.

There were many cultural misunderstandings for me in Paris. When I was not yet married, but just living with my future husband, the postman who was delivering certified mail, asked me if I wished to sign for it. I told him we were not married and he then asked if my status was that of a concubine. Visions of courtesans and harems came to my mind and I threatened to sue him and call the post office to inform them of his derogatory remarks. Later I realized it was an oft-used term to describe a woman living with a man and had no negative connotation. I still see the poor postman hurriedly running down the stairs, escaping my outraged remarks.

The fashion people were making a lot of money in this crumbling neighborhood of Reaumur Sebastopol. Every nook and cranny of the neighborhood were rented out for preposterous sums. All you needed was a designer or some fashion instinct, a cutting table and then you could send out the pre-cut fabric in big black garbage bags to be assembled by underground sowing rooms. These assembly rooms were often headed by hot headed Turks.

Most of the fashion company owners were Jewish Tunisians. They are the most flamboyant type of Jews you can find. IF one can generalize, which I have been told all my life is not a nice thing to do, but when you have been in branding all your life, you do tend to think of groups of people as distinctive brands with codes and identities. The environment of course has an effect on groups of people and their flamboyance was a product of several influences. They were inhabited by a "joie de vivre" that comes from having lived in sunny Tunisia juxtaposed with their situation as immigrants that made of them born hustlers. Add to that mix the influence of leading a life in Paris, the city that had the best bling to offer in the moneyed eighties.

The women would come to work dressed in Chanel and lug the garbage bags full of cut fabrics ready to be assembled towards the Turks that came for pick up, tottering on high heeled strappy sandals. Our head of production, Martine, was a typical Tunisian product. She wore tight miniskirts, thigh

high boots and heaped jewelry on. She swore with great fervor (on the Torah) that she was very religious so would never come to work on the Shabbat. Martine negotiated with the tough Turkish assembly line owners and stamped her patent leather high heeled boots when they did not accept her price. They eventually gave in and she would reward them with a wink and dashing smile. "Ok Sifti, mon ami tu me ramenes ca quand? N'oublies pas les boutons! Quel h'mar! "(Arabic word for idiot). She would then look at me with an air of complicity and a wink that spelled, "What would you guys do without me?". She had slanted green eyes that added to her very coy cat-that-swallowed-the-mouse demeanor.

The men indulged in the coolest sports cars, that were unfortunately not made for the narrow, arched entrances built for horse-drawn carriages. They drove in very slowly with many workers guiding them inch by inch. It was the only thing they did slowly.

Indeed, the action in the neighborhood was very fast-paced. People from all over France and other countries would pile in to buy goods that we replenished just as quickly by sending out garbage bags with pre-cut fabric to be assembled and then a few days later new goods flew back in to be inspected and sold. And the money flowed in.

Wonderful movies were inspired by this neighborhood such as "La Verité si je mens", which is a pun exposing the exaggerated lies and hustle of this community, that means "It's the truth, I lie". Another classic is "Coco" based on a real character and his the-sky-is- the-limit-attitude towards his son's bar mitzvah. I witnessed the existance of most of these characters in real life. Right down to the boss that enters a room and adds an insignificant detail to a logo or a dress. He then playfully tells the designer that has been poring over his work for hours, "sometimes I wonder what I pay you for, I always come up with the ideas ", punctuated by a martyr-like sigh as he walks out.

Egos were big and so it ensued that competition for more money was intense. Three well known sisters in the neighborhood had started rivaling companies. Stories of them cheating on their husbands with customers, fabric cutters and sales reps flowed through the neighborhood. I remember staring in awe at the most successful of the sisters as she ambled down St. Denis with a tutu like skirt and cowboy boots.

Competition reigned in bar mitzvahs and weddings as well. The most beautiful halls and party planners and haute couture dresses were paid for by all the Sentier cash. Huge orchestras, belly dancers, fortune tellers, caricaturists and other entertainers were hired for elaborate party schemes. Overwhelming decors of starry nights in jungles filled Paris's most beautiful halls. Endless foie gras selections, sweet tables and specialties from varying countries were offered. Still, it was not enough. At one event given by one of the most flamboyant couples the Sentier had produced, the whole family lined up on the stage facing us next to this community's iconic singer, Enrico Macias. The parents, bar mitzvah boy, sisters and grandparents all surrounded and sang along with him:

Le Mendiant de l'Amour
By Enrico Macias

J'ai de l'amour plein la tête, un c'ur d'amitié.
Je ne pense qu'a faire la fête et m'amuser.
Dans toute la ville, on m'appelle le mendiant de l'amour.
Moi, je chante pour ceux qui m'aiment et je serai toujours le même.
Il n'y a pas de honte à être un mendiant de l'amour.

Moi, je chante sous vos fenêtres chaque jour.
Donnez, donnez, dodo-onnez,
Dieu vous le rendra...

The Beggar of Love
By Enrico Macias

(I have a lot of love, a heart of friendship.
I only think of parties and fun.
Throughout the city, they call me the beggar of love.
I sing for those who love me and I will always be the same.
There is no shame in being a beggar of love.
I sing under your windows every day.
Give, give, giiiive,
God will give you back ...)

Even though the song sang of love it, seemed as if they were asking us to give them more material possessions when they all sang the chorus line with great bursts of energy. Especially the grandmother, notoriously known for being the mother of the three competing sisters. She was wreathed in a gold toga-like dress that revealed her humped over silhouette and that gave her the allure of always running forward, in the search for more. She wore thick eyeliner on drooping eyelids and her arms covered with diamond bangles gesticulated eagerly and emphatically towards the crowd. She smiled uncovering a mouth full of oversized teeth and sang proudly next to the star of the community Enrico:

Donnez, donnez, dodo-onnez,
Donnez, donnez moi,

Donnez, donnez, dodo-onnez,
Dieu vous le rendra...

(*Give, give, giiiive,*
Give, give, giiiive,
Give, give, giiiive,
God will give you back ...)

Memorable. In spite of the ridicule of the situation they were all an endearing lot. They loved life, money, love and laughter above all.

I realized years later that the barmitvah boy had suffered from intellectual disability. His challenge had not transpired one moment of this majestic and opulent and well-orchestrated festivity.

Using the same fervor, love courage and willpower that made them a success story of the Sentier, they had raised and surrounded the young man with the best care, so that his disability was hardly present. Years later I witnessed a friendly exchange between father and son, while standing behind them waiting for my turn at the Tabac.

There is something to be said for drive; the motor can bring power to many realms in one's life. They invested in business, festivities and all life had to offer with great intensity. This intensity and fierce determination showed in their son and the way they had willed him out of his challenges.

As a Jewish Moroccan, in this mostly Tunisian neighborhood, the perception of my identity underwent a great change. In comparison to Tunisians, Moroccans were seen as low key, refined and distant. Back home that was the way we Moroccans perceived the Ashkenazi community.

"You, Moroccans are classy, plus look at you, you are

educated. You should not be getting your fingers dirty here". Martine would say to me with her flattering, manipulative tone. She would say this and plop herself on my husband's side of the desk, playing Boss Lady, whenever he was out, every chance she got.

When I complained about this to my husband, he would shrug it off and say, "You just cannot beat the cheek and impudence of those Tunisians. Better to have them work for us than next door".

Lunchtime came, and we would go to Chez Juliette, the most famous restaurant in the neighborhood. Juliette greeted us with couscous platters in both hands, wearing figure hugging Azzedine Alaïa designs.

"Voila, Alex y'a une table pour toi là", she would say as she kissed him on both cheeks even if she was simultaneously balancing platters.

I never understood why Juliette never greeted me but was once explained by other women in the neighborhood not to take it personally. She never wasted time saying hello to women. Men paid the bills.

Life passed in the fashion district of Paris was a far cry from the glamour I had dreamt of, but the financial compensations were there. And Paris was there.

Bonpoint Birthdays

I was living in the center of Paris in a 2700 square meter apartment right on Monopoly's best street, boulevard de Courcelles overlooking the Parc Monceau's pretty pond. I was shopping at Prada's, sending delivery boys on the spur of a whim to get me that checkered shirt from Burberry's that I saw in the Jalouse magazine.

Not to mention the pleasure of going to Bonpoint to fill up my daughters' wardrobes, each season. They would be dressed in identical or matching sweet-as-can-be-dresses for parties. We would adopt hippy chic looks to hang out on Sundays at Mariage Freres, sipping the best tea and pouting in front of their St. Honoré, with their friends who were just as unabashedly elegant. The fabrics were dark tweeds, rich corduroys, velvets and flannels to be worn with liberty floral prints and checkered cotton underneath casual cashmere sweaters in the winter. Their silhouettes were topped off with wool duffel coats or velvet collared coats in dark tweeds. Even for children, the hues were sophisticated prunes, greys, browns, taupes, cobalts and burnt oranges. In the summer we selected starched cottons and gabardines for day with liberty prints in lighter tones. Organdi was a favorite for the wedding season and puff sleeved dresses were graced with sashes tied in the back into generous bows, underneath a row of matching raw silk covered buttons.

It was a real treat to see their clothes wrapped in the signature pale pink tissue paper, then slipped into cotton bags and vaporized with their trademark heavenly scent. This package was then slipped into perfect pink bags with the Boinpoint logo in gold letters on the white crest. Boys had pale blue packaging so for my beautiful daughters, we always left with clouds of pink bags. The pale blue was reserved for the gifts we made.

At Christmas time the tissue paper was exchanged for gold gauze and these folded packages were slipped into red cotton bags stamped with a gold Bonpoint logo. The most beautiful windows replete with traditional, luxurious and refined Christmas window decors greeted us. Whimsical elves, fairies, thrones, crowns and magic wands adorned the windows and store interiors. I never envied presidential favors but when I heard that Bonpoint St. Germain had been closed to greet solely the Obamas and their daughters for one magical Christmas shopping spree, I did feel a little pang of jealousy. This was well before Paris started feeling the economic slump, so the saleswomen were cold and obnoxious and even haughtier if you actually spent money in their store. Because in France spending money is slightly vulgar, so there is always a tinge of disapproval and distance when you are a good customer. But it didn't matter because the clothes, decors, lights accessories and windows were so enchantingly beautiful, it probably would have been ridiculous and syrupy if they had been nice. Like an extra sweet and soppy fairy tale.

All this was unpacked in their pretty Gustavien style bedrooms, equipped with furniture from Bonpoint and finely embroidered, perfectly starched sheets.

Birthday parties were under the sign of pink helium balloons and rose petals leading up to our apartment where we greeted the guests in their "col Claudine" dresses. It was not uncommon for little girls to bring a bouquet to the birthday girl which was a charming portrait to vision. I remember Iris Deschamps (the literal meaning of the name is "Iris from the fields"), our first guest at my eldest daughter's fifth birthday party, arriving with a bouquet of tiny roses. My daughter accepted it graciously with a sweet "you shouldn't have". I watched this prettiest of scenes between two five-year old's in awe, my breath held. It was all as delicate and fine as crystal with the sun shimmering through.

Birthday tables were decorated with great care, laden with silverware piled high with pink macarons, strawberries and puff pastries on starched lace tablecloths. We started a week before the party, by decorating the apartment with brightly colored paper decorations, so we felt the start of the party prancing upon us and made the pleasure last longer. One of the birthday musts was the pink helium balloons we filled the apartment with. Once I let them go inadvertently in the street and all the passerbys stopped to watch them prettily floating away. I also stopped and admired how pretty they were against the blue sky. Then ran back to the store to order more. Pale pink balloons were a must.

My parents had made memorable birthdays for me even though we had just arrived in Canada and had limited means. I wanted to maintain this tradition. In Montreal my legendary birthday parties consisted of bringing all my girlfriends to Ponderosa steak house ; the style had been very different, but the effect had also been immense. My birthday is in October but as soon as school would start in September, my classmates eagerly asked me how far away my birthday was.

So Parisian life was steeped in prettiness and finery. Of course, there is a price to pay for everything.

My help recently told my daughters that she was a cleaning lady, so her children would not have to be one. Sometimes, I feel I married a wealthy man, so my children would not have to. I sometimes saw in people's eyes envy because my husband was wealthy. I wanted to be able to say Do you think it's EASY? Cause it's easier said than DONE. Easy to envy me but you have no IDEA. You see if you can put up with him. How dare these people envy me when they are NOT paying the price. Would YOU pay the price I pay every day? Today I see Melania Trump and my heart goes out to her. (Ok, he was not THAT bad...but I wasn't living in the White House!).

The main problem with a wealthy man is his demanding, egotistical nature. When to make matters worse, he is an entitled Sephardic macho, you get a result that is hard to live with. Especially when he comes complete with the wicked mother and sister duo.

Nevertheless he was not all bad and sometimes he actually tried to be a good husband. But our programs were too different.

He was kindest when business was difficult. He would curl up in bed and not want to leave the apartment. Ironically that is when I found him most endearing. But when business was good, he was unbearable. His ego came crashing down with full force and obliviated everything and most especially me.

(His)tory

My father told me many wise things. One of the wisest things he told me was, "It is never the person's fault. It is the situation's fault".

That is why it is important to think of a person's story when you think they have wronged you.

Alex had arrived straight from Israel, where his family had emigrated to flee the end of the colonialist era in Morocco that spelt uncertainty for the Jews.

He had been raised in Morocco with a complicated family history. His father had been married to a woman and had six children with her, when he fell in love with Alex's mother, a young woman who had never been married. I got to meet her when she was a bitter old mother in law, so I was never fully able to understand the charms she must have had back then. He left his wife and six children and married this young woman. At the time he was a very successful businessman often travelling to Europe to buy fabric for his store, so morals and money were no object. A wealthy man could and still can do what he pleases. The couple had two children, first a daughter (who was to become the most wicked sister in law of the West) and then Alex.

The father was soon disappointed by his new wife and her

bad character. He kept running back to his first household where he was revered by the six abandoned children for some unfathomable reason. Back then, no matter what parents did they were revered. It was way before the era of therapy where one could indulge in blaming everything on your procreator. After several years of a tumultuous and unpleasant marriage, Alex's father did the "pack of cigarettes trick". He said he was going out to buy a pack of cigarettes and didn't come back. He took off to Israel where his first family was waiting for him. Now to his credit no one ever said they were going to Israel when they left Morocco. In fact, in Morocco no one ever even mentioned the word Israel. People would say, "so you are going to t**he country?** ".

Alex's mother soon enough noticed his absence and went running to his brother and partner. He was the good brother with a kindly wife and extremely well brought up kids. One of those families where absolutely everyone is kind. He could not have found favor in his brother's scheme, but nevertheless had nothing to say. And probably admittedly found Alex's mother a terror. He doled out money to the abandoned wife and children until they found their way to also go to **the country.** Alex was 12 at the time. His father was living with his first family, but somewhat helped them establish themselves in Israel.

Life was tough for them there and his mother soon had an accident with a bus that ran over her and left her in the hospital for 6 months. By then her wealthy ex-husband had lost all his money. There is a saying that if you want to be a millionaire in Israel you must go there as a billionaire. A country that is always in a period of war and survival makes for a lot of tough and ruthless businessmen. Alex soon left school and tried to flee as much as he could this all (hysterical) women's household made up of his mother (whining), sister (overbearing) and grandmother (the one he called the saint). This is no doubt where his contempt for women was born.

In his late teens, he left for Paris with promises that once he would become successful, because there was no doubt he would, they would all come join him. He had been greatly in love with a young woman, but problems arose when she did not comply with his wishes to find an excuse to avoid the army. He had been excused from doing his military because he was supporting his family and therefore felt she should also find an excuse. If he wasn't doing the army, why would she? He promptly left her. Just like he left me many years later when I refused to abandon my beloved job at BCBG. Lol.

In Paris, he lived in his uncle's small apartment crowded with his aunt and four cousins and shared a small bedroom with his favorite cousin. He was on a hunt to make money. His sister joined him soon after and she started dating a young man from a wealthy family of the Sentier. Alex accompanied his sister and her new boyfriend to Parisian nightclubs such as Regine and Olivia Valère. The same ones that my father had enjoyed in his time. He took one look at the expensive whiskey bottles, they were ordering, figured out that the money came from the fashion district and enrolled the next day for night classes at Esmod, a renowned fashion school. A few weeks later he got hired as a designer, quickly became a partner in the company and eventually bought out the company some 18 months later. Typical hungry guy achieves the success story of the '80s.

By the time I met him, he had taken on the polish that money gives.

His success had been hard-earned. And me with my dreams of career, self-fulfilment and realizing my full potential...well this was all useless blabla and Jewish American princess spoiled brat talk to this guy.

I had taken the easy way out and even before we married, I started working with him in his company. After the internship at Femme, I was never able to find anything except for a very poorly paid job assisting a woman that tried to put French film production budgets together. She never succeeded and was highly aggravated all the time. The easy way out presented itself. But deep down I felt that this was a failure, a betrayal of the American dream of the fulfilled, independent and strong woman I should be.

Especially since even at the office our different backgrounds and cultures clashed. When he asked me to convince a client to buy merchandise that was perhaps not ideal for her, I refused. I was the scrupulous Canadian, I had established a rapport with this woman, she trusted me, etc. He, of course, blew his top. He had come to this country with nothing, but his survival instinct. Aa spoiled American brat only could have the luxury of such rigorous principles. He was robbing no one and could not understand how I was not putting his needs and requests at the forefront of all my actions. I tried to be true to myself, but at the same time wanted to please, like the good student, I had been. I wanted to be efficient and take the example of his success.

I had my wonderful daughters and with their father's position, they should hopefully never lack anything. I reasoned that it was important to have a flexible working schedule that allowed me to organize a household filled with nannies, piano lessons, ballet classes, birthday parties, play dates, tutors and High holidays.

Unfortunately, the High holidays were usually great cause for distress. My husband's mother would come live with us for the duration and growl at me and my help. For weeks before, my mother would call me and ask me if as a dutiful wife I had ordered the meat at the butchers before there was no more. I always waited till the last minute because I wanted to push the stress-laden ordeal to the back of my agenda and mind and yet never once did the butcher have a meat scarcity. Yet my mother called me incessantly about the holiday meals I had to organize, and my aunts would call to wish me the best holidays and try to sneak in a few recipes, probably dictated to by my mother. I would immerse myself in work to try to forget that I was now the head of a household, I had to entertain these horrid women, I had to live up to the demands of a macho, Sephardic, demanding husband. My mother was relentless and soon enough my mounting stress was faced with the reality of the holidays.

Here I felt I was living in medieval times with a difficult mother in law and sister in law. My husband played referee and we got through the ordeal best we could.

Needless to say, once the holidays were over and his mother finally back in her house, I was happiest back at work.

India

We had Indian suppliers that manufactured clothes for us, and they invited us to their daughters' wedding in Bombay. It was a one-week affair with dinners, dancing and classical music played in hotel ballrooms. Each foreign guest had a family member attributed to them to organize transportation to the affairs and to make sure they were seated and served. Every member of the bride's family was attributed to a member of the groom's family to take care of. I shivered at the thought of such a thing happening with a woman like my mother in law. I could just imagine her sulking while being fawned over.

Our hosts were so attentive they sent me a beautiful gold and red sari to wear to the peak event: the religious wedding that would be followed by a dinner served in the center of a polo race-horse track. We arrived (after 2 hours in Bombay traffic) on the field that had been furnished with antique pieces of Indian furniture. The guests strolled from one couch to the next, conversing and forming new groups. The women wore richly embroidered saris of dazzling colors. It seemed like each sari was an ode to a different bright color or palette and represented a new play of embroideries running through the fabrics, thus displaying endless creativity. I had already spent hours admiring the sumptuous saris in stores that ranged from the inexpensive brightly colored offerings to heavily embroidered ones that were kept for security behind glass doors, each one costing tens of thousands of dollars. Now they were all before me and I spent the evening in awe at the beautiful silhouettes strolling by.

We advanced towards a big stage at the far end of the field and waited in line for our turn to walk to centerstage where we could congratulate the bride and groom. We were blinded not only by the beauty of the bride but also by the customary family necklace worn by the groom on his wedding day. Traditionally this necklace represents the family heritage and is composed only of diamonds. This is a strand of diamonds that increase in size towards the center. Hanging in the middle of his necklace throned a huge and dazzling diamond.

The buffet spanned the full length of the field and was composed of only vegetarian dishes as Hinduism dictates. The diversity was so overwhelming that one wondered how this was possible with only vegetable, grains and dairy food groups. Each dish was more succulent than the next.

India is a country of disturbing contrasts. When we left, we saw a huge line outside the football field. It is customary for the poor to wait for leftovers at these lavish affairs.

Throughout my trip, I had been very disturbed by children in rags holding out their hands in the middle of highways, near cars that raced too closely by them. I saw mothers begging with skinny babies in their arms. I would ask the driver to stop so I could give them money or to find that woman who had just disappeared into a side street with a sickly-looking baby and he would laugh and say, "never mind, many like that, I find you more". After the first days, I feared venturing into the streets, feeling increasing helplessness. The only refuge was offered by the stores filled with saris and the sights of women walking in the streets enveloped in their bright garb like an armor against the environing poverty.

Our host was elegant, a real product of British colonialism, complete with impeccable manners and elegant clothes. He always looked like he was going off to play polo.

The hostess was less refined in her ways. I had noticed when she came to Paris that she never addressed our personnel directly as if they were lesser beings.

"We are not of the right caste," they told me laughingly, her manners were so evident.

When we brought our suppliers to a very chic Indian restaurant, she embarrassed me by giving very abrupt orders to the Indian waiter as if we were in her home and he was her servant. He seemed to know and expect this attitude from people from "back home" and served us unflinchingly.

Now in India, when they drove us to our hotel one night and she saw me look out the window aghast at what seemed like hundreds of people lying side by side in the street she waved in their direction with her pudgy hands covered with bulky diamonds and laughed,

"But dey are happy like dat".

I had never seen anything like this. I cried silently.

"Stop it, you are embarrassing the suppliers", was the only reaction I got from my husband.

Bali

Alex and I were different in more ways than one. In his mind, because I was the woman, I always had to be second best in every domain at the office. So, when the children and I accompanied him on a design trip to Bali with his core team he did not understand that I wanted to go to the design offices with him instead of staying at the pool all day with the children. I insisted, and he ranted, roared and complained that it was not professional, that he needed to concentrate with his team, that I was never happy, etc., etc.

On the last day of the business trip he said I could come with the children. As soon as we arrived at our supplier's design offices, I came to life in the presence of the linens and bamboo buttons. He had ordered over 80 samples designed by himself and his team. I asked if I could design a small group of 6 items. Because I asked pretend-timidly, no doubt, he acquiesced as if he were indulging a child's whim. My group was delivered with his samples. In the end, although he never admitted it, this became the only group we produced from that whole trip. This is one example that represents our whole marriage. Two rivaling egos, cultures, intentions and objectives that made everything difficult.

The arguments were frequent and explosive. I understand now that our differences were due to paradoxical cultures and self-branding.

We both were born in Casablanca, but besides that, a

common birthplace stamped on a passport and the same cultural *background*, the things we had in common were few and far between.

I was a product of the North American culture that encourages women to find their way, to be independent and fulfilled above all.

He was a product of the Israeli culture that dictates survival above all and to boot had been exposed to a man, his father, gone bankrupt, which gave him the example that the only way out was to earn money.

The identity or self-marketing that I wished to expose to the world and myself was that of a successful, creative and independent woman.

The identity or branding he wished to impose on me or any woman at his side was that of a sweet woman whose major preoccupation was to help her husband continue to prosper, to exist through his success, to cook the most perfect edition of his mother's handed down recipes and to care for the children. Only once these tasks were accomplished, this ideal woman could run to the office and be of use with utter selflessness. A woman who would call him "Cherie" and check his shirts.

As one of my best friends, Bianca pointed out many years later, even our linguistic differences did not help. "Cherie" was reserved for my parent's vocabulary. I needed to name affection with Love, babe, darling, honey but that did not correspond to this man.

I wanted to create? To use the skills and knowledge my masters had taught me? I could just throw that diploma down the toilet for all it was worth. After all, he had dropped out of school at the age of 15 and was lording it over a minimum of 50 employees.

Between these two differing ideals and the linguistic gap, our marriage could not survive.

One day after having served the legendary Dafina dish, I was cleaning up at the sink and he came to gratify me with a kiss and a hug. I tried hard not to throw up because this image repelled me so. I had to be washing dishes after serving Dafina to deserve admiration and affection.

Besides these issues, we were simply always at odds. When I was sensitive, he was not. When I was enthralled, he was not. What he liked, I didn't. What he wanted to do, I did not. Whom he liked I did not. Like in all dysfunctional marriages.

All this through no fault of either of us.

Figured you out
By Nickelback
And I hate the places that we go
And I hate the people that you know
And now I know who you are
It wasn't that hard,
just to figure you out
(Now I did, you wonder why)
And now I know who you are
(Gone for good, and this is it)

My Stroke Of Insight

I knew something was wrong, but I did not dare to do anything about it. I was able to raise my daughters practically alone as he was always busy at work. I was able to face his wicked mother and sister (worse than in any Cinderella book). I was able to solicit customers laden with clothing samples in the metro and repeatedly knock on their door till they gave me orders. I was able to run and hustle and jump loops as all women do. But I was not able to leave this marriage that did not suit me one bit.

And yet there were signs that I could not avoid. Very potent and significant signs.

One night I was up in bed and although I am usually a very good sleeper, I could not sleep. I silently asked G.d to send me a sign. Was he or not the right man for me. Should I envision that this was the man of my life and that I would stay with him forever or was I living a lie?

At this very moment, (I swear), he emitted the loudest and longest flatulence I had ever witnessed. My question has been explicitly answered, I thought and stifled a chuckle.

To this day this story elicits lots of laughter from my best friends, especially beautiful, dainty, elegant Tia who grew up with three brothers and loves all the vulgar body emitting jokes best.

But it is the solemn truth.

Now what? I pondered, staring at the ceiling and feeling even more alone in my bed, now that I had my answer.

Alone And Married

I was married but had never felt so alone. It did not help that his mother and sister were Wicked witches. It did not help that my own family and extended family were so far. Each time they came to Paris or I brought my daughters to Montreal to visit them my heart was filled. Otherwise, I tried to keep busy and pushed my constant loneliness to the back.

During the summers of my childhood, I had run to Israel to feel the security blanket of our family: my grandparents, aunts and uncles.

And now, during these summers, I ran to Montreal to revel in everyday life and pleasures with my parents, my sister, brother in law, nieces, nephews, cousins, aunts and uncles. Nothing made me happier than to see my daughters putting on plays with my nephews or going to an American style day camp as if we lived there. This was now my security, my warm and generous blanket.

Once summer was over, I landed abruptly in beautiful but cold and grey Paris. Yes, I had my darling daughters, but felt so alone with this cold and demanding husband and his unwelcoming, to say the least, mother and sister.

I was too far, too suddenly, right at the start of my adult life and often worried about my parents. Especially about my father whom I loved so much. I was born like him on October 22nd and had always felt that our souls were the same. If I called home and my parents didn't answer because of the time difference I would creep back into the kitchen in the middle of the night and call again and again until they were home safe. It was one o'clock in the morning in Paris, but only 7pm in Montreal. Now I realize that this obsessive behavior was because I felt so estranged by a marriage with a man that I did not have much in common with.

Cell phones were not around, and I did not always want to call my parents from the apartment in my husband's presence. Also, he would have seen how ridiculously high the bills were. I often went down to the public phone booth like many other immigrants on Sunday afternoons. And felt even lonelier and isolated in the phone booth but needed to be alone with them.

Chanter pour ceux qui sont loin de chez eux
By Michel Berger
Celui-là passe toute la nuit
À regarder les étoiles

En pensant qu'au bout du monde
Y a quelqu'un qui pense à lui
Ils sont tristes à la fête,
Ils sont seuls dans leur tête,
Je veux chanter pour ceux
Qui sont loin de chez eux

Sing for those who are far from their home
By Michel Berger
(That one goes out all night
Watching the stars
Thinking that at the other ends of the earth
Someone is thinking hard of him
They are sad at the party, wherever they go
They are alone in their heads
I want to sing for those
Who are far from their home)

I kept busy with my roles in my husband's company each time trying tirelessly to find personal fulfillment to my husband's disappointment. I kept busy with the children, with dinner parties and lunches and trips. Each season also brought the joy of new collections to shop, one of my happiest moments, I must admit, fashionista that I am. Upon entering Prada, Paul & Joe, Marni or Miu Miu, my heart would seem to beat with more excitement, and I would forget what a disappointment my marriage was. We did our rounds starting avenue Montaigne, St. Honoré and then St. Germain. In St. Germain we finished off with the cherry on the sundae : Miu Miu. In the '90s, it was still a little store on the Rue du Dragon, named after Miucca Prada's nickname. As soon as you entered the store you saw that she got to play with this line. No doubt because this was an escape from the huge responsibility of Prada, by now an institution, and its numbers. Eclectic prints, embellisments and extravaganza made you feel as if you had uncovered a closet in a fairy tale. Ever see grown women play dress up? It was wonderful, especially accompanied by my shopping partners in crime.

Pascale And Azzedina Alaia

One of the most glorious souvenirs of all those years in Paris was lunch with the girls and shopping. The perfect day consisted of shopping, lunch and more shopping. One such day, one my best friends Pascale and I headed out to the must-have-brand of the late eighties; Azzedine Alaïa. There we both fell in love with a jacket with a tribal chic edge that had a pinched in corset waist from which straw fringes shot out. She opted for this style in a sand tone and I went for the camel tone. We were paying the heady amount that makes one's heart race even more and completes the guilty love affair we have with clothes. To our surprise the saleswoman told us that Azzedine was not totally satisfied with the end product and we should come back for a private meeting with him. True passion! The sale was made, but in spite of that he was not happy! An appointment with Azzedine himself was booked. I went back the week after and marveled at this discrete perfectionist as he twirled around me and gave instructions to his assistant to take apart the whole corset and add more fringes. The fringes jutted out creating a more pronounced volume and thus accentuating the waist. It was perfect.

Pascale was her usual lackadaisical self and did not come back. That was part of her charm. She had a brand-new car in the garage but, could not be bothered to try to retrieve the driver's license the Parisian police had withdrawn because of too many unpaid tickets. She was one of these women that reveled in the bathrobe moment after the shower, taking time to get ready. It seems I was always running after something all those years in Paris and her laid-back ways seemed to have a philosophical European edge...as if to say, "What for?".

But with what energy this cool, laid back women wrenched her older son from drug dealing and addiction many years later attests to the great inner strength and determination that erupted from her like a volcano where her sons were concerned. She threw kilos of stashed hash found in her apartment down the toilet, confronted the dealers and sent her son off to boarding school, psychiatrists, mentors you name it. She saved the situation.

That is the power of women. We may have our light, superficial, self-indulgent side, but when we need to be a warrior, unsuspected forces appear and help us rise to the occasion. Of course, we prefer not to have to use them and just indulge in lunch, shopping and pink tinted sunglasses. But beware.

The only other time I saw this woman's carnal instinct was when my delicate, fine boned friend, wearing the latest and trendiest of Parisian fashions would face her favorite plate of steak tartare. Such a delicate looking woman wolfing down raw meat was fraught with the wonderful paradoxes that inhabit and benefit women.

Bianca And Prada

Bianca my great friend from Montreal had moved back to Paris, where she had originally been raised, a few years after I was living there. Our fathers had been the greatest of friends way back in Casablanca and we even have a picture together at her one-year old birthday party. She was raised in Paris, but when we were teenagers, she moved to Montreal to join her father who had left Paris and a wife and three children who did not want to follow him behind. Bianca was the only one who eventually wanted to try living in Montreal and we soon became great friends doing all the silly things teenagers do. We experimented with nightclubs, dying our hair, smoking cigarettes, etc.

Many years later as I was walking by Prada in Paris, to my surprise Bianca ran out of the store and surprised me. She had spent a few years in New York after Montreal, but by now had decided to come back to Paris and had very recently been hired by The Brand of the decade: Prada.

We were teenagers again, but with more pocket money and now Paris was our playground. She wasn't married because "no man she had met was good enough to impress by Anna Wintour standards."

Our favorite past time was shopping on our days off. We would whizz around in my Citroen and on the spur of the moment double park, erupt into stores, run in crazy circles, scatter in different directions, each following our attraction for a print, a color or detail and then recoup in 40 seconds if something was worth trying. "Did you see this??". "I knooow its great!!" or "No way, too last season". And if there was something that passed the first glance test and that we wanted to try on we were giddy with excitement as we rushed into the dressing room.

Some months I would tell my friends "I am not spending a franc this month on any clothes, I swear" and then bump into the perfect blue shade in a coat graced with a bow and think to myself "why, I could get hit by a bus tomorrow and what will have been the use of depriving myself?".

One such day, a perfect spring day that only heightens the excitement and promise of Parisian shopping, we set out first to the super trendy A.P.C store, a very confidential, off the beaten track store on the rue de Fleury. This street is off the grid of the busier part of St. Germain, so I had no queries about leaving my car double parked outside. I decided to try on a two-piece gabardine bathing suit at APC. Only APC could be daring and crazy enough to make a bathing suit in rigid gabardine. As I was evaluating the look in the mirror, Bianca shrieked,

"A bus, your car is blocking a bus!"

I threw on one of the brands signature cotton raincoats, left my bag and clothes in the waiting room, yelled at her to watch my things and raced out of the store, clutching the coat over the bathing suit. The salesgirl was quite upset, even if I had left my clothes and purse behind. Her gaze dismally followed my frenetic actions. I freed the bus from its position behind me and started driving in search of a parking spot.

I was, to say the least, very frazzled at this sudden interruption. I found myself driving around in a bikini that did not belong to me (slipped on top of my oversized comfy cotton underwear of course). To make matters worse, there was a constant and screeching beeping sound in my car. I worried that perhaps something was wrong with my car. That was the last thing I wanted, to have car problems. In Paris the smaller the car the better and my "fun" money did not have any priorities other than fashion shopping. (I had no problem entering the beat-up Citroën with my rearview mirror held up by band aids and a bag from Colette with 3000 euros in clothing). The noise was incessant as I circled for proper parking. I finally parked the car and ran out into the street. Things were getting worse: the noise was not stopping. What if this noise was in my head? "Bianca!",

I screeched erupting into the store, "Can you also hear that horrible noise or is it just me?"

"You idiot! It's the security tag on the bathing suit".

The Parisian salesgirl stood there sulking as they often do, reacting very disdainfully to my relieved, "I'll take the bathing suit."

The great thing about having a best friend that worked at Prada, besides getting me on the list that granted me an official 10% discount were all the funny insider stories.

In the 90's Prada was THE place to shop and work at. Bianca worked there, and I harassed her with phone calls when I could not physically be there to know what incredible pieces had just arrived, bringing in a flurry of excitement, and what I should splurge on. Each new piece arrived with ceremony and was greeted as if it had been accompanied by hundreds of beautifully fluttering pastel butterflies. I called her so often she loved to pick up and say, "Is that my customer from hell?"

She had a lot of customers from hell. She would often come to our home after work and relay to my daughters and me all the crazed stories of the day. One of her most avid listeners was my husband even if he would beg to differ.

All the manufacturers from the Sentier would go to Prada on Saturdays, their pockets filled with thick piles of cash made from selling their cheaper brands and to be spent at Prada's. Of course, the clothes they bought at Prada's were often first brought to their teams to be studied and copied so it made the purchase worthwhile. Once it was copied, it was worn. Sometimes it was worn on the weekend and then flung on Monday morning on the patternmaker's desk. So usually on Saturday afternoons all the owners of the Sentier brands were there.

Tara J., the picture of wasp perfection came with her husband, the epitome of the ambitious Sentier businessman who yearned for success and then crowned it with a trophy wife who was not only beautiful but could also design. Many contrasting cultures met at the intersection of fashion and thirst for success in the '80s. Before meeting this graceful wife, he was giving all his energy to a man's line. The smart man that he was no doubt quickly surmised that this picture of natural style and grace should be given the design reins. The line that ensued reflected her taste and values. Years and a lot of money later she was to leave this fruitful marriage and partnership for some chic seaside resort city in the USA where she could live for real the lifestyle images of her brand: cable-knit sweaters on yachts and couture-inspired LBD's (little black dress).

The two top brands of today that shall remain unnamed belong to two sisters. The sisters would look over the Prada collection with a fine-tooth comb, then whisper to each other emphatically in the VIP dressing room while they tried clothes on together. A lot of their collections were inspired by Prada. The younger sister had divorced and was plotting with the help of her sister and fashion/love affair accomplice to marry the heir of a huge button manufacturer. To say that a lot of buttons (and zippers, shoulder pad and hundreds of other items) were needed in that neighborhood is an understatement. An empire had been built. The older sister was married to a very laid-back Ashkenazi, who was known for spending a lot of time at the café next door to their wholesale operation while she worked diligently. Her marriage made up of two extremes worked well, so the younger sister followed her example.

The Ashkenazi heir of the button empire ended up marrying this ambitious young Sephardic woman. The son of a wealthy Ashkenazi man is no match for a determined Sephardic woman from a modest family. It is like comparing a gentleman farmer from the English countryside to a female politician from Manhattan…or Caracas (lol); she will get her way. He confided to his friend many years later that he did not always feel comfortable with the ever-present family, religion and superstitions that came with having a Sephardic wife but no doubt he must have admired their success.

Many Ashkenazi Jews of France have distanced themselves from religion, especially after the horrors of the Shoah traversed by their grandparents. They see religion like a distasteful but ever-present poor relation that one must put up with. Sephardi's coming from North African countries had a very different experience with religion. In Arab countries, the practice of each community's religion, Jews and Arabs, side by side, came as naturally as the preparation of meals and the raising of children. It was an inherent part of the lifestyle, never to be questioned, where traditions and even some superstitions were part of the mix. Religion was synonymous with parties and high holidays and rules were respected as this guaranteed "parnassa" or material rewards. Thus, the M… sisters, no doubt under the influence of their parents and ancestors, never opened the wholesale stores in the Sentier on Saturdays. Unlike the renegade Ashkenazi families. For this Ashkenazi husband, having in-laws that always had a Rabbi in tow, were Shomer Shabbat and hid from the evil eye was not his cup of tea. But a wife that was in Vogue with all the benefits must have been impressive for a man of taste.

The Prada fever thus ensued among the Parisian crowd of moneyed fashionistas and jewish-parisians from the Sentier. Women dragged in their husbands, their parents, their boyfriends and begged for a piece of the Prada action. One woman nearly pinned Bianca to the wall," I need this dress, my mother will come pay for it tomorrow". She was known for having a coke addiction but in that instant, she transferred it to Prada.

Patrick B., the most popular singer of the moment was dragged into a store one day by his very pregnant girlfriend. Like many men about to be conned into spending money, he did not give in to the exaggeratedly polite smiles of the salesgirls. He walked in hurriedly and told his girlfriend to quickly try on the (damn) dress, seemingly trying to reign in his exasperation. She came out of the dressing room elated and expectant like any woman who has achieved the feat of dragging her man to a Prada store with a credit card in his pocket full of possibilities. He glanced at her and uttered the cruelest words:

"This is what you dragged me here for? I am waiting for you in the car". He made a hurried exit. Crushing and cruel. Her face fell. I was told the story and could never stomach his songs after that.

The craziest of the bunch was undoubtedly the heiress of the most well-known chain of stores selling appliances in France. She would start her day at Prada practically every morning and then continue shopping all day, ending the day with the cheaper brands. Her chauffeur was sent to pick up clothes and do other random errands like "bring back this perfume bottle to Bulgari, I can't believe it: the spritz broke".

She was obsessed with what she was getting at Prada but even more preoccupied with what her friends were getting. In St. Tropez, her best friend and next-door neighbor was the founder of a brand that she had somehow convinced LVMH to buy out, even it was still in the very early stages of brand creation. If a Prada box was spotted being delivered to her friend and neighbor in St. Tropez, a phone call to Prada Paris would ensue. The heiress would casually call Bianca:

"Hi, how are you…my help just told me Renata got a box

from Prada. Her help told my help. Could you please discretely ask Fabio what he sold her? I neeeeed to know what she got. Pleeease." she wheedled. Like many competitive businessmen, she did not focus on what she was making, but rather on what the next guy was earning.

Bianca, dying of laughter would go see Fabio and they would laugh about their crazy customers.

Renata, the director of the fashion brand was a terror herself. No one even tried to avoid her calls and demands. After all, she had been shrewd enough to sell her brand, originating from the Sentier, to the LVMH Group based on only ONE style she had come up with: the kaftan dress, inspired by her jewish Tunisian background and updated with her Parisian chic. That and her strong personality, confidence and persistence had been enough to push one of the corporate heads into a corner until he bought her brand.

I can imagine her harassing the elegant French director of LVMH and dazzling him with her charisma and directive personality. She must have entranced him with her whirlwind of activities, dinners, laughter and rambunctious friends. The purchase was made, she got loads of money and her brand was written off as a failure by LVMH soon after. Today, this woman who must be in her 60's lovingly posts pictures of herself wearing the best brands in the hippest vacation spots nearly every day. The look on her face is that of a cat who swallowed a mouse. No wonder the LVMH director was no match.

She often brought men that she cornered into coughing up their credit cards. Some women mysteriously have the magic touch. Heavy-handed, but still magic. After she brought a man to Prada, she asked that his credit card be kept on file. Then she would call in and order purchases to be put through on the new victim's credit card. No one dared say no.

The Prada crew were victims of the success of the brand and thus were continually harassed by these women and their incessant demands. They would call and say that they "absolutely need that bag...did you check in Venice??? In LA? New York???"

Our heiress had two nieces. One day their mother dragged them into the store sulking and ordered them to pick out a gift for Aunty. They did not seem to put their heart into it. The aunt came the next day and willingly gave the rundown.

"My sister dragged them here to buy me a gift? Haha. I want nothing of their gift. Here take it back! You know what they did to me while I was away with Jean ??? (French motor sport executive of Ferrari who shall remain unnamed).

"They had the keys to my apartment, wore my clothes out every night and then proceeded to sell my clothes in the depot ventes across Paris to make extra cash! Jacques the chauffeur is scouring all the depot ventes to get my clothes back! Some I will never retrieve! They even took my underwear! " (no wonder, it was only La Perla).

You never do know though with children. Later, one of those nieces ended up being an award-winning writer.

The executive of Ferrari eventually left her for an Asian that hardly ever uttered a word. Probably to his great relief.

"How can he be with her: she looks so oooold!" That was all our heiress had to say.

Bianca also told us stories of fraying with the Kennedy's. The most elegant customer I ever caught a glimpse of was Caroline Kennedy. Her tall, thin angular figure with that tightly wound bun of gleaming blonde hair spelled Wasp Nobility. She came numerous times to the Prada store and even before the news hit the press, she told Bianca of her upcoming wedding to the most eligible bachelor of the planet: John Kennedy. When

Bianca once remarked to Caroline that she loved the jeans she was wearing, a few days later she received two jeans from the said label in an envelope that had been mailed from the George magazine whose editor was John Kennedy.

She often lunched with her customers, notably Lee Radziwill, sister of Jackie Kennedy. The Kennedys were known to abide by Truman Capote's famous quote: "You can never be too rich or too thin". I think Lee loved inviting Bianca because she ate so little herself, so she loved watching Bianca eat and devoured vicariously through her. She would reminisce about her young glamour days while looking with great fascination and near admiration at Bianca savouring her Costes Club Sandwich and fries, while she herself nibbled on a sucrine lettuce or green beens.

One rainy day the Prada crew was all standing around the store void of customers except for the tenacious and reliably present appliance heiress. The bodyguards suddenly pointed to a figure at the far end of the store. "Be careful of that woman. She looks suspicious. She has a huge bag."

They all looked her way. Only Bianca recognized this small, dark, and non-descript woman.

"My God that is Miuccia Prada!!!!!!!"

Bianca went over to welcome her, the sales team and the heiress trailing behind.

Very flustered and impressed, they all gave her the welcome she deserved. Miuccia Prada, had an extremely busy agenda and had never set foot in the avenue Montaigne store although it had already been opened for several years. She was in Paris and had suddenly decided to "take a look".

Our very impressed heiress wanted to make a good impression on this stature of the fashion world and quickly said:

"I loooove what you do. I have nearly everything you do!!" She gushed over her.

"So what? "retorted lackadaisically the number one world designer of the moment. She shrugged her shoulders and might have even repressed a yawn. "So do I. " And on this note she bid them farewell. She was earthy Italian stock in spite of being the number one in our fashion world.

Nocturnes Aux Printemps

When our days were filled with too many obligations, we still had our Thursday evenings at The Printemps. I was used to stores staying open late on Thursdays and Fridays in Montreal. But the French never got used to shopping in the evenings and so the "Nocturnes" that the Printemps instilled never took off. Which means I had all those fabulous floors practically to myself. Later when I would come to get Bianca at Prada's to go out for lunch one of the salesgirls told her "what were you doing with Mme. Anonyme? I remember her from my stint at Printemps; she was one of our rare customers on Thursday nights."Bianca laughed and replied that before being Mme Anonyme I was her childhood friend and Montreal had instilled in us the nocturnal shopping habit. By then Bianca also accompanied me to the Printemps "nocturnes" one of our favorite outings.

What a rush of adrenaline inhabited us as we entered the big department store and rushed to the designers floors. Armed with Printemps credit cards which boasted "3 months no interest fees", everything was possible. We felt a heady sensation that I always evaluated must be similar to the way hunters feel as they enter hunting grounds. We would frenetically roam on all the fashion floors until closing time excitedly looking for our prey… or life-transforming-piece of the season. First we would head to designer's floor and wether we splurged or not on that top floor, we would then make our way down to less expensive lines, bags, accessories…. "ooh cannot wait to get to shoes"! We would run in different directions and then we would call out each other's names to come for an opinion which was usually met either with an emphatic yes or no. Sometimes we would call each other on cell phones "Where are you? Come now! Chloé!". "I am here! Behind you! Wow, sooo cool!" or "no, so last season".

Suddenly the loudspeaker would start announcing the countdown to closing time and we would hurry to finalise our purchases. We felt an even greater rush when we purchased a brand name with a hefty price tag. Our hearts would race as the bag was handed over to us and there was mixed with our sheer pleasure a little feeling of guilt, no doubt at spending such an amount on *clothes*. (Perhaps once again similar to what hunters must feel when their prey is caught!)

We left the Printemps regretfully, still stealing glances on our way out at a lipstick, a scarf, a bag while the guards practically escorted us out, calling out to us to follow them out towards the only door open by then, the employee's exit. We filed out, still elated by our purchases, slightly embarrassed to be the very last ones out.

Recently my eldest daughter was blocked on the top floor of another Parisian department store, "Au Bon Marché" with her husband, while visiting the store for their wedding registry. There had been a demonstration, of the "gilets jaunes" under the Macron presidency, in the streets of Paris and some unruly participants erupted into the store. The sitation was thankfully minor and security announced that all should stay on the top floor while they escorted these people out. She calmly made the best of it and ran from one department to the next. Her husband marveled that she could continue shopping at such a moment.

Her mother's daughter, she patiently explained there were worse places to be stuck.

September 11ᵀʰ

I cannot write about that era without remembering September 11ᵗʰ and where I was that day. I never remember dates or years, but everyone remembers where they were on September 11 th when they found out the horrible news.

I was shopping. Twice a year my husband would give me a generous amount of money to shop. The bills could be tax credits because we were in the fashion business. No, he was not ALL bad like I already acquiesced.

I started the day on avenue Montaigne, relishing those first moments of a beautiful sunny day when you go on a shopping expedition and you have money to spend in all the glimmering stores. Of course, it is always tricky because there is never enough sunshine (or money) to spread among all the brands you love. Every purchase must be based on directions from the heart and the mind. But usually, the heart prevails. Some wonderful pieces of course will reach your very soul! As I was passing by Louis Vuitton, two Asian men stopped me very discretely and asked,

"Could you buy a bag for us at Louis Vuitton and we will pay you?".

I had heard of this silly black market. Louis Vuitton sold very limited quantities of their wares to Asians because they would bring bags back home and sell them cheaper than in their stores by not paying import duties and taxes. Sometimes also this was to copy them. Our friend Gerard had told us how in the eighties every time he needed cash, he would head to the hotel Nikko and find some Asian at the bar in need of Louis Vuitton.

Empires were founded with the first francs this impromptu business offered. I had always been fascinated by these stories and now was my chance to test it.

"Ok, give me the price of the bag and add 100 euros for me."

"Yes, please follow me".

I walked to the side of Louis Vuitton, we both looked to our right and left and then stopped in front of the nearby Chanel store. He opened a well-thumbed Louis Vuitton catalogue and showed me the bag and wallet he wanted me to purchase. I nodded that I was ready for my mission. He handed me the euros from his coat pocket. Feeling like a spy on an illicit mission I headed towards Vuitton.

A busload of Japanese customers stood in a single file in front of the store and they were granted access to the store five at a time. They opened the door for me and waved me in as if there was a quota for Asians and one for Caucasians.

I went straight to the counter and asked for the bag and wallet. I was being paid 100 euros and wanted my time to be cost-efficient. Plus, this little adventure was interesting, but I did not wish it to unduly delay my favorite mission: personal shopping.

The salesgirl took me aside and to my surprise said that the store manager wished to see me and enquire on a matter.

"Hello Madam, I do not want to be indiscrete, but today there are many characters in the street sending our customers on errands and we are assuring ourselves that purchases are not made for these people".

"Well, that is indeed preposterous. I have always heard of this black market but never understood it. It is most certainly not my case."

"Would you mind therefore coming back tomorrow to make your purchase? As a matter of precaution we are asking this of our customers."

Wow, I really must work for these 100 euros I thought.

"I absolutely cannot. I am taking a flight to Montreal early in the morning and these are gifts for my sister and brother in law."

She pursed her lips, looked slightly contrite but complied. I think my fresh-from Canada-good-image helped. I was out of there in 10 minutes.

My "boss" and his companion were waiting nearby on Avenue Montaigne under a tree. I got a kick out of walking straight out of the store, sunglasses on and giving them a very discrete nod to my left, thus indicating where the exchange of goods would be held. He saw how seriously I was taking my mission and by the time he reached me with his accomplice, near the Chanel store, they were trying hard not to laugh too loudly. The goods were handed over to him and he asked me if I would come to meet him at the end of the day at the Louis Vuitton on Champs Elysees for another mission. I told him I would bring a friend, thinking Bianca could enjoy this as well. We agreed on a time and parted.

Bianca came to join me, and we shopped and had lunch on a beautiful Parisian terrace. Then we went to Galeries Lafayette and then the world turned.

We were in the middle of the shoe department when my mother called me.

"Where are you? The twin towers have been smashed into by planes and destroyed."

That same minute Bianca got a similar call.

We were glued to the spot not knowing how to react or what to do. Of course we did not fully realize what was happening, like the rest of the world. Nearby American tourists overheard us speaking English and ran over to us.

"Did you hear, did you hear?".

Galeries Lafayette was never so silent. We each rushed home to witness on tv the new crazy reality.

The Louis Vuitton adventure of that beautiful morning seemed so far away and of course we never went back to meet our new partners in fashion crime.

Manhattan-Kaboul
By Renaud and Axelle Red
Deux étrangers au bout du monde, si différents
Deux inconnus, deux anonymes, mais pourtant
Pulvérisés, sur l'autel, de la violence éternelle
Un 747, s'est explosé dans mes fenêtres
Mon ciel si bleu est devenu orage
So long, adieu mon rêve Américain
Moi, plus jamais esclave des chiens

Manhattan-Kabul
By Renaud and Axelle Red
(Two strangers at the end of the world, so different
Two strangers, so anonymous, but yet
Splayed on the altar of eternal violence
A 747, exploded in my windows
My sky so blue has become storm
So long, goodbye my American dream
Me, never again slave of dogs)

Americans In Paris

Being an American in Paris was not easy. My husband and I would often go to dinner with two wonderful couples whose wives were English speaking. Tia from back home and her husband Gerard, who loved asking for bread, butter and jam at the end of a fancy meal to the French waiters who often took themselves too seriously. And Jean Jacques and his wife, my great friend Kelly born and bred in the US of A.

Both women were often frustrated by the French's rude attitude towards anything not French.

They seemed to particularly abhor Americans or anyone English speaking.

"Listen to this ", Kelly would start with deserved indignation, "I asked her in French 'ou est l'ascenseur' and she pretended not to understand my accent and made me repeat it three times! Ascenceurrr....like that! You get me, right???".

I agreed because even if my dear friend's accent was not perfect, she was an example of the kind, childlike earnestness that is often present in the American culture. I quickly surmised that the snarky French clerks of Galeries Lafayette were, as usual, unwilling to make an effort.

"Did she tell you BONJOUR in the loud voice they love to use? They love to subtly reprimand you for not having started your sentence with a Bonjour? They love teaching us civility lessons," delicate Tia would add.

It was not easy indeed to live with the negative-a-priori most people had of Americans.

I would speak openly about it with my photoshoot team. One always has a certain degree of intimacy with a team taking pictures because hair, makeup, photographer and stylist are all in this together to meet the unfathomable demands of impossible to deal with customers. To boot, we always spend a lot of time waiting around...for make-up, hair, lights, etc.

"Why do you guys not like Americans? May I remind you they saved this country? Look at that war victim's graveyard we saw last week when we were shooting in Normandie!"

"Becauuuuse….", evidently searching for words "they always think they know better than us".

"And we don't want to become like them….with stores open 7 days a week and Sundays spent in shopping centers".

"Yeah, Sundays we have a French way of life. We have a big family lunch. We fight with each other and are bored. That is France!".

"Yeah, even if we complain about it! That is what we do, and no one will change that!".

Nearly every French movie I ever saw was dedicated in great part to scenes of family meals. Everyone would seem vaguely irritated or spit out truths to each other at these meals, but they remained faithful to Sunday lunch. After lunch, in most movies, they ran over to the next-door neighbor's that they were having an affair with or tried to corner their illicit love while doing the dishes. No one ran to any shopping malls, so I had to admit defeat and eventually gave up telling them their reactions were quite unfathomable.

Veronique And Entertaining

I had my fashionista friends, but I also had friends that were refreshingly not into fashion. My new friend Veronique was a lawyer. The first time we went shopping together, to my surprise she bought clothes because they were practical. I discovered a whole new way of thinking. If the pants fit right, she got them in three colors. This would never happen to me because there were so many different wardrobe and pant options I wanted.

But where she excelled in creativity was at home and specifically at the table. Her tablecloths, dishes, flowers and way of entertaining simply sparkled.

When I had married, I had obtained a nice sum from

the gift registry of the Printemps and I had chosen the finest names in silverware, porcelain and crystal. Christofle for silver, Bernardaud for porcelain and Lalique fot crystal. But I was most excited by the Chanel purse that my husband allowed me to purchase with the registry funds.

Now Veronique made me see the table and its finery in a different light. She gave life to the art of entertaining. We spent many an afternoon at our favorite neighborhood store, quite appropriately named "Champagne", oohing and aahing over tableware and accessories that would complement our sets.

We organized elaborate dinner parties with flowers and candles and ran around town for the finest chocolate or teas. One of our friends, Pascale B. had been raised in Paris and supplied the oldest and most reputable addresses of anything ranging from equipment to linen, produce or flower arrangements. With a no-nonsense practicality these women explained how to prepare a feast for 16 and how the summum of chic was to set an elegant table by mixing by mixing Monoprix and Lalique. To this day I remember Pascale B.'s dinner invitation, in her immaculate modern apartment, where she served an entire fish whose scales had been reproduced with thin slices of cucumber. These women could tackle anything.

True calling always finds its way. Many years later my friend moved to the States and could no longer practice law. This was to benefit her greatly. With the great resourcefulness that women possess, she became a reputable party planner endowing parties with her distinctive style and flavor. Pascale B. was to use her style, good taste and addresses as a top Parisian designer for Saudi Arabians with beautifully unlimited budgets and for beautifully chic Parisian hotels.

The introduction of this newfound passion reminded me of the shopaholic in the book "Confessions of a Shopaholic", that suddenly discovers the pleasures of stationary. The horizons of a new world of pleasure are discovered. Oooh, how did I spend so much time without knowing how beaaautiful stationary is. (I do love stationary by the way). It was a whole new floor to cram into my trips to Printemps and to distress even more the always-in-the-red-bank-account I had.

But like I told the "banquier" who gently reprimanded me on the sorry state of my bank account in spite of regular input, "it is not my fault sir, this Paris is too filled to the brim with temptations lurking on every street corner."

Driving In Paris

On one of those glorious, sunny fall days with a crisp edge in the air, I was coasting down Boulevard Iena when a man honked at me from his car. To my great surprise, he shouted out to me, "I feel sorry for your husband!"

I might have inadvertently crossed a rule of road etiquette or cut him off. (Checking out botox effects in my rearview mirror??). I had no idea, but even less did I understand the referral to my husband. He was a complete stranger: how did he know I was married. Perhaps I had been oblivious and self-absorbed on the road....and in my marriage no doubt. I had not seen the crash was coming.

But let's get back to driving in Paris. It had taken me a long time to get my driver's license. As a foreigner you must transfer your driver's license in your first year of residence. If you fail to do so, you must try the impossible: pass your driver's license in Paris. Unaware of this rule, I went to validate my driver's license too late. My request was turned down and although I tried to pass the test, it was impossible. My theory is, they wish to encourage public transportation and so they will point out every wrong move that is off by half a millimeter to refuse to give you a driver's license.

Luckily, it was the '80s and clothes were highly evaluated. By total happenstance, we were vacationing in Corsica in the same hotel as the Prefet of Paris. His wife was rotund and when she found out that we were owners of the renowned plus size fashion brand she showed great interest. She came a few weeks later to pick out a wardrobe, for which we graciously refused any payment. My husband hoped this would help with his French papers. He still had a Moroccan and Israeli passport. I begged him to ask for my driver's license. He was vaguely irritated by my request but complied. (Miraculously) a few weeks later, I received a notification to go pick up my driver's license at the very same Prefecture de Paris that had refused my application. It's not what you know, it's who you know.

After several years of metro, I discovered how exhilarating it is to coast along the Seine, drive through wrought iron gates and zoom by the imposing Louvre. Even figuring out how to get to a little Parisian street, with all the one way streets was like figuring out a labyrinthe.

Driving through the Louvre archways when coming from the left bank was reserved for taxis, but several times I gave myself some adrenaline by driving the forbidden route. I was once caught driving in this illicit direction but pretexted a tummy ache that made it urgent for me to get home and the kindly policeman let it go.

Parisian police is charmingly human. I have observed that Montreal policemen are usually better looking men with healthier smiles but implacable.

The hairdresser of avenue Victor Hugo, where I lived, once saw me hand over a beautiful enticing plump peach on a hot summer day to a policeman who canceled my ticket. «

Les pêches sont magnifique en ce moment; prenez en une. Meme avec le ticket! ». (Have a peach. They are in season. Even with the ticket!) As the hairdresser looked on mouth gaping, the policeman canceled the ticket, and bit into the peach. Charmingly human.

There was an unforgettable incident when I found myself run dry out of gas on the highway. It happened to me several times, but when it happened in Paris, I would call the delivery boys.

"Please send someone to a gas station. Buy a canister. Fill with gas. Bring to the café located at 126 Boulevard St. Germain. Please do not give me that silly story about couriers only transporting important papers. There is nothing wrong with transporting commodities".

But this time it was on the highway. Kindly police officers happened to drive by and stopped. They decided to push my car off the highway to the nearest gas station with their police car. I was, after all, a hazard in the middle of the highway. It was my first car and it was a dump. My macho husband had reasoned, "Let's see how you drive in Paris, before we get you a new car". The front license plate had fallen off for some reason. Once the car had arrived at the gas station, I placed myself strategically in front of the car and happily waved off the policemen as they drove off, so they would not see the lack of a license plate. This does not happen in America.

The drivers though were tense and aggressive. I was once caught in a traffic jam on a highway. Cars inched their way so slowly forward that my car bumped very lightly into the car in front of me. A man in his early 30's erupted from his shining sports car and came to my car window to explode in anger. I excused myself meekly, fearing for my safety, stuck in the middle of the highway with an angry driver. He went back to his car, after one more menacing look. We continued to inch forward, but I was upset at this man for his aggressivity in a situation where I had been so vulnerable. I was perhaps not the best driver, but such excessive and threatening behaviour was uncalled for. At a fork in the highway I noticed a police car. I abandoned my car, which was still stuck in the slow moving highway and ran over to them.

"You got the call from your station?? I just called your station to alert them. There is the man in the car in front of me. Dangerous individual. He threatened me. May be armed! Wow, I can't believe you made it here. You guys are the best".

They obviously had not received any calls but were so happy to comply with an already satisfied civilian. (No one ever answers the phone in Parisian police stations).

They ambled over to the angry man's car, with me hovering behind and smiling smugly. Ecstatically. They made him get out of his car, check his trunk, car, etc. He looked at me incredulously.

"How dare you threaten a woman alone on the highway, you vile man. "This was whispered with a big smile.

Then as he was being checked, in order to leave no loose ends, I walked over to his girlfriend, sitting in the passenger seat.

"You should be ashamed of yourself for lacking female solidarity and letting him threaten a woman alone".

Nothing was found in the car, but my point was made. So rare but so nice when justice prevails.

I finally got a new Citroën and each time my lease was up; I would call the garage.

"I cannot come. I have no time. Please order the exact same one in another blue."

"But Madam, you cannot order a car as if you were buying a pack of cigarettes!".

That is the thing with French salesman: they do not even care about making the sale. They want to give you a long process, really talk to you and shuffle papers. I made him understand I would buy it like a pack of cigarettes.

A few months later, my car had arrived and so I had a taxi drop me off at the dealers. The saleman started the car for me, and I entered my new car.

"But it is manual!! I hardly ever drove manual".

"I told you, you cannot buy a car like a pack of cigarettes."

"Ok no time for this. Off I go."

I stalled, but I learned. And when I finally reached the office, I had to call him, embarrassed to ask him how I would start the car.

Eac And The Canadian Embassy

As a way to escape my husband's business, I decided to go back to school in my late thirties and obtain a Mastère (imitation Master because from a private school) in Cultural Enterprise. I enrolled in a private school and here I was able to closely study the followers of the Gauche Caviar that make up a good chunk of the Parisian intelligentsia.

These are people who favor a socialist France but only want the cream of this France. They are often involved in politics, culture and art but have a proud distaste for money even if in reality they have high paying jobs in the said museums and ministers. In America, it would be called something like Champagne Democrats.

Most of my classmates were my age and already had jobs but came to enrich their profession with this Mastère that was usually financed by the institutions they worked for. They came to be intellectually stimulated, not as a contribution to their careers. Displaying ambition openly, especially in the realm of Culture was held in contempt and of poor taste. They were French for the most part and this hungry ambitious style was attributed to immigrants and Jews.

At least that was the image and ideal they wished to reflect. I soon realized that they were *obliged* to reflect these ideals otherwise they would not be accepted by their pack. There was a certain hypocrisy in representing themselves as an all-inclusive left that claimed to embrace diversity and freedom but only on their terms. If you did not wear the same lumpy sweater and play the part of the impoverished artist/student, you were scorned. Finally, it seemed that this "gauche caviar" was more confining and conformist than any other social class I had encountered.

Members of this pack smoked cigarettes at each break, wearing always the same well-worn, plush filled, drab sweater and complained of the high cost of everything including lunch nearby even if their mothers owned buildings in the center of Paris and their fathers were gentleman farmers in family estates. I wanted to fit in and discover a new horizon across this group. I limited my wardrobe to two sweaters and even tried smoking a cigarette with them (I have occasionally been a social smoker) but smoking during the day made me feel nautious so I gave up. I tried to wear the same coat every day because I knew who I was up against but by the second week of school, I could no longer stand the monotony. Then to make matters worse, my husband handed me down his old jeep and the leader of the class/pack once saw me drive up in it and nicknamed me "the bourgeoise".

I was as irritating to them as the sound of squeaky chalk.

I stood for what was in their eyes ignorant American

capitalism. I did not understand their will to fund dusty marginal plays and theatres that no one wanted to go to. "If no one wants to go to these representations then maybe they just aren't good and so taxpayer's money should not be spent to support them. "I dared voice this thought that they would qualify of obtuse American pragmatism. They looked at me with disdain and exasperation. Yes, they stood up for freedom of speech, but once again only on their terms.

I was not the most popular girl in school, to say the least. On top of my differing ideals, my culture made for a different personality. I was too outspoken in class. In America, we are taught to participate, to share opinions, to contribute, think out loud and express ourselves. The French look at you as if you are indulging in a vaguely nauseating display when you voice your thoughts or give the right answer to the teacher.

Years later when my daughters went to Canadian universities after prior studies in France, they remarked on the outspoken behavior of their classmates in disparaging tones.

"I can't stand these students. They are always raising their hands and saying, "I think so and so or I observed this", who cares? I want to tell them just let the teacher talk: I am not here to listen to you!" My daughters enthusiastically agreed with each other that this display was nauseating.

I thought back to my Mastère days and realized why I had always felt dissimilar. The "good Canadian student ", I was must have seemed so overzealous, involved and exuberant next to the coolly detached French students. I explained to my daughters that it was a question of culture and that if I was in the same class as them, they would probably find their mother very irritating.

Indeed, I marveled, you can love your children, they can love you back, but you can come to the realization that if you were the same age, they might not like you at all!

Rainy Day In Paris

A photographer I had worked with on my husband's fashion brochures asked me if I was up for an artistic project. He was getting together the usual fashion photoshoot team composed of a stylist, a make-up artist, a hairdresser and himself, but this time we would not be commissioned by a customer: we would indulge in a free for all session composing the images we wanted of women. The idea of expressing our art on women thus transformed into blank canvases that we could reinterpret according to our visions appealed to me. As an added benefit, I made this book project my end of year assignment for my Master at Eac. I contacted my favorite designers such as Azzedine Alaïa, Paco Rabanne but also Paris' best florists and props and costume addresses so we would have a wide range of accessories and themes to choose from. We met once a month in a café near Republique to discuss upcoming shoots and themes.

One particularly rainy, dreary Parisian day, I had just landed in Paris from Montreal where I had been in the cozy cocoon of my family when the phone rang. Thankfully, I have noticed that sometimes when I most need it, the phone rings or an email of hope of a new work mission or exciting opportunity arrives.

"Hello, this is Mr. Lemoult from Christian Dior Haute Couture. I see your request is dated from six months ago, but I finally worked down my pile of papers to it. I am interested in lending you Dior Haute Couture for your book. We will have to work out the details and send items with a security guard, etc, etc".

My dreary day was transformed. I walked down to my favorite florist to discuss an upcoming shoot, my energy and purpose renewed after this long-awaited phone call.

Deschamps was one of the most beautiful florists in Paris.

His creations filled dotted and striped hatboxes so that the tops of flowers peeped up at you. He sometimes added fruits and small props amid the flowers for extra enchantment. It helped that he was extremely good looking. Later he married and had little girls whose names were Rose and Lily. Rose and Lily Deschamps.

The most beautiful song that symbolizes Paris played inside and I froze enthralled by the music, flowers and promise of Christian Dior Haute Couture, simply savoring the moment.

Je ne veux pas travailler
By Sympathique
Je ne veux pas travailler
Je ne veux pas déjeuner
Je veux seulement l'oublier
Et puis je fume
Déjà j'ai connu le parfum de l'amour
Maintenant une seule fleur
dans mes entourages
Me rend malade

I don't want to work
By Sympathique
(I don't want to work
I don't want to have breakfast
I only want to forget
And then I smoke
I already knew the scent of love
One million roses would not smell so strongly
Now only one flower in my surroundings
Makes me sick)

Although I don't smoke anymore, (such a taboo in North America compared to Europe!) this song nearly makes me wish I did.

Much later, by chance, I ambled into the Art & Book store Artcurial avenue Montaigne and after buying a book, I exchanged a few words with the head librarian. I mentioned that I was part of a team that had a coffee table book in the making. She told me to come when it had advanced and she would see about organizing an exhibition and book sale.

A year and a half later, my book was in the process of being published and I walked in, thinking she had probably forgotten me, but ready to present her again with my project.

To my astonishment she quickly replied,

"I remember you, send me some pictures, meanwhile pick a date for this spring."

I was told later that the "Tout Paris" knew of this extremely intelligent and professional woman. Besides being head of one of Paris's most beautiful art bookstores, this purposeful, direct and efficient woman was known and admired for having defeated a very bad case of brain cancer.

I could imagine that it took a smart, concise, efficient and strong woman like that to do so. She must have calmly grabbed the cancer, twisted its arm with a karate gesture and whipped it around and slammed it on the floor with her calm purpose. "Out of here, you, I have no time for this". Perhaps she gave it a little dispassionate kick for good measure, to make sure it was inanimate. Then she must have readjusted her suit, pinned her hair back in place and walked out leaving it very defeated so she could continue to catalogue books.

A remarkable woman.

My Stint At The Canadian Embassy In Paris

During my Mastère, because I was "reinventing" myself, a Canadian friend I had made at my daughter's school helped me get into the Canadian embassy to do an internship in the Cultural department. I was very impressed by this woman from British Colombia. For me, she was a "real" Canadian as her parent's origins attested. Her father had even been made Honorary Indian Chief! He had a picture with an authentic headdress. They probably had a hallway with hooks for raincoats, a plaid covered bench and a cane with a duck's head. She also had a real career and was not dependent financially on her French husband and that was enough to merit my admiration.

Years later I bumped into her coming back from the Fnac with a pile of books she had recently bought. She confided that her husband had found out that she had had an affair with her kinesitherapies. He would wake up in a cold sweat in the middle of the night, so disturbed was he at the thought of her intimate sexual relations outside of their marriage. He was trying to forgive her for the sake of the children as he also wished to avoid divorce, but thoughts of her infidelity drove him to distraction. She had bought him a few books on how to cope with adultery at the Fnac hoping this would bring some serenity to his tortured mind.

I marveled at the civilized way this was playing out and was embarrassed to confide that if my husband, the Sephardic macho had been the betrayed party and I brought him home books from the Fnac he would have made me eat them like most Sephardi's.

Thanks to this woman, I started an internship at the Canadian embassy.

Here I observed the life of the political officials. It was not uncommon to see two men of high rank discussing for minutes on end if a doorstop should be added in a corner of their offices on Avenue Montaigne. Details, processes and an aversion to change was the keyword in these offices. I was in my late thirties and I was interning? They found this very suspicious. Was I vying for a position? And then I dared suggest new promotional items by saying that perhaps we could find other gifts to give than pens or ties with Canadian flags. Couldn't we try for something trendier? Why did we as Canadians not have the sophisticated image and branding that France, England and Italy had? These suggestions were greatly balked at.

After having participated in a Canadian event at the Science center I proceeded to write a report complete with all the successes and challenges of this event and submitted it to my superior before sending it to my school. A few days later, to my surprise, I was convened by the Consulate himself. Of course, I let imagination get the best of me and hoped he wanted to offer me a position!

The next day I went to the top floor where I had never ventured till now and was greeted by the Consulate himself. A funny detail I will always remember is that he was wearing a skimpy but nevertheless Burberry tie with the signature tartan. And I in Sephardic fashion lover style was wearing a Burberry duffle coat in the same signature tartan.(Probably bought with the three-interest-free payment card from the Printemps) His slightly startled gaze looked over my coat and no doubt wondered how an intern could afford such an item when as a consul he had splurged on an item made with all of 30 square inches of Burberry tartan.

I thought of my friend's Ashkenazi mother back home who once said to me "How come those Moroccans who just emigrated to Montreal don't have a house or a car and yet can all afford leather pants?".

To each his priorities my dear.

He led me into his office and proceeded to disapprove very strongly of my report. I could not believe that the Consul, himself, had convened with a little intern, the lowest position on the rung for a school report.

"How dare you mention any challenges or find fault in any event organized by the Canadian Embassy?".

"I mentioned very few points and it was just constructive criticism", I stuttered, very disappointed that my dream of being hired had clearly been an illusion.

"Do not give us here that art school talk of expression and ideas. We are an embassy. Your report is rejected. We will not keep a copy here and we will not pay you the amount (of 100 euros) that we usually pay for reports".

"But we are in Canada! What side of the iron curtain are we in?" I added aghast certainly but still adamant even though I was simply an intern and he was the Consulate. Was it my oversized Burberry coat looking down at his skimpy tie that gave me the courage?

"All of that is cliché! You do not impress me! I tell you this report is not accepted and will not reside here. Good day."

Thus, ended my brief career at the Canadian Embassy.

My friend comforted me when I called her, still startled, to explain how my report had been received.

"Don't worry. I read your report it's great and there is absolutely nothing wrong with it. It's just about differing mentalities between the art world where we are allowed and encouraged to voice opinions and find the pros and cons to all experiences and the political world where we aren't. Where everything must be tight-lipped perfection". Another culture discrepancy.

Later that evening, I explained to my husband how I had unknowingly disturbed the Consul. I was seeing a discouraging pattern in my life and somehow I seemed to always be getting in trouble by being part of the opposite trend. It could be so trying, I despaired, to always circulate in the opposite direction, against the wind. He then unexpectedly gave me probably the nicest compliment he ever gave me.

He said, "but you must admit there is never a dull moment with you."

BCBG Encounter In La

Even when I was still working for my husband deep down, I dreamed that one day I would be something else than the boss's wife. That I could claim a career to be my own.

This niggling thought was on the back burner for a very long time. Many of our friends started moving to Los Angeles. Jews were leaving France and at dinner parties the usual conversations of "where are you going on vacation" (which happened every 5 to 6 weeks and which I usually answered with "I feel we just got back") had been replaced with "Where are you moving to?". Between the murder of Halima who had been tortured for 10 days and the attack on a Jewish school in Toulouse and countless terrible incidents uncertainty had come back to France.

Our summers were spent renting villas in Malibu to be near our friends who had moved there. We were also doing business with Max A. and Gerard G.

I had called Max from a pay booth phone in New York, my husband, by my side, prompting me. This was before cell phones in the early nineties. We had one thing in common: work. And on rare occasions, he was happy to benefit from his success-driven ambitious wife. I jauntily asked for Max, telling the secretary that I was in from Paris for a short time and we had common friends. Piqued by curiosity, he accepted my call. I told him I had never yet had the pleasure of meeting him but wanted to show him the Next Big Thing. No matter how successful a man is he always wants to know what the Next Big thing is. In front of my amazed and slightly disconcerted husband, I jotted down a meeting time with him and two days later we lunched together in Los Angeles.

Nothing came of it, but we eventually met Gerard G., his best friend, with whom we embarked on the adventure of creating a collection for Beyoncé. My proud husband took many pictures with her. One evening, during their stay in Paris Beyoncé's mother came over for dinner. It happened to be a Shabbat dinner but she liked the family atmosphere. She explained that her close-knit family was her priority. She then proceeded to tell us funny insider stories of competitive designers. Among the most competitive was Donatella Versace, not to my surprise. She related intrigues on how the designers and their teams were not above manipulating to get Beyoncé to their shows and away from the competing shows.

With all these business adventures we were often in Los Angeles. The American dream was getting to my husband's head and I was thrilled to be back in North America. Summers were spent in LA and frequent business trips were made in the winter for fairs and meetings with buyers.

The fairs were full of crazed energy and each brand wanted the most flamboyant stand and to take out the biggest buyers for the most extravagant meals. I was used to fairs in Paris, although in comparison, it now seemed a quiet elegance reigned there. Here it was as if Disney World had invaded the clothing fairs. One season the owner of the most-successful-brand-of-the-moment was irritated by the managers of the fairs asking him to lower his music, so the season after he booked a hall across the street and created his own fair. I can hear the guy saying "Je vais les eclater fils! "(I am going to blow them away bro). He had started from nothing with a baseball cap that everyone wanted after being pictured atop an actress's head. Now the brand of Ed Hardy adorned anything from activewear to suitcases, shoes, leather, watches, you name it. Businesses begged to buy him the rights to his line and thus get a piece of the action. He threw the wildest parties and even had his childhood hero from when he was a poor child in Marseille flown in for his birthday party: the legendary king of French rock, Johnny Halliday. To his credit, he also had flown in for the fiesta, the heavily tattooed and impressed cronies from his young and broke days, who were still struggling financially back home.

The exuberance was in the fairs, collections and expenses, but even more so in the wild characters that dominated the scene. You could overhear phrases such as, "You should have seen X (the owner of a clothing brand) making out with Y (the buyer of a huge chain) right at the dinner table at the Bellagio; he would do anything to get his ordered renewed." To my amazement, the Sentier crowd from France looked subdued and restrained in comparison. They had never gone around throwing numbers like these guys: "we did X million, billion dollars we sold to that chain x hundreds of thousand styles and they have x hundreds number of stores and x number of square feet". It seemed to me that the words billion, million were constantly sputtering forth from their mouths accompanied by wild gesticulations.

They were proud of their successes. They were proud of their cunning and how they had made it with so little baggage. Once I found myself on a beach with my husband and a few of these characters measuring themselves up to each other. They even bragged about how early they had left school while they puffed on their cigars.

"I left school in grade 6".

"I left school in grade 4! ", his crony proudly overbid.

A lot of these flamboyant types played at the casino tables in LA. They were so hooked on the adrenaline that it was known that often the worst ones would call friends who were still lingering at the tables from their hotel rooms and say "Immediately, now, I can just feel it:place 5000$ for me on the 26 red." And then more often than not lose the money via a phone call, not even live.

Gerard G. lent us his jet, his houses, his cars (yes, he was the friend you want in LA) and we often rented Malibu homes, brought the girls shopping to loud Abercrombie stores, rented limos, Hummers and Mustangs and entertained our new Los Angeles friends in our pool over Mojitos. It was quite exhilarating. Especially the summer when my husband's employee did not comply with all the regulations to get his mother a visa to come to Los Angeles on a vacation with us. Alex had to get on the plane without her, after the officials noted she needed a visa to visit the US. When he landed alone, he forlornly recounted the dilemma to my uncle who went to pick him up at the airport. My uncle called my aunt who was waiting with me and my parents back at their house to tell her the "upsetting" news that his mother was not going to make it. All summer I had dreaded her arrival as she had always been extremely difficult to deal with. The gardeners in front of the house saw me suddenly jumping and dancing with my aunt and mother and joined us without knowing why.

We all pulled adequately disappointed faces when my

husband arrived. Life sometimes delivers the most unexpected and pleasant surprises.

After the birth of my youngest daughter, came the summer I finally pulled away from being my husband's employee and was hired by Mr. Max of BCBG himself. My husband and I were invited to a dinner party in his home (along with about 100 other people and two TV chains) and at what you can call an opportune moment I sidled up to him and told him I was looking for a new challenge and that he should hire me. I added that I was the best marketing/branding specialist he could ever find.

He responded that he was looking for designers.

Without batting an eyelash, I replied that I was the best designer, he could hope to find. I just pretended that the previous sentence had not existed. It worked. He liked that I was Canadian because it just so happened that some of his best employees were Canadian.

"I will be in Paris in September. Take down my number and call me". I was to call him a total of 22 times. Each time he would say, call me next month, next week, tomorrow, in an hour….and finally one day came the magical, "can you be at my office in an hour ?". With great emotion, I jotted down his address.

That is where I nailed him.

He had just bought the chain of stores A. Manoukian. I knew instinctively that a Tunisian/American would be seduced by a mix of superstition/spirituality. I told him that my father had been a consultant for a firm that had imported A Manoukian in the eighties. I had grown up with that brand. I might even have shown a moist eye. He asked what my horoscope was and approved that I was a Libra. He asked what my age was and proceeded to explain that he was bringing down the average

age of the company. I have never approved of ageism but diplomatically omitted from pointing out that he was bringing up the average. He then asked what salary I wished for and I balked because I had thought of everything but that question. I gave him a reasonable enough number that tempted him. I was hired after a total of 22 phone calls and 12 emails, but the experience was certainly worth the effort.

Months later my friends saw a French tv documentary featuring Max's American Success Story that was partly filmed at the very dinner party where I first tried to land my job. They joked that they could have sworn they saw me in a corner holding my resumé and pushing it under Max's nose. Lol.

Why I Was Able To Lie To Max A

There is something called Moroccan exaggeration. I exaggerated because I was not a full-fledged designer. Yes, I had dabbled and did a year at the Paris American Academy but then realized it was a rich American girl's school with a very light, nearly make-believe program and asked for a full refund. That day, I was inspired by more than just Moroccan exaggeration. I was inspired by Tunisian Hallucination.

My husband had a friend, named George, who was part of that whole Max, Gerard crowd of "heavy duty partying, mixed with business, casino players and lots of women "type of men. Alex once bumped into George in Paris who told him he had just started a manufacturing firm.

"Next time you are in Hong Kong, come check out my outfit for your manufacturing needs. Wait till you see it. I have over 100 people working for me, beautiful design offices, conferences rooms. I have two Ferraris there and I just love it in Hong Kong." (Note: not one but two Ferraris).

A few weeks later my husband was in Hong Kong and decided to look him up. He went to the address on the business card he had been given by George. To his dismay, George greeted him in a rudimentary 1000 square feet loft where 6 employees were crammed into with all the paraphernalia this business demands. No Ferraris in sight. Not even one.

But what impressed me the most in the story that Alex relayed to me was the way George greeted him. Without the slightest embarrassment at having been caught in a lie. As if he were greeting him precisely in the space he had described. Some call it Tunisian Hallucination but in America, it is called the Power of Positive thinking.

And it worked because when my husband heard of his success a few months later and went to visit him again in his headquarters, this time the reality before him resembled exactly what George had described. And yes, he had not one but *two* Ferraris in the garage.

When in Rome do like the Romans. I decided that I had to adopt a Tunisian Hallucination attitude if I were to work with one and it was to serve me many times.

Manoukian Gets Bought Out By BCBG

I was to be the right hand of Mrs M. of the brand A. Manoukian that Mr Max A. had just bought from her and her husband. They were to stay on for a few more years, as is the custom in many businesses. It is always difficult to leave fashion for many reasons. Fashion can be a very emotional and extremely fun-filled business.

I was very excited by the challenge. I went to get my new-job-wardrobe with great happiness and intrigue for all to come.

But very quickly a major problem surfaced. War was declared between the new team that consisted of one, (me) and the old team. The outcome was that Mrs M.'s team simply connived constantly to make me look bad. For the first time in my life, I found myself in a dream job but very alone and vulnerable. It was tough, but finding a job like that was even more challenging, so I wasn't willing to give up and go back to my husband's company.

The delightful Flemish sisters that had inherited the original knitting firm from their parents were quite a pair. Denise, the older sister, had married "the Armenian" who eventually baptized the business with his name : Manoukian. Mrs. M (or Denise) and her husband were a total mystery to each other. They came from such different cultures. She laughed at his heated and passionate side because she could look at you with the brightest blue eyes and very coolly throw a racist comment about how this was "du travail a l'arabe!". The one Muslim girl she had hired in the whole company would tell me sulking, "she thinks I don't hear her". Denise would swivel her head from right to left to make sure the sole Muslim employee wasn't an earshot away and exclaim her racist comment when she was dissatisfied with the manufacturing of a garment or any presentation. For Denise, everything was based on reflection, processes and hard work. His style of management was a lot more impulsive and flamboyant, to say the least.

Denise's sister, Nadine, would come in just before lunchtime with her aloof manner dressed from head to toe in killer designer outfits. She said that until she was at least 80 she would wear bloomers. Indeed, why sacrifice herself and deprive herself of the pleasure of wearing bloomers or any other fashion statement she loved. She had cashed out her share of the company early, so she was technically an employee. She would enter quietly, late in the morning, fully decked out, looking like she was wearing 3- or 4000-euros worth of clothes, long blond hair perfectly blow-dried and manicured and sit by her sister's side during designer meetings. Denise would pick her selection of designs from the ones that the designers would lay in front of her and pass them to her sister. Nadine had the sacred responsibility of cropping these drawings with very straight lines and pasting them meticulously on big sheets and adding style numbers. This was her responsibility and she did it with great care. Annik, one of the art directors Max had hired when he bought the company asked her politely, "Do you want me to help you with that?". She seemed to feel bad that elegant Nadine had absolutely no say in picking the designs that we would create and was stuck only with a task that seemed too menial to be attended to, when decked out in so much glory. Nadine looked grimly right through her and said "No Annick that is what *I DO. I* cut, and I glue". She took this role very seriously. Annick came from the most reputable Courrèges. Over there, everyone had to dress in white, every last deco, piece of furniture, pencil last down to the paper clip, had to be white or one got reprimanded by Mr and Mrs Courrèges. In spite of the excessively neat fashion environmenr she came from, Annick was always nibbling messily on something. Crumbs flew down all over her mac, and Nadine practically handled her A3 sheets with cotton gloves.

When Max bought the company for the first six months, he let everything under the sign of status quo. No changes were made except to impose me as an assistant to Denise. Denise was upset at having sold her beloved company even if it was for some 60 million euros. She still wanted to select styles, and her sister still wished to cut and glue. They did not want anything to change. Max just observed. And slowly sent in his people.

Then he would call us and ask us questions on the goings-on. We were forced to be somewhat double agents.

Denise complained: "If he bought Manoukian it is because he loves it. If he loves it, why would he change it?", she wailed. I could not, of course, bring myself to answer her that her beloved company had been losing money for the past five years and so Max was perhaps right in hoping that change would bring an upward trend to the numbers.

Meanwhile, Denise loved her company so much and during the first months, with Max tucked away most of the time in LA, she continued to act as if (and probably convince herself of this) nothing had changed. She continued devoting herself to the company and asked this of all those around her.

"Nadine ce soir on travail tard." (Nadine we must work late tonight).

"Mais Denise, je ne peux pas je sors diner avec Ginette, c'est prevue depuis longtemps." (But I cannot Denise. I planned dinner with Ginette).

Belgians speak extremely slowly so even when they were arguing it was in veeeery soft, very subdued languorously draaaaawn out tones. The exchange was so comical that I always hoped that they could not notice our shoulders shaking with laughter in the open space where we worked.

"Nadine le traaaavail paaaaasse avaaaant tout. Tu le saaaais." (Nadiiiine wooork is our prioriiiity. You knooooow it).

"Maaaais Deeeniiiissse, j'aaaai ce dineeeer." (But Denise, I haaaave this diiiinner).

And then two hours later

"Deeeniiiissse j'ai annulé mon diner." (Denise, I cancelled my dinner).

"Bravo Nadine! J'aime bien quand tu me parles comme ca!"

(Bravo Nadine! I liiiiike it when you talk like thaaat).

All around them in the open space you could notice shoulders shaking as they stifled laughter. All this, in order to slowly and meticulously cut and paste.

Corporate Spending Habits

Denise was very involved in the company and was not happy that Max was sending in his people and I was the first sign of change. Something about this woman, her intensity, love of her work and the childlike quality of her bright blue penetrating stare made me like her in spite of myself and her latent animosity. I wanted her to be happy with me and accept me, like the teacher pleaser I have always been. I soon discovered her weakness. She loved saving money. She regularly made pit stops at our desks and surprised us by checking if we had a pile of "brouillon paper" nearby. Anything that had erroneously been printed on one side should be used on the other for scribbling.

Denise and her husband loved saving on small things. They would only hire through interim agencies, thus spending hundreds of thousands yearly, but would ask us to take as many pens as we could when we were in hotel rooms to save on office supplies. They would ask us to work through lunch and then order for all 14 people in the design team an expensive lunch at Lina's. To add to the expense, the lunch hour was not really efficient because we would be eating most of the time and perhaps discuss a few buttons for over an hour. But if one dessert was left untouched, Denise would obsess over who had dared order it and not eaten it. She would call the secretary on the interphone and ask her to bring the list of what we had each ordered. I would silently pray that I had not forgotten that I had ordered that pecan pie?

On one occasion, her husband sat at the head of the table and lectured to us like he loved to about upcoming trends or something else that the design team would criticize and scorn over while smoking their after-lunch cigarette outside. Denise kept prodding his elbow and pointing in the direction of his untouched soup. He dismissed her with an impatient gesture and resumed his monologue. On the fourth prompt from her he exploded defiantly. "I don't want that soup!".

"Albert, you ordered it ; you eat it!" and she pushed it back in one sharp movement glaring at him with her bright blue stare.

He took a spoon. We jumped on the chance to file out.

I quickly surmised that to gain her approval I should show ingenious economy. The first time she sent me to buy samples we would use for inspiration/copying, I suggested I would buy them at the Printemps because if there was an article she did not like I would bring it back and get a refund.

"What?? They will refund us if we bring them back?"

"Of course, Denise. We have 30 days. You even have enough time to send them to China, copy them and bring them back to the store."

"Trop forte!" I could see in that bright blue stare her racial characterization. She was most evidently thinking "these Jews are just too cunning. Better to have them on our side.

Nadine and I had already shared observations on Armenians versus Jewish reputations. She was also married to an Armenian and considered it had rubbed off on her. One day she confided to me:

"You know the Armenians say it takes two Armenians to make one Jew because you guys are so smart". She said "smart" with great diplomacy, but she meant cunning and crafty.

"Well, that is funny", I retorted." When I started working

here my father told me jokingly of an expression that we have: that it takes two Jews to make an Armenian".

Thus, we flattered each other about something else than what we were wearing.

Denise and Nadine did not like any new addition imposed by the new owner because we were constant reminders of his existence. But they loved my taste in spite of themselves and often asked for counsel and so I started influencing the direction of the collection. Amid their court, jealousies started to arise. Indeed 6 designers, and 6 assistants held court to them every day.

We would all sit around a big table and ponder for hours on what each delivery should be made of. On Max's request we were no longer doing a summer and winter season but one delivery for nearly every month with 30 new styles. Each of these capsules needed a common thread or main inspiration. Usually each capsule was named after a city. The customers never got to know the city names that inspired us, but we picked them with great care.

"We need a name for this capsule. Valerie, is there a chic Canadian city we can use for this capsule?"

"Let's just call it Toronto. Not so important is it?" We had been talking about the name of the capsule for over an hour and not yet picked a style. I could just imagine what the cost-efficient Max back in America would think of a staff of 14 based in France with all the additional taxes paid on each salary was costing him, to simply pick the name of a capsule that the final consumer would never hear.

"But it's VERY important", she exclaimed, bright blue eyes wide open.

Fashionable French Working Women At War

The French designers used every meeting for showy displays of their culture and rambled names of cities from arty films, dim theater plays and classic literature. Years after when I found myself in the Canadian fashion world, I missed the abundance of cultural references. There was a (deserved?) superiority complex vis-à-vis North American lack of culture. One day, I overheard a French designer I had been on friendly terms with, mock me and these North Americans and their limited culture to Denise. I quickly chalked her up on the enemy side.

There was so much competition and internal warfare going on that I marveled we got any work done.

Denise's team was very charming with me when I started. Especially their leader Adèle Amour a tall French girl with porcelain skin, hard eyes, Mick Jagger's mouth and a prominent chin that belied her strong and willful character.

She knew as they all knew that I had been hired by Max and he was the new boss. These women had held court to Denise for years but were willing to toss her into the Seine and now hold court to Max. As soon as Max was around, they would all in unison pull out their lipsticks like fresh artillery to spear him with. And paint the lips over their extremely long teeth.

Quickly it was evident that these women did not want to be friends with me. They wanted to eject me and become Max's right arm. Adèle and her best friend Sabine, who was a gothic with black lipstick and bought absolutely anything adorned with skull and bones including rain boots and hair pins, were always going for cigarette breaks and plotting. Their favorite designer Yelena played on the fact that she was also Flemish to make nice with Denise. But she hid from her very knowingly that her husband was black. Everyone knew that Denise favored white and French backgrounds. Between the Parisian office and the head office outside of Paris, in Mercurol, we were 300 people but only one Muslim and one newly arrived Jew; me. And of course, the new owner Max.

Now the team's efforts were concentrated on Max. They continued to play up to Denise but like a nanny does with a slightly annoying child that has decidedly fallen out of favor. They answered to her with cold exasperation that it took greater and greater care to conceal, especially when Max was around. He had the power and they wanted to convince him that they were his answer and he need not hire new people.

I once asked if I could go to lunch with them and caught Sabine's reflection in the beautiful Hausmannien mirror signaling "no" to the others. It was that childish. If the company was not doing well it was because of Denise. Throw her over, reach out to Max and all would be fixed.

Slowly Max sent in more of his people. He hired two new Art Directors. Martine and Annick arrived. We were three newly arrived and quickly joined forces against the old court. Now I had friends to plot and plan with and their company was very welcome. I had valiantly held court to Denise and Max all by myself for months.

Max would make a brief rock and roll star appearance every 2 months with 3 or 4 of his assistants holding court, we would have a lunch, a dinner, ply him with smart comments to impress him, show him styles and he was whisked off. He was the owner but could not be bothered with taking care of Manoukian on a daily basis. Mrs M. wanted to test her powers like one tests the waters. After hearing that we had sent in our double agent spy report on the present design team, asked of us by Max's right arm, she decided to fire all three of us. She had dipped her big toe in to test the water.

The fatal day came. Mrs M. invited me into her office to say, very softly and politely that I had one month's notice. She added that to every situation there was a silver lining and I should look for it.

After two initial days of shock it came to my spirits that the company no longer belonged to her and that Max should be the one to fire me. During that months' notice I called Max who shouted into my ear from his boat on the Riviera, « She cannot fire you! I hired you! The company belongs to me now! Don't worry my main man Barry will fix all this! Call him. »

I alternated calls between both. Max and Barry were very difficult to reach, but I finally was able to reach them by calling incessantly until they answered. It took sheer perseverance. These men are always doing three or four things at the same time. You must try their number 10 times for every time you reach them. When they finally answer, you had better be in top form. A bit like a runner before the pistol signals departure. Your bit must be communicated clearly, efficiently and very quickly so as to not lose their constantly solicited attention. Every second counts.

Then I would come home and be greeted by my daughters. My career was often discussed at home and they followed my adventures. They would be buttoned up in their pj's, hair still damp from their showers and ask : "Did you speak to Max A. today?". I couldn't help laughing at how he had become a household name.

I finally reached Barry who assured me « it's all good, I spoke to her. Go back to the office; they are expecting you. »

Mrs M. with the pure strong spirit of her Flemish heritage (weren't they Vikings?) was never to go back on her word and mention to me that I was rehired because this would wound her pride. I should simply show up at the office on May 1st, even if officially I had been told that my last day was April 30th. « It's an insult to Max and me if you don't go, because we hired you. So by firing you, she overstepped her powers.», explained Barry to a very grateful me.

May 1st when I would walk into that office 20 sets of ferocious women's eyes, would look at me with surprise, to say the least. They would not be informed by Mrs M. of the fact that she had overstepped her privileges when firing me, and that I would be coming back. This situation was as complicated, ambiguous and as embarrassing as things got in the corporate fashion world. But for each complicated fashion world situation, there is a fashionable answer.

The Power Dress

I needed a dress. A dress that exuded confidence to help me face this situation and make everyone realize that I was not so easily defeated. A dress that would help my normally timid self overcome this day and give me the courage to stay on and face corporate hostilities.

I needed the perfect dress. BCBG had built part of its reputation and business on the perfect dress. I wanted to make my entrance, wearing the dress that all future BCBG clients would want to wear. The up and coming dress.

BCBG focused on the dress and attributed all dresses to one of close to 20 categories of dresses that we needed to always provide. It is said the **Inuit** languages have around 40 to 50 words for snow, depending on the dialect. BCBG had cornered the dress market with close to 20 names for dresses:

the bridesmaid dress, mother of the bride dress, day dress, work dress, lunch dress, Sunday brunch dress, etc.

Diane Von Furstenberg's Summer 2006 collection was inspired by the power women of the 80's. You just looked at those printed shirt dresses and you saw Joan Collins from Dynasty behind her huge mahogany desk. She would be unclipping her earring and flippantly tossing her hair that never really moved to the side, so subdued it was by hairspray, to free her ear for the phone, so she could deal in million dollars. And Diane's whole campaign was based on comic strip images of a Wonder Woman scurrying around New York and appearing in defeated women's minds saying: « Be the Woman you Can Be ». This dress was made for New York corporate women. Normally it takes two French corporate women to equal the feistiness and battle of ONE New York corporate woman doesn't it? I could face at least 100 corporate women with this dress! As I tried on that dress in the Paris DVF store, I walked to and fro in front of the mirror and said to Bianca who was now manager of the DVF stores, « Do I LOOK like a woman who cannot be defeated? Do I LOOK like a woman who has a very successful career?"

"BE THE WONDER WOMAN YOU CAN BE!!" My friend, the salesgirls and customers chanted in unison at the back of the little DVF store of the rue d'Algers. For one brief moment, all of our chests were filled with enough confidence to rule the world and our heads were light with the dizziness that too much power and the right dress can give. We broke into laughter but that heady sensation stayed on.

That's what a dress can do. And that is what it did for me the next morning on May 1st when I strutted into that office and just walked over to my beloved desk with 21 pairs of eyes looking in astonishment at the woman with power and confidence oozing out of her dress.

"One does not get rid of me so easily! Just ask my husband."

Of course, when my divorce arrived years later, I came to regret that sentence but that is another chapter.

Human resources called me on my desk phone and asked me, "What in the world are you doing here?".

"Ask Mrs M., I believe she has had a conversation with Max", I curtly replied.

And twenty minutes later, I went to see Mrs M. and we talked softly about the upcoming collection as if nothing had transpired.

Sweet victory, when it occasionally comes, must be savoured as slowly and with as much pleasure as a chocolate mousse.

In London We Shopped Till We Dropped

In spite of her, I began to grow on Mrs M. This was before the internet, so we had to go to stores physically and take pictures to see what the competition was doing. This fun mission was to "inspire" the designers. I excelled at fashion espionage. I put myself in the shoes of bored saleswomen and reasoned that if we would not disturb them, for the most part, they would not bother looking at us. They were probably immersed in their thoughts and lives, no doubt thinking about the argument with their child, fight with their boyfriend, what they would make for dinner, etc., like all women. So, I just fearlessly clicked away inside the stores at the displays with my little camera. We would come into the store heavily wrapped in our winter gear, complete with puff jackets, chapkas and tightly wound scarves, go into a fitting room with a generous selection of clothes, take 15 pictures of clothes still on hangers and walk out one minute later still ensconced in our gear and say sweetly "sorry! nothing fits".

It was wrong, but someone had to do it. There are weird ways indeed of making a living. I reasoned that the saleswomen were probably happy that the clothes were still neatly on the hangers at least.

I was good at this fashion espionage because I had a knack for picking the right styles and the cheek to take the pictures. Once Mrs M. realized that she was stuck with me, she took me on her trips to London. We would shop, lunch, shop, have dinner for three days straight. Paradise.

Security was tightening in London stores with the onset of terrorism. In the Ted Baker store, I noticed a man that looked very obviously like Sherlock Holmes spying on me and justly surmised he was the house detective. I made for the door, knowing that if I was outside, he could not confiscate my small camera. Phones with camera features were just starting to become available. Mrs M., who was docilely following me, ran out after me, oblivious to what was happening. He came running after me, but I was already safely outside.

"You were taking pictures! You cannot do that! We are protecting our stores and city from terrorists!"

We quickly engaged in a dispute. A very bemused Mrs M. placed herself between the two of us, unfamiliar with the English language but trying to fathom what was going on. She made for a very comic figure as her head swivelled left to right and back with her wide-eyed stare. She looked as if she was at a Roland Garros tennis match.

"Does she look like a terrorist?! Do I look like a terrorist?! You have no right to retain us! We are no longer in your store! Goodbye, sir ". Mrs M. could not wait to get back to Paris and recount this type of adventure. She was endearingly childlike in spite of her 60 plus years and her 60 plus million euros tucked away from the sale of Manoukian.

. I did finally grow on her because years later, I was one of the very fortunate few that she invited to her goodbye party. And that was not under Max's orders.

I Love New York

With the team of designers, we were to go shopping all over New York, London, Los Angeles and of course our hometown Paris, in search of inspiration. On my first business trip, which was to New York, I was worried I would have no time for personal shopping but was soon reassured. On our first day of espionage shopping the designers informed me that we always started with the shoe departments. Personal shopping, I breathed with relief: we didn't even design shoes.

It was during that first business trip to New York, that I became familiar with the cheerful cast of characters that held court to Max. I had connived my way into the trip by telling Mrs M. that the Americans wanted me there. One of Max's close aides, Candice, the Head of Retail, had taken some interest in me and was still in the process of evaluating if I could contribute to the company in spite of the disparaging remarks that my wicked colleagues had made about me. Candice had simply asked me if I was going to be included in the trip.

I "exaggerated" and told Mrs M. that Candice had strongly suggested I go. She told me to book my trip with the Travel department. I triumphed and thus my first real business trip was finally going to happen. My husband was not happy. He was starting to feel that my life was more exciting than his.

"I am sure you manipulated your way in".

"Of course not. I can show you the agenda with my name on all the meetings!"

"Our youngest is only two! How can you go!"

"It's only 5 days!". And I have been waiting my whole life for a full-fledged business trip.

When I got to the airport, my colleagues were way ahead of me in the baggage drop off line, so I ran up to them. Truth be told, I tried hard not to skip, I was so happy to be part of a real business trip.

"Oh, hi guys can I wait with you?"

They all graced me with a sullen look: they were so upset I had managed to get into THE business trip. I didn't care that I was ostracized. I was just so happy to be there.

We arrived in New York and after waiting an hour at security, one of the French fashionista's voice resounded in the airport

"PUTAIN J'EN PEUX PLUS JE VEUX UNE CIGARETTE!!!!"

(I cannot fucking take it anymore, I want a cigarette!)

Finally, we arrived at Max's favorite hotel, the French-speaking Sofitel where our rooms were reserved. There was an initial flurry at check-in because our rooms had not been paid for and although we were traveling with Mr and Mrs M. they were not going to pull out their credit cards for a company that no longer belonged to them. These are the type of situations that happen when companies change hands. None of the employees wanted to pull out their credit cards and advance funds that were reserved for personal shopping in New York. It was all soon straightened out. I had found out just before the trip that I had been paired in a room with Yelena. We disliked each other but I figured that is exactly why the spiritually inclined Americans had decided to put us in the same room, so we could overcome our mutual dislike and work out our differences. I reasoned that Yelena probably hated me more than I disliked her and that she would get us out of this mess. She did.

When I landed, I discovered I was now paired with one of Max's numerous ex mistresses, a very pretty and fun-loving young woman who had become Retail manager. She constantly displayed her lingering power over a kindly Max by booking suites when she toured the stores in France and taking her poodle on the job. She was a Canadian from Vancouver and was now dating an eligible Jewish Moroccan bachelor. His family was from Meknes a city in Morocco and although she was from the other side of the world, she was aware of the rumor that all Meknasi are very stingy. I marveled at the power of cultural stereotypes that travel at the speed of light. She was now going through conversion to humor his parents. I had become acquainted with her the week before in the Paris head office, when she asked me if I thought she could borrow a shawl from the showroom to be modest for her weekly meeting with the rabbi. I was very pleased with my new companion.

Our first meeting was held by Max's right arm, Barry Cohen who had been my savior when Mrs M. had taken a stab at firing me. Every person who surrounded Max was a character and he was certainly no exception.

He was a tall man with regular features, perfectly brushed back hair and was always wearing the perfect suit and tie. He boasted of a Swiss education which left me perplex, because I distinctly remembered him from Montreal: he was one of my first boyfriend's cousins. He did not seem to remember me from our past lives, but I did not take it personally. If there was one person whose good side you wanted to be on right after Max, it was Barry.

On our very first trip to New York, he had the whole Manoukian team led to one of the most impressive conference rooms with huge glass walls overlooking Manhattan. He then proceeded to subject us to a three-hour "shmatology" session. Barry loved to hear himself talk. He was the best salesman Max had ever had, probably because he loved to hear himself talk, but also because he truly believed all the tales he spun and so the buyers gulped them down thirstily. They gulped down the heady numbers he promised. This item was the winner, this fabric was the hottest, etc, etc. If the guy seemed to truly believe he had gone to a Swiss boarding school, he could play make believe anything. Who were we to contradict him? Certainly not I! He was my job savior!

That day he locked us up and subjected us to a shmata lesson, complete with diagrams drawn on a smartboard, representing trends.

"So, first a designer comes up with a hot new item, so it is reserved to the high-end market here." Arrow drawn at the top. "Then all the medium-priced brands copy it, so it goes down here." Flippant turn of the head with perfect strands of hair swept back, to jot more on the smartboard, "and then the style is copied by mass distribution and so it is distributed here." More energetic scribbles at the bottom of the board. He had it all down to a perfect science, gestures, hair movement, chalk and all.

All eyes on him. We had no choice. His boss had bought the company and even Mr and Mrs M. were playing the role of the eager beaver first row students. They had at least 60 million euros in their pockets, but they would have been bored back at home without an office to play in, so they were so happy to participate, learn from the Americans and even be part of Max's court.

At one moment Max graced us with a two-minute visit. He pulled us from our context of intellectualizing and theorizing about shmata theory. He sauntered into our ultra-luxurious, ultra-sleek conference room holding up a very material sneaker.

"Les enfants, ecoutez moi... I just want to tell you, I can get this sneaker for two euros".

"Max! Why are you interrupting! Now I have to start all over", from a very exasperated Barry, chalk in hand, who did not want to share the limelight.

After 4 hours of listening to Barry we were nearly faint with hunger. Not to mention that we were dying to hit the stores. Finally, as an afterthought, he mentioned ordering food. I gave my food order with my perfect English accent and was graced with, "Hey, where did you get that accent?".

"In Montreal"

"What I am also from Montreal!?"

"I know. I remember you, I dated your cousin Charlie B. for a year." I was happily forsaking all my dignity but being rewarded with the gaping mouths of my fashionably sworn enemies. Intrigues and confrontations between the old and new team members of the Manoukian team was at its peak during this trip.

"Wow, that's crazy!" Just like in school, I had made a notable impression on the teacher on the first day of school. My classmates - uhum I meant collegues- were extremely upset. Call it high school – uhum corporate life.

Do Not Drink On The Job

I was so heady with my new-found independence, that on that first business trip to New York, during the first dinner I got tipsy. Even a bit more.

It was so exhilarating after all those years of being part of a couple, and what I felt to be the smaller part of a couple. I had not existed solely for so long. All of a sudden, I was on a business trip, part of a team and was included in meetings based only on my independent existence. The feeling of new-found freedom and power was exhilarating.

Limousines were sent to our hotel to bring us to the fashion shows at the Bryant Lane Park situated in the middle of Manhattan. We were particularly fortunate because we had a fashion show for each division: Hervé Leger, BCBG and Max Azria. The shows were all fast-paced, spectacular and filled you with longing for each silhouette. We knew the collections on display were ultra-glamorous mirages and that when the real collections were produced for distribution, they would become diluted, pared-down, cautious and price conscientious versions of what was on stage. But during the fashion show, all whims and luxuries were allowed. We would run backstage afterwards to congratulate Max and Louba and then run off back to the limousines bringing us to the "after parties". Movie stars like Kevin Costner and Nicole Kidman came from LA to honor Max and of course, there was always a generous helping of reality show tv stars posing and ooing over Max.

During every evening in New York, our generous boss organized a dinner outing. This time it was in the Sofitel restaurant. We had just arrived, and with the prospect of fun-filled days ahead of us, we were a particularly unruly crowd. Some of the undisciplined French even lit up cigarettes in the restaurant to the horror of the Maître D who kept running over. We sang and joked and laughed and I must have indulged in two (maybe three!) drinks. This was above my usual quota.

The next morning, I got up feeling queasy and started scolding myself. "You finally get to your first real business trip at the age of 39 and you screw things up by having an extra drink and feeling sick on the first business trip day?

I whipped myself into shape letting the shower stream on my pounding head. Water revived me and I was able to make it down to breakfast in time. Washing my hair is often like a new lease on life.

I walked into the dining room, as discreetly as possible, to take a seat at the same table as my favorite colleagues, the designers who were my allies in all the intrigues happening. Mrs M. screamed from the other side of the dining room.

"Et bien vous etiez POMPETTE hier soir Valerie!"

(You were wasted last night Valerie!)

I winced with embarrassment

"Don't worry she is Flemish you know. It is quite a "spectacle" to see her guzzle down beer when we go to Belgium!" one of my colleagues cheerily comforted me.

How About The Clothes?

It soon became evident that Max was the kindest, most charismatic and generous boss you could wish for, but he didn't know much about clothing.

At one of the least attractive clothes presentation, Yelena, by now the Head Designer of the Manoukian collection, thanks to her little friends in high places, had put together a collection with thick fabrics in egg shapes. He raved over the collection. Even her close allies like Adèle Amour had doubts about the collection and had tried, the night before the presentation, to leave what she estimated was a sinking ship, change sides and come over to our side. I ignored her insinuations, smiled brilliantly and walked off. Turncoat, I thought. The next day Adèle smiled brilliantly when Max congratulated them on this atrocious collection. Indeed it was to bomb six months later in the face of the final judges; the customers.

When I was in New York with the design team looking at trends and inspirations, Max urged us to go to a specific store he heard was making a ton of money. When we got there it was very contrary to our brand direction. This store had mannequins from the eighties and clothes were hung with fishing thread to our dismay. This was a far cry from the Barney's, Bergdorf's and Saks where we chose to go for inspiration.

Like a lot of businessmen, even if he had 1000 stores, 400 of which were designed in the most glamorous and contemporary fashion, if he heard of one store that was raking in money, even in the dim side street of a doubtful neighborhood, we had to go look at it.

This was similar to my husband and his friends' way of always calculating the turnover of any restaurant we went to even when their businesses were far more successful. A businessman does not see how much money he is making but sees how much money the next guy is making.

At BCBG the design aspect was the property and responsibility of his wife. And at BCBG, you were either a protégé of Max or his wife. If you were a protégé of Max you had humor, style, you were flamboyant, fun to be with and you probably worked 60 % of the time. If you were a protégé of his wife you worked for 18 hours straight and occasionally nibbled on lettuce. On the pictures of her with her team after the fashion shows, she is usually a foot higher than all the hardworking Asians that she surrounds herself with. She had a distaste for food and the time-consuming activity it can be, when one had a collection to put together.

As for Max, it sometimes seemed that fashion and the business were just a great excuse to enjoy life with.

The Take Away From New York

Max had hired two of his best friends to take care of the Paris operation and they were also on the same flight to New York. They had noticed that the Parisian girls always kept me at more than arm's length. Feeling sorry for me, they tried extra hard to include me and back in Paris they plied me with missions that I ably filled, and we soon formed a cheerful trio. Basically, I took care of rebranding, designing windows, packaging, internal fashion communications and all the visual identity such as ads and brochures. They gave me one mission at a time and were satisfied with the results to the huge dismay of the competing colleagues.

Candice, VP of Retail came to the Paris office and announced that Max had remarked that my assistant and myself were handling singlehandedly all internal and external communications as ably as his team of twenty in New York. My wicked French colleagues tried to smile, but it was so evident that they were glowering.

If some of the French feuded with me, I found friends and allies among the Americans.

The extremely elegant Caroline, director of Hervé Leger, encouraged me to take on responsibilities and was of a great support against the conniving French women. She was efficient but very philosophical and laid back at the same time.

The mean girls (women) never irked her because she preferred focusing on the good rather than the bad, on the fun that fashion brought rather than the negative environing energies. Those unwanted energies she swept aside with an elegant gesture that would end by sweeping up THE right Prada bag in the store we were shopping in and she would say,

"tu vois, tu as des jeans, un pull gris et tu fous ce sac sous ton bras" (you see, grey sweater, jeans and you top it all off with this statement bag)...and all of a sudden that was the too-die-for-bag. I once left New York with two Prada bags : the one I made her walk 12 blocks for and the one she swept up with that elegant gesture making it so desirable.

"Yes, you need that shirt! What you already have three white shirts? Even 12 white shirts are not too much. This one you nearly need two of, because when it is in the laundry...". Her taste, style and philosophical view on life are till this day unfailing.

By then I had learned how to handle the mean girls. If I learned that Adèle was speaking badly of me and then she called me, I would simply hang up on her with a huge bang. She imagined that if I dared hang up on her I probably had more power than I let on. It never failed. That was when she would come around my office cooing and cajoling and asking me why I had hung up.

"Because I am not French like you. I do not say ugly things about people behind their backs. I hate these intrigues. So, I hang up to your face".

"But Valerie, do admit it is not professional"

"I have other ways of being professional. Do not worry about my profession"

"Max has plans for you?" Instantly alert.

"I cannot say anything". In reality I had nothing to say, but Tunisian exaggeration and visualization had brought its fruits. I was learning.

Corporate life can be like playing poker. Even if you do not have a full hand, smirk and pretend you do.

Cultural Discrepancies

By now Max's Los Angeles team knew that I was the token Canadian in Paris and I officially became the American correspondent in Paris. Visualizing power had given me a certain power. Hard work too, but who are we kidding, working in fashion is not hard work. I had made my place.

Every time that the Americans had something to explain to the natives, they would call me. And when the French wanted to ask about the Americans habits or bizarre ways of being, they questioned me.

From The Americans

"Can you please explain to them that there is already a ridiculous amount of bank holidays in France and on Labor Day, we work because we celebrate Labor!"

"Can you tell those wicked union people to stop sending out three hundred-page reports that everyone is printing on company paper and reading all day".

"Are you serious? That designer has not designed a stitch in years, and she is now a full-time union member which gives her immunity? We cannot fire her??"

"Why did that sales team from France show up at the trade show without make-up or manicure? How can they show a line without a manicure?".

"I told her that even if we do not get along that is not a problem. If I need to get the job done, I can work with the devil!". (overzealous and drama loving American corporate women in fashion).

From The French

"They cannot be serious? We cannot play these inspirational games; the personnel will laugh at us. We are not oversized children like those Americans".

"When are the Americans coming?" This from Mrs M. who made me feel as if we were all in the middle of war.

"We are to work late again? We have a life! Life is not just work".

Indeed, I was the go-between of the divergent cultures.

On the one hand were the Tunisian born/raised in France /emigrated to America crew that Max headed. They were a fiery, hurried lot that answered emails with short brisk sentences often peppered with grammar mistakes. The French excused their French mistakes because they thought of them as Americans and didn't know English enough to notice those.

Most of the emails I got from Max's team consisted of the word "Oui" or "Non".

They played as hard as they worked and constantly made jokes. Max indulged in hiring his friends and family, so he could have them close by. His vice president was his brother Simon who loved giving money to charity and generally helping the Tunisian community. "We know these people since Tunisia and Max promised them that we were buying their company" he wailed", what are we waiting for?".

Max and his crew were always "enhancing" information so there was never a dull moment. On one of our New York trips, while we were having breakfast, Max hurried over to our table.

"Did you all hear the good news? We are number one at the Paris Fair. We made over a million in turnover. Come see me in my office, all of you".

We hurried to the head office and waited outside his door, till he saw us and then seemed to vaguely remember that he had asked us to come.

"Did you hear? We made 700 000$! We are number one".

By then I was familiar with Tunisian exaggeration. I had already spoken to my colleague holding up the fort in Paris, who admitted that the fair was very quiet but of course omitted pointing out this boring truth.

I just smiled, congratulated him and ushered out my stunned colleagues.

"Valerie how did we just lose 300 000 $ in half an hour".

Yes, that was my role. Cultural correspondent and translator.

Lunches and dinners were always on the agenda and Max loved being at the head of a big table, surrounded by his friends and colleagues. Conversations ran all over the place.

"Si ta soeur est deprimée Max fais lui les saints."

"Quoi? Peleriner les lieux saints?

"Non, fait lui refaire les seins. Ca va lui donner un coup de jeune".

After six months of reporting to Yelena, I was very grateful to be transferred and was now reporting directly to Jean, Max's close friend and ally. Yelena had been a chilling superior. She once summoned me to her office and asked me in staccato tones made even harsher with her Flemish/German accent,

"How dare you have asked Simon for a blackberry? I am your superior and you must address your requests to me. I see no reason why you should have a blackberry".

I tried my best not to show that I had broken out in a cold sweat and that I was chilled to the bone by her piercing cold eyes and tone.

What a merry change to now be part of Jean's team. He

constantly made jokes, approved all my requests and hard work while puffing on a cigarette and generally made work seem more like play than work.

As Head Designer, Yelena had her say in window decors for the stores and suggested to Jean that all the window decors for fall 2007 be inspired by "Les Parapluies de Cherbourg". With full knowledge of a Sephardic's superstitions, I ably pointed out to Jean, "do you think Max will be happy **about open umbrellas inside the stores?**"

"What? Yelena are you crazy! Already our numbers are not good! all we need now is open umbrellas in the stores! Ok, from now on Valerie is in charge of windows!" Max had superstitions like all Tunisians and to know of them and the general culture helped me in my work.

Max never went anywhere without his assistant, Marilyn because he said of her that she was like Aladdin's lamp. Rub her occasionally and the money pours in.

Indeed, Max's crew lived mostly in Los Angeles and excelled at talking in numbers. Numbers of stores, numbers of turnovers, numbers of cars and sometimes numbers of women.

For these men, it wasn't about the woman. The women were not important: It was about impressing the other men. Men impressed other men with women. We women impressed each other with our tastefully chosen clothes.

Max always had a flavor of the month assistant. You could tell who the new assistant was if you spotted a really pretty woman and asked her what she did.

"Well let's say you want to say something to Max, you come and tell me and then I will tell him".

"Got it! Welcome!". That is how you knew she was the new favorite.

Invariably, after a while, a new favorite appeared and last month's flavor either got a real job in the company or disappeared. The men that surrounded Max were very competitive about women. They loved to bring trophy girlfriends. It seemed that the shorter they were, the more willfully they wooed super tall girlfriends and came accompanied to Max's parties by willowy, extra-long women that towered over them. As we entered one of the company's best parties, Max's vice president introduced me proudly his over six-foot tall girlfriend. She was a very sullen-looking young woman with a tough look and cropped hair. "You know she is the ex-girlfriend of so and so football player. Putain, are they all going to be impressed by me tonight! Wait till Max sees her. The only problem is she swears an awful lot".

It seemed as if these women could make up for their own lack of height. In one documentary film on Max, when asked how good he felt about having succeeded so well he retorted philosophically that, "It is very nice, but still I will never be immortal, and I will never be tall."

And then there was the Parisian crew with designers who spoke eloquently of their far-fetched inspirations and even our very own highly intellectual and intelligent librarian/historian of fashion. Mrs M. proudly exhibited her to Max as if she was showing off a relic of ancient times, a symbol of European culture that she proudly still had the means, will and good taste to support. Our librarian put together thick and intense trend reports replete with historical information and cultural references and even sociological aspects of fashion that were impressive if sometimes dull and very long to read. Hélène would walk in and converse with Max, slyly observing this product of America with slight distaste. Yet you could tell by her twittering movements that she was valiantly trying not to be impressed by his success and power or succumb to his charm like her lesser colleagues. He also observed her as he would an exotic and amusing animal. Two very different cultures mystified by each other.

"The problem with these Americans is that they might have money but no culture at all". She scowled, brushing off cat hairs from her librarian style corduroy skirts.

Denise M. approved of Helene's condescension with a beaming face and her brightest blue eyes.

These women were extremely smart, cultivated and quick but way too often they used their acid tongues and quick reflexes for the cattiest of remarks.

I was grateful that they had never noticed that Max's "library" at home was filled with fake books, all-white spines like the ones that were used as window decors in the stores. When Life and Work overlap, I guess this type of faux pas happens, I thought indulgently, when I discovered this during a party at his house. Just because he was so nice.

Finally, a whole other mentality/culture reigned at the **head office in the South of France.** Parisians are not well-liked by the rest of France, who attributes to them a superiority complex. They have never liked the Parisian's hurried airs, but these were nothing in comparison to the Tunisian/French/American hurried airs that left one dizzy. Mercurol, was little more than a village made up of very down to earth people living in a place where Manoukian was part of the country heritage and made for nearly all the jobs in the area along with Valrona chocolates. When I needed to recycle the BCBG suitcases for my window decors, they rounded up extra hands at the local bar to help us place the luggage on a field and spray paint. That is how informal and tightly knit community life was in the village.

As you pulled up to the imposing wrought iron gates

surrounding the beautiful stone structure that was graced with a fountain and cherubs, one realized that in this part of the woods Mr and Mrs M. were the equivalent of a Duke and Duchess. The first time I pulled up, I marveled that I was doing so exactly as my father had twenty years earlier. It was one of those splendid moments when Life seems to fall into place as it should.

Mercurol, had its fair share of characters, love affairs in the parking lots and feuds with the union. It was known to all that Mr M. had an affair for over twenty years with the Real Estate Manager, a stocky woman with a deep smoky voice who defiantly wore miniskirts and low-cut blouses. Her face was as harsh as her clothes were blatantly sexy. It was rumored that they would ride all over France together to visit stores and occasionally recline the car seats. After twenty years of an illicit relationship that had not given her much, she fell into depression and Mrs M. herself went to pluck her out of her house and bring her back to work. One can imagine her encouraging her to pick herself up and come back to work:

"Ma petite Bernadette il n'y a que le boulot qui compte!". (My dear Bernadette, only work counts). Her attitude revealed that she enjoyed her duchess role but did not wish to get her hands dirty with her husband's primary needs. She left that to the personnel. She liked being in charge of logistics. I was in the car next to her on one occasion when her husband called to ask where the American phone charger was and she very efficiently indicated where he could find it. Everything was always in perfect order in her homes and offices, she assured me. When she hung up, she proudly remarked, gracing me with her most self-satisfied smile, "Oh these men they are nothing without us".

The Mercurol office was constantly subjected to a feud between hot-headed Mr M. and the equally hot-headed Union workers. Most of the union workers were exempt from any "work-related" responsibilities as they were allowed to give their time to their union duties and benefitted from immunity. Their duty was to protect the personnel against the capitalist owners and so they were always complaining about having only 5 weeks' vacation or thirteen months of salaries. In France, it was not unusual to get double salary in December to afford all the extras that Christmas celebrations required. On one occasion, as certain union members were picketing, Mr M. raced in with his jaguar and grazed the knee of a picketer. Max had just recently bought the company, so he still had illusions that he would be able to seduce the union with his charm and thus succeed where Mr. M. had failed. Having grazed the knee of a picketer was bad form. So, he seized the opportunity to ask Mr M. to leave the company permanently. This got him a few points with the union, but Max and the Americans were soon to also lose patience with each others demands. Especially since in the Americans perspective, any French worker already had way too many rights.

Mrs M. was so in love with her work she still showed up every day, even after her husband was asked to leave. Max finally found the courage to ask her to leave. As is usually the case, the purchaser wants free reign in his company. And previous owners sometimes have a hard time leaving. A visual metaphor came to mind. It seemed as if Max had slowly but surely disengaged one clutching finger at a time held tightly to the edge of a roof.

All of these different cultures, cities, personalities and allegiances made for a lot of intrigues. And extremely funny situations.

Max bought a small hotel in Mercurol and that was where we went for dinner and stayed overnight when our agenda required several days on site. The hotel was in the center of the village next to the post office, the Boulangerie and overlooking goats grazing on the mountainside. Soon after he bought the place, his brother had kosher meat delivered there from Paris. There were no kosher butchers in Mercurol. And so, when we ordered steaks from the waiters, these men who had never seen a Jewish person in their life held their pens poised over their order pads and queried "kosher or non-kosher?".

When we slept there, Simon brought delicacies from the best kosher caterers and set a table as if we were having a Shabbat dinner filled with all the Tunisian specialties. "Close the windows," he would say "we don't want the policeman on duty to see us smoking or he will fine us!" We were like teenagers having a party.

Ch...Ch...Changes

One year after I was hired, members of the Paris office were gathered for an announcement: the Paris office would be permanently closed and if we wanted to stay on, we had to move to Mercurol. Max was trying to minimize the cost of running this operation and it was the easiest way to fire 70 people in a country that was overly protective of employee's security. He knew that no Parisian would move to Mercurol and so they would have to give up their job. By then my work was being chaperoned by Max's two best friends, the very pleasant and competent Abel and Jean but also by the powerful Candice Head of Retail based in the LA head office. She called me after the meeting to say that they were finding ways to keep a few of us in a small Parisian office and so I need not worry.

To avoid the Union's complaints that no one should be favored, I was also fired and then became a consultant. My job remained the same, but instead of being on payroll, I sent invoices for my services. The other person they were keeping on was Yelena. Candice asked me to pretend that I was also leaving the company at the end of the summer just like everyone else. All summer I kept up the pretense. Yelena had her doubts and would sneakily ask me what I was doing with my files etc. I would forlornly comment that I guess I had to throw them all out.

On September 1st after the holidays when she saw me at a desk in the smaller Parisian headquarter that Max had installed for his reduced Parisian cohort, she was very upset. She asked if I was the new Mme Pipi signaling that my desk was not far from the washroom.

70 people had gone. Two had survived. The Union decried that it was scandalous and that I had received favored treatment. On my next trip to Mercurol, I denounced the head of the Union in the open space with over 200 people looking on. I felt attacked by her suggestions that I should not be kept on. I officially gained my title of 007. In France, people rarely say openly what they feel so this was a cultural faux pas.

In the end, I had to give an apology to the head of the union, but like Simon A., our Vice President said to me with American practicality

"What do you care as long as they aren't asking you for a check".

I did as I was asked to rectify my impulsive behavior. Indeed, it was a glorious job, and this was a small price to pay, I reasoned.

Max

One Hanukah I found myself in Mercurol with Simon, Max's brother, Candice, Jean and Abel. We lit the Hanukah candles and marveled that perhaps that night we were the only Jews in all of Mercurol and probably this was the only Hanukkiah lit in the whole department of Mercurol. Perhaps that was our mission that evening; to ensure a Hanukkiah would be lit in the 26600 department (26 is a mystical number in the Jewish religion).

My colleagues started reminiscing on the start of BCBG and Max's early days.

Like many French businessmen from the Sentier, often of North African ascent, the American dream was predominant. Some felt that France was too small and confined and that a big success story was only possible in the United States. Some simply married American wives or cars and brought them back home. Others went all the way to America.

L' Amerique
De Joe Dassin
Mes amis, je dois m'en aller
Je n'ai plus qu'à jeter mes clés
Car elle m'attend depuis que je suis né,
l'Amerique
J'abandonne sur mon chemin
Tant de choses que j'aimais bien
Cela commence par un peu de chagrin
L'Amérique, l'Amérique, je veux l'avoir et je l'aurai

America
By Joe Dassin

(My friends, I have to go
I just have to throw my keys
Because she has been waiting for me since I was born, America
I give up on my way

So many things that I liked
It starts with a bit of grief
America, America, I want to have it and I'll have it

A whole crew of French Tunisians found themselves in Los Angeles.

Max had many ups and downs and at one point had a real low. His first wife, who looked exactly like Sylvester Stallone's wife, that tough blonde with razor-sharp features and a personality to match, had left him for their son's karate teacher. She had shoved all his clothes in a garbage bag and at the ripe age of 40, he found himself with a partnership in a small boutique, living a small rental with his two daughters. She had kept only their son, so she could continue bringing him to karate lessons. It is to his credit that he jumped back up from that situation, started BCBG, hired his second wife as a designer and together they reached their great success story.

What was even more to his credit, was that he never had an ill feeling towards his first wife. Every Shabbat dinner or party I went to she was there among the guests, immensely enjoying herself. She confided to me that she benefitted from the houses and the reapings of the business even more than Max and his wife, who were always busy working. She would pop in and throw a crepe party for her kids and theirs or could be found working out or water-skiing while they were on an endless business trip in Asia.

General Washington said, "A nation is judged by how well it treats its veterans." I would like it to be said, "A man is judged by how well he treats his ex-wife."

Max Sets Sail Into A Documentary Film

It did not look good that 70 people were let go from the Parisian headquarters, and this at the untimely moment of one week before Christmas. Making matters worse, our attaché press had allowed Max's vacation to be filmed the previous summer, as part of a docuseries, and it aired on French tv at this untimely moment. "Capital" was often a lure for the successful that wanted to show off their accomplishments and lifestyle.

Businessmen who were featured on the show, would give away too much information, so willing were they to flaunt their success. Soon after, inevitably they would be victims of tax audits or they would realize that they had unknowingly supplied information of their sources to their competitors. The lure to shine can be dangerous.

Just like in the fable by Jean Fontaine where the crow is flattered by the fox and lets his prey drop by opening his mouth.

It was a very bad decision. 70 people had just been let go and the last thing they needed was to see Max spending 300 000 $ on a summer vacation.

The first part of the documentary consisted of following him in his LA office, making phone calls to reserve the yacht.

The reporter asked the fateful question, "Do you think anything can go wrong?" Later I watched the documentary film with my colleague Sylvie and her parents who were Max's closest friends and hence part of Max's chosen few during this trip.

"There! ", her mother shrieked "That is the exact moment when she gave us the evil eye and our whole trip was ruined! Une catastrophe ce voyage!".

The first stop was in Capri and there was a not-so-flattering side shot of Max licking ice cream cones with his friends. And then everything went downhill from there.

First, they were all seasick and green. You could see Max and his crowd dragging themselves from one luxurious room to the next. Max was the worst off; he could not even get up. And then the yacht stalled. Just like that. They had to be taken to shore on the rescue boat. They were brought to a beach shore and waded in the water to the shore. Unfortunately, they had not brought their shoes and "ouched" their way achingly to the shore on the beach's rollers.

The boat was fixed after a few days whiled away in a hotel suite. After finally getting back on board the yacht stalled again. Max was lying down on a couch, seasick again and oblivious to the camera that was filming him, he roared into the phone, "I want my money back: je veux mon pognon! ". This was the mood of the whole trip.

It did make you wonder about the evil eye, even if you weren't Tunisian.

And throughout the whole documentary, there were snatches of Max's ex-wife having the time of her life with the kids in the Miami apartment, water-skiing and whizzing by the camera laughingly.

It was to the man's credit. It was said by George Washington that a country's greatness can be evaluated by how it honours the heroes of its history. May I add, that a man's greatness can be evaluated by how he honours his ex-wife.

Paris St. germain And Herve Leger

My new office that September was in the beautiful St. Germain head office. Inside a courtyard proudly stood the hotel particulier ; four stories of intricate stonework and ornate iron gates. We were lodged between Shiseido and the very reputable Café de Flore, the renown gathering places of French authors.

One day I met my girlfriends there for lunch and dressed up with the full cliché: black beret, baguette and Pléiade leather-bound book tucked under my arm. They all shrieked with laughter as I walked in.

When that office was undergoing renovations, we moved to the equally chic St. Honoré and I met Bianca for lunch at Colette's, the iconic multi-brand store filled with every designer from YSL to Balmain and back. Funnily enough, the owner came straight from the Sentier where she had already excelled in being a great picker and creating original windows. I remember one window with '60s inspired clothes surrounded by close to 100 barbie dolls dangling from ropes Tarzan style. The Sentier must have been a good breeding ground because that Colette store became the toast of fashion Paris and the obligatory stop for fashionistas from all over the world.

I met a lot of very competitive women, but thankfully some special ones were out of the lot. Women like my new friends Sylvie and Caroline were not obsessed with power and competition and were of the most pleasant company. We enjoyed together what this fun fashion environment had to offer.

Caroline would come in from Los Angeles always with an ingenious idea. She would be decked out in Chanel but would knowingly pair it with a Petit Bateau t-shirt. Caroline was at a very high level of fashion and taste and this came to her instinctively. Her mother had owned one of the most prestigious shops of the Champs Elysees in the glorious fashionable '80s. She would walk into any Parisian high-end store and was recognized as an authority in fashion.

I attended Caroline's wedding (by the time we were friends it was her second wedding). The perfection of her ultra-chic Courreges dress attested to her superior style and taste. Squares of silk were sewn together and unfolded into a marvel of style and perfection of design. I also attended her mother's second wedding when she was well into her 70's. She entered the picture-perfect Ritz Carlton gardens, where the affair was held, dressed in black like any fashionista of the '80s: it was black or nothing. The groom though conceded to tradition and was decked in white.

Caroline would run in and exclaim, "Hey, girls! It's the Hervé Leger Press days…Everything must be in mauve and gold, the brand colors. I bought paint. If no one else can do it, we will paint the window shutters gold ourselves."

And there we were, dressed in Marni and Prada, tentatively dipping brushes in pots of paint and lovingly spreading gold on the window shutters. We decorated the beautiful building in St. Germain that housed our showroom with little tables and gold Napoleon chairs and flowers. I went to buy the macarons at Pierre Hermé and decided to get only one flavor: matcha tea and ginger because they were a beautiful mauve, the Hervé Leger brand color, speckled with gold. The flavor turned out to be so sophisticated that we observed at least two very elegant women spitting them out daintily on gold paper napkins. But we didn't care, the visual effect had been achieved; our brand colors were respected. We were happy and Max was proud that we had painted the windows ourselves.

When I recounted the pleasant incident to my husband, he sulked," for Max, you would do anything, even labor." How could he understand that when you mix women, fashion, gold and macarons everything is magical?

One day we went to spy on Hervé Leger. After Max had bought the name from him, Hervé and Max had a falling out and split up. They didn't know what to do with the flailing line at the beginning…there was even talk of relegating the name to the "plus sizes fashion". This would have been an acronym because Leger means Light in french.

Max had bought his name from Hervé and with it the exclusive right to produce and distribute the signature bandage dresses. Max gave us a mission: we were to spy on his new store, now named Hervé L. Hervé no longer had the right to use the name of Hervé Leger since he had sold it to Max. We were to make sure he was not producing or selling bandage dresses. So he had no right to his name or his invented bandage dresses: business can be so cruel.

My colleague Sylvie and I, full of a giddy self- importance because of our mission ordered by Max himself, crossed St. Germain to do our spying bit. We entered the charming store that resembled a" bonbonnière" in a very quaint side street of St. Germain, rue Jacob, graced with antique stores, the finest names in home fabrics and Ladurée macarons.

Hervé himself greeted us with a French-accented, "Hello". Often in Paris, it is a common misconception that if you are wealthy enough to be entering a fashionable store you must be a wealthy American. For some reason, you cannot be French. You are contemptible because you have money, but you are spoken to in your English tongue because you might spend some of that wicked but welcomed money. In those cases, I always kept up the pretense and answered in English, thus reveling in being a foreigner in Paris for a few moments. Even more so for this spying role and so I answered his query if any help was needed, with the norm: "thank you, we are going to look at your collection". I laid on my thickest English accent, as an extra cover to our spying role.

Sylvie, very uncomfortable in any illicit situation looked pointedly ahead and buried her head in the clothes on the racks, pretending to be very engrossed by the collection. Later this same extremely discrete Sylvie was to find refuge behind a camera as a spy and this would lead her out of the chic and safe neighborhoods that were here natural habitat. She would be pulled into near illicit situations and forge ahead into new neighborhoods in her search of subject matter. Driven by her need to capture strong and beautiful images she became very adventurous and a very talented photographer. Women never do cease to amaze me.

But this day, as we looked through the beautiful dresses exposed, he turned his attentions back to a woman that was seated on a small couch next to him.

For some reason, he was flattering this woman. "You have such beautiful skin", he remarked. This woman was quite overweight, so it was a smart thing to say to a woman in a store filled with tiny form-fitting clothes.

"You must tell your friends at Harrods the truth. Max puts all the beautiful dresses from the vintage collections I did in the windows and then he sells his shit inside". It was a good thing we had our faces hidden in the clothes. Our eyes became huge circles of amazement behind our incognito sunglasses. We hurried back to the headquarters, even giddier now, with the self-importance of our full report. We called Max in Los Angeles and relayed to him that there were no bandage dresses in sight, but that Hervé was still filled with lots of ill will (perhaps not surprisingly so as he no longer had his name or signature style). Max was like a teddy bear; he was sad. He just wanted everyone to love him.

And for the most part, they did. Especially women. He flattered them, brought them on plane rides and showered them with BCBG bags. Even when they were no longer the flavor of the moment, he showered them with kind attentions and protection. One of his assistants came back to visit once she was established with husband and child and he loved it when we said that the little Asian child she had borne revealed a little" je ne sais quoi" of Max.

From Porn Star To Fashion Model

One summer he insisted that he was going to be producing the Manoukian ad campaign and brochure in Los Angeles. He delivered it back to us and to our surprise, the model had a sexy, curvy figure, not at all in line with the criteria of a fashion model. The truth soon came out: she was a porn star whom Max had made promises to. Our CFO was probably a fan of her movies because her identity was revealed through him. I had been upset that Max had taken the ad campaign responsibility away from our team. With an extremely indignant look on my face, I brought the list of movies this actress had been featured in, to Simon, Max's brother, after a Google search. I told him that this situation must not repeat itself; going forward all brochures should be shot and produced in Paris! What if our customers found out?

With his charming French accent, he read the list out loud oblivious to the meaning of his words.

"Dee noty garl next dor" : The Naughty Girl next door.

"I vant mie loli...pop??" : I want my lollipop.

"Fack me": F.ck me.

Hmm the situations one finds oneself in. I often thought our corporate slogan should be "Never a dull moment at BCBG."

Dancing Queens

There were many dinners, parties and nightclubs. Yelena and I continued to be extremely wary of each other. She was upset that I had "survived" instead of her friends. I never trusted her because of the way she had ostracized me and treated me harshly for three months when she had been my official superior. Nevertheless, there was one moment when we put hatred and rivalry aside. When an Abba song came on, we were immediately on the dance floor, filled with positive all-encompassing energy. We equally reveled in the music and could sincerely smile at each other while we danced. Abba had been big in Montreal during my teenage years and no doubt also in Belgium during her teenage years ...during the time of a song we were on the same cultural horizon.

Dancing Queen
By Abba
You can dance
You can jive
Having the time of your life
Ooh, see that girl
Watch that scene
Digging the dancing queen
You are the dancing queen
Having the time of your life

Los Angeles

My first business trip to Los Angeles was just before the notorious Black Friday. The date was chosen because it was customary for the Americans to rev things up and motivate the troops at this timely moment. This strategy paid off because store managers and their best sales associates would be motivated at the seminar and then go back to their stores roaring to go in for the kill to sell, sell, sell just in time for the long-awaited Black Friday.

Max summoned the French directors to come and "see how things are done in America so that after you can do the same in France". Ha. Ha.

We arrived just in time for the three-day seminar.

Breakfast was served on a rooftop hotel for over 400 of the sales staff arrived from all corners of America fully equipped with blow-dries, French manicures, perfectly applied makeup and cheery dispositions. These women and men (because there were a few), were very excited and felt privileged to have been selected to attend this seminar that was more like a BCBG field trip. They had probably gotten up at 6 am to work out and get ready for this power breakfast. I looked at my French colleagues summoned from Mercurol and they made for a dismal lot in comparison. Their hair had probably met a comb at best and did not seem freshly washed, manicures were still largely unknown in France. Why call them French manicures when France discovered manicures in the late nineties? Their make up was usually composed of mascara and some hurriedly applied rouge. For the most part, they were wearing neutral tones that looked out of place in the fierce LA sun that called for bright colors. And as for working out most of them had gone outside to light up their 3rd cigarette that would accompany their power breakfast of black coffee.

"Those French women have a lot of nerve", Candice, Head of Retail, took me aside." How dare they not respect Max and show up dressed like that! They cannot motivate personnel by looking like that…so…uh. unenergetic looking. One of them is wearing jeans! ". (Uhm didn't Americans invent jeans I thought grasping for excuses but deciding against it).

The French personnel looked on dazed and confused as the 400 sales managers chatted and giggled emphatically. They cooed excitedly over how wonderful the collections in the stores were while the French mustered a few brave compliments.

"Pff these Americans! How excited can they expect us to get over clothes? It's just a dress!".

We were asked to file into a spacious conference room with top to bottom glass windows overlooking LA. Everyone was seated, and we faced our inspirational speakers, corporate-level sales directors for the most part. They were generously applauded.

And then the real fun began.

"It's about YOU today! So now we want you to share with us some of your best practices," the MC exclaimed zealously.

It started timidly.....the first hand went up and the director nodded, smiling approval in the direction of this first brave participant who was willing to generously share her gold nugget of best practice.

"Well, I come early in the morning and precut ribbons, so we don't waste extra time preparing gift packages."

A hearty round of applause was met with a gratified smile. Another brave hand went up.

"Once a week we get together for a team meeting and quiz each other on the product knowledge."

The emotion was palpable. Whistles and loud claps.

"Well when I go to other stores and notice a really brilliant sales associate with that 'special" talent, I give her my card and encourage her to come work for us! We love welcoming new talents in our team".

Here the house was practically coming down. I feared the standing ovation and perhaps even a teary eye moment.

But what I rightly feared even more, was my French colleague's reactions. They looked at me with horrified looks.

"They cannot be serious. You must explain to the Americans

that we cannot do this back home. We will never ever be able to live down the ridicule."

Other activities awaited us.

Different halls in the hotel had been accommodated for fun-filled games.

One hall boasted a reenactment of "The Price is Right" complete with screens displaying best sellers from our collections, booths for participants and buzzers to bang down on if you had the answer to:

"At what price is selling our Brighton sweater? 300? 350? 500?".

In another hall, women were shrieking and racing around in high heels to win relay races. The objective of the race was to dress a window in the shortest time possible. My French teammates stuck out like a sore thumb. It was visible they had no desire to put their effort into the unpleasant and trying task of dressing and undressing mannequins "for a game" with no real business incentive in mind. In France work is not play! Even Jean and Abel, our directors whom always encouraged us to adopt dear Max's American way ("cause come on, Max is so good to us and he knows what he is doing, look at the success he built,") were very reluctant to set an example. I surmised that we would be spotted very quickly for our lack of enthusiasm and participation so I begged them not to eclipse themselves to smoke a cigarette, but to compose a team.

"Come on guys! Let's beat the Americans". I searched unconvinced for something that would set them off. We did not beat them but got a few points for participation from Candice who noticed our efforts and smilingly nodded to us in approval.

"Isn't this great fun!", she added with enthusiasm to cheer us on. She seemed to be sincerely enjoying herself. The French tried valiantly to muster up smiles and fake enthusiasm.

Luckily the evenings were reserved for outings and general bonding.

Max booked the best restaurants and even threw memorable Shabbat dinners where we were usually close to 100 lucky few. He invited directors and his family and friends. It was a dinner party with people of many religions, but there was always a solemn moment when everyone was hushed and Max or his brother recited the prayer over a microphone and broke bread. As part of the personnel, if you were invited to a Shabbat dinner in Max's home then you were extremely privileged.

The next day we met at the Los Angeles Studios. The very fortunate ones got to kiss Max on both cheeks and even take a picture with him. And then we filed into the studio. A well-known MC proceeded to show a slide that showed BCBG as number 3 in America (after Bebe and Marciano). But next year we will be number 1! The audience roared.

A very well put together corporate video was presented with testimonials from all of the top people on what it was like to be part of the BCBG team and all the wonderful things that were coming up.

Finally, a video was projected on the huge stage showing planet earth slowly turning on its axis, to the sound of,

We Are the World
By Song by U.S.A. for Africa
We are the world, we are the children
We are the ones who make a brighter day
So let's start giving
There's a choice we're making
We're saving our own lives
It's true we'll make a brighter day
Just you and me

And out came Max, dressed in head to toe white, pulling a seemingly reluctant-but-loving-every-moment-wife equally dressed in head to toe white. Max, characteristically happy, waved at all of us to the sound of the music, like an eager and proud child waving to his parents. The standing ovation I was expecting came and we were all overcome with emotion and tears. Even my French colleagues seemed to be filled with as much emotion as if Johnny Halliday had been in front of them.

No expense was spared. Max showed us during that trip that he could play hard. An airport hangar had been converted into what looked like an ultra-sleek, ultra-chic lounge complete with plush white carpet, lounge areas and dinner tables. Fantastic figures on stilts walked around us adding magic to this hangar transformed into party land. Musicians entertained us all evening and women complimented each other's evening dresses while men smoked cigars, crooned and flirted with the newly arrived female staff.(waaaay before the #metoo movement).

Max observed all this and smiled benevolently at all of our gracious thanks and admiring comments. Indeed, he deserved it.

We are the world
We are the children
We are the ones who make a brighter day

Price To Pay

I would not have missed this all for the world.

Although the price to pay was hefty, even during some of the hardest times, later when I looked back, I knew I it was all worth it in the end. I had waited all my life to have a fulfilling career and the demands of a macho, self-centered husband just could not get in the way of my dream. I was finally living my dream of a fulfilling (and glamorous yes, I am not embarrassed to say) career. I had been programmed for this ever since I was a little girl. Didn't I work hard at school because we were programmed to one day reap the benefits and have a glorious job. Wasn't this my due?

The first price to pay after my first ever fulfilling business trip was at the customs in France when I got back from my "business and yes shopping" trip. I could have seen this as a sign. The customs department must have been rubbing their hands eagerly while they waited for all the fashionistas arriving from New York's Fashion Week. I flew in oblivious to all this with my all-black obviously fashionista shopaholic look and overweight bags. I was quickly singled out. To my horror, the contents of my bags were scrutinized. I shrieked in dismay and haggled with customs over what had been bought this trip and what was ages old.

"What! That is not new! I most certainly did not buy that bag this trip. It's last year's Prada! ". I glared at the customs agent getting back at her like I could by pointing out her ignorance. In vain.

I was presented with a bill that I had no choice but to pay.

"Pay this or leave the merchandise here".

There was blatantly no choice.

And then with as much dignity as one could muster in such a situation, I presented customs with all of my overused credit cards. We tried one after the other even combining amounts and juggling until the hefty sum was paid and I could leave with a shred of dignity and more importantly my Fashion Week's treasures.

The second price to pay was the reception given to me by my Jewish Sephardic husband who had not been programmed to have a wife that was having more fun than him.

He was supposed to have all the action, business trips, fulfilling career, stimulating relationships. (I have heard many a male business trip is extremely stimulating).

While I was now off gallivanting, attending Max's parties, networking with businessman that were impressed that I now worked for the "King", something was slowly breaking inside of him.

Our last summer together in Los Angeles, we were invited to Max's for dinner along with other colleagues. A male ego does not accept that someone like Max greeted me, the mere woman first. He made his entrance into the living room calling my name and telling my husband how happy he was to have me on board. My husband smiled that empty smile that signals uncertainty; similar to the expression people wear when they are unsure of the punch line of a joke. Then we were seated with the top brass from the office (according to my position in the company). Not with Max's friends and top businessman (according to his position).

Arguments started.

"Again, a business trip".

"You are contributing to someone else's business".

"You are neglecting the children".

Then detachment. From one day to the next I did not exist. I had not complied. I was banned. It was my birthday and he was in Hong Kong.

He called to wish me Happy birthday and sang a few words. But something was wrong with the tone. I understood what it meant to hear a thin voice for the first time in my life. A thick voice is one that is covered in love and thus becomes voluptuous and rich, throaty and thick. This voice was so thin it was at the same time hollow and metallic. I can still hear that tone, when I close my eyes. It sent a chill through my spine

Then he started going out. Or coming late. Without me and he had never done this before. He said he needed space. This is when I started to feel the abandonment. I was gratefully busy all day, but when I left my office and my busy fulfilling days, I felt new loneliness in my chest on those cold winter evenings. I could not breathe. We had never gotten along extremely well, but he had been a strong presence in my life. Now I came home and it was the girls and me. He would come very late and sometimes not answer the phone. If he did and I asked when he was coming home, he would hang up.

And then he started my trial.

"We never got along"

"You never got along with my mother. Yes, she is crazy, but you could have made efforts with her.

"You exhausted me with all those horrible fights. I felt out of a boxing ring each time".

There is a lot of fear but there is also real power in the act of divorce. You are separated, and you become "one" again and you must survive and thrive this way. Soon after the divorce, one of my aunts remarked: "Oh no all your children are going on vacation with their father and you will be left alone?"

Not wanting anyone to feel sorry for me, I gave us both a reality check and answered, "but one day we will all be alone. Sooner or later. We come alone, and we leave alone". But of course, it took me a while to overcome the fear and feel the power.

Trials

Trials and efforts started "to get my husband back". He was here, he was home, but it was as if he was covered with Saran

Wrap. I could not reach him. He was cold and detached. But I was on a mission, albeit with knots in my stomach.

TRIAL 1: Manipulation

Ok, let's play hard to get. I am going to start going out too. He will wonder where I am, I thought, and the tables will be reversed. The age-old trick. The only problem was I did not feel like going out. But I tried, I went out with my single friend Bianca. I soon found all those trendy restaurants boring and devoid of interest, so I decided to stay late at work. Once I was indeed very lucky. I stayed at the office till 11 pm and who arrived just as I was leaving? Max himself, straight from a Hong Kong trip on his way to Los Angeles, had decided to come by with a fellow traveler to pick up something he needed. He was very surprised to see me working so late.

The next morning when I arrived Jean and Abel were grinning.

"Max says you are the pillar of the company. He said that you are the only one that works here! Ok warning you though! A promotion does not mean a raise! (Promotion ne veut pas dire augmentation!)".

Working late was great for my work situation, but never did save my marriage. No matter how late I worked, he usually came home after me.

TRIAL 2: Marriage counselor.

He came with me a few times, but quickly tired of these two women who always seemed to be on my side. It was a new technique in France. For one couple, two therapists. My duo happened to be composed of two females. It was not such a good idea for a man that already had a problem with women.

TRIAL 3: The Rabbis

First, I reached out to an organization whose goal it was to discourage divorce. The rabbi met my husband a few times but to no avail. My husband was respectful but closed.

My mother's friend had a difficult husband but had discovered a rabbi/counselor that could help me. I called him. He assured me that all would be good. The problem should no longer preoccupy me." Just ignore it and when you feel uneasy call me." 80 euros an hour.

My friend Bianca said to me "all the rabbis in Paris are spreading the word...I have a tip for you they are telling each other. There is a good business opportunity to be had at 28 boulevard de Courcelles." Well, I tried 500 euros worth. Maybe a bit more. There was not much result but some Saturday nights speaking to this "professional" gave me some comfort and temporarily soothed my nervous palpitations.

One rabbi, gave my husband great sustenance (and received donations). He explained to him that I was like milk and he was like meat. In Jewish religion, both must never be consumed together so clearly, we were incompatible. My husband was an easy victim for these simplistic formulas that he clung on to and repeated. To him it was so easy to digest and explain away the mess of divorce and incompatibility with the pretense of wise words. I preferred humour. I went to the "biggest" rabbi in Paris and relayed what the other rabbi had said. "Does that make our children like cheeseburgers? Not kosher?? G.d forbid!".

I could never resist a joke that would be a story to tell (much) later.

TRIAL 4 : Tarot card readers.

None of them said there was another woman. Not one. Most of them said this would all go away, and I was going to stay married. Another 400 euros.

TRIAL 5 : Bewitched

My aunt in Morocco asked me to send a few hairs. The man could certainly be bewitched. It was something that women did in Morocco. There were specialists. My mother had always prided herself on the fact that we had evolved and had nothing to do with this penchant of our culture. Even her mother had been very rational. "We sent you to university, didn't we?" As if university explained and solved Life. I decided against this. Especially when the good witch in Morrocco said it wasn't a lock of his hair she needed, but sperm. Years later, I laughingly recounted this request for sperm to a friend, also from Morroco. She looked at me with a straight face and said, "It wouldn't have worked anyways. If you sent the sperm to Casablanca, it crosses a big body of water, so the power is lost, the spell is broken".
Well live and learn.

TRIAL 6: Leave him alone

I wanted to check out a bookstore in Brussels that I discovered in a Design magazine. I bravely took my children alone and off we went for the weekend. It was my birthday gift to myself. I thought he would feel lonely and miss us and stop living his own life. It was my first trip as a single mother. I felt very lonely, taking all the decisions and full responsibility for everything alone. I kept us in constant movement, visiting the library, going to museums, sightseeing, reserving restaurants, buying a dollhouse. The constant thud in my chest and the feeling that my heart was in my throat would not go away. Sunday night he came to pick us up at the train station and seemed really happy to see us. But twenty minutes later I was obliged to admit to myself he was still his new distant self.

TRIAL 7: The Children

Let's do things with the children. He had probably noticed that our three older ones were more independent. Perhaps he felt less needed. We needed to unite the family. Let's all go to Disney especially since our youngest has never been. We all went to Disney. On the long road there he was still coated with Saran Wrap. He seemed like a teenage child that had humoured his parents, had come along for the ride, was going through the motions of joining the family outing but was not really there. His life was elsewhere. In the car on the way to and from Disney, I was frustratingly sitting next to a man who was not present. Amy Winehouse was very popular at the time and the song below was playing on that car ride. It took me ten years to be able to listen to it and not feel any sadness. Many years later, one of my daughter's brought up how the negative innuendos attached to that song had tainted it with the bitter taste of that time.

Tears dry on their own
by Amy Winehouse
He walks away
The sun goes down
He takes the day but I'm grown
And in your way,
In this blue shade

My tears dry on their own
I don't understand
Why do I stress the man

The Finale

Sometimes the growing distance between us and the constant thudding in my chest would give way to an explosion. When would this end? When would things go back to normal? Out of my desperation came futile attempts to stop all this. I needed to give way to the explosion of my fears.

"Where are we going like this? We cannot continue like this? You don't really want a divorce?"

He was calmly shaving in the bathroom. He answered and continued shaving, with imperturbable composure. Chin lifted, gazing into the mirror, he shaved meticulously with great attention.

"Why not? Other people do it all the time." He lifted his head and delicately concentrated on his neck. I wished he would cut himself. I am not a violent person. I have a total aversion to violence, but if I said that I did not wish physical harm on him throughout this period, I would be untruthful. My daydreaming went so far as to fantasize about hiring a hitman more than once. Of course, this was pure daydreaming: I knew I would get caught...lol.

At that moment, I was in shock. I felt like I was on the edge of a cliff. I was dizzy, shaking, and felt that my knees would give way. I felt simply scared and lonely.

Soon after I was called to Montreal. That phone call came from my uncle. He urged me to come immediately. My father was "not well". He had told my husband the horrible truth: that my father had passed away. My husband did not think one moment to accompany me. He booked tickets for my youngest daughter and myself and we were off. I was greeted at the Montreal airport by my cousins who told me the most awful news I had ever had in my life so far. When they had called me, my father had already passed away. October 8th. A few days before our common birth date. For the first time in my life, my father and I would no longer share the day and our complicity by wishing each other happy birthday.

The horror I had dreaded for the past twenty years had arrived. The person I was closest to in the world had passed away.

I went through the motions of the next week like one goes forward through a dark tunnel because there are no other options. I cried and smoked and talked.

And cried and smoked and talked mostly with my aunts and cousins. My mother, sister and I sat Shiva for a week. I had always visited other people in this sad situation and observed all this incredulously. The day I had dreaded all my life had arrived.

The only light in my life that week was the presence of my youngest daughter. She was oblivious to what was happening around her and thus pulled me towards the ordinary motions of life with her two-year-old demands. I understood why my mother had sent the message that I bring at least my youngest.

Meanwhile, my husband with his usual lack of emotion had announced to my daughters, soon after I left, that their adored and very special grandfather had passed away.

And he proceeded to live his life as if nothing had happened. He went out to dinner and even invited friends over for dinner and asked my listless daughters to come and smile and welcome the guests. Ironically the guests were some of Max's acolytes that were often present at his fashion shows and parties, basking in Max's glory. He just loved that.

I knew deep down that my husband had been jealous of my fast-paced fun life. He was not jealous that I was less with him or ever doubted my fidelity. Rather he was jealous that he was not living my life. He had reached that mid-life crisis and was bored with his business for plus size women. He spent days with his employees of twenty years that he no longer found amusing. I was always coming back with fun stories that happen when 10 flamboyant Jewish Tunisian men are brought together to work and play.

I was in a new and fascinating environment. I was part of the "King's" team. Max was the biggest success story of our community and he was having a lot of fun with it. I was invited to the parties, the meetings, the lunches and trips with all of these characters. People that he would have loved to have as friends. He had grown up with too many responsibilities and he had missed out on carefree male bonding days as a teenager or young adult.

I recently read Fire and Fury on Trump. I found many similarities between Max, my husband and some of my bosses. The narcissist macho type always has the same traits. They are never truly in love with a woman because they love themselves so much. But they are capable of a good strong man crush. Trump had a man-crush on Putin says the author: I believe it. My husband had a man-crush on Max and his friends. He was frustrated that I was having all the fun and he was being neglected.

Right after Fire and Fury, I saw a four-part series on Netflix about Trump. It was difficult to avoid the subject. In part two, Ivana has finally come into her own and proven that she can be a smart businesswoman. She arrives at a benefit in her honour upon the completion of the fabulous work she did renovating the Ritz Carlton. She is glowing and seems so proud of what she has accomplished. Finally, she has done something on her own, and of course, wants to show her husband that she too is worthy of (his) admiration. Donald, on the other hand, seems ill at ease and even upset at all the flurry of excitement around his wife. In the film, we are told he pretexted a headache and left early. Shortly after they divorced. He left her for an aerobics teacher, I believe.

When I came back from Montreal after that horrible trip, still not quite coping with the reality of my father's death, my husband was odious. He went so far as to refuse me the comfort of my bed, pretexting that I was in mourning so I could not sleep there. He did this so that I would tell him to leave. He wanted me to liberate him. That is what I did.

And then because I have always been a finisher, I knew that I could not stay in an ambiguous situation. I could not let him be free and have his cake and eat it too. I needed something violent to make a clean break, so I proceeded to ask for the divorce. I felt all the fear of abandonment and extreme sadness and anguish but went ahead. Again, like in a dark tunnel with no escape.

That was when he served the cruelest blow he could, to a woman with abandonment issues. He agreed to the divorce, packed his things and left the house. He abandoned me right after my father's death. I can still hear his steps resounding on those Parisian wood floors and in my head and then the cold click of the door closing and the empty silence my daughters and I would hear for a long time. The silence of abandonment.

Reflections
By Diana Ross
Through the mirror of my mind
Time after time
I see reflections of you and me

Reflections of
The way life used to be
Reflections of
The love you took from me
Oh, I'm all alone now

Money

Tia who is as smart as she is delicate and well-bred, told me very wisely, "Be smart, take him for what he is worth". I listened dismally. I was only half- convinced that this was important in the face of this devastating divorce.

How could I think about money and lawyers and fighting when I couldn't even breathe?

But when Tia's husband said to me, "Let go of all this, just get out of it and do not argue about every detail," my survival instinct resurfaced.

"Gerard, did you ever see the War of the Roses? Did you see the part where they swing on chandeliers? Do you see all my beautiful chandeliers? I will hang onto each one of them and not let one go."

The problem with women {and I certainly am no exception), is that we are too romantic. We listen to love songs. When we should just be thinking about money when we divorce. That is one real word of advice I wish to give women out there. Probably the smartest and most useful thing I will have said in this whole book.

Just take them for what they are worth. Nice or mean, short or tall, tough or sensitive, weak or strong. Because as they get older, they cling more and more to their egos and their money as both are directly linked and become unequivocally interdependent.

As for women we wisely relish the certainty and comfort that is afforded by the small pleasures of life that become more meaningful: flowers and pretty tables, bath salts and candles, Vogue with espresso. But realistically, note that these pleasures all have a price tag.

So just like Joan Collins says, tell them to,

"Sell the pipeline".

Money
By Pink Floyd
Money, get away.
Get a good job with more pay and you're okay.
Money, it's a gas.
Grab that cash with both hands and make a stash.
New car, caviar, four-star daydream,
Think I'll buy me a football team.

Going Through The Motions

So, I went through all the motions and cried and smoked.

I went to work every day and when I couldn't take the thudding in my heart, I did one of three things alternating these options throughout the day. I either went to the bathroom to cry a few minutes or went to my friend Sylvie's office who had gone through this horrible divorce thing many years earlier or I called my future ex-husband to ask him if he was sure we had to go ahead with this.

The worst moment was when I left the office to go home. Walking to the parking lot, getting my car, driving home: these moments were unbearable. I felt the full force of the abandonment at these moments because I knew my husband would not be having dinner with us, would not be calling to ask me if we should have dinner out with friends, would simply no longer be part of our evenings or life in the same way. These were the moments I felt the loneliness and the most frenetic pounding in my throat. I was greeted by my daughters who now had an absent father and a very dismal, depressed mother.

During evenings, I smoked, and it seems I was always on the phone with someone who had a useless two cents worth to give me.

"Beware of rich men, they will take your children away. I know a woman etc."

"Remember you will now find out who your friends are".

"Of course, your financial situation will change, it always does."

"Well you will just have to leave that beautiful apartment you have, and each get a smaller one." This from a frustrated rabbi's wife.

"He will regret this. I know a man who got very sick 6 months after his divorce. Men realize after."

"Don't worry he will never leave you in the street." How comforting.

"You have a strong abandonment issue. That is why it is so tough for you". My therapist.

"Stephan says you are lucky he stayed with you so long. Most wealthy men move around a lot more." Meanwhile, Stephan is gay and has had the same boyfriend for over twenty years. What a jealous bitch to say that.

"You never got along, you never loved him really, you don't speak the same language at any level." Bianca was right, but still.

"I just hung up with him. He said you made his life miserable."

"No big loss."

If he were to leave me, I was going back home. It takes a village…I needed my roots, my surrounding and a close-knit community. I could not raise the teenagers alone and then fight back the tears in the presence of my youngest one in the Parisian Park Monceau. Ever since he had left the house, he only wanted to see the children on his terms and visits with him would be very frustrating. I could not reconcile myself to this new situation of having to live under the schedule of a divorced couple's visits. The worst was Sunday nights when he took my daughters to the restaurant and left me behind. I cried, smoked and talked on the phone. But when I asked him to help with responsibilities, even on his time, he flatly refused. Leaving the country would dispense me of that horror and thus offered an escape route. My girls pressured him, and it was settled.

Our lawyers talked, and the amount was settled. I did not put up the fight I should have because money seemed to be of lesser importance; I was so dazed by what was happening.

Ironically while I was divorcing, one of my cousins from Los Angeles was marrying a girl originally from Paris and they had decided to wed in her hometown. The girl came from another "King of Shmata", the Naf Naf empire. The Naf Naf brothers had launched a sportswear line in the '80s. One lucky day they created a cotton jumpsuit that became the biggest "tube" or hit, thus propelling this small manufacturer into a multinational brand of huge proportions. My whole family was coming for the wedding and most of them were staying at my house.

I had given my room to my aunt and uncle from Los Angeles who were marrying their son. I had given one of my daughter's rooms to the groom, and the other ones for other family members. I had taken a smaller room and only left my eldest daughter in her room because she was in the middle of studying for her Baccalaureat Degree. I had given various couches to teenagers and booked nearby hotel rooms for my mother, sister, brother in law, nieces and nephews and other aunts and uncles. In all, I had over a dozen people sleeping over and my home was the general meeting place for close to 30 people. I ordered blankets for 12 and then we were hit with a heatwave so when I opened the door to the mail by order salesman I explained "Sorry wrong color, please send back," in one breath and just ran from one errand to the next. I organized a Shabbat dinner for 50. I gave full control of the kitchen to my aunts and help but just organized provisions. I gave instructions to my help to hire a cousin of hers and tried to maintain order best I could. My aunts cajoled and flattered my help. They were so worried she would eventually not show up.

"Gladys, you look so fine today. Wow, I love that lipstick on you," exclaimed one of my aunts. They were generous with compliments each time she bravely showed up. "What brand and number is that?". My aunts were preoccupied with cooking more than anything. I knew they were just schmoozing her.

"What are you crazy, forget it; it's never going to look like that on you. Did you see the sexy lips, she has?", the other aunt chimed in, adding another layer on.

I laughed at their natural charm routine and at the same time I cried and consulted therapists and lawyers. It was July and my daughters and myself had planned to be in Montreal for our new life by the end of August. I had already sadly handed in my resignation to my dream job.

I kept busy organizing all my house guests and joking, "Well, I am glad to see you guys are not superstitious about throwing wedding festivities in my apartment in the middle of my divorce."

I would come back from another appointment with the divorce lawyer and find 30 people in my kitchen cheering me on, one uncle encouraging me to have a drink and another uncle lighting my cigarette.

My future ex was mildly frustrated to be missing out on all the fun and wondered if he should come back home. For all the wrong reasons. After all, this was going to be the wedding of the season; the Naf Naf daughter was going to be married and he did enjoy the company of my fun-loving family.

My cousin got married. They all had kind prayers for me, the perfect hostess in spite of it all and then they were off. The silence and inactivity were deafening, especially in the heart of summer in Paris. We had never been here before in the middle of summer. All the Parisians desert Paris and only the tourists occupy it and it becomes a very heavy and lonely place.

Reprieve In Casablanca

My dear cousin Paula invited us to Casablanca. Every family needs a therapist and even before becoming one officially, Paula had all the makings of one with her listening skills, analytical mind, good sense and natural empathy attributes. I took my daughters to Casablanca for four days. Three of my best friends came with us and we had a welcome reprieve from the painful last weeks in Paris and before our uncertain future in Montreal.

We had women and children time. For lunch, we gathered at the restaurants of the Tahiti of my childhood. We enjoyed big tables of women and children as was always customary in the history of our culture. These moments were very soothing, as if I was safely encompassed in the habits of women long before me. I lived in the moment with the comfort of my past around me. The beach was the one my father had spent his summers in and had earned him the title of the "playboy of

Casablanca "and where my mother had won Mrs Tahiti prizes. In the darkest moments to contemplate a reassuring past can be of great comfort. Even today when I feel nervous or uncertain, I think of everything I have gone through and lived, and I derive strength from it. Living for a moment in my reassuring past, allowed me to put the present in perspective. It was a welcome reprieve.

Be Brief, Be Brilliant And Be Gone

The day I dreaded had come. Even ten years later, it has been several days now that I have been putting off writing this part. I incessantly delay it and write other passages.

Our short trip to Casablanca had been like an eye in the tornado, but we reluctantly had to leave. These days had afforded us a welcome respite filled with sun, laughter and the special soothing love that emanates from women and children only zones.

We had to face Paris. The movers would be coming to disassemble our lives and ship everything to Montreal. I had to grit my teeth and go through this.

We landed in Paris late one evening. When one is anguished, it is always harder to land in a city at night and I was struggling with my dread of the few days ahead. As we were leaving the luggage claim, I bumped into one of my best friend's sister. She had always been the type that put her foot in her mouth. She had divorced two years earlier, so I was very careful not to bring up her ex or any of the hurt he had caused her by running off with a twenty-year-old he had met at a Club Med. The twenty-year-old had been on vacation with her parents and he had been vacationing with his wife and children. Not nice.

She was less careful.

"Hi, how are you?! I cannot believe the news! I heard that your husband is with so and so! Wow she is something; a real snake; capable of anything: he will be in for a rude awakening.... oh sorry you seem surprised...you didn't know? Wow I really put my foot in my mouth."

I quickly ushered the children away to the taxi stand. I had to get out of there.

My pain was immense. I couldn't breathe, I was overtaken by the pain of the betrayal. I felt lonely, abandoned and a huge pang of sadness overwhelmed me like a wave. I fought to hold back the tears and called my husband who was in Hong Kong at the time, praying that he would tell me that this was not true. It was so ugly and lowly and cliché. This only happened to other people. I was actually being left for another woman. How ordinary. Of course, he did not answer the phone and left me to deal with my immense hurt and frustration.

And then you find out all the sordid details. How they were taking the same flight to Israel. How her husband had left her 10 years earlier, and she was desperate to meet a man. How they flirted on that plane ride. Exchanged numbers. How once she was settled in a friend's apartment in Israel, she showed up at his hotel and told him she had nowhere to go; her friend had argued with her and she was kicked out. I want to throw up. Ten years later it still kind of makes me grimace with distaste. The word "gross" just comes to my mind.

It is the well-known story of flattering the man to get to him.

"What?? Your wife cares more about her career than you? If I had a man like you all I would do is take care of him. He would be my first priority, etc, etc.

Because my ex-husband is a narcissist, this talk went straight to his head and heart. As an added benefit, she was in real estate and he was looking for a new field to jump into. Years later, after he opened a real estate business in Israel, he told my daughters he wanted to leave her. He confided, as part of his reasoning "she hasn't even sold one apartment!". Practical guy.

He did not do the typical-leave-your-wife-for-a-younger-woman-thing because that comes with certain obligations. If you leave your wife for a younger woman, it goes without saying that you will have to spend a lot of money. You will have to cater to her rather than have her cater to you. Not all men are up to that. Especially not a self-loving, calculating man. This woman was perfect for him. An ego soother that would not be demanding and that would focus on him.

The ugly painful truth was out. When he came back from Hong Kong, I confronted him. To my horror he did not deny it. She is a companion, he replied. No big deal.

The words hurt. Not because I loved this man, but because of the abandonment. Perhaps the ego too. That is what it usually is. After all, like I said, how and why would anyone love a man that does not love you back?

We were leaving in a few days. I had to do something to vent my feelings. Bianca and I did a Google search and found out where "the other horrible woman" worked. A few days later we were in the car with my daughters and found ourselves in St. Germain. It is a big regret of my life that I was blinded by my tears and the craziness of those past few days and that what I did next was in the presence of my children. I parked the car, sent one of my daughters to buy eggs in a nearby restaurant. Then, from the car, they saw me walk into the real estate office in a beautiful stone building with glass walls.

I asked for her by name. The woman behind the desk answered with a smile that it was her. Bianca looked on incredulously with my daughters and she best described the scene.

"There you were with your 1950's style Prada pale grey cotton dress with the full skirt and peach cardigan, your retro bag held in the crook of your left arm, looking like you were going to a ribbon-cutting event. Then you threw an egg at her with your left arm as if you were throwing rice or flowers at a ceremony."

I missed her. I was always the worst in gym class at aiming anything. I left her and the whole agency flabbergasted. I told her whom I was and told the agency they should be ashamed to be hiring an immoral woman. To go with the 1950's dress. We drove off in the car. Laughing and crying. My ex husband-to-be found the whole thing amusing. There is nothing quite as potent as the ego of a man.

Years later I was watching for the umpteenth time one of France's cult movies, "La Boum", starring the legendary Sophie Marceau as a teenager. I had forgotten the scene where her mother, played by Brigitte Fossey, erupts into the perfume store of the mistress. She breaks every single glass shelf and perfume bottle in sight. She looked so fashionable with her long hair and slim silhouette buttoned up in a typical French sand coloured raincoat. The classic lines of her smart and strict raincoat contrasted with her loose curls and her wild gestures. Smart to wear a raincoat when smashing all those perfume bottles, I thought. I always liked Brigitte Fossey.

The next day the movers came and three days later we were on the plane to Montreal.

CHAPTER 5

THE BOOMERANG
IMMIGRATION

My migrations so far had ensued in the following way : Casablanca, Montreal, Paris, Montreal. Would I one day end up in Casablanca ? We eventually go back to where we come from one way or another.

Je reviendrai à Montréal
By Robert Charlebois
Je reviendrai à Montréal
Dans un grand Bœing bleu de mer
J'ai besoin de revoir l'hiver
Et ses aurores boréales

J'ai besoin de cette lumière
Descendue droit du Labrador
Et qui fait neiger sur l'hiver
Des roses bleues, des roses d'or

I will return to Montreal
By Robert Charlebois
(I will return to Montreal
In a big blue Boeing
I need to see the winter again
And its aurora borealis

I need this light
Coming straight down from the Labrador
And which makes the snow in the winter go from
Blue pinks, pink golds.)

Here I was back in Montreal. I had missed my city all these years away. My therapist had assured me that leaving behind the city of the Break Up would make things easier. Most women stay in the same environment and then the man they shared a life with comes and takes away the children every two weekends or as he pleases. This seemed even more heartbreaking. I was avoiding a big part of the pain, but there was still so much left. I was on my own and needed to organize a whole new life for us. The momentum of constant movement dulled some of the pain. I had so much to do. If one must rebuild a new life, I had reasoned, better to do it in a new environment.

Montreal had not changed much. If anything, it had lost the glamour and aura of the eighties. The separation that French Canadians had clamored for so ardently had benefitted Toronto: all the businesses that did not want to deal with the complications of using two languages had moved to Toronto.

Over the years I had often come on vacation, but living everyday life was an entirely new perspective.

To my surprise, the rift between the English and French-speaking still existed. And many of the French from Quebec felt no affinity with the rest of the English-speaking country and still spoke of separation. Which had stalled the country. If you are living with your boyfriend but are talking about moving out every day, how can you go ahead and make a life together? You can't: everything just stays frozen in time. Even if the separation was not obtained, living in a city with an eventual separation looming over was an ambiguous situation few wanted to cope with. To divorce or not it seemed to say.

The Frog song
By Robert Charlebois
Ton beurre est dur pis tes toast sont brûlés
Ton lait est sûr, ton jaune d'oeuf est crevé
T'as pus d'eau chaude pour te faire un café instantané
Sept heures et quart, t'embarques dans l'autobus

Ton sightseeing tour pour aller travailler
Un beau voyage en groupe organise comme toué matins,
You're a frog I'm a frog, kiss me,
And I'll turn into a prince suddenly

The Frog song
By Robert Charlebois
(Your butter is hard and your toast is burned
Your milk is sour and your egg yolk is flat
You have no more hot water to make yourself a coffee, instant
A quarter past seven gets you on the bus
Your sightseeing tour on your way to work
A nice trip in an organized group, like every morning
You're a frog I'm a frog Kiss me,
And I'll turn into a prince suddenly)

The Religious Divorce

The civil divorce had been taken care of but since we had married in a synagogue, we also needed to formalize the religious divorce. All my friends assured me that the religious divorce, called Get in Hebrew, would greatly benefit me.

"As soon as you receive the 'Get' you will feel light".

"You will feel as if a big weight has been taken off your shoulders".

"That is when your new life will begin. Until then you are stuck".

I called the religious institution of the Vada Ir and made an appointment.

Usually when the husband and wife are in the same country they meet at the local Vada Ir and there is a heart wrenching ceremony. The woman must hold her hands open like the recipient she is (sigh, in soo many ways) and then the soon to be ex-husband (disdainfully?) lets this paper drop into her cupped palms. The text states, "You are hereby permitted to all men", which means that the woman is no longer married and that the laws of adultery no longer apply if she engages in another relationship.

I was once again saved by the distance I had put between us.

I showed up at the Vada Ir and stood alone before a council of 6 men. There were many deliberations over the exact spelling of my name and if I had a nickname. They kindly explained that to divorce the "right people" they must inscribe our names correctly in this 12-line document, written by hand by a professionally trained scribe under the proper supervision of a Bet Din, or Rabbinic Court, and signed by two witnesses.

Because my ex husband-to-be was not present to hand it over to me, the Rabbis indicated a man in a beard and said that we would stand in as my husband. I would walk towards him, open my hands but not push them towards him and wait till he dropped the paper into my hands. Then the divorce would be declared. 800 $ later, I was free.

It has been done this way for over 5000 years. I did not question or discuss the formalities, even if I did find the whole process quite surprising. I tried to feel all the things my friends had assured me I would feel. I didn't.

The Professionals

Like the bellboy said at an Israeli hotel we once stayed in, when he arrived to pick up our 5 pieces of luggage with a tiny carriage," This is what we have and with this, we will win....".

So, what I had was a divorce, a lump sum and a lump in

my throat but most importantly a new life to build with my daughters.

What did I do? Rally up around me all the possible professionals and experts the modern world had to offer, of course: rabbi, psychologist, healer and fortune teller for the spiritual and real estate professionals, mortgage broker and headhunter for the material. And then top that off with a matchmaker for everything in between.

These professionals are not miracle workers but running from one to the next kept me in a whirlwind of activity. This activity allowed me to think less. And each upcoming appointment held the promise, at least beforehand, that the answer would be found and my pain relieved.

But there was no magic potion. Time had to be gotten through. I remembered a very wise but temperamental French doctor I had called over to my apartment one sad Sunday when the nervous palpitations were too strong to bear. This was just before leaving Paris. I had never met this doctor previously. I had called SOS Doctors, a doctor dispatch service, which is kind of a lottery service because you never know who you will land on.

Bianca was often at the house during those difficult times and she had opened the door and brought him down the very long hall to my bedroom. I asked if he had any miracle antidepressants that could work or a quick and efficient therapist "But Madame, I am not a waiter in a restaurant that you can impatiently ask to bring your order! You cannot simply order me to make you feel no pain!" he said, looking at me aghast and irritated. He was right.

It was a rainy Sunday and thankfully Bianca and her boyfriend Anthony had come to spend the day so that my children and I would not be left alone with our fear and feelings of abandonment. Me especially. Anthony had walked him to the door slightly bemused and greatly admiring the man.

"Wow, pas mal (not bad) this guy is brilliant! He is right! you think you can just find a professional to order your pain away!".

And that is the hunt I went on. One therapist after another, one self-help book after another, one method after another. I compared notes with my other divorced friends.

"Did you read the book by Louise Bourbeau? We each have one of five wounds, totally based on our body type. The wound we have is the one we were put on earth to face and conquer. My wound is abandonment...see my hips? That is clearly my wound. THAT is why I had to be abandoned in this life. To deal with it and overcome it. Just having a hard time understanding the last chapter about how to overcome it!!.....Hmm? Your tummy represents the wound of humiliation? Indeed, your ex was humiliating! It all fits!".

One had to make sense of this great break in our lives and while we made sense, they all made cash. Like one of my best friends, Bianca had wryly remarked at the time "all your miracle advisors/wedding counselors are spreading the word :Fresh new divorce in the 17th arrondissment. Cash to be made."

It is a whole economy that lives and thrives off of a divorce. There are rabbis that promise to pray for your husband to come back. Spiritual healers that hurl at you that your marriage was a lie and lies do not survive in the twentieth century. Therapists that relate your divorce to a growth experience. And some specialists that swear by black magic.

And then on the practical side, there are lawyers with their well-oiled conveyor belt...come this way dear, first meeting, second meeting, three calls, all good, next date, first contract, agreement, all done, out this way, good luck, goodbye, here is your invoice wham bam thank, you ma'am. One home becomes two so real estate agents and brokers have their fair share.

And if you don't want to go crazy the best option is to cling on to a trainer, a sport, a gym and because you are back on the market, make sure the Botox budget is consequential. Not to mention restaurants, bars, etc..... what would the economy be like without divorce?

Once I had gone through the therapist for my mind, the lawyer for the divorce contract, the real estate agent for a home and the headhunter to help find me a job, I proceeded to contact the next professional: the matchmaker. All this with the goal of survival.

I Will Survive
by Gloria Gaynor
At first I was afraid, I was petrified
Kept thinking I could never live without you by my side
But then I spent so many nights thinking how you did me wrong
And I grew strong, and I learned how to get along
And so you're back, from outer space
I just walked in to find you here with that sad look upon your face

PLAY

Matchmaker, Matchmaker Find Me A Catch

When you marry you become a couple and not an entity all by yourself. Then you divorce and suddenly you are no longer a part of a whole. You must be a whole all by yourself. The void must be filled. So, you try to date.

Like the French expression says if you want to get rid of a nail, hammer another one on top. "Un clou chasse un autre."

I was not a believer of the theory, "it's too early to meet someone." Why wait? To purge myself? One of the fashion district sisters had told my friend Bianca, "it is too early for her to meet someone else" but I remember that she had been plotting in the dressing rooms of Prada on how to throw the net over her second husband to be. It is reprehensible when women do not recognize their weaknesses and lack female solidarity.

It seemed to me that to quickly forget my ex, the best solution was to occupy my mind, heart and time with another man. I was in a flurry of activity already, so it was just another note to add to my agenda: find the right matchmaker.

But soon I had to face the truth.

Another recession was hurting divorced women even more than the economic recession (which had already diminished our net a porter.com budget) and threatened to be a menace to our womanhood (nearly as much as a diminishing wardrobe budget). Like other women, I had to face this harsh reality.

The male recession.

I was faced with the reality that singledom is a man's market!

Whether in movies, TV series or books we all see the reflection of today's recession. Bridget Jones was our first heroine who bravely resounded the grave news that men were a scarcity. Men of all ages, shapes and sizes. And not just the first time around. After a divorce too!

The TV series "Sex in The City" portrays four women chasing men in various ways and showing different degrees of desperation in this occupation. (Lucky them; no diminishing wardrobe budget). Remember Charlotte actually pondering to become ultra-orthodox when sleeping with a rabbi or poor Carrie chasing Mr. Big named as such because in a male recession-era like ours a man that can support a woman, especially in a place like New York, deserves no less than the title of Mr. Big.

Alaska is one of the very rare places where there are more single men than woman. I always hoped that somewhere in Alaska there was the equivalent Mrs Big to even things out. Alaskan bachelor's websites often portray bachelors posing on fur rugs in front of fireplaces in their beautiful and homey wood cabins so desperate are they to find single women to meet. Could this be a good TV series "Sex in the Juneau, Alaskan capital"? Just imagine portrayals of the trials and tribulations of four bachelor men in the very rare heterosexual men-majority capital. I remember reading an article where one thrilled, single woman who landed in Alaska had said with refreshing candour, "There are so many men here it is great. Back home I am a 6, here I am a 9 out of 10!!". The problem remains for those of us that do not wish to live or travel to Alaska.

In most places around the world, singledom seems to represent a majority of women. Montreal was no exception.

Now, if we look statistically there are as many women as men. So why did it seem to the naked eye that there were more single women than men out there.

I once went to a bar in New York, where I counted 23 women for 7 men. I was with my husband at the time and as soon as I got up to go to the washroom, two women pointed their index at him and tried to lure him over to their table. As if he was a little puppy that might run away and hide in his owner's legs. Here, here doggy. Being a bit (lot) of a macho man, he found this behavior distasteful.

"Elles sont folles ces americaines", he said to me when I came back and related the incident to me. (They are crazy these American women).

But then again, he had hated "Sex in the City" like the

Sephardic macho he was and was shocked when Samantha Jones called the doorman up to have sex with her. If it had been the other way around...

To get back to the problem at hand: once women are out of High school where did they meet men? Especially the second-time round after a divorce. Or the third...

Because besides the fact that they are a scarcity, there is the problem of quality. Especially in later years, the ones out there that are of interest to us are widowed or divorced. Divorced men are usually divided into two categories.

The ones that were nerdy growing up and couldn't get any girls in high school. Suddenly (partly because of the scarcity of men, partly because their average looks have given them a certain demeanor with age), they become successful in life (meaning make money) and thus popular with women. It all goes to their heads and they break up their marriage because all of a sudden, the world is their playground. Forget those men, they must be left to play.

Then you have the men that are truly the good fathers and want you to help babysit/cater to their children or grandchildren every Saturday night. Babysitting is 15 dollars an hour, so he may also be the unthinkable, unacceptable cheapskate.

What are we left with? Men that seem a lot like the ones that we or our friends divorced. Unfortunately, the men out there cannot compare with the quality of the women I see, for the most part.

Of course, that doesn't mean there aren't ANY wonderful men and men-for-the-future out there, but I am just saying there is a frightening proportion of men that aren't prizes. (Perhaps especially among divorced men?)

If we analyze the situation there are two problems.

Scarcity and Quality.

To each situation an expert.

Matchmakers for the male crisis.

Without a matchmaker, I would be leaving an encounter to chance. Especially since I was not in the sit pretty and wait mood. I was running around in circles to try to disregard that constant lump in my throat.

When I was married, I had urged my single friends to take the situation into their hands and reach out to websites and matchmakers in the quest for Mr Right. Now I had to practice what I had preached from atop my mountain of a married and established (lol) woman. Dating sites, I quickly saw would be too time-consuming and who had the time to sift endlessly? I needed that dress - oooh sorry- man *now!*

Matchmakers offered a real service. They sifted through the offer of men and would introduce me only to the ones that corresponded to my demand. Offer and demand. Like an economics course. No, I thought reasonably, one shouldn't go overboard with their demand. Like the women in the eighties who went to the hairdressers with thin, limp hair and showed a picture of Farah Fawcett declaring "this is what I want".

So I had evaluated that it was the safest way to meet someone. It was also the only way to meet someone outside of your circle of contacts. The agency knowingly insisted on this point in their favor with good salesmanship, just before making me sign on the dotted line of their contract and hand over the check.

One matchmaker explained this to me from her desk, in front of bay windows overlooking our city from the 22nd floor of one of Montreal's high rises. I felt like I was in investment banking office so the conversation we were having seemed surreal.

"You are right here, with your network around you." She

drew me in the middle of a circle, "and he is here", another circle on the other side of the page. How else do you meet?

Hmm, indeed I nodded. But still my practical side won over and I proceeded to negotiate the hefty sum she was asking for. Yes, a man would be nice, but not at ANY price. Ah, the cynicism of divorced women. She excused herself to run to another office and asked her "boss for permission to lower the price". I felt more and more like I was at the bank. The negotiating tactics confirmed that dating was based on offer and demand just like all goods or services on the market. She returned shortly to inform me that I was lucky they were in an exceptional slump period and didn't have many female candidates. My offer was accepted and we had a deal.

My criteria was established with an objective and realistic manner. The agency must tick off all the boxes of my criteria before introducing me to someone. Sometimes one unchecked box could be a deal-breaker. And like at the restaurant one must place an order in a very precise and concise manner.

It happened to me. It was an ironically funny situation when I forgot to tick off a box.

I found myself on a Monday morning, on the way to the office, calling the agency from my car and hearing myself say, "Yes, I had coffee with him, but I had specifically asked for a Jewish man I am sure." Otherwise, my life would just get too complicated.

The agency replied, "No, you said you had a PREFERENCE, not that it was a deal- breaker." Oh yes, I vaguely remember that after the disappointment of my divorce I had rebelliously thought, what difference whether he is Jewish or not!

Another time yet, "you told me he was an 8, he was a 6!" Or "he says he is 59 but looks more like 73." To which the agency, who always covered their bases, would answer cautiously, "well, that is in the realm of the subjective....".

Usually agencies reflect the "market" and there are many women and not enough men in agencies. Single men are not as adventurous and outgoing as single women. Just glance around at the tables in restaurants. You will often find tables of 3 to 4 women, but fewer tables made up exclusively of men.

Matchmakers know where and how to sniff them out. Often the men that are signed up in agencies did not go willingly sign up and pay their subscriptions as the women have. They were approached in an airport, a parking lot or at the local supermarket. Or forced to go by a family member.

I remember an anecdote one of my father's friends had shared, that reinforced my theory of the scarcity of men of all ages. He was in his early seventies at the time and innocently walking down a street in sunny LA. A woman in a limo thrust her business card at him, "Are you single? Please call me, I have a deal for you." This retired and slightly bored man called and soon after found himself sitting in the luxurious Los Angeles office of a highflying corporate woman.

"You see I have a dating agency here and I have many older women signed up, looking for companions but not enough men. You don't have to pay the entry fee and I will set you up on dates."

There is nothing dishonest about this; this professional just had to find the offer to meet the agency's demand. After all, there was nothing wrong with this bachelor; he just wouldn't have taken the initiative to sign up (and pay, let's be honest) like most men. Men of today are less inclined to be outgoing, so she went out of her way to fish him for her clientele.

My father's friend ended up accepting the deal until his first date ordered 4 glasses of champagne and he realized that even with a free subscription it wasn't worth it.

My first date ended up being reeled into the agency in a similar fashion. The agency I had called came to my home to interview me. She was assured by my career that I was not looking for a man that would be a source of steady income.

"No, that I do not do", she said with the quiet, firm manner that is so fitting for a matchmaker. "I only work for women who work. Men do not sign up to support someone." Oh, the cynicism of divorced men. "But you have a career, so it is all good. I will find you someone."

I found out later that she had no one (in stock) so she called THE most renown bachelor of the city. "David, PLEEEASE do me a favor …take out one of my clients….". Hmmm.

And we did end up dating for quite a while.

Bachelor Number 1

David White should have been patented. Even he admitted it. He was the type of pleasant bachelor that woos and seduces you and that you need when you come out of a divorce. He had been divorced for nearly 20 years, so he was good at the game. Nearly too good.

"I was never told you were drop-dead gorgeous".

"If this is the way you look in the morning, I need to make this for life".

These were some of the generous lines he had uplifted many a divorcee with.

I started dating again. The sudden freedom of being on my own again and reliving the dating of my much younger years was very enjoyable.

After 20 or more odd years of married life, you find yourself on a couch next to a grown-up man who has some glimmer left in his eyes from teenage days and you wonder how he will make the first move. You observe the scene as if you were looking at it from the outside, because you still have not fully registered that this is you on a *date* ? You observe him make the same moves, he could have made lunar years ago. You smile inwardly as he puts his arm on the couch behind you. The chit chat is there still although it is slowly tapering down it is no longer the real focus here anymore. Then he takes off his glasses with a "casual" gesture. Aaah, he is turning his head towards you. For a second you are thrown off by the situation and you must adjust (also to the fact that he looks very different without his glasses). You are still bemused that is you on the couch in this relative stranger's house. It is all so weird and surrealist, yet it is all vaguely familiar at the same time. It is so crazy because just yesterday the couch was a place your husband occupied while he watched the soccer game and you ran around the house and now a couch holds a different purpose...

You hesitate, exactly as you would have lunar ages ago. Then you just.... let loose. More so than x years ago because now there is no "reputation' to preserve and no "worries about the future" and how your life will roll out.

Crazy. Divorce is not ALL bad. But it is not simple, and neither is dating all over again...

I still had a lot of ill feelings towards my ex-husband. And way too often I still found myself so frustrated by the divorce, that I would share my resentment with David. That is why what happened was no doubt my fault too. He was an incurable bachelor and when he pocket-dialed me while wooing another woman, I thanked serendipity and realized that he had served his purpose. This type of situation is always painful (our poor egos), but I was relieved. I had known he was not exactly the type of man I wanted or needed, but at the same time who was I to ask for perfection? The universe took care of things for me. I mean, how crazy is that? A man who pocket dials you at exactly the right moment? When a relationship is meant to end, it does. Exit bachelor number 1.

After a divorce one heals a lot more quickly. And life becomes a study for which we find reasons for everything. He had been there for me during my divorce. That was perhaps the "raison d'etre" for this wizened bachelor and now he had to continue serving his purpose because there were a lot of other newly divorced women that he could woo, date and help free their minds of recent divorces.

WORK

The Web Window

May I point out that my new life was not solely about men. I was also juggling the move into our new home, new schools (soon to be discussed) and a career. All this was a lot to handle at the same time, although being busy again saved me from thinking too much. The very day that our container of furniture and other belongings was scheduled to arrive, I had a job interview. I was thankful again for my extended family. One of my uncles married a wonderful down to earth French Canadian, the only sign of our assimilation to this wonderful country and she was the perfect relative to have in moments like this. This nonsensical, extremely practical and organized woman (she has worked in banking all her life to prove it) came to my house early and shooed me off to my job interview. She directed the movers with my daughters and started unpacking all my belongings.

"You took everything but the kitchen sink! No, I do not feel sorry for you one bit". This did make me feel good. And off I was to that job interview.

I had to adapt from being married to being single and I also had to adapt in my communications and branding job from traditional to virtual media.

I realize now that the best way to cope with the major change that ensues when one moves from a big city like Paris, to a much smaller one, like Montreal is to go virtual. It was very fortunate that I moved back home at a time when the internet thrived and so I never felt confined to the smaller-in-comparison-to-Paris-city-of-Montreal. I had access to the window of the world through my mac. I could still shop my favorite designers, if I had the money which I didn't anymore, but that was beside the point. I could travel virtually to my favorite Parisian concept store Colette and even find inspiration at Chaumet of Place Vendome for my first web experience ; the rebranding of Ice and Diamond.com.

My first web experience was fraught with frustration and anxiety. My mother was willful and tenacious in exhorting big sums of money from businessmen for charity purposes. She was one of the best fundraisers in the city and one of her favorite donors was Judy Ginzburg.

Judy Ginzburg, was a religious woman who came from an established, Jewish orthodox family of Montreal and had, in a very adventurous way married an immigrant rather than the son of another established family. Among Ashkenazi families it was good form to marry a Steinberg. The family was known for the huge grocery chain that existed before thoughts of separation appeared in Quebec and brought us IGA, while the Steinberg family fled to Toronto. That is what one of my friend's mother said to her when she married a Sephardic: "why couldn't you just marry a Steinberg?".

Judy and her husband started out with a lot of love and modest means. Happenstance and her sense of adventure brought her to explore goods from Asia and import a few pearl necklaces at a time that she sold to her friends. I will skip the details, but the American dream occurred and twenty years later she was at the head of a jewelry business that sold to the big North American chain stores. Her husband, children and grandchildren worked with her.

The family men would meet in the conference room for business meetings, but more importantly to pray and discuss Torah every day. In her office were pictures of the whole beautiful family. They were all lined up in neat rows by category. All the daughters and daughter in-laws in one row would be wearing the same pink v neck, all the sons the same white shirt, kippah and long beards, all the granddaughters in pink and grandsons in blue. Judy and her husband rightfully throned in the middle. It was all so neat and tidy I never tired of gazing at this order while I waited for her in her office.

This religious woman reminded me of that joke on Bill and Hilary Clinton.

Bill and Hilary are at a gas station in their hometown. Hilary says, "oh I remember that man pumping gas, I think he was my first boyfriend". Bill scoffs, "well if you had married him, today you would be married to a gas station employee instead of the President of the United States."

"Oh no", she matter of factly replies "today, that man would have been president of the USA."

Any man Judy would have married would be fortunate to be at the head of the beautiful family, business and life she had built with her soft, gracious and well-mannered ways.

Judy was extremely generous with those that were less fortunate. Besides selling to chains across North America, the business also ran a wholesale jewelry store in the same building as our headquarters. The older salesladies would shuffle over to her in slippers (who could see slippers behind the jewelry counters? our gracious and indulging boss reasoned) and would say, "Another rabbi is asking me for an exceptional discount to give his wife a gift for the holidays! I really think he is exaggerating". The saleswomen were always protecting Judy's interests.

"Give it to him," Judy would gesture helplessly "It's the holiday". There was always a Jewish holiday around the corner.

As down to earth as she could be with the less fortunate, if a customer asked for her advice on the purchase of jewelry she would simply yet eloquently reply.

"The bigger the better".

She hired me to help her with branding. After a few months of working with her, I confided that although she was very pleasant the environment was not challenging enough for me and I had another proposal. I was a one-woman marketing team and had no team to brainstorm or interact with. She calmly replied,

"Yes, I thought of that. I think you will be happier at my son's company, Ice and Diamond.com".

I changed floors in the same building and discovered a real startup. The vibe I discovered in awe was "we are web, we are cool, we get together to eat freshly delivered bagels and brainstorm in our cool kitchen, every morning".

I forsaked on bagels remembering that one bagel is four slices of bread and if you start with this habit on Day One you are hooked forever after. But I had another problem.

I had been a PC user and now I not only had to learn Mac,

but all about banner ads and web content and social media. In Paris, I had overseen a web division, but it was a small addition to my main responsibilities.

"Eh Valerie tu peux t'occuper du web?" had added Jean, Max A.'s best friend in charge of the Paris head office and the European division of BCBG, Manoukian and Hervé Leger. He added it as an afterthought which was exactly what it was in the fashion business of the early 2000s. "Je te mets en charge d'Etienne et Stephanie, deux petits jeunes très sympa, qui s'occupent du web." Sure, with pleasure. Whatever images we ran in brick and mortar we transferred to the web and they adapted.

In Montreal, at this company the experience was 100 % virtual. The transition did not come without pain. After all I was in my mid 40's when I landed into the virtual and I was not born with a computer. Like my university friend who became television fashion critic, Steven Cojucaru wisely once said, "our generation is devoid of interest…before us they had the excitement of Woodstock and social revolution, after us, they are born with computers as natural to them as extensions of their minds and we have what exactly?". Hmmm. Steven always had a great grip on how to sum things up with candour and a piercingly clear analytical mind.

The exact term of what we were I discovered in Joel Mitch's book "Control, Alt, Delete" many years later. I was a digital immigrant. But when immigrants take stock of their setbacks and weaknesses and face them with will, perseverance and more hard work they can sometimes go farther or as far as natives. Or at least it is encouraging to think so.

You know the story of the little choo choo train that can. Well that type of inspiration was given to me one day by a colleague Leila, who saw my frustration and said to me these simple words "You can do it. The girl before you was not a rocket scientist, no one here is, so if they can do it, YOU CAN DO IT." The power that thought gave me was similar to that of clicking the "on" button. I realized indeed that it all was in the realm of the possible and it was thanks to her that this whole world opened up. The power of women. The power woman can give each other when not competing. After Paris and the crazy competition among women, the kindness, concern, care, authenticity and generosity of this young woman, was a welcome boost. She represented the good side of Montreal: the clean ethics and "roll up our sleeves and help each other spirit." It is more difficult to find this culture in big cities filled with people trying to make elbow room for themselves at the table in the conference room.

So even if I felt a little in nowhere land after Paris (sorry Montrealer's) I was part of the web world and that is not measured by where you are geographically located. It is measured in terms of followers, data and dollars used.

After the uncontrollable turn that my life had taken with the divorce, the web offered Control. Because with access to Photoshop, a Wi-Fi connection and a web address anything is possible. You can create whatever your heart desires and the sky is not the limit. You are not tied down by budget constraints or held back by external factors and you do not have to adjust to the schedule of other people like the workmen in brick and mortar stores. You have total control of the outcome. You can be in bed, watching Mad Men and create the next store window or home page with nothing physical to manage. Create an ultra chic no expenses spared environment with red carpet, gold dust and crystal chandeliers and project it on the screen. Just press the publish button.

Power, control and freedom (hmmm I feel like adding pink

flamingos or a silver moon right there) was given to me through the web. Everything my divorce took away from me the web gave back.

Ice.com And Diamond.com

All of a sudden creativity was escaping from my pores. I started as an assistant to the Creative Director. The Creative Director was Brandon Green. He didn't have a chance. He didn't even follow the international rule that any self-respecting Creative Director *must adhere to:* wear a black turtleneck. He wore short sleeved plaid shirts and chewed gum, very emphatically. He was a pro technically, but we were selling jewelry and we were not making our consumers dream with our daily 30% discounts. I happily zoned in on this and started proposing ways to bring our jewelry in contact with the world of fashion and luxury.

Soon the new CEO came on board and I started pestering him to give me more responsibilities, each time following the precepts of "The Secret" and envisioning myself leaving his office with promises of promotion obtained from him. It worked. He gave me my first assignment. Later he admitted he had assigned it to me simply as a way to be rid of me. He hadn't taken me seriously and the only observation he had imparted me with was "you looked very different from everyone else here". It was not meant to be positive or negative; a simple statement. No wonder I looked different ; I was still wearing my favored "confidential" brands like Marni with oversized necklaces, loud prints, pink jeweled collars and woollen bloomers in an environment where most people were wearing gray sweatshirts and carried lululemon lunch bags. I always dressed for myself, oblivious of my environment. Nevertheless, he liked the assignment I brought back on how I would build the personality of Diamond. Com. Who was Diamond? what was the personality of the brand ? Who was the aspirational muse of the brand? By what dog/architecture/car/fruit could it be best represented?

Soon Diamond.com was defined by a strong image and doing better than Ice, so I was given the care of Ice. Brandon was lightened of his job as Creative Director and it was offered to me. I did feel a twinge of guilt but a very small twinge because that is the corporate world. And happily, I later heard that Brandon found a job as a Creative for a big dog food group that was more brand coherent with short sleeve plaid shirts. I know, sometimes I am not nice.

Diamond.com became a brand for the sophisticated, successful woman that was perhaps lonely at the top, or even if she had someone in her life, she still earned enough money to pamper herself. My muse was the appliance heiress that used to shop at Prada. I remembered that once she had proudly showed off to Bianca a huge cocktail ring she had bought for herself. She had taken the pains to get it engraved for herself with the simple yet so eloquent text, "From me to me". This was my muse: a self-indulgent woman fascinated by luxury and status. The jewelery was photographed in still life environments composed of fruits, flowers, minks, branches and macarons. I was oblivious to the marketing's team's information that one customer had emailed "wow, those are really cute pink hamburgers" about my macarons. I waved it away, "they will learn". Recently I saw macarons in the advertisement at the Scotia bank and chuckled.

I went to buy fruit for my shoots with great care. And laughed when I thought of how my over demanding husband would criticize the fruit I hurriedly bought.

"You don't buy fruit with Love. I love fruit and you don't know how to pick the right fruit because you aren't doing it with love." I had found his tedious demands so exasperating. What a high maintenance man, I would think to myself.

No, I retorted in my mind. Because I wasn't buying the fruit for a photoshoot. This thought struck me one day when the fruit vendor eyed me suspiciously because I was looking at a pear from all angles for a photoshoot. Wrong casting, I thought. It was just the wrong casting.

When I was finally given Ice.com, the muse was a younger woman with a sense of humor who bought jewelry because she loved it, was attracted to it but took herself less seriously. She loved everything that glittered and winked at her. Here the jewelry was exposed on ice cubes, lipstick, Lego, society games and anything from coke bottles to colorful straws.

They were no longer taking the usual stock photo of a woman holding a phone and photoshopping in a ring from Brandon's days.

Marketing Versus Creative Feud

Needless to say, I also lived the usual corporate struggles that keep you on your toes, even in Canada, the country of friendliness, respect and the politically correct. France had been very far from the politically correct: when I lived there, they still named a certain chocolate pastry "têtes de nègres"!

My predecessor had been dictated to by the marketing team. He had executed their visions. They had gotten used to this relationship and enjoyed it. At the start of my mandate, I determined that all creative assets should come from my team based on the brief coming from marketing. We would provide several options and then they could select from our generous selection. The first mission had come: Mother's Day. I went into the meeting with my team. Thankfully now at the head of my team was Leila my savior. We showed our idea. Jewelry with speech bubbles, Lichtenstein style, thanking Moms. The team was aghast. You could have heard a pin drop. How dare we come with ideas and reverse the power balance. Finally, a young man named David (many Davids in my life then) stood out from the pack.

"I like it. The jewelry is talking".

The others argued, "How could you have started without waiting for our brief?".

What brief? You have to explain to me that it's Mother's Day and so you want it to be sweet and tender and corny? I need a brief for that, I thought?

Nevertheless, I won that battle, but there were many more to come.

Sometimes marketing would try to say we were late, and Leila and I would walk in fully prepared to defend ourselves. Scalpel? Knife? I would say as if we were walking into an operating room. Marketing Emergencies.

My cult movie 99 francs depicts this feud between marketing and creative. It is the story of a Creative Director and an Art Director that brainstorm, smoke an occasional joint and are thoroughly fed up with marketers trying to be creatives. One of my favorite scenes is the one where the CEO of a huge yogurt company plays at being creative.

"So, yesterday I was at my granddaughter's dance recital and I thought lightness, grace, elegance. All of this is in a yogurt. Let's have ballet dancers in our ads!".

The creative director ends up so frustrated that he films an anti- consumerism activist film instead of an ad on yogurts and broadcasts this instead. It is an extreme representation of the feud between the departments.

When a team member from Marketing would try to impose their ideas, I was not yet used to the "Canadian" way of doing things with calm, poise and a lot of political correctness. In France when the women wanted to compete or get the best of you, they did it even if it meant excluding you from lunch. It was manipulation and secrets. Just like the European history of kings and queens, one Human Resources director adroitly pointed out to me in Montreal. But in Montreal, it was done with such calm, quiet pose and political correctness that it seemed insidious to me and I needed to voice the issue.

"If you want to start imagining creative then you must be in the wrong field…why are you in marketing?" I would query.

This would send the poor marketer crying into the arms of the CEO, making me look very mean and brutal. I was just being a temperamental European to the others.

It was difficult to be a European creative against a Canadian marketer.

And predictably, the memorable Christmas (50% of yearly sales) battle came.

Christmas had to be planned and our team had come up with 5 beautiful ideas. At our presentation, I played my favorite Christmas song and handed out candy canes to get the marketers into the right spirit and then we proceeded to present.

All I want for Christmas is you
By Mariah Carey
I don't want a lot for Christmas
There's just one thing I need
I don't care about the presents
Underneath the Christmas tree
I just want you for my own

More than you could ever know
Make my wish come true...
All I want for Christmas is you

One of our proposed directions was banners in silent movie style stating, "All I want for Christmas" and then our jewelry intermittently flashing on the screen. It was later my huge regret that they did not pick this option because it was that Christmas that "L'Artiste" based on silent movies came out and was to win five Academy Awards. The main actor, to boot was Jean Dujardin my alter ego who had played the role of Creative Director in 99 francs. Serendipity has always been my favorite word, with reason.

We were all sitting in the conference room and at the head of the room throned our CMO via a screen since he was based in San Fransisco.

"Well," he addressed me with his habitual drawl, "interesting presentations but none of these really follow the marketing brief".

What bullshit those briefs I thought. I need someone to explain to me what Christmas is about? Yeah, I am Jewish but Jews have a special connection to Christmas. Maybe we yearn for it more than anyone. Wasn't it a Jew who wrote the best Christmas carols? I may be Jewish but if you look at how I decorate Christmas trees you would never know. Each year I have carefully planned a new theme. Chanel inspired with pearl strands, gold ornaments and black bows. Authentic Austrian with red and green wood ornaments. Ice castle with crystalized ornaments and oh so many glorious lights. You name it, I had run the full gamut and even decorated coffee tables with acorns and holly branches. My early days under French colonialism had taught me the magic of Christmas. Even when we moved to

Montreal, there was always an uncle willing to dress up as Santa. These conflicting influences had cost me some embarrassing episodes like when the rabbi's wife asked me on Facebook, after I had proudly posted my tree, "Is that tree in your house??". To which I had responded, "Well, actually it is a Hanukah bush".

"Really?" I answered the CMO, "Didn't the brief state that it was about Christmas and we are supposed to pull all the right heart strings? All five proposals are very emotional. You have a Benetton direction with children of different nationalities offering jewelry, you have a Christmas morning still life direction with all the trimmings and you have here our favorite based on Silent movie nostalgia."

"Yeah but Nancy came up with an idea....". And he proceeded to explain his teacher's pet's (or CMO's pet's) idea about a woman sending a text message about a ring she wants. He was reducing Christmas to cold technology.

"We would like you to try this idea."

"Well", I drawled back "Today, I am inspired by Steve Jobs". He had just passed away. "Steve Jobs said, never do anything you don't want to do. I could get hit by a bus tomorrow and so on my last day on earth why would I do something I don't feel I should or want to do."

Everyone looked at me aghast. Of course, I had gone too far. Even I didn't know how I was going to get out of this. I did need the money and loved the job.

And then something incredible happened. Just before our CMO could react there was a loss of signal and the screen went blank. No more CMO. Everyone looked at me aghast. I could not resist.

"I swear, I didn't pull the plug. "I said with the sweetest fake look I could muster. I had mentally though.

The reunion disbanded. The tension broke and the CMO

probably had time to calm down because he called me on my desk phone and asked me to be reasonable. It was easier for us to make concessions without being in front of everyone. I had owned my diva moment, so I graciously executed their request. Weeks later he called me.

"You were right. It was a shitty idea. Back to the drawing board, please help me save Christmas in time."

I abstained from pointing out that the marking team members had nearly been the grinches that stole Christmas, even if that vision was furiously dancing in my head.

Like the Eagles said in my favorite documentary, sometimes when things happen you don't understand in the moment, but years later, you look back and you understand. Life is like a novel and it is only when you finish a chapter that you can look back and understand, if not everything at the very least, a few things. Thanks to my move to Montreal, I discovered the beauty of open horizons and the limitless creative power of the web.

CHILDREN

Schools + America = Cult(Ure) Shock

The after-divorce-dating and web-work were not the only new epiphanies in my life bringing with full force the realization of the many cultural differences I had to cope with.

The schools were a whole other ball game.

I looked on with amazement at the environing overzealousness in my youngest daughter's private grade school. When I dropped off my youngest at school everyone chirped "Have a Grrrreat day". In the school halls of Parisian schools, they could hardly muster up a "Bon Courage" which means I wish you a lot of courage to face the day.

All the little girls wore a lot of bright pink and leggings and t-shirts. One day my eldest daughter Raphaelle dropped off her little sister Lisa, wearing her Marni inspired egg-shaped grey flannel coat over a sweater, cardigan and pleated skirt. Lisa looked like a Bonpoint back to school window, although I had forsaken the beret deeming it too Parisian for Montreal. She noticed the carelessness with which the others were dressed that set off her sister's difference.

"Is today pajama day?" she asked a mother, worriedly, wondering if I had missed this information.

"No!", the mothers replied visibly offended. Just a few weeks after I had to succumb to Lisa's outrageous demands to add a screeching pink sweater to her wardrobe. After a shopping spree Lisa had with her father during one of his trips to visit the girls in Montreal, I had lost total control of the clothing situation. My elder daughters and I would look at Lisa wearing her miniature Mackage coat we deemed so vulgar for a child and her furry leopard printed chapka with great distaste and laugh at "that North American child from the suburbs". The Marni inspired coat soon went into hiding for the winter to my great dismay.

In France proper parents meeting consisted of at best of three or four of the most entrepreneurial, educated and articulate mothers standing in front of the school and looking vaguely bored while puffing away on their cigarettes and mildly remarking, "We really must fix that staircase ramp this year".

In Montreal though, the private Jewish school, I had enrolled my youngest in boasted 14 Parents Committees each with a different and enriching part of school life zealously organized by them.

At the beginning of the school year, all the parents would meet for a breakfast reunion and each head of committee would get up and encourage us with a speech to join their committee. The Lost and Found Committee greeted us with a song about how it made them so happy to help each little cap or sweatshirt find their proper owner. I looked on in shock and thought with nostalgia of those French existentialists of yesteryear schoolyards who had been so detached in comparison. They had great philosophy I thought. They knew that where children were considered their micromanagement was in vain.

Hot lunch, Parents day, Art night, Teachers Appreciation, Bazar, Fundraising, Lice check (this one I appreciated even if I never joined, after a few mishaps encountered in French schools) committees all encouraged you to join except for one... the pride and joy of the school, The Play. Here a mafia-like ring of mothers valiantly fought to stay among friends. High school friends. They did everything to keep you out with the most politically correct smile plastered on their face. When I expressed my interest to join, visions of High School Musical in my head and what a real American Play experience would be for my daughter, they wheedled and claimed, "but don't you work?"

The word work was always pronounced with the slightest disdain, so it was NEARLY imperceptible. In Paris, all the women had valued work. In a small town like Montreal where you could still feel a hint of the '50s, if you worked you had done something very wrong along the way. You just hadn't played your cards right in the game of life. You had not married a man who could support you. You were not a perfect Stepford wife. Some excuse could be made for professionals like doctors or lawyers.

"You know this play is extremely time-consuming..." they coyly added. I was back in the manipulative atmosphere of BCBG but now it was for a *school play*.

It was a cross between corporate struggles and being ostracized by the popular girls in high school.

I realized later that they had visions of the Prize for mothers getting involved...getting lead roles for their daughters...Yes, star ambitions were extremely potent in American schools. They only looked laid back with their informal attire of Lulu Lemon sports outfits, constantly lugging around the oversized Starbucks thermos. If you looked closely you could see that the gum- chewing was quite frenetic.

Candice Caron de la Carriere, the head of the play committee, back in Paris had also favored her friend's children. My eldest daughter was still saying three lines after 4 years of being enrolled in the school play. When I casually pointed this out to her, she had told me with disdain, "Would you like to PAY me for a role for your daughter", referring of course to the fact that I was Jewish Sephardic and therefore prone to displaying lavish spending and even bribing to obtain my means.

I had then retorted the worst insult you can give a French woman from noble descent. "Please do not be vulgar ". The exchange had been swift and to the point. The play had not been a yearlong production. Usually, our children would recite a few lines from Balzac or Moliere, and we were never involved. The only thing asked of us was to show up and clap. Which I did each year in the mostly French amphitheatre with mostly French, blonde children because the immigrant parents stayed away from Candice Caron de la Carriere and her imposing ancestry. A few years later she did what most very French people of noble ancestry end up doing; buying an authentic "mas" somewhere in the countryside, renovating it and raising her children on solid French ground.

In France, money had been considered distasteful and to exhibit it was extremely vulgar. In Montreal, I discovered on the first day of school a huge apple tree made of cut out Bristol board in the front hall, bereft of any apples. Soon apples appeared with names on them. I realized that even if we had paid full and hefty tuition, for my daughter to see her family's name on one of these tantalizing red paper apples, alongside her classmates, we had to donate to the school. Extra money. In France, the parent's economic sitaution would never be displayed in such a manner because being rich was nothing to brag about. It was better to be cultured and articulate and wear frayed shirts.

The overzealousness of American mothers who were involved in every nook and cranny of the school's existence made me nostalgic for the French mothers. In comparison, they now seemed to have been enlightened with a deep intuition that control over children is not really possible. Their philosophy on life and children was steeped in a certain debonair elegance that did not allow them all this frenetic dancing through hoops that probably led to the same result in the end, where the children were concerned. Parents were heard talking about their ascension to the board of directors as if it were a relentless pursuit, likened to job climbing in a corporation. "We have worked long and hard to get here. We started at the very bottom with Lice check."

In their involvement, especially the hiring and firing of new school principals, they were relentless in their search for perfection. Parents would nearly chant together that a member of academia must be fired because "Her way was not our way." I shuddered at the vaguely eerie resemblance with certain other organizations that also pretend to act and exclude for the good of all. It was unsettling to witness this will to control the school at all costs and to maintain a status quo. This will to direct had never been visible in lackadaisical European parents whose philosophy was that control was impossible so why bother.

I often wanted to tell these overly involved parents to grow up and go play in their own courtyard.

White Picket Fences Are Trampled Over

With everything going on in my life, I often felt like the heroine from the Netflix series "Weeds". The one that becomes a weed dealer to maintain her way of life in suburbia. Like her, I often felt very out of place as a divorcee in a small suburban town. I found myself in crazy situations to maintain the status quo. Like the time my friend recommended me a French-Canadian man to represent my Inukt line.

"This is what you need for our business to take off: a real French Canadian with ties to this city".

He took some samples for "promotional" purposes. A few days later he admitted he had given them away to some female stripper friends of his.

"You know you cannot rip off a divorced woman ", I scolded the French Canadian. "it will throw a curse on you. It's called Karma. How will you pay those samples now?"

Luckily, he must have had some sense of superstition or just ethics.

"I can fix your back porch for free. Get me new tiles and I will take care of it".

"Deal".

"I can also help you bring your stock to the flea markets across Quebec so you can sell it".

That is how I found myself atop a U-Haul going to meet my new partner and his girlfriend who were staying in a motel nearby for a plumbing job. By now I had found out they were both strippers. These are real Canadians I thought, as I picked them up at the motel, brought them to Tim Hortons and watched them light up their first Export A of the day. I felt so far from Paris. Even farther from Casablanca.

They helped me set up booths in little villages where we paid 25$ a day to rent a table and sell off my stock. I felt so bad for the stripper, imagining the tough life she must have had to land where she was, that I kept gifting her anything she tried on.

We greedily counted the cash that poured in and I gave him my promised cut. That was how I was going to pay for my five-star hotel that summer in Israel.

I invited another divorced girlfriend to come with me. My daughters came to visit their father, who by now had also moved back to his hometown and although they were supposed to stay with him, most nights they preferred squeezing in my small room.

The next mornings I was so grateful to lounge in the pool. Especially when I thought of all the U-hauls and resourcefulness I had used to make it to this hotel. On my dime, I thought proudly, without any husband in sight.

"I don't know how you girls can stay in this heat," a spoiled married woman we bumped into from Montreal saluted us as we happily lolled around the pool. "I cannot move from the air conditioning of the business lounge".

I had to hold my tongue back to not say:

"If you were divorced like us dear, you would be so grateful to still be hanging by a thread and be staying in a five-star hotel, never mind the extra business option."

With a smile of course. And a new porch to boot.

Little boxes
By Malvina Reynolds
Little boxes on the hillside,
Little boxes all the same,
And the people in the houses
All went to the university
Where they were put in boxes
And they came out all the same
And they all have pretty children
And the children go to school,

One summer, a few years later, I noticed that a few of the perfect white-picket-fence-families from my youngest daughter's private school were being infiltrated by the dirty divorce word. Many of the perfect white picket fence marriages started crumbling.

What struck me was that the families that were the subject of the rumours, always had the most beautiful gardens in front of their homes. The lawns were perfectly manicured as usual, but it seemed as if there was an overabundance of flowers and colors. Like a face with a screechingly bright lipstick that seems to be trying to persuade itself and others that everything is wonderful. Ironically it was the hottest summer since I had moved back, and it seemed as if the neighborhood team of gardeners worked tirelessly to stop the flowers from fawning and rotting. In vain.

The perfect god-fearing Jewish families let go of their façade.

It started with a Facebook post where the wife put a picture of a crashed into red Lamborghini…exactly like the immaculate red Lamborghini her husband drove but totaled and with the caption WATCH OUT.

I remembered their children from our first carpooling days.

They had been entitled and loved to boast about how big their homes were.

"Lisa's room is smaller than mine." Would comment smugly the five-year-old.

And I would compete with the five-year-old and retort with all my maturity and the wounded pride of a recent divorcee who wants to cling to the status quo:

"Yes, but Lisa has a country house", annexing my boyfriend's house as our own. One of the David's.

"Oh, but we have a HUGE country house". "Perhaps …but she has an apartment in Paris".

Looking fixedly at those cold stares even my ex-husband became my ally.

The children had indeed appeared so much colder than the French children who showed up with smocked dresses and bouquets.

At the first all pink bubblegum, loud music, beading, bowling, non-stop bouncy castle birthday party I tried to make Lisa feel comfortable and had approached those beady eyes. "Will you take Lisa by the hand?"

"No" the child had simply retorted. No further explanation. Take that.

My daughters, who had accompanied me to drop off Lisa at the first birthday party she was invited to had indignantly told me,

"Let's take Lisa and leave immediately".

"No. Veni, vidi, vici. This is what we have and here we will win. We cannot leave a bubble gum, bouncy castle birthday party defeated.

And long after that first birthday party, we had tried to adapt, and I had thought that this family was the perfect American family dream. Ironically their name in French meant

"The idiots". We joked about that after the birthday party that had left me cold as I stared into the cold eyes of an entitled North American child.

Now a few years later I realized it was a mirage. The mother was miserable, took a nerdy but nice married lawyer for a lover instead of her demanding Donald Trump- like husband, and moved into a white picket fence home with the lawyer a few convenient houses away from the lawyer's now divorced wife and children.

Oh, and that same week, one of the most religious, god-fearing successful men in our suburban heaven was caught cheating with his wife's friend.

A third one took off with his assistant of twenty years.

White picket fences trampled, crushed and defeated.

Recently my sweet seven-year-old niece came to visit. We asked our darling guest what she wanted to play with. Our beautiful real wood doll house, of course.

I heard her pairing figurines.

"...and she is married to him..."

The dream lives on.

A Log Of One Day Filled With Single Mom Responsibilities

Like all single mothers I did so much more than take care of the children, work and think of men. Some days I logged everything simply because I was so amazed at how I was constantly juggling (single) handedly all my responsibilities.

Work, appointments, hassles. And more hassles and endless details.

Buy ink, fix printer
Iga grocery store, make dinner, change lightbulbs
Negotiate and juggle bank account to get a deposit for plumber
Negotiate birthday party animator
Speak to ex-husband
Speak to 3 friends about latest boyfriend incident
Email therapist
Look at high schools

Generation And Cultural Differences

One of my friends suggested I write about the drastic change in my life, that I underwent by going from being married to single, and the funny experiences it had brought in its tow, such as dating through matchmakers and all the general craziness in my life. I had first balked with, "But think of my reputation… I would have to disclose all my intimate life and secrets …as you know I do have some in my life, even if in moderation Sex, Drugs and Rock and Roll".

"Who cares? In this age of terrorism where we could get wiped out any minute everything has changed. Who cares?".

Hmm. Yet when I turned on my favorite radio station, playing rock music of my teenage years, my daughters seemed uncomfortable. They would ask me to stop singing so loud on the treadmill and when I was in the car with my youngest daughter she would switch the music channel to a news station.

As if they sensed that Rock music was only the visible tip of the iceberg…that more was hidden. And they did not want to know. Where was the classic married Parisian mother? Who was this American that listened to this music?

Most of the issues we have with other people in our lives stem from cultural differences. Immigrants move from their country of origin, but still maintain the values from back home and then they find themselves confronted with children that have grown up in their country of adoption and thus espoused the values of the new environment. Clash of cultures. I had lived through this clash of cultures with my husband and now, because of all of the complicated back and forth in my life, I was going through a clash of cultures with my children.

I was born in Morocco to parents who had overprotected me. Then I had come to adopt Canadian values that push a woman to be independent and self-fulfilled. Not feeling quite capable of this, perhaps held back by my inherent culture, I had married a man who exemplified financial protection to the point of being overbearing and macho. We had raised our children in a very French catholic neighborhood where little girls wore col Claudine's and used the respectful "vous" for teachers and elders and went to a school where they were taught to value restrain and discretion. For Show and Tell in a French grade school, one of my daughters brought the book titled "The Secret", preaching positive thinking, that had been a great success in North America. The teacher promptly gave her a zero decrying it as an American sect.

And then we moved to Canada after an alienating marriage and intense divorce so quite naturally my yearning for freedom, expression, creativity and even North American rock and roll wildness sprouted forth from where it had been repressed. This was judged and confronted by my teenage daughters whom I love more than anyone. The move made our cultural differences and values all the more screeching with contrast.

My children were Europeans growing up in North America. This was the mirror opposite of my experience. I had been a North American adapting to Europe. That is how we came to become diametrical opposites.

Where they valued restraint, I valued unbridled expression. Where they valued reason, I valued desire. The issue of men was a very delicate one. Yes, in theory their mother had to start dating again. But in practice they wanted it to be done moderately and reasonably. I was never either of these. Now that I was back in America, I sometimes felt like I was the North American teenager with overly reasonable and cautious old-world European parents. All this was in the context of the divorce and the resulting hurt we were all feeling which made it all too intense. Even rereading this passage feels too intense and I feel my breath quickening at the tension this brought into our home. It is hard to be pulled in opposing directions of those you love most.

Thankfully, our love, unity and commonalities helped us reconcile our differences. We quickly forgave each other and wiped away the tears more often than not.

After one particularly intense fight and make peace session I remember wiping my tears as we all calmed down and having the presence of mind to point out to one of my daughters:

"I love how you accessorized those pants today". We all laughed. Humor is a big savior and a moment should never be lost to crack a joke. That and putting a grosgrain bow on everything is the legacy I aspire to leave my daughters. Probably the only bits of knowledge I can claim to pass on.

Showing A Glamorous Made In Canada Line

I was discovering the web, renewing with the North American culture, with the music of my roots and with Canada. I had come back home and found things had changed very little. The web was the greatest thing I had discovered, but my hometown was still not the big cosmopolitan city I had hoped it would develop into by now. Due to the separatist movement, Toronto had long ago beaten Montreal but still, could this sole factor account for the way the city seemed to have stayed at a standstill ? The mentality and evolution of the economy seemed to have not changed much.

And what about the Canadian identity in itself I pondered. Why is a Made in Paris or Italy blessed with a more "chic "connotation than a Made in Montreal? I had seen the underground truths of how some Parisian clothes were made and they were as far removed from Glamour as could be. It was all a question of branding and perception. I remembered my stint at the Canadian embassy and how obstinately they wanted to put the Canadian flag on pens and (ugh) ties. This country needed to be rebranded.

Some aspects of Canada rivaled with French beauty: the landscapes and the way extreme and beautiful change swept over them each season. How the vivid greens of summer became orange, fuchsia, purple and then a clean blank white slate would bring us back to the initial stark and empty canvas that was just as beautifully extreme.

I got a kick out of the extremes that inhabited this country. I would observe everyday occurrences like a teenager walking her dog in a light attire of shorts and tongs. Then I would imagine that in six months, at that same spot, the picture of this young woman walking her dog would be so different. She would be muffled in layers from head to toe and her revealing tongs would be replaced by the armor of snow boots. The landscape of greens, golds and bright colors would be replaced by a piles of shimmering ice-covered snow. The latent humidity and heat that surrounded this teenager would be replaced by harsh winds and extreme below zero temperatures. All this in the exact same spot. There was something crazy and near-magical about these extremes.

Having just come back from Paris, I was very inspired by Isabel Marant, the first fashion globetrotter. I loved the way she took inspiration from artisanal crafts and then modernized them with her urban ultra-cool flair. I imagined her in the mountains of Peru, discovering an old tribe of women producing time old jewelry worn by their ancestors. She would land in the midst of them and transform their beautiful but rural wares, in a flash, into items worthy of the coolest fashionistas.

"You see that bright red there you are weaving into the basket? Can we replace it with orange? The orange from Hermes…who has the Pantone color? Oh… they don't use Pantone?" slightly perplex but braving cultural frontiers.

Thus, came the idea to renew with the landscapes, history, culture and codes of Canada, while reinterpreting them fashionably, giving them a contemporary edge and exposing choice artists and artisans that were the New Canada.

I started my research and looked for artisans that were still creating original First Nations wares, but that were opened to reinterpreting them with me to add a fashionista flavor to them.

Hence the philosophy of Inukt was born. Introducing a Canadian inspired collection reinterpreted with an urban edge. Four basic rules were established.

1. Rigorously made in Canada.
2. Handcrafted, high-end standards.
3. Dedicated to giving back.
4. A line that is tied to the History of Canada with a silk bow (no, Grosgrain is much better).

My beautiful adventure started while still working at my

day job at Ice.com and Diamond.com. I hired a company to help build the website. I reached out to local Canadian artisans and designed products in line with my philosophy. Inukt would become the Ralph Lauren of Canada.

It was the time for my American (Canadian) dream. I would finally become very rich and self-sufficient and my divorce would be justified.

Beware Of Second Marriage Pendulum Swing

As I was elaborating this plan, I met husband number 2. He was everything my first husband was *not* and he was not anything that my first husband *was*. Thus, the attraction. He also fit very well into the new trend board of my aspirational life.

He was a third generation Ashkenazi Canadian where the ex had been Sephardic. He was an educated dentist, while the ex was too much in a rush to make money to linger long at school. He was intelligent and well informed where the ex had been bright but focused mostly on business. He had the calm poise of the son of a rich man who never worried about money while the ex had fought for money and usually entered a room with the pounding feet of a man who has no time to waste, because time is money. He had stopped practising dentistry to dabble in other things that were of interest to him while the ex would never put on hold a financially lucrative situation. He was extremely docile, quiet and gentlemanlike while the ex was extremely overbearing.

I realized later that this marriage could be qualified as a pendulum swing. Just the way a pendulum swings from one extreme to the next at the beginning of a movement and thus countries can swing from extreme right to left until the movement tapers down and they find themselves in the middle.

I was still swinging dizzily and thus landed in an extremely different marriage that seemed to be appealing...at the time.

Part of the appeal lay in the fact that in his family, the mother/women were the princesses whereas in my ex's family the father/man was the king. In a Sephardic upbringing, it is the man who must be greeted like a king, unlike the Ashkenazi culture where the women must be catered to, protected and admired.

Once a year Mike's family had a Family Day. His mother entertained the in-laws ONCE A YEAR. I had suffered nearly every Shabbat with my in-laws. At these occasions, the whole family was invited to the country house for the day. May I add the whole family consisted of Mike's father's only brother, his wife and their three children, respective spouses and grandchildren. In Sephardic families entertaining the whole family means an average of eight or nine aunts and uncles and a generous helping of cousins of all ages. At their family meetings, the hired help (usually a team of three locals) would put tables in place, then they would help Mike's mother and her daughters-in-law make a few salads and potatoes. Mike's father, assisted by his sons, would barbecue the meat. At Sephardic affairs the display of food and complicated time-consuming dishes was endless, and lunch would turn to happy hour and there were always more than a few that would linger for supper and stay late into the evening. I watched with wonder as Mike's sister in law sprinkled pita chips on a salad and said she loved cooking. In our family, a woman had to baste, marinate, chop, grill, boil and make pastries from scratch for this to qualify as cooking.

When Mike's mother took something out of the oven her husband scolded her that she would burn herself. While I looked on with amazement. She usually did burn herself, being unpracticed with the chore and then she would get more attention. I looked on with admiration, thinking of how my lineage was getting ripped off.

After lunch, the moment of Mike's father's speech would arrive. He would stand up, glass in hand, and thank his wife whom he would say had been pouring for weeks over recipe books (for a barbecue) and who had put together this wonderful event thanks to her energy, devotion and good taste.

This would never have existed with a Sephardic husband like mine. I was in awe. At barmitzvahs, it was the same thing. Ashkenazi men would thank their wives for choosing the tablecloths. If I had cooked from scratch for a whole batmitzvah assembly of 200 people, I would not have been thanked so profusely and my ex would never admire and respect me for spending his money! In the Moroccan community of Montreal, it was common for women to organize gatherings after their children's weddings for 100 to 200 people, to cook for weeks beforehand and yet I had never witnessed such speeches.

I was in love. I thought. And I wanted to get married. This seemed like a happy ending solution. This was the type of man I should have always married and there would never have been any incompatibility issues. The moment to rectify the wrongs of my life was here; this marriage felt like an epiphany. We would be like his parents. I was a Canadian after all, I had been raised in this country and I needed a Canadian. I needed a mild-mannered, intelligent and polite husband. He was indeed so mild-mannered that he didn't have the nerve to propose marriage, but that did not stop me. I suggested it and we were married at a very elegant ceremony in my backyard.

Fifty people, small ceremony, brunch, a-line, to the knee, '60s inspired dress and hair. The perfect second wedding gig.

Then off to our honeymoon and once again, my newly branded Life was consistent with my trend board. We were greeted at the quiet but elegant boutique hotel with fresh coconut drinks made with produce straight from their garden instead of the glitzy empty-calorie champagne of my previous life. We went to museums instead of the devoid of interest constant clothes shopping. We spent our days quietly reading books under the shade of a parasol instead of sunning with unsubstantial trade magazines. We kept to ourselves behind polite but distant smiles for the other guests instead of fraying with the loudest and most prominent members of Club Meds.

We were that discrete, pale-faced bookish couple that goes unnoticed in a pool corner.

When I came back from the honeymoon, I learned from the teachers that my daughter, who was in grade 4 by then, had been asked the routine back to school question, "what special thing did you do this summer". She had announced to her class that her mother had gotten married.

"We find her so calm and confident this year. Perhaps this is somehow reassuring for her." I smiled sweetly. We nearly blinked back the tears at this happy ending story as we all smiled at each other. Confident that Life had meaning.

The stories we women tell ourselves, I thought not much later, when I recalled that moment. Because the epiphany and the welcome energy of the pendulum swing did not last very long.

But the teachers and I had a nice women "bonding" moment. Perhaps that is what makes it all right somehow : the little moments and big feelings.

How A Jewish Moroccan Woman Got Attacked By Natives

Meanwhile, my Canadian dream was taking place.

Suppliers were delivering, the website was shaping into place and Mike and I had put our energy and money into this new business. He put a lot more money than I had. I put a lot more energy than he did. Of course, that was not helping our marriage either because I saw how lackadaisical he was about my American/Canadian dream. I grew very impatient with this son of a rich man's poise and calm. What had seemed like debonair elegance now seemed like a lack of energy.

The trend board of our marriage that I had composed in my mind was slowly coming apart.

We had traveled across Quebec to see suppliers and elaborated products ranging from boots to statement furniture, t shirts art and ice wine. I got to play Isabel Marant in Wendake with the sharp owner of a third-generation boot company. I called her and told her I loved what she did but wanted to come to her showroom and bring certain modifications to her styles by changing the colors and trims. She answered, "Wow that is funny, there is a Japanese group that has recently contacted me with the same objective". The Japanese have a flair for refined fashion, so I knew I was on the right track.

I put up the website and social media. I hired a photographer for campaign pictures and used my daughters as models. By then I had done so many photoshoots in my life I had grown tired of "rented humans" as models. I posted the pictures and wrote everything from the About us to the mission to the product descriptions. I created a full brand and website. And then one day we walked into the Museum of Fine Arts and showed our concept, products and website and the charming store's curator agreed to launch our line. A beautiful event took place at the Museum one evening and was followed up with an article in the Montreal Gazette. And then the problems started.

Canadian Brand Dilemna

The elegant store at the Montreal Museum of Fine Arts was hosting the Inukt launch for us. Our wares had been selected and there was a selection of our statement chairs, pillows, boots and accessories displayed for the evening, to be sold afterwards in the store. One of my future projects was to make an Inukt ice wine in collaboration with a Canadian winery and so, our new friends from Pilliteri ice wine of Niagara Falls had graciously sent us their ice wine. We had ordered dark chocolates and other made in Canada goodies.

My guests, friends of the museum and the press gathered to admire our collection. The launch was a success: events with free wine usually are. The next day there was a write up in The Gazette about our line and the mention that a French woman had bought a $2000 fur bag from our line. No doubt an Isabel Marant aficionada who understood where I was coming from, I thought.

That is when the criticism started to pour in from all sides. We were accused of cultural appropriation. I had been away for twenty years and had not done my research properly.

When I had left Montreal, no one saw anything wrong with the term Indians or with playing cowboys and Indians or with getting inspired by "Indian" handicrafts.

But times had changed and in the new era of political correctness, frontiers were being erected all over the place of what one could or could not say or do. My Made in Canada line of handmade luxury goods was guilty of cultural appropriation.

This was the first I had heard of this. I had even invited the Chief of Youth, Josh Iserhoff and he had loved the line. I had picked him, especially because he had written a very fashion savvy editorial in the First nation's magazine (that stuck out

like a sore thumb to my delight), where he mentioned loving
Alexander McQueen stilettos among talk of caribou hunt and
education in Buffalo. Talk about juxtaposition of cultures and
identities.

During the event at the museum store, a few intellectuals
had mentioned something about my not being an Indian and
that the United Nations passed a bill stipulating that their
culture and the use of it in any shape or form was reserved only
to natives. This was explained to me over a glass of ice wine,
but I had innocently smiled, nodded and patted a pillow back
into place.

I came from a world of free inspirations and since I was
changing and reinterpreting the First Nation codes nothing
prepared me for the backlash that started the next day.

The museum started by calling me every half hour to tell
me they were getting calls from Native organizations all around
North America demanding my line be pulled out. Then they
said that a Native exposition scheduled for the month after was
threatening to cancel their delivery. By 4 pm the picketing was
being organized in front of the museum by the First Nations
representatives. The museum direction called and explained
that he had to give in to the pressure and pull my line out of
the store.

Still, the noise was not over. Write-ups in the Gazette, the
main English-speaking paper in Montreal and in countless
other online and print magazines appeared with my name, all
accusing me of being a shrewd businesswoman. I was banking on
the First Nations culture and making light of their history and
suffering while becoming heavy with the cash I was amassing.
That was their version, but far from reality.

The single fur bag I sold was being transformed in their minds
into hundreds. The illusion of the web is such a smokescreen,

that everyone imagined Inukt.com a company with a huge team behind it when in fact it was all emitting from one single Macbook: mine.

My Facebook page had become a ready target for the insults from all the natives. I was subject to torrents of insults. First my daughters and their friends defended me and retorted to each negative comment. Soon though cracks were to be seen in my defense team. Some of them began to have their doubts.

"Mom you put an image of their Chief that was killed in a massacre on a t-shirt and recolored it Warhol style. Imagine if someone did that with one of our rabbis?"

The Aboriginal tv called me for an interview as well as the radio. Funnily enough, the radio called me on Halloween day when I was on the way to an office party dressed as a disco queen. I was in a panic, because I had just been sent the link to a video of a little girl, that was going around social media, asking people to respect her culture, and to please not indulge in stereotyping by dressing up children as Indians. What was remarkable was that the little girl had an uncanny resemblance to my youngest daughter. I called the house shrieking in my disco costume (thankful I had not dressed as a native myself).

"Did you guys see that video on Facebook? That girl looks like Lisa! Did the Indians get her!!? Is she home?"

The next day the Aboriginal tv came to interview me, but I made them promise not to divulge my address. I felt paranoid by then. I once came home and found a banana peel near my doorstep and wondered if an Indian rights defender had placed it there for me.

Finally, in the middle of this whirlwind, I breathed deeply and emailed my response to the Gazette. Montreal is a village and nothing else was happening, so they called me two minutes after I had pushed on "send" saying they wished to publish it in the weekend edition.

"I am puzzled, to say the least by all the paradoxes and situations that have faced me in the first year of starting my business: a simple fashion brand named Inukt.

On Wednesday of this week, the Montreal Museum of Fine Arts said it was removing my Inukt line of First Nations-inspired clothing, furniture and décor objects from its boutique because some First Nations artists found them offensive. At the same time, I have been accused of "cultural appropriation."

In fact, the Inukt brand is about positioning Canadian heritage as a whole in the fashion landscape. I recently returned to Montreal after working for 20 years in Paris, in the fashion industry. I worked hard to ensure that Inukt's first collection was put together with help and sourcing from aboriginal communities here in Quebec.

As a result, I could never have predicted, as a humble fashionista or style hunter, that some First Nations communities would protest against our line. I had never imagined that in order for me to be allowed to be inspired by First Nations culture, *I had to be a descendant of the First Nations myself.*

That has been a recurring question that I have faced: Do you have indigenous ancestry? If I did, I would be allowed to be inspired, in ways that I am not allowed as a non-aboriginal? That was the first paradox; that the credibility of my line depended on my nationality and place of birth.

By this logic, should people not accept Julia Child writing about French cuisine because she isn't French? Or should the Orientalists have not been allowed to paint the Orient because they were European? Please note that I do not have the pretension of comparing myself to these painters. But this assertion whereby we are not allowed to be inspired, without showing qualifying birth credentials, is puzzling for a simple fashionista like me. Maybe it was the fact that my launch was in a boutique associated with a major Canadian museum that afforded me all these intense reactions.

In the fashion world, inspirations can arise under a variety of circumstances and no amount of opposition can, or should, stop freedom of inspiration. Freedom of expression is guaranteed by our constitution. The people who have been insulting me every day on Facebook should go visit Simons or Forever 21 and all the other podiums of the fashion world that are inspired more routinely than we realize by Hassidism, the military, punks, burkas and a host of other cultural cues. That is the real world of fashion. That's what some of my First Nations critics need to realize.

I realize that this whole situation and the torrent of hatred that I received on Facebook is not really directed at my humble brand. Some First Nations communities have been short-changed and their challenges have made me a visible target of their discontent. My brand is not the real problem. Let's try to separate the two.

I have closed my Facebook page not because I wasn't open to dialogue but because I have been subject to inappropriate language and even hatred. I'm just a fashionista who wants to make some cool clothes and was hoping to show potential buyers the richness of First Nations culture in the most respectful way.

This whole experience, for me, has been a growing experience, and I will use it to revisit my line and plans for a second collection. New encounters with First Nations communities have been opening up for me in recent days and with them have come some constructive criticism.

I cannot change the fact that I have no First Nations ancestry. I am a fashionista who appreciates First Nations culture, its symbolisms and especially its people — and who looks forward to continued, close cooperation with First Nations people in a mutually beneficial fashion."

I was eventually graced with some positive comments and support. Particularly a remark that appeared in the Gazette about Othello having been played by a Nigerian and that it had been an interesting and beautiful juxtaposition of cultures.

Some First Nations people said they loved what I was doing and that they appreciated the new twist given to their wares.

The important thing I learned in all this was that I was still different no matter where I was. I had left Casablanca because I was Jewish. I had left Montreal because I felt drawn to the European culture that had been mine in my colonized place of birth. In France, I had been the Canadian and felt out of place. Now I had come back home and just when I started feeling "Canadian", I was being attacked by the First Nations because as a Jewish Moroccan I had no right to be inspired by a culture that was not mine.

It was very puzzling. As it is no doubt for many citizens of this planet.

Oh, there was one nice comment from my ex when my daughters recounted our adventures that summer, "That is the thing with your mother…one is never bored."

Canadian Marriage Dilemna

I had loved the Canadian marriage too. Until I started getting bored.

We would go to the family country house on weekends, but the tepid conversations, overly civilized talks, routine lunches and dinners with prompt beginning and end times left me restless. The property next to the in-laws belonged to a very well-known Moroccan family and I looked with longing at their assemblies of over twenty people lounging around on their lawn while we were usually 5 people at best.

My daughters were persuaded to come a few times, but only when they could bring a party of at least twelve. One memorable weekend, they brought nearly twenty cousins in from out of town, but the in-laws left the scene immediately looking slightly dazed and confused and pretexting an event they had forgotten about in the city. Then my mother in-law called Mike and plied him with warnings and instructions to heed on the running of the household in their absence. Our differences were not fun anymore. As for our similarities they seemed to lessen each day.

About a year later I realized I had not married him for whom he *was* but for whom he was not. And I had to admit to myself that I had even a bit fallen in love with his ultra-chic mother. Who was also the opposite of the sullen, bitter mother in law I had during my first marriage.

My friend Yolanda, who has always observed everything with her distinctive but spot-on outlook shared this observation with me one day: "After you left Mike, we bumped into him one day on the lake and he invited us all over to the family home for drinks. I saw part of what you fell in love with right before my eyes. Those pictures of his mother when she was young, that was you. You both had the same love for receptions and decorations and atmospheres. All over the house in every pillow and piece of china, silverware and furniture, I saw the very same style that inhabits your home. Those were all your signature prints. This marriage was not a meeting of the minds. It was a fusion of fabrics. Don't tell me her style didn't pull all your heartstrings. You didn't want to be Mike's wife. You wanted to be his mother's daughter in law." Hmmm, interesting point of view.

When Russell Brand married Kate Perry he realized very quickly after, that he had made a huge mistake. That she had absolutely nothing to do with him. Look at the pictures and the story they tell. This complicated and extremely intense man seems to be sulking all the time while she was thrilled at being caught by the paparazzi. After the divorce (that Russell asked her for by text, cad that he was), he said that whenever he caught a glimpse of her in a society paper or party he would think with distance: oh yes, that woman I was married to for a year. That is how great his feeling of alienation and distance was from her.

I am embarrassed to say (among many things written in this book), that is how I felt about my second husband soon after I asked for the divorce (not by text). That is the man I was married to for a year or so.

I went back to the Vad Air for a divorce, but just like my both my marriages were very different so were both my divorces.

A few days after I decided that this union was not one that had any reason to last, I was on my way to the office and I casually called to book a divorce. The rebbetzin made it sound long and complicated. "Yes dear, come see de rabbi, ve vill discuss, ve vill see, ve vill then see your husband, ve will discuss, ill see." I politely wished her good day, hung up with her, veered the car around and found myself, ten minutes later, hovering over her at her reception desk.

"Hi there", I breathed in and tried to smile as calmly as I possibly could, while hanging over her reception counter. "I am the one that just called you. I thought I should come over and explain. I have been through this before. I do not need a long and meaningful drawn-out divorce. This is a second marriage. The pendulum swing, you know? You must have witnessed this before here. I went from one extreme to the next. But it's just a light second marriage. No children together. We just want a light second divorce. Nearly casual. Let's do this quickly and airily. I am so happy you seem to understand. But you must meet all kinds here and be a great judge of character. So, we don't need many meetings with rabbis etc. What's the rate? Still 800$?. Great thanks. Like Nike says, Let's do it.

The pleasure of a tepid marriage and divorce are only attainable with a mild-mannered gentleman. The second time it is simply liberating without the fear or sadness. I went home and did a little dance.

Girl on Fire
By Alicia Keyes
She's just a girl, and she's on fire
Hotter than a fantasy, lonely like a highway
She's living in a world, and it's on fire
Feeling the catastrophe, but she knows she can fly away
Oh, she got both feet on the ground
And she's burning it down
Oh, she got her head in the clouds
And she's not backing down

Day Job With Quebec's Dragon's Den Lady

Truth be told it was not the Indian's fault Inukt was not pouring in cash like they thought it was. After all, they were not my target customers. My target customers were the Europeans. When I lived in Paris and I mentioned that I came from Canada, people suddenly got a dreamy look on their faces. I could see reflections in their eyes of romantic visions of prairie landscapes, sleigh dogs and a rugged but nature-filled lifestyle. I could see the allure these landscapes offered, as their visions were diametrical opposites with the charming yet confining and overly busy, bursting with activity streets of Paris. Those were the people I had designed my line for, but I realized (a tad too late) it would cost me too much money to reach out to them and market the line via the expensive web highways.

The conclusion was that I needed a job. Back to my mother who had a new career woman in her contacts. My mother was an intrepid fundraiser for the Jewish community. There were two types of community members for my mother: the ones who saw her and crossed the street to the other side, hoping she hadn't seen them because they didn't want to offer a donation. And then there were the very generous ones who made donations willingly. Some gave such huge amounts that my mother graced them with gifts of home-made jams. Sometimes the jams were given in exchange of $100,000 the pop. These were extra sweet jams.

Dalia, the hostess of Quebec's equivalent of Dragon's Den or Shark Tank, otherwise known as the Queen of the Beauty Industry had met my mother because she was "honored" at one of the events my mother hosted for successful entrepreneurs. Usually when people of our community are honored, they are quick to understand that they should follow up with a thank you donation. Few escape the rule. Dalia, was one of the very few and very shrewd who graciously chose to ignore the rule.

My mother referred me to her and when she saw my Inukt, although she was in the Beauty industry, she told HR during my interview,

"See what she did? She did something beautiful. So now she will work for us and do something beautiful here." Thus I proceeded to rebrand her beauty empire on the basis that she was selling Intelligent (because non-invasive) beauty.

What was interesting about Dalia, was that like me she

was a Jew born in an Arab country but the similarities in our upbringing stopped there.

She was born in 1956 in Oujda, Morocco, the child of a Jewish Moroccan woman and a German soldier that she never met. Her mother, according to Dalia's autobiography was of fiery and strong-willed temperament. In that era, to marry outside of your religion was not customary to say the least. Especially not when you were a minority Jew living in Arab lands. Between having a child with a German soldier and then raising Dalia and her brother (son of a Muslim) singlehandedly as well as being a business partner in a garage, Dalia's mother was not your typical pampered and sheltered Jewish Moroccan woman. They had no doubt not been very involved in Jewish community life.

Her mother, half-brother and Dalia moved to Algeria for a new opportunity during her teenage years. Dalia eventually distanced herself even more from the Jewish community by marrying a well-established Muslim with whom she had 4 children. She was hired by the US Embassy to issue visas and with her relentless spirit, energy and ambition she rose to become an advisor to the United States Ambassador to Algeria for 12 years.

In the early 1990s, feeling the political climate deteriorate in Algeria, she decided to immigrate to Canada. Dalia who had inherited her mother's temperament refused to put up with certain comments and messages she was receiving about wearing or imposing the hijab on her daughters.

She left Algiers to settle in Montreal with her husband, mother and children and with her zeal and energy started a new life. No matter the job she took, whether it was in a health center or selling lingerie, she invested herself thoroughly and with gusto as she can and does proudly recount today. One day, after a very tough day selling door to door, she dreamed of the hammam moment from back home that could wipe out all the efforts of the day and leave you feeling renewed and re-energized thanks to the horsehair glove that accompanies this ritual. But no hammam was in sight. That is when the idea came to her to import and distribute these gloves. Her eldest daughter was enjoying her job at Le Chateau, a Canadian fashion brand, advising clients. Dalia yanked her out regardless, for the good of the family and made her help launch the business. With Dalia you did not discuss. When one of her daughters had a rebellious moment, having just discovered their newfound North American freedom and told her that if she reprimanded her she too strongly she could call 911 on her mother, Dalia reprimanded a lot louder. She said if anyone called 911 she would break the phone. 911 was not raising her children. She was not buying into all that the Canadian culture had to offer. And her daughters respected her for it as well as for the example she set in many ways.

Shortly after the hammam gloves took off, the Quebec Dream ensued and Dalia was expanding the empire and selling everything from the gloves, to beauty creams and finally beauty machines. When she first reached out to LPG France, the world-wide renowned leader in beauty machines, in order to become their distributor, they informed her that all distributors had to be doctors. They soon enough found out that Dalia never took no for an answer.

Her success led her to become the hostess of the French Canadian business tv show, earning her the name of La Dragonne. She was also rewarded with her own editorial section in the magazine Les Affaires.

By the time I came on board, she was a source of inspiration to Quebecers. She represented the immigrants' dream. Women especially poured out their love and admiration for her on her Facebook page and she rewarded them graciously with wise words of inspiration. Many asked for money or to partner with her on their own dreams and those too, she rewarded with wise words of inspiration.

Her husband had not fared as well. Like many immigrants as soon as he landed in their new country of adoption, he realized that his important position and diplomas were staying behind on the other side of the Atlantic. He did not have Dalia's resilience. While she was knocking down doors, day after day, relishing in discovering Quebec, he was having a hard time bidding goodbye to yesteryears life made easy with chauffeurs and honors and private club memberships. He was faced with harsh winter and the realization that at best he would become a chauffeur himself. He did not take well to starting afresh on the bottom rung and the experience did not give him the adrenaline that it seemed to give his wife. Throwing oneself off a cliff can provide a heady sensation of freedom for some but can be filled with dizzying uncertainty for others. The way we approach a situation often defines the results we get from it as we know too well.

Eventually, their new life and perspectives created a distance and they divorced. Later she married a Jewish businessman, but always lavished attention and great respect on her first husband. "If he has a headache, I have a headache. He is the father of my children and I kiss his hand", she said in her speeches to show that everything must have its place and even ex-husbands were dealt with in the correct way in Dalia's orderly world.

She had embraced her new life with unparalleled enthusiasm and energy. This she roared to her followers who readily breathed in this source of inspiration, whether live or through her social media channels.

"I came to this country and had to learn EVERYTHING.

I had to learn how to talk (indeed she spoke French in Algeria, but she was shrewd and quick to notice that French Canadians were more prone to bonding if you adopted their accent).

I had to learn how to EAT.

I had to learn how to face the COLD.

I had to learn how to WORK HERE.

I had to learn how to be the HEAD OF THE FAMILY.

I had to learn how to RAISE CHILDREN HERE.

I HAD TO LEARN MY LIFE all over again.

The French Canadians were not the only ones that were fascinated with her. The Muslims too, even if their admiration was tinged with a bit of jealousy as it usually is when one of the same crop flourishes more than the others. After a year of working there I became restless. Branding of slimming and youth gets repetitive after a while. I was looking for a way out of this dragon's den and was open to job interviews. One head-hunter made me go all the way downtown and then centered all his questions around D. and remarked that he didn't "get" her success.

"How do these French Canadians gobble it all up? How much is she worth?" Walid was just jealous and frustrated like many men from back home. I was frustrated that he was wasting my time because of his unseemly pettiness.

But like Dalia said of anyone who envied her or had even tried to do her wrong, "I have no time for that. I rush away because I am going places. No time. Have too many things to do, people to see and places to go".

The woman was indeed admirable and controlled us all with a hand of steel in a velvet glove. She loved to lecture the estheticians while she laid down in the cabins and they rolled the LPG handle over her body clad in the white bodysuit. Very much like Cleopatra must have done when the women at her service massaged her every limb. She was not a beautiful woman in a classical way, her features were too bold, but she held herself as such and could fool any man or woman into thinking she was very beautiful with her shrewd and confident demeanor. And when she threw back her throat and roared her powerful laughter, heads would turn.

If anyone left something untidy in the kitchen or a conference room, they were severely reprimanded. We were often all gathered to be reminded that it was with a lot of BLOOD, SWEAT AND TEARS that Dalia had obtained her beauty empire and we had better respect it. She treated her employees like the children that she loved and that admired her but that also sometimes deserved a good old-fashioned scolding. It was not uncommon to have one of the estheticians erupt into our Marketing or Human Resources department holding back tears.

This was particularly paradoxical as I often viewed her appearances on tv shows and witnessed her delivering wise and enchanting words to the TV host.

"See Jean Claude, my thing is I love PEOPLE. That is why I take your hand and I hold it and I look you in the eyes because its PEOPLE I love and want to listen to." All this was delivered with the right gestures and with the perfect French-Canadian accent that ensured delivery right into the Quebecois heart. When she said it, I am sure she was sincere. But like all women her feelings and their expression were extreme. We love our children, but do they get us mad when they mess up the freshly washed kitchen floor.

To the French Canadians, she never denied her Jewish and Muslim connections, but knowingly put the accent on her Christian roots. She touchingly spoke of the little angel that had been given to her as a child and that stood for the effigy of the Lord and never left her bedside.

With the Muslim workers and her numerous cousins, she bantered, joked and reprimanded them in their Arab dialect and with ample gestures.

And when she went to the Jewish fundraising events she came accompanied by her second Jewish husband and spoke of her past, raised as a Jew in an Arab country.

I admired this woman and if she was a bit too harsh sometimes it was so evident that it was the situation she had evolved in and not the person that was to blame.

Her mixed cultures gave her a very distinct identity. Her numerous religions also mixed with superstition. During one of her trips to Europe, one of the goldfishes, that she kept in the huge aquarium at the office died. In Middle eastern and North African cultures, fish are attributed the power of protection against the evil eye. This incident greatly upset the office staff who trembled and feared the moment they would have to announce this news to her. There was animated talk about whether we should just buy another one and replacements were brought for scrutiny. It was finally decided against. You just didn't pull the wool over this woman's eyes.

Her Jewish, Muslim, Christian, multicultural background and French-Canadian success story all contributed to the highly colorful and interesting person she was. A woman made from her story and with her story. Like every one of us is.

Some things about her were an example, other things less, but like most people, she was a package deal and her resilience, strength, impudence and overzealousness could not be disassociated from her success. Here was another woman trying to make her way in this world and using everything at hand to do so. If one doesn't squeeze every possible drop of where we come from and who we are, it would be a waste and a pity. And even more difficult. When one is surviving divorce, it is a great asset to run into examples like this woman.

Art Versus Science

It was not always easy to work at Dalia's. Paris was not so far behind and sometimes I would look out the window overlooking the ugly highway and think of how not long ago my office had overlooked the beautiful streets of Paris. The thing one should never do is compare present with past. Also working on brands focused on beauty (mostly skin because yes, beauty IS only skin deep) was becoming repetitive. It was all about focusing on faces and buttocks that had incredible results thanks to all the skin tightening machines and creams distributed by Dalia. I played with the idea of Intelligent Beauty and Smart & Beautiful because it was non-invasive treatment but after a while, I felt that all the beauty ads looked the same.

But everything always happens for a reason and it was thanks to that job that I was able to bounce to the next one.

My new boss had laboratories that analyzed blood and when I was interviewed by him, I was able to say that Dalia was in Science & Technology as well. She even had a Food Intolerance Laboratory.

I had made a big jump from Fashion and Art to Health and Science. In the end, it was all the same because the main subject everywhere is Business and Math. What I had not calculated was that Religion and Faith were also going to play a big part.

Health And Science

Leon had a dream: to build the Zara of Medical complexes with an Apple Identity. The blood poured in to be analyzed and so did the money to invest in Medical complexes. Later I realized that in the Jewish religion blood is compared to money. Without money, we are bloodless and lifeless. Is that why the new boss was making so much money, I wondered. Because he was dealing with blood? Connections will never cease to amaze me.

This project had a lot of money to invest. I loved it. Affordable health care in clinics that would look like they came out of Star Trek. I envisioned white curves, stainless steel accents, futuristic ribbons of light with nurses walking through glass bubbles in silver boots and high collared white vinyl jackets right out of Courrèges and Paco Rabanne. Those designers had always mastered the eighties vision of what fashion should look like in the futuristic year 2000.

That is what we proceeded to do. My boss loved luxury as much as I did and although he was a businessman when something was beautiful, he agreed to pay the full price. Much to his partners' dismay and my pleasure.

The partners would lament: "What are these uniforms you are buying for the receptionists?? But at Walmart's they just have a t-shirt with the logo on!". How to explain to them that we were trying to communicate the clean-lined, ultra-cool graphic efficiency of the Star Trek staff through their outer appearance and outfits.

Later, once the clinics were built, the boss and I were the ones to be dismayed to see the personnel wearing their immaculate white blouses comfortably open over a multi-colored striped t-shirt or checkered shirts.

"We are not at Couche Tard," I would whine inwardly and ask them with a smile to zip up their white uniforms.

It took us two years to build these clinics. I was in branding and when I was hired, I thought my responsibilities would be confined to the communications field: website, brochures, stationary, social media and any necessary communication tool. But a few days after I was hired my luxury-loving but business-savvy boss informed me that I was going to help him design and build the clinics as well.

"You were at BCBG …you helped with store décor…it is the same thing".

I could not resist the challenge. I started putting together trend boards and bringing home architectural plans so that my daughter in architecture would help me make sense of them. I googled builder's legends and found out that those little white objects in the ceilings were sprinkler system in case of fire. The architect we had hired designed the plans for the clinics and finally I followed the contractor who was my boss's brother in law. My imposter complex was at its highest, but I continued to pretend/play as we do all through life.

The office environment was All in the Family. It was the first time that I was immersed in the Sephardic community that Leon, my boss, mostly surrounded himself with. Everyone seemed to know each other, to go to the same barmitzvahs, to have the same cousins and know each other's brother in-laws and aunts. I had left the community for over twenty years and now I was immersed in it, feeling part of it but also feeling like an observer. I loved the easy familiarity and the respect the younger girls had for the older executives even if they were sometimes disgruntled by their reproaches. It was as if a Hebrew teacher were putting them back on the right track.

My new boss was an aesthete. I marveled at how he loved

fashion and luxury. Even where his personal shopping was concerned.

"What?? These are the shoes he delivered? Yes, they are made with the finest leather, but I assure you these are not navy, they are black. Look I am putting them in the light next to navy as I speak to you, and I can tell they are black. No, send them back to Italy. I have twelve pairs of black shoes! The whole point was I needed navy".

His reactions were the same during the clinic's design. "That wallpaper seems a shade darker than the sample you showed me...hmm...are you sure? Where is the sample? Ahhh you see...what not the same batch? But still such a difference?". It was impossible to remind him that doctors or patients would not notice the slightest shade difference in wallpaper. He wanted perfection....much to his partner's dismay.

"Look at that suspended ceiling... they could have put it six inches higher. The rooms would be airier. Tell them to rip it off and start over. Wait, let me go up on the ladder, bring me a tape. Ok, tell them they can bring it up 7.5 inches. Yeah, rip out the whole thing and start over. I prefer to delay by a few weeks and get it right".

"Listen", the partners would argue, "the patients will never notice, the doctors don't care...". Their voices trailed off because they knew it was to no avail. The majority partner was the visionary and his vision demanded we attain perfection.

I often felt like we were building a high-end fashion store and told him more than once he should have been in fashion. And when I missed fashion, somewhere deep inside, I dreamt that our boss would one day come in and say that he was starting a fashion line with the finest fabrics from Italy. After all deep down, all Sephardic Jews should be in fashion, I thought with humour.

But Leon had been too smart for that. He had wanted to be successful and had tried other franchising concepts before. Even a chain of frozen yogurts parlors in Israel that had been successful, but that he had abandoned when his loving mother told him "enough, please come home". After that he continued to search success methodically and with the focus that I had already seen by then in many businessmen: my ex-husband, Max A. and even Trump from a distance. All these men had vision, faith, focus and turned a blind eye on anyone that asked them to be realistic or reasonable. These were all men whose narcissism empowered them, so that they never doubted that they deserved to succeed, and that come rain come hail in the end, they would succeed.

His partners were not as driven or as confident as he was. I was having a great time spending money on designing these clinics, designing and ordering custom reception areas and desks, using only gleaming surfaces for cabinetry, choosing paint colors and wallpapers and leather seating to match the turquoise of the million-dollar blood testing machine from Laboratories Roche. I put together power points to convince partners and doctors that you could spend money on boring walls, furniture and stationery or spend 30 percent more but what a difference…and in the end what could you buy with the difference in budget? A quarter of a Mercedes was the final slide of the powerpoint presentation.

My presentations did not convince the majority of partners to spend more. The doctors did not have esthetics so high on their priority list.

They did not care about the wallpaper nuances or the plush

beauty of Italian leather chairs in the most perfect taupe by Knoll. The doctors did not understand the expenses. They hunted me down bearing ripped out pages from suburban newspapers featuring faux leather chairs from Staples for 99$.

"Extremely depressing chairs; not reflective of a positive environment for you or your patients", I argued. Leon nodded approval at my arguments. But differing cultures have very opposite views on how to spend money and the differences seemed irreconcilable.

One day Leon swept into the office at his usual Ferrari speed, (this luxury lover alternated between his Ferrari and Range Rover) smiled and told me he had great news.

"All of the other partners pulled out. It will be easier now. Decisions will be made faster."

Indeed no one would be around to discourage me from uninhibited spending at full speed. Which we proceeded to do. Finally, on opening day, one of the first patients came to congratulate us during our very first rounds.

"I was told you are the Director and you are the designer of this clinic," an elegant older gentleman nodded to us. And then he proceeded to gratify us with "Madam, Sir, my congratulations. No one told me I had to wear a tuxedo to come to this beautiful clinic'. We felt amply rewarded. We had won the battle against the investors and the doctors for the benefit of the patients who duly appreciated the shade of wallpaper.

I often found that the majority, if not all of the doctors, had huge egos and marvelled at this. After having been so immersed in the fashion world, I was used to hearsay of the egos of Donatella Versace and John Galliano. I had witnessed through firsthand experience the inflated egos of some head designers and fashion editors I worked with, but nothing had prepared me to expect that doctors felt they should be entitled to huge egos. I was again discovering a new world.

"What I wish to explain to these doctors", I once explained to my boss's wife, a very down to earth and pleasant dentist that did not adopt the affected ways of her colleagues, "is that Science may SAVE lives but remember it is ART that makes these lives WORTH living!".

Religion And Science

My boss was as religious as he was successful in business. He juggled all day long between his chain of laboratories, the chain of medical clinics and a pile of additional responsibilities he had attributed to himself in the form of charities. These ranged from fundraising for unprivileged boys who needed a bar mitzvah ceremony, to heading a religious school, determining programs for his synagogue or becoming president of a huge gala event in favor of a village in Israel. Everything was important. He could spend hours arguing about whether a young unruly boy should be expelled from the religious school, he sponsored, and forget the scientists who came from France to update him on their latest technology to wait interminably. The children in that school were so unruly that his own wife never let him put their children there, because even if she was as generous as him, she was more objective.

The whole experience indeed was as dedicated to Science as it was to Religion. On my second day of work, Leon informed me that my work on the clinics would have to wait a few weeks. One project was more important than the clinics.

"You see I was in Israel this summer and I met the parents of one soldier that was killed during Operation Protective Edge. I was so touched by their loss, their courage and this young man who gave his life for our country that I offered to donate a Sefer Torah in his name. And then I thought to myself that ALL the soldiers that were killed during Operation Protective Edge should have a Sefer Torah in their name. Plus, the three young men who were killed last summer. So, we need to put together 76 Sifré Torah and B'H (meaning G.d willing, used abundantly to punctuate all phrases) and organize a ceremony at the wall in Jerusalem for this coming summer."

This seemed quite unreal. 76 Sifré Torah multiplied by 25000$ because it takes a good 6 months to be written by a scribe. Then there were the logistics of getting them to Israel. Lastly, I imagined that one does not book the wailing wall like a hall at the Ritz.

"Don't worry, when I was in Israel, I got the blessing of both Chief Rabbis. Here are their contacts".

And that is how I met again in my life the Power of Vision and its exponential energy when coupled with Faith. No matter the difficulties and frustrations and multitude of details to be seen to, Leon never once faltered. He always came in smiling and confident like a sailboat that knows the wind will always be in his back.

There were indeed barriers. Letters had to be written, a logo created, a website with our mission, donors to be found, more donors to be found, logistics organized, and the Ministry of Defense in Israel had to be contacted. They didn't answer emails or call back or have meetings: they were too busy getting real stuff done like defending their country and taking care of the soldiers and their families.

When I finally was able to reach them through a simple, friendly phone call at an opportune moment, I often thought of my stint at the Canadian embassy and how two colleagues would be found leisurely discussing if a doorstop should be placed or not, and how this or other details would be the subject of numerous emails. In that situation, I was able to observe how countries, cultures and situations are often more than a world apart.

Two weeks to be dedicated to the project turned into three and four weeks and still work had not started on the clinics. Leon would sail in, always holding down his kippa as if he feared the wind in his back would make it fly off and say, "By the way, I just bought the building next door so we will have to design that too. Don't worry, very simple, Apple look, glass partitions, Corian desks, kitchen for twenty people, bathrooms, new blood testing machine coming in from France, etc. Here is the color of the machine. See a very particular shade of turquoise. But after the Sifré Torah project. B'H. That is the most important. That has Hashem's blessing."

I panicked, felt overwhelmed and often found myself very depressed looking at the pictures of the young boys who had lost their lives. I did not have my boss's faith that the Sifré Torah would elevate their soul and comfort their families.

His faith kept us all going. He had a committee around him of four other donors in the community and we met with them every week along with two other employees who had many responsibilities in the office, but whose primary responsibility had become this project. The other committee members showed up or not, donated or didn't but there was one force, one vision and it was Leon's.

He would often jump out of the Ferrari, bolt into the office and say in passing as he ran into a meeting, he was late for, "Laura, Sandy, add two more Sifré Torah to the list. This weekend at the synagogue David Bensoussan promised to sponsor one, Josée Bitton also promised one if I pay him a trip to Israel, and

Albert Berdugo says he is sending us a recently restored Sifré Torah from his synagogue in Casablanca...How much are we at? 18 you say?? No, no we are at 20 I say, remember we had 12 then 2..."

The most remarkable incident happened during that year. Enough to make me wonder about the strength and possible existence of the Higher Power. As I already mentioned, I did not have the same degree of faith as my boss. I walked into the office one day, weighed down with samples and tiles and saw Leon on the phone waving me over.

"I think I just found the solution," he said into the phone while looking pointedly at me. "Hold on". He addressed me, "I am on the phone with the rabbi. He has collected from different donors 18 Sifré Torahs for our cause in his synagogue. They cannot be sent to Israel for another 15 days and he is nervous. He had a nightmare about them, and he is not insured. Can we move them to your house? I cannot have them at our house; our youngest boy just scribbled all over the walls of the house, he is too fast for us".

"What an honour. Of course."

18 Sifré Torah in my house meant that I had more spirituality than 10 synagogues put together. I have always been more spiritual than religious and these handwritten scrolls, duplicated by our religion for over 5000 years were potent with spirituality.

I marveled because the week before, through Airbnb my house had been rented to the spiritual leader of the Sikhs in Montreal for a seminary. I had rented out my home a few times for extra cash, before renovating the kitchen, rather than selling weed like my alter ego and favorite divorced heroine from the Netflix series "Weeds". He had left a message for me with one of his disciples.

"He said, to tell the owner of this beautiful home that even if he sees you follow another religion than ours, (he had noticed the picture of Rabbi Shneerson in my home) all of our spiritual leaders are united together up there and he blesses you and this home."

In a way, I felt the kindly Sikhs had "cleaned" my home to prepare for the Torahs.

I had the Torahs installed on big tables in the basement. My daughters and I solemnly covered our heads and went downstairs to whirl around them and pray. I felt electric energy coming from these 18 accumulated scrolls of wisdom, history and religion.

A few days later, Leon called me to his office.

"The rabbi just called me. He is so grateful you took those Sifré Torahs. Last night at the exact spot where the Torahs had been placed, there was a huge leak from the ceiling. They would have been splattered with the ceiling, water and paint!'

Decidedly this was a potent project we were working on. I still do not know to this day what I believe in, but a Higher Power was blessing this project.

In my mind, the Ministry of Defense of a country deals with the military over religion, but they had great respect for our cause. The Sifré Torahs were delivered to them and it was with wonder that I arrived in Israel with my boss and the committee and saw the Sifré Torah in the middle of the government building handled with great care by the military. It was fascinating to see the bond between Government and Religion.

This experience also taught me that in the end it all gets done. The end always comes. One year later the clinics were built, the building renovated, and we were all in Jerusalem at the Wailing Wall witnessing our boss delivering a touching speech. We looked on in amazement at the 76 Sifré Torah enter the stage held by soldiers to the music of Israel's finest voices and orchestras, in the presence of the parents of the fallen soldiers, Mrs Netanyahu (Benjamin had a private ceremony for security reasons) and many dignitaries.

As Leon gave us his speech, I realized that anything can be achieved if one has absolute certitude that it will be accomplished. That is what happens when one has an abundance of energy, optimism and drive that can be attained from feeling the certainty that the wind is always in your sails.

Meeting At The Wailing Wall

The day of the long-awaited ceremony, honouring soldiers had arrived. We had arrived at the Wailing Wall, I had installed my daughters a few rows behind my seat and had gone to look for my seat in the section reserved for committee members. As I was trying to figure out how I would decipher my name on a chair, as they were written in Hebrew, luckily enough someone read my name out loud. I walked towards the first row and a photographer that had come to solicit us in Montreal called to me, "Hey, lucky you; you're first row! A few words for the camera?"

I looked at him very quickly, he seemed so out of place with his Bermuda shorts and rumpled shirt. "Sure". I gave the camera my brightest smile, a few appropriate words on the power of the event, the fallen soldiers and my gratitude for being part of this momentous ceremony and as soon as the camera was turned off, I looked away.

The touching and beautiful ceremony occurred: 76 Sifré Torah filed on stage in front of the Wailing Wall. The Creative Director of the Ministry of Defense orchestrated visuals, musicians, speeches and a ceremony that linked the history of Jerusalem to the present.

Many months later I fell in love with that very photographer and he showed me the rushes taken of me that evening. "See how you looked abruptly away at the end of the speech; you were so uninterested by me. That is when I vowed, I would chase you down and seduce you as soon as we were back in Montreal."

When we were all back at the office, that fall, after the intense ceremony at the wall, he came to present the film and pictures he had taken. I had not forgotten my first university dream to make documentary films. Since I was in charge of branding I was called to the meeting with Leon and Laura his right hand. I proposed a storyboard during the meeting and Leon asked me to work on this project with David.

He was wearing rumpled cargo Bermuda shorts and saying he was sorry he was late because he had a dental appointment, I smiled politely and tried not to show my scorn." What are these idle men that book a dental appointment in the middle of a working day and run around in leisure clothes on a weekday? A lazy artist", I thought.

After the meeting and the prospect of working on a documentary film, my vision of him changed. It was as if a new trend board had materialized before my eyes. He was no longer a lazy photographer. He was my partner in a documentary film about religion and culture. He was no longer just a broke photographer. He was a partner in an intellectual endeavor. I was goaded partly by Laura, my colleague, who remarked, "Didn't he mention he just went through a divorce? He has really nice blue eyes…. he could be cute if you fixed him up…".

Fatal last words that women always fall for. Fix him up. We

are deep down all nurses or rebrand specialists. Yes, the haircut, the clothes, the shoes especially…hmm.

And that is how my new rebrand project came to life.

All of a sudden, I became the Power Woman that was going to write the storyboard and make a film out of his unorganized video rushes. I was also going to rebrand and relook him, so he wouldn't look like a rumpled artist but like a trendy photographer. I would be the woman behind the man and a Power team could arise.

He had started seducing me with admirating comments and so I played back and suggested he come over for a work séance. We were alone in my office and the air seemed electric.

"You want me to come over…but this could lead to something…"

"We do not know. Let's wait and see".

"Mixing work and play? I want you to know, no Porsche is waiting outside for me. Just a broken-down station wagon".

"I know".

"How do you know".

"I graduated from Concordia in Communications. I know all about the broke artistic types, money-is-not-important-way-of-life. I do not mind".

I sighed and remembered that when I was a teenager, so long ago, he had been the type of man I had been attracted to. Deep down, I had felt I could not assume such a bohemian, free-spirited, no borders, no rules or security type of life. My upraising as an immigrant child necessitated drive, ambition, success and stability. In my teenage years, I felt I could not afford to be attracted and pair off with a man like that.

How could I explain to this man that now I could finally afford to? Thanks to my first marriage with a hungry self-made Israeli, I could now afford to pair off with an artsy, neurotic

Ashkenazi. I smiled smugly at the thought. Revenge on my ex, I thought. Hypothetically I could even shelter a sexy artist type in the home he had bought me. What an interesting spin on this situation.

And thus, started our affair. After a few months, he turned out to be extremely inconsistent, selfish and self-centered. As unreliable as I had imagined. We would see each other and then he would close off into his shell for a few days, running off to take pictures by himself. He was just as unreliable and sporadic about getting the documentary film completed.

Work And Play: Not A Good Combo

Until he found out that I was hired as Creative Director by a chain of 100 fashion stores whose name shall remain unknown.

This is how it happened. David had introduced me to a rabbi /painter/spiritual advisor, he had just met through the grapevine. He brought me to see the famed artist named Haim. We soon became fast friends and to my surprise, he warned me to stay away from David.

"He will hurt you. He cannot feel anything for any woman. He is emotionally blocked", he told me as he painted. And then he gave me an amulet with a mini Torah inside to protect me.

Very soon after, my cell phone rang with one of those calls you wait for all your life.

"I am in Human Resources and just found you on Linkedin. I see you have a great fashion background and we are looking for a Creative Director for a chain of 100 clothing stores across Canada."

I could not believe this. Ever since the end of my BCBG days, I had reasoned with myself that my fashion days were over. Leave clothes branding to the younger generation, I thought. I am lucky I found a job in Beauty and now the Health industry. It is a natural evolution for a woman my age. And now, I thought to myself, somehow the hope must have stayed aflame in a tiny corner of my soul and ignited this new opportunity.

One month and four interviews later I got the job and went to tell Leon that I had to leave the company.

"Leon, the concept is built, I leave behind the Clinic's Bible of standards, so you can reproduce these medical clinics endlessly. You can always count on me; I will be there for any questions. I will always be grateful for the Sifré Torahs. But Fashion is calling. I cannot say no."

The big day arrived. First day on the job. I marveled that for the first time in my life I was getting THE job I wanted. I was not going into a company where I had to fight to climb a corporate ladder. My title was exactly what I wanted: Creative Director for two fashion brands, owned by one Canadian company.

Perhaps it is because I am a Libra that I have often worked for companies with two brands, two extremes, two identities that I balance like the plates on the scale.

I was shown to my office, my staff and my parking spot. Meetings were booked for me as well as trips to accompany my boss to visit our stores across Canada. No more taking care of endless details alone. I only had to come up with ideas and watch them materialize. Instead of coming up with boring copy on health, I was now concerned with fashion. It was like slipping back into comfortable old slippers.

The first day at the office, I was invited to a collection meeting. We all sat around a big table, just like when I was at BCBG back in Paris and analysed all the styles I would be shooting.

I wanted to rub my eyes. I could not believe my good fortune.

I had reasoned myself that I was no doubt too old to get back into fashion and I was fortunate to be in health. And here I was helping with the rebrand of a chain of over 100 stores.

My days were filled with one effortless project after another: getting involved in the new store designs, window sets, brochures, new website, emails and social media. I wondered how I had been so lucky to land such a job and thought that perhaps in one corner of my soul, I had never given up my desire and the vision had stayed lit and rekindled the flame of possibilities. It was the only explanation I could find for such good fortune.

But there was one problem: we needed to hire a full-time photographer. At the same time that I was enjoying my new job, I observed that I was obtaining very favorable attention from David the photographer. No doubt because he knew that I was going to be needing fashion photography and it was his big dream to get back into fashion.

He had had his share of success as a fashion and even rock star photographer in New York in the '90s. Due to his disorganization, he had burned out, fell out of favour with a very important woman in the social scene (one he no longer wanted to date) and all had come crumbling down. Now I could give him his chance to resurface.

I started by hiring him as a freelancer and reveled in my new-found role as power woman hiring the artsy photographer. What a turnaround from when I was the meek boss's wife.

I had to rebrand two lines and had begun to establish muses for each.

For the less expensive brand, I decided the muse would be the friendly, approachable woman next door. The good friend with the listening ear that wrapped herself in comfy clothes and adopted practical layering. She worked to supplement the family budget rather than for self-fulfillment. She cooked from scratch and was the family pillar with the cheery disposition. (if she does all that when does she have her nervous breakdown I thought, but adroitly omitted from voicing this during my presentations). Oh, I must add she was saved by the library card that gave her access to escape.

For the other more expensive brand, M.L., I naturally opted for glamour. In her family, she was the first generation to earn as much, if not more, than the men in her family. She was a food assembler, she loved beautiful tables, spectacular homes and clothes that had a wow factor (studs and fringes and leopard print come wither). Even when she went to the gym it was with a manicure and a cute work out outfit. I had fun doing a brochure with a really good-looking male secretary running around behind her.

The only problem was that I mixed up my muse and real life.

I Thought I Was An ML Woman

I wanted that male secretary. It became my obsession to hire David full time. I needed a full-time photographer to help me build and equip the studio so why wouldn't it be him?

We would be the cool creative director/photographer couple. We would work in fashion, he would work for me, he would earn less than me thus firmly securing my place as the Power Woman I always wanted to be. Even if he didn't have a lot of money my trend board was now filled with a Road trip, a 3 star hotel and healthy, vegan food and rock music that was so much more Rock and Roll than 5 star hotels with men you either bitterly fought with (my first ex-husband) or men you were bored with (my brief ex-husband).

And that was when my scheming and manipulating began.

Greater men have fallen for secretaries and trophy girlfriends. It was to be my turn.

First, I placed him in a favorable light and gave him free-lance missions. Then I hired him. To his dismay (and my delight) he was TWO rungs below me on the corporate ladder. By a strange twist of fate, the Studio manager who was to now supervise him had worked for him many years before and she knew of his failings. She was worried he was not focused enough to handle the monotonous, e-commerce photography that was also part of his responsibilities. I brushed away her preoccupations and told her not to worry.

My boss James, son of the President, grandson of the founder, an Ashkenazi woman who had opened a first (shoppe) in the '60s, also had reservations. "Let's give him a 15-day trial and reevaluate".

Meanwhile, I was traveling across Canada with James and he was greatly pleased with my work. So, I felt (oh so wrongly) that I could hire my "boyfriend photographer".

There I was, the Power woman of my dreams having the time of my life. Arriving every morning and first passing by the studio where I made sure my boyfriend would click relentlessly away and then going from one meeting to the next with him calling me to ask for advice/favors/permissions.

"No, David," I sighed exasperated but at the same time no doubt smiling smugly from my superior (high horse that I was soon to fall off of) position," we are not buying that latest video camera. Let's first show results with what we have".

"How many did you shoot today? Not enough!"

"Go back to your studio immediately. I have a meeting with James."

It amused me that he would complain he was not invited to

meetings or why were we still keeping the Star photographer for main campaigns.

"I feel like the Cinderella photographer", he would lament.

"Be grateful you have a job!" To my surprise, I started reminding myself of my ex-husband.

Roles had shifted in my life. My ex-husband used to be the bossy, directive, head on his shoulders guy and I had become him.

I loved this new role and it seemed to justify all the pain and soul searching of my divorce. This had been what was waiting for me. I had unearthed the real me. I loved nothing more than to give a corporate presentation to the team in my navy or black tailored Kooples suit and then drive off on autoroute 66 (lol ok 15 north) with my boyfriend for a weekend of hippy chic flea hunting, having now donned a loose floral dress and floppy hat. Ok, I admit, I didn't wear a floppy hat, but you get the trend board.

The only problem was that I was PRETENDING. Because if I had a head on my shoulders, a REAL Power Woman's head, I would have never hired him; I would have come to the conclusions that he was not disciplined enough for corporate life. And evidently, I was not professional enough for corporate life...

The bosses had evaluated, saw this weakness in me and made the decision for me; David was out.

James called me to his office and told me coldly I had to fire David.

"How did I get myself into this mess I thought?"

I called him over to Human Resources to give him the news. He sauntered in unknowingly wearing navy bermuda shorts to my dismay.

"How do you fire a 54-year-old boyfriend on the day he is wearing navy Bermuda shorts," was all I could think.

Aided by Donald, a trim, neat small guy from HR, I explained to David that he had not come up to par with what was requested of him and that he had thirty minutes to leave the building as gently and diplomatically as possible.

After that, the relationship understandably went a little sour.

Exit ML Woman

I should have suspected that these new American Jewish Ashkenazi bosses were not the fun-loving, wild and crazy Sephardic Europeans that Max was. He had loved the little weaknesses in his personnel, that made us all human. He loved to hear about who was dating whom and who had an argument with whom. But Max loved to party and drink and smoke. James was proud that he never had a drink.

"I used to like it in high school, but now it makes me feel sick, so why drink?" he confided with his slightly nasal voice.

I realized cultural differences were many and even visible in color schemes. I once suggested to his mother, who was 2nd generation of the clothing empire across Canada, "Aren't prune and beige a wonderful combination?" to which she retorted with her equally nasal voice:

"It is too European, in America we like prune with grey".

Brr so cold.

She turned out to be colder than I thought....

"Is she hiring all the Sephardics in the city", she would complain when I hired a stylist and assistant from my community.

There have always been rifts between our two communities because the cultural differences differ as much as religion is the same. Especially in older generations, the Ashkenazi looked down on Sephardic Jews. This was not a current event, but it takes a while to wipe out things one has heard from past generations of our family. These comments from an albeit distant past remain in small corners of the mind like dusty unswept corners that are stirred up by a gust of wind or a fresh breeze (like me lol). One woman once told me that many of the Ashkenazi mothers told their children to marry anyone they pleased, a Chinese, a Muslim, a catholic but Never a Sephardic Jew.

It was the beginning of the end.

But truth be told it wasn't their fault they couldn't accept my 15% craziness.

One day neat, little, trim Donald from HR called me over to say it was over (just one week before my 6-month trial was over). This was one of the worst days of my life.

As a parting slap, he explained it had nothing to do with my work. That was impeccable.

"This whole mess with the photographer, and also feedback from the buyers".

I realized too late that I had not sucked up enough to the buyers.

I cried all the way home and called everyone from my ex-husband to my girlfriends. Thankfully my daughters were vacationing with their father, so they did not witness my great distress firsthand. I found myself empty of my Power woman role, missing my team and my muses. Stripped of everything from one day to the next. It was another divorce.

Similarly to after the divorce, I tried to take stock and survey what I had done wrong.

1. Hire a boyfriend photographer (I got fired because deemed irresponsible to have hired this quasi gigolo

by my Puritan bosses although my work was highly commended).

2. Not sucked up enough to the buying teams. I never took seriously the oversized ego of a team that seemed to me to be making really ugly clothes for the most part clothes. But egos there were as potent as Chanel. Unfortunately, I realized this too late. James had slipped some comments and I should have heeded these as warning signs:

"They didn't like it that you looked at your computer during their three-day presentations". (I am a ferocious multi-tasker. I used to do math homework in French class and science in English).

3. Not wear clothes from the company's brands. Now that I thought back there had been a memo circulating about having to wear company clothes and I was even given a budget. But I gave the budget to my mother and aunt, never thinking for a moment that I seriously had to wear these clothes. Even at BCBG, I could never muster up the desire to get dressed in the house's main brand....

4. I just did not fit in the box and like the French Canadians say of the Anglophone in this country, they are "des têtes carrés" or square heads with little room for anything that does not fit perfectly into their square corners.

5. I came from a very different work culture, Where James never drank, Max had partied all night. Where James did not understand "promiscuous" relations between colleagues, Max had encouraged them. During one meeting, he had distributed photocopies of essays written on the Zara culture and how employees were encouraged to develop relationships and marry among themselves.

324 A Divorcee

It was an easy way to keep them happy since the Zara headquarters were in a very small city in Spain. And Max loved nothing more than hearing of relationships among his employees and partaking in in-house gossip. He was, to put it simply, a charismatic leader with a great sense of fun and his joie de vivre was a close second to the priority he gave to his business side.

The other day I called and asked my help if there was a round plastic jar of Breakstone's whipped butter in the fridge. She replied no. I purchased some along with nuts and dried raisins that I needed to make chocolate Florentines. I had to drive back home just to put the butter in the fridge. On my way home, she called in her usual lackadaisical way to say, "I just found the butter." As she does all the time. I was irritated as I often am by her. But can I fire her because she doesn't fit in my scheme of things? No. Ok not comparable to my error.

Decidedly some cultures are just colder and less forgiving than others. Corporate cultures? North American cultures?

What was left after this? A huge effort on my part to forgive myself. The first morning after I got fired, was nearly as bad as the first day of my divorce. The divorce was two people's fault, but this was entirely my fault. I had failed all alone and now I had nowhere to go to. No more parking spot, office, team, ideas, meetings, brainstorming, presentations, trips, trend boards, newsletters, fashion shoots. Emptiness and a huge feeling of failure. I could not believe I had done this to myself and I knew it would take a long time to forgive myself. This opportunity had come out of the blue and it had vanished into thin air because of my vulnerabilities. I had made a huge 140,000 $ a year mistake in hiring him. He was tall and good-looking: the trophy boyfriend for a woman who grew up with

Robert Redford and Ryan O'Neal as male ideals. Although what should have been blonde hair was thoroughly grey at 58. Was it my fault? Was it the person's fault or the situation? Poor, vulnerable divorcees are easy prey for fallible situations.

The Power woman trend board that was my inspiration had made me fall flat on my face. Beware of heady sensations that come with a power trip and an ego ride.

If nothing happens without a reason, then I tried to understand why in the scheme of things I had to trip up on this "obstacle" like a horse that fails a very high jump. It was very timely that I met this man just before my dream job and that because of him I "failed" the test. We must make sense of what happens to us and try to convince ourselves that it is for a reason. It is called storytelling so we will never know if it is the truth or not, but we need stories to justify what overwhelms us. I had made sense of my divorce, now I needed to make sense of this failure.

Here were my abandonment issues surfacing again. I had been fired, rejected, stripped of my identity and my activity. I missed my muses. I could no longer make them live through my work and I felt empty.

Perhaps it was a lesson to learn that a man is always an accessory and should never come before a 140,000$ job.

I paid a whole lot to learn that lesson. But it is said that life is a novel and we only understand it when we get to the end. I guess I needed that humility lesson. Or the lesson that priorities should be children, self-sustenance and then men in that order.

I also needed to try to accept and like myself without being part of any trend board. I had been stripped of being the wife when my husband left me. I had been stripped of being the head of the family when my girls became teenagers. I was now stripped of being the superpower career woman I had always wanted to be.

Like my friend/rabbi/artist told me "You must exist outside of your career and all the outer superficial layers". Easier said than done but that was perhaps the lesson that had to be learned.

Ok, I see a new trend board appear. It involves less superficiality and material goals. On this trend board, I see earth tones, green plants, linen and cotton, vegan food, Zen attitude, meditation, kindness, charity work. Hmm... maybe I should start sprouting?

Mes Emmerdes
By Charles Aznavour
Tout ce qui fait, je le sais (Tout ce qui fait, je le sais)
Que je n'oublierai jamais (Que je n'oublierai jamais)
Mes amis, mes amours mes emmerdes
(Mes amis, mes amours mes emmerdes)

XO

After the shit hit the fan and we both found ourselves fired, the relationship dwindled as could be expected. He was not tamable and dispersed and I was understandably depressed. Still, we saw each other occasionally.

And then one day I saw him write XO on a text to a woman with a pool. It was the middle of July. The woman he was going after always had to have something useful, I thought. He said that she was only a friend (of course) but right before my eyes the X transformed itself into a pair of scissors that snipped the silk ribbon that had tied me to him...and the result was a 0 ...no more feelings for him.

My therapist was relieved I was over him even if she seemed

surprised at my description of the effect of the XO on me. After being fired, I didn't bother calling all the round of specialists as I had done after my divorce. I just called the therapist, (and the naturopath and the astrologer...not the rabbi, the matchmaker or the real estate agent so I was getting better). The therapist enlightened me by informing me that everything I was going through was because I had married too young...had not been a teenager long enough. And the divorce led me to a second teenager crisis entering my life. Indeed, girls just want to have fun....

I took stock and realized that after my divorce I had dated three David's.

"Jamais deux sans trois" we say in French. I breathed with relief. The era of the Davids was over.

Their Ashkenazi North American mothers all call them David I thought. As if by calling them the name of our King that would be a sufficient armor, honor and attention and thus they would be equipped to fend for themselves and leave their mothers preoccupied with self-absorbed activity. Their mothers could not really take care of them. They had too much to do between running to therapists, masseurs, fundraising and table setting events. The very opposite of Sephardic mothers whose priority was raising and treating their sons as Kings. (One Sephardic mother I knew, would go to her son's side, or throne, whenever he wanted her to watch him watch tv). These Ashkenazi mothers ran around so they would not think...of the hardship of growing up with parents who had suffered from the Shoah. This made it impossible to truly give. Thus, the sons always stayed thirsty of attention, in spite of bearing the name of our King, and were for the most part more neurotic and anxious than other men. They often barricaded themselves from any real relationship with the opposite sex. These relationships were often born from convenience and calculations.

Many indeed, like David were effeminate. Being competitive with me about who had the best clothes! "Why do you always out dress me?" He would wail in his beige wool coat and prune sweater…. yes, that was my styling.

Love Yourself
By Justin Bieber
For all the times that you rained on my parade
And all the clubs you get in using my name
You think you broke my heart, oh girl for goodness sake
You think I'm crying, on my own, well I ain't
And I've been so caught up in my job, didn't see what's going on
But now I know, I'm better sleeping on my own
'Cause if you like the way you look that much
Oh baby you should go and love yourself

Street Smarts

To survive as a divorcee means you need a generous quantity of street smarts. Yes, here I do think of my Netflix mentor, the heroine of Weeds. And I did everything short of selling drugs, organs or other highly unethical options.

Today thankfully, a variety of options appear in our digital world.

AIRB N B

I rented my house on air b'n' b which was not in itself without some risks.

I had a group of Sikhs coming to Montreal for a reunion,

which made my neighbor call me over in a frenzy in the middle of the day.

"No this must stop! All these veiled women are entering your house, the neighborhood is in a panic". I ran over from my day job to find smiling women peeling vegetables for their vegan meals in my garage. All this to keep my kitchen clean. All the guests had lined up their shoes at the entrance and one woman was taking pictures of how my delicate objects were laid out so that she could "store them and put them back the same way".

Of course, there was the time that two teenagers tried to pass off as nice Jewish boys looking for kosher restaurants when in fact, they wanted to rent my house to throw a huge party.

I was vaguely suspicious when they uttered the wrong Jewish expression during the conversation but I let it go. Instead of saying "God willing" they said "Thank G.d" in reply to my questions about their plans.

My daughter's boyfriend was thankfully over and recognized them as well-known party animals that would have destroyed the house. Once I was out of earshot, he made them hand over the keys and admit they had booked with a stolen visa. As a divorcee, one must sometimes count on the angel that protects divorcees.

TURO

I rented my car on the Turo rental app and found myself renting it out occasionally and dropping it off in far off neighborhoods, then taking the metro back home, coffee mug retrieved from my car and bumping into another neighbor.

"How are you? Yes, was just having coffee at the neighbors! So nice to walk sometimes!".

SELLING STUFF

Here the options are plentiful. One divorcee spent 600 000 glorious euros on Fendi, Prada and Hermes over a period of 3 years. A Fendi fur coat is 30,000 euros, Hermes bag minimum 20, 000 euros, a Prada outfit, shoes included, around 8,000 so it all adds up quickly. She then spent the next two years surviving by selling to secondhand luxury stores that are plentiful in Paris and on the web. (Love that web savior). Of course, this was not my example, but I did permanently sift through my stuff to sell what I did not need or want and to bring in each time a few dollars that would pay off a bill.

It is just important to be resourceful and get down and dirty.

This has been rewarding because often I have found myself with 11$ in the bank and then a Turo payment or any other welcome sum comes to the rescue just in time. I have mastered the art of juggling, interac transfers and positive thinking that a "surprise" sum will appear. It works.

Pause

My job/photographer combo was over. My cool Creative Director dating photographer trend board had vanished into thin air and just like Cinderella, I fell with a bump on my behind. I bumped into a nosy neighbor:

"Are you still working at that job?".

"No. they fired me because I hired that guy I was dating".

"Are you still dating him?"

"No, it fizzled out after we both lost our jobs."

"So, you lost the job and the boyfriend?", she said with a smirk (I swear).

"Yes." (makes you happy?? I repressed myself from adding.)

When necessary, one must simply admit defeat. There is something bittersweet about it.

In those times I remember this: when we are young we worry about what people think about us. Later we do not care what people think of us. Later still, we realize no one is thinking about us. They have their own stuff to handle.

And then because I had no choice, I started from scratch. Which in our era means going to Apple. The job took back the computer I was using: a laptop and 36-inch screen they had acquired just for me, do not remind me, ooh that hurts. I then proceeded to bravely reinstall all the Adobe suite software and office tools. All this with money that my mother embarrassingly enough lent me because, of course, I had started right away leading a 140 000$ a year lifestyle. Trip to Paris. Marni bag. Valentino shoes. I now realize, I think I thought I was working for Chanel and not for a commercial Canadian brand. No wonder they said I did not fit in.

I found a freelance mission at a super cool brand that designed a very fashionable mostly leather brand.

The owners were friends and their kindness was very soothing after the traumatic firing I had been subjected to. It was a small team and I did some part-time consulting. After the all-encompassing directorial position in a big firm, this small but high end and edgy brand was tinged with an artsy melancholy. I worked mainly alone, interacting sporadically with two ultra-refined designers and occasionally went to the car during lunch break to meditate all that had spiraled out of control, smoke (whatever I had) and listen to bittersweet songs.

Trouble
By Cage the Elephant
We were at the table by the window with the view
Casting shadows, the sun was pushing through
Got so much to lose
Got so much to prove
God don't let me lose my mind
Trouble on my left, trouble on my right
I've been facing trouble almost all my life

I knew that this mission was not full time and was just a pause before I could bounce back. Indeed.com, Isarta.com, Espresso.com, linkedin.com for a job and match.com for a boyfriend. When I say the web saved me, I know what I am talking about.

Hilary R. And Hilary Clinton

Just at the time that I was hired by the Hilary R. clothing brand, Hilary Clinton published a book trying to explain why she had lost the elections and displaying to the world the hard time she had "letting go". I made a parallel with my own failure.

I had to get a prescription for 20mg a day anti-depressant when I lost my $140,000 director job. She lost forever the opportunity to be the FIRST WOMAN PRESIDENT of all time! How does your ego ever get over that? What measures up to that afterwards? I tried any reasoning I could to put my little defeat into perspective.

I had been hired by the owners of the group that owned the Hilary R. brand, probably because I had uttered the magic word "Michael Kors" during the job interview thus putting visions of fame, glory, success and dollar signs in my future boss's eyes. Michael Kors after all, had similarities with Hilary R. It had been a very successful, glamorous brand in the seventies, then had dwindled into the land of forgotten brands with sporadic attempts at survival through licensees (shoes, glasses, sheets whatever you could plaster a brand on). Michael Kors had undergone a total rebrand and resuscitated the glamour of the eighties through its original DNA: clean-lined elegance sprinkled with splashes of gold and logos. These are non-fail ingredients that appeal to a woman's first tribal instincts to shine in the jungle or forest thus increasing her attraction for the male species and the ensuing capacity to mate and reproduce. This is part of the evolution of mankind and Michael Kors had cashed in on this big time.

There was no reason why we could not do the same with Hilary R. It was a question of unearthing the original DNA, reinterpreting it with a modern, contemporary twist, reviewing the "story" and thus creating a distinctive brand that would have its personality in the maze of competition. All this and of course throwing in a lot of money for getting the brand out there.

The Hilary R. line was now being designed by one of the group's designers who of course was in rivalry with the real Hilary R. Hilary R., just like Hilary Clinton, had understandably a hard time letting go. Even if she was busy between Mexico, Stowe, her 70th birthday party, etc. etc., the appeal of fabrics, color and glamorous fashion inspirations kept pulling her towards the head office where she would make appearances and ply us with ideas and (creative) direction. Of course, the in-house designer resented this. Especially since she was trying to appeal to a diversity of women, by creating a collection that would reconcile the tastes of Southern soccer moms going out for a Saturday night dinner with sparkly cocktail dresses and shoulders covered with furry shrugs, with that of the big-city women desiring immaculately elegant clothes bare of extra fuss and reflecting power.

The timeless (as in timeless fashions?) question arises: when does one let go?

How to leave behind the excitement of shopping for ideas, of looking at a magazine not just for enjoyment but for active, involved inspiration. How can one stop betting on what will be the new color and pondering endlessly between two blues?

So, I had officially entered middle-aged fashion and all of its complexities.

This involved finding models that were thin but not thin enough to offend the customers, young but not young enough to offend the customers. Which means that for some strange reason you hire 35-year-old models, but then paradoxically you end up photoshopping the disgraceful wrinkles. Very confusing. Note that 35-year old's who have overdone the Botox trick are not an option either.

It was an all-women environment and once again I found competition and strife among certain women. But now we were in 2017 and this seemed to be a thing of the past. When the big boss on campus noticed my work and expressed the wish to promote me, my direct superior had a hard time concealing that she did not approve of this plan. She had no desire to see me evolve, even if it was in the company's interest. I could no longer fight, compete, manipulate and take offense like I had in my BCBG days. It seemed like a distasteful trend you wore once but cannot bear to wear again. I mean, if you wore bell bottom pants in your twenties and the trend comes back 15 years later, in my humble opinion, you should abstain this time. I had no patience for this lack of elegance at our age and in our era. Especially since the women that were the most competitive and manipulative lamented Hilary Clinton's loss in favor of Trump.

I did try to communicate the parallel. "Women should stick for other women. Especially divorced, single women (80 percent of the women in this company). If women stuck for other women, Hilary R.…uh I mean Clinton, would be President today". I hinted, slyly, I thought and was quite proud of the parallel.

Unfortunately, it seemed lost on my audience: too second degree. In Paris the eloquent bitches would have gotten it, I sighed. They seemed bitchier but smarter, more sophisticated. I yearned for the battles of what seemed like a distant youth now.

But then look at how first-degree advertising is in Quebec. "Vive la bouffe". ("Long live food.") IGA slogan. Really!

Needless to say, I left.

Back to the computer.

But this time with more calm, which is welcome, even if it is accompanied with one-part resignation. Is that what they call maturity? Let go and let G.d.

Web Dating

After the whole incident with the photographer-that-ruined my career who spent the summer lounging in the pool of a fresh on the market divorcee (another one who sadly needed male presence whatever the price was), while I looked for a job, I needed to get my mind off of the stress of finding a job.

I also simply needed to get the Photographer- got-us-both-fired-incident out of my head.

At the moment it was of little consolation that I knew for sure he would end up on my doorstep or at least on the other end of my phone as soon as pool season was over, come September, with the prospect of coming to my High holiday festivities….

which he did but thankfully I had enough self-love to send him away.

The matchmaker era had come and gone. I had met my first boyfriend through her and indeed the fun of being courted and dated had helped me start to get over my divorce. It was time to continue moving on. My first after-divorce-boyfriend had become a friend. I probably have more exes than future mates at this point in my life, so it is best to be friends with them all. We laughed together about his perfect wooing bachelor aptitudes and agreed that he should be patented and quickly reproduced to fill the demand for increasing divorcees.

Soon after "the incident", I bumped into him at a party and asked him why he had broken up with his most recent girlfriend. Two fifty-year old's having a conversation we used to have as teenagers. Even now that we are older, I see in everyone who they must have been in high school. That aspect is still undeniably part of whom they continue to be, under all the accumulation of all these years. We are more and more like archeological artefacts that can be dusted so that the splendor of yesteryear can still be perceived in a mischievous smile or the glint of an eye.

"Because she was hooked on dating websites" he confided as he coughed over the joint he was inhaling.

I had indeed become a teenager again and liked to occasionally indulge in the fumes myself. I even relished in sometimes being a teenager again. Especially after having been married to an overbearing Sephardic old fashioned husband, the dating and occasional puffs were welcome liberations and made up for the setbacks of the divorce.

Hmmm if she likes it, why wouldn't I, I thought?

"We went to see Suzy the sex therapist" he explained. I

remembered her from high school: who would have known she would become a sex therapist. - but she did have a way of showing people how she had an innate ability to flap her tongue rapidly.) "Suzy said I shouldn't accept this. If she was checking out dating websites while dating me, it was unacceptable". Hmm, I guess that is what a wizened bachelor deserves, I thought, but diplomatically refrained from saying and smiled politely. Are two fifty-year olds really having this conversation?

And he proceeded to show me pictures on his phone of five girls he was simultaneously texting with on match.com.

Hence my website dating days started. Why go negotiate a fee with a professional matchmaker when I had become a savvy digital immigrant and for 40$ a month I could have a wide selection of men at my fingertips.

It's Raining Men
By the Weather Girls, Chocolate
Get ready all you lonely girls
And leave those umbrellas at home
According to all sources
the street's the place to go
'Cause tonight for the first time

It's gonna start raining men
God bless mother nature, she's a single woman too

It did help that as a Creative Director, specialized in websites and web communication tools I had a fantastic Seo (search engine optimization). My portfolio was on Behance.net, my Linkedin was updated, my line of designs had numerous references to myself, Facebook, Instagram...Hence anyone in the vicinity (close enough for GOOGLE) could type my name and city and there I would pop up right away. Google images made it even easier at the time with pictorial recognition, but 50-year-old guys usually were not quite that web-savvy. I was living proof that with purely organic content one could be found on the web. Just make sure to have a low bounce rate I thought. Not to be a rebound. Lol. So many similarities.

I thought of all the similarities between web presence and web dating.

Between branding lines and how we brand men in our minds. Between creating muses and trend boards for customers and how we also create trend boards of the men we meet and fall in love with.

Working on one brand after another is like going from one man to the next.

In order to keep one's sanity one should allow for some breathing space between missions. (and men too).

Otherwise, the experience can be quite muddling.

Too often I have been preoccupied with the outside envelope (of men and brands), rearranging, picking a new font and logo colors, making him change style of shoes and his haircut...only to realize that the brand, and even more unfortunately the man, has no soul....

That is where one should begin, sometimes when you are caught up with branding or external envelope you can easily forget.

You can meet a man (or a brand to rebrand) and decide that he (or it) is a sexy hippie chic style or an immaculate contemporary, bold and powerful style and get caught up in the image that you are creating in your mind.

Like one of my mother's friends said to me one day, "These men we build them up in our minds and adorn them with ornaments like Christmas trees but once the season is over and we take away the glitter, gold and crystal that we created we are left with a puny senseless tree". That woman knows, she was a four-time divorcee.

Meanwhile, I was using my communication skills to write on dating sites.

"I was born in Casablanca and grew up in Montreal then lived in Paris for twenty odd years before coming back with my 4 daughters. I love my job, that basically consists in assembling words and images to create a brand identity for a firm that needs a sprinkling of magic in order to make what they sell, goods or services, very desirable.

I love to read, travel, go out (do not say shopping, save that for later). I enjoy meeting people. I prefer big city travelling and going to museums, bookstores but can also enjoy the beach.

My ideal match must be ambitious, driven, smart and very well read.

I prefer he have some sense of religion to none at all. I prefer tall and lean rather than large and muscled.

A sense of humour would be extremely appreciated."

Upload a picture of yourself, not one that shows you cropped out an ex boyfriend, and off you go for another branding exercise.

The web window was just as good for dating as for branding.

It did not lack humor that my first web site dating relationship started with the Executive Director of the conservative shul of a Canadian city I will not name. I met him during the Rosha Shana peak period which in his field was equivalent to Fashion Week in my life (in Paris).

The texting stretched out in anticipation......for weeks.... because he could only come to visit after the High Holidays.

The anticipation added charm and spice to this virtual relationship. The virtual relationship eventually fizzled out.

With such experiences there is the 80/20 rule, or may I

say even 9 to 1. It took 9 bad dates, fake dates (the guy posts a picture of a male model but then doesn't show up to literally lose face), or even dates where everything seemed right, but nothing clicked. But like one friend was told when she declined a blind date, pretexting she was fed up with the dating scene, "you must meet a lot of frogs till you land on Prince Charming". By the way, she finally agreed on that blind date and he did end up being Prince Charming!

Jeff The Name And Man

And then one very magical day, someone asks you to go for a drink and you enter a bar, looking vaguely lost, not knowing if you should turn right or left and then suddenly he is in front of you and it seems like you have known him all your life. He is approaching you and he greets you with encompassing arms and takes you to your seat. You have a drink and the conversation doesn't stop and the next thing you know you are irresistibly drawn to stroking his hair (yes, what a bonus he has hair!) and he keeps holding your backside with a very casual but proprietary gesture that makes you sit there like a content, purring cat.

Then he walks you to your car and comes into the car just for a quick good night kiss… and visions of pale blue, silver and pale Prada green butterflies appear before your eyes because you simply cannot get the teenager out of you. Thank G.d. You are still reveling in each other's company and just can't wait to meet again. Your phone rings and since this is your daughters mini because you didn't want to drive up with the carpool-I have-so-many-responsibilities-car, all of a sudden, your mother's voice comes blaring through the bluetooth signal and she is hurling:

"Where are you!! It is a week-night! You told me one hour!"

Etc. etc. You have just met the man of your life and your mother just won't hang up and put an end to your embarrassment.

But if he really is the man of your life, then he will find this all a bit messy, but endearing and will text you the nicest things later when you are in bed reliving every moment of this magical evening.

It was wonderful that his name was Jeff to top everything else onto his so appealing 5"11' height (especially right after shorter men). Well yes, they say it in evolutionary science :tall men are desirable. As an immigrant child with a complicated first name inspired by French colonialism, raised in an English neighborhood of Montreal, I was in awe and admiration of names like Jeff, Michael, Susan and Sally.

I marveled at anything Anglo Saxon in that first-grade school by the name of Russell, just like my mother had admired all things French. "Why couldn't you have named me Sally?" I implored my mother who had been influenced by French colonialism.

Thus, had begun my identity confusion crisis.

Jeff was the Anglo Saxon that fit in but by now and it was none too early, he was much more than that. He was a man with a real soul. It was no longer a branding experience.

When several months after we met, he had to move to Miami for a business opportunity he could not refuse and we had to impose on our relationship long distance ties, I read a sign into it. I got used to telling myself stories by now.

The powers that be, the mission, the karma, whatever it is that rules this planet, have determined that I am not yet independent and strong. My mission to grow is not complete. I must continue to strive and grow to merit this relationship? Is that really so one wonders? All the single women are single because they must grow? And all the married ones are strong and independent and do not need to overcome this mission? One wonders about these stories.

Clouds Across the Moon
By The rah band

"Good evening. This is the intergalactic operator. Can I help you?"
"Yes. I'm trying to reach flight commander P.R. Johnson, on Mars, flight 2-4-7
Ooooh...since you went away, there's nothing goin' right!
I just can't sleep alone at night... I'm not ashamed to say
I badly need a friend...or it's the end
Now, when I look at the clouds across the moon
Here in the night I just hope and pray that soon
Oh baby, you'll hurry home to me

CHAPTER 6

THE BEST FOR LAST: WOMEN

I have written about men and work, but indisputably the most important are the children and the women. When I think of the most meaningful lives, it is that of the women. Perhaps because they give so much more. The intensity, resourcefulness and sincerity of women is our strength and our weakness.

I think of my sister who managed to motivate and control her very turbulent boys, so often kicked out of school, but who finally, to everyone's surprise, made it into Med school.

I think of her mother in law, whom she would call in spite of being divorced from her son and who would say "So what they got suspended. Ok I just landed in Dubai for a business meeting but will be back in two days, book an appointment with the director." And to keep my sister's spirits high she would add jokingly. "Don't you get it? That director is in love with you; that is why he keeps kicking them out, in the hope of seeing you".

I think of my mother who emigrated to this country with my father, the wonderful dreamer, and found herself taking the bus in snowstorms. And then helped her 5 younger brothers and sisters emigrate to Canada with their father when her beloved mother, the other pillar of the family passed away.

I think of my rebellious great grandmother who lived intensely before her time.

I think of my grandmother who gave love to her 11 children, endlessly sowing sheets and dresses for her family and making her husband proud.

I think of my aunts and cousins and the love they give our family, the bond they create and maintain among themselves and through their children.

I think of my friend Pascale, who pulled her son away from drugs like a mother tiger pulls her son with her teeth away from danger.

I think of impulse women shoppers who buy dresses online

in the middle of the night, just for the dream of it, and send them back the next day.

I think of that elegant French woman who refused to tell her daughter and mine her age as we walked from school. "A mother is never 40", she smiled softly as she walked gracefully on high heeled pumps that French women master like none other.

I think of my friend Veronique who emigrated to America, left behind her lawyer's robe and donned the chic evening dress of the refined party planner.

I think of my friend Yolanda, who wants to sing and dance all the time as if she were right out of an Ernest Hemingway novel because she was gifted with the intrinsic knowledge that this is what counts the most.

I think of the women that I shopped with, worked with, entertained with, laughed and sobbed with, sometimes from one minute to the next.

I think of my dear friends that support their children, their health, their weaknesses and I remember the without a care-princess-teenagers we were and how life has put us to test.

I think of all these women who were tested by children, men, careers, health, traumas and financial ruin, but still painted lipstick on their faces most days.

I started to write all this because divorce is underrated but so is all of life and its struggles.

I think of this song written by a woman of course and am sure that it would melt the heart of the most insensitive terrorist. But then again, I am a woman so what do I know? Only a woman would think that.

Comment te dire Adieu
By Jane Birkin

Il faut que tu m' explique un peu mieux
Comment te dire adieu
Mon coeur de silex
Vite prend feu
Ton coeur de pyrex
Résiste au feu
Je suis bien perplexe
Comment te dire adieu

How can I tell you good bye
By Jane Birkin

(You have to explain to me a little better
How can I tell you good bye
My heart of flint
Has quickly caught on fire
Your heart of pyrex
Resists fire
I am very puzzled
How can I tell you good bye

CHAPTER 7

NOW WHAT?

The Railroad Crossing

I went to visit a friend who literally lives on the other side of the tracks. As often happens when I go visit her, I got stuck waiting for the train to cross. The train was making its usual noise ringing in my ears and the red lights of the signals were filling up my vision as I sat there and waited.....and waited. My fingers were drumming impatiently on the steering wheel and I felt taut, readying to change gears any second now. Finally, the coast was clear, the red lights turned to green and all of a sudden, my vision was filled with the white headlights of cars crossing from the opposite direction. Everything was flowing again. In a flash, I realized how irrelevant the long waiting period seemed now. Nothing was left of it. It was a thing of the past. Most things that seem so important to us today will soon be irrelevant. The thought seems comforting.

Intensity And Posterity

I always knew I would write but thought I would do so at least at the age of 70. But living in this digital era everything is quicker and more intense. Sometimes I say today's 50 is yesterday's 40 to reassure my friends: we are still young etc. But sometimes I feel that today's 50 is actually yesterday's 70 because our lives are so fast paced and intense and by the time we reach 50 we have had 15 jobs, 3 husbands, 8 homes and lived in 4 countries. Intense.

"Wow that was intense", I breathed in and quickly exhaled as I black Adidased it (narrow black lapel blazer with slim-fit pants suit from Kooples) into the office. Unfortunately, my Parisian understated elegance outfit was totally lost on my colleagues from yet another Mary Sue Jane Kay label for Mary Sue Jane Kay label I was trying to revamp as was my comment. Oh no, I thought, I have again landed in an office with minimal communication. It is difficult for a multitasker like me who loves to work, watch YouTube seminars and talk at the same time. Especially difficult after coming back from one of my best friend's father's funeral.

It didn't matter that we were not talking at the time because of a story over a boy and about a girlfriend just like when we were 16 except that now we were 53 (me!) and a couple more for her. She would probably hate me more for pointing that out.

Anyways it had all been a lot to digest. The loss of this man, yet another of my father's generation, was placing us all, each time a little more ahead in our lives. Equally sadly, it represented the slipping away of an era. Our carefree, young years, sheltered by of our parents, blessed by blissful ignorance and wonderful oblivion are all gone. The only things left from that era, are the values that our families and that past generations will leave behind. The ethics and values we hang on to, are all the good we can possibly hand over to our children. In spite of all the craziness of our lives, some good must come of it. That is what I was telling the grandchildren of the man who had passed away. To hold on to that. After all, they were the future and they had the obligation, like my children and all future generations to carry on the good of their families and of generations past. I knew they would carry this on, I reassured them, that is how their grandfather would live on.

As I was finishing this wise thought, I turned around and saw their father. My friend's ex-husband. Oh no, I forgot about the crazy genes coming from that direction I thought. Someone else's ex-husband smiling smugly at me.

Is That All There Is?
By Peggy Lee
Is that all there is?
If that's all there is my friends, then let's keep dancing
Let's break out the booze and have a ball
If that's all there is
I know what you must be saying to yourselves
If that's the way she feels about it why doesn't she just end it all?
Oh, no, not me
I'm not ready for that final disappointment

This End

Recently I went back on a trip to Paris to visit my eldest daughter. Try as I might to keep us all together in Montreal, she has been attracted back into Paris's arms. The allure of this beautiful city she grew up in was understandably too strong. I had even tried to be a Teresa, my mother's skillfully manipulative friend who had artfully controlled and planned her children's lives, by introducing her to a nice young man in Montreal, thinking she would establish herself there. These things cannot be improvised: cannot be a Teresa whoever wishes to be one. To accept this is part of the wisdom of life. I do not seem to have that willful, focused personality because it did not work. I am sure it is better this way. And when I miss my daughter or think that perhaps my other daughters will leave me for another country, I reason that we lead digital pixelized lives and that we are no longer established in any one place anymore. We are in several places at the same time. By the time I reach the last homeland I might well have lived in three more cities.

Meanwhile, on this trip, I had errands to do for my friends in Montreal and knew I wanted to do them at the Monoprix situated Place des Augustine's where I often went when I lived in Paris.

I remember often walking in there for some errands, after a workday, before going home during my divorce. I remember the cold, lonely evenings and the lump in my throat that stayed permanently along with the palpitations I felt. I had difficulty breathing; my fear of the present and future was so strong. As if I was on the edge of a cliff before falling. Even worse had been my loneliness, the emptiness and the great sadness that came with this feeling of abandonment.

But today was a beautiful spring day. We had visited the Louvre and danced in the streets with the legendary gay pride parade.

Well, I thought as I walked into the Monoprix, I have come a long way, remembering the fearful, sad woman I had been nine years earlier as I walked, no doubt hunched over, into this same Monoprix. I felt so free and light as one does after long and tiring travels that are safely tucked away in the past. There would no doubt be relapses and other moments I would want to hunch over. But for now, it was enough that I was free of that terrified panicky feeling that had once overwhelmed me. That is true wisdom and all we eventually learn to ask for. To be fine just this minute.

Enjoying that realization and reveling in my present lighthearted feeling, I looked up and realized I had never noticed how lovely the beautiful old clock was on the facade of the Church of St. Auguste. Its face looked at me glistening with its gold patina. As I breezily turned into the Monoprix, with a certain lightness in my step and in my heart, I could not hold back a chuckle.

Signed,
A divorcee

The Windmills of Your Mind
By Noel Harrison
Round like a circle in a spiral,
Why did Summer go so quickly,
was it something that you said?
Pictures hanging in a hallway
Or the fragment of a song
As the images unwind,
like the circles that you find
In the windmills of your mind!

Printed in the United States
By Bookmasters